He straighte a nervous stall, wanting to grab her and flee from her at the same time.

His eyes had darkened like a stormy night as his warring needs fought inside him. He didn't bolt.

But he made no move toward her, either. Instead, he fisted his hands at his sides. A slight hitch in his breathing was all that she needed to know that she had a chance to win this battle.

She rose to her feet, keeping her eyes locked on his the whole time. Slowly, she padded across the thick carpet to stand in front of him, with only a few inches and the heat from both their bodies between them.

"Colton," she whispered. "I want you."

He swallowed, his Adam's apple bobbing in his throat. "We're working on a case. We don't have time—"

"We do have time. Hours to kill." She slid her hands up the front of his chest, delighting in the feel of his muscles bunching beneath the thin fabric of his T-shirt. "And I've got the perfect way to spend at least one of those hours."

"Silver. . ." His voice came out a harsh rasp. He cleared his throat and tried again, still not touching her, hands at his sides. "I'm not what you're looking for."

"Now, that's where you're wrong, Colton."

DEEP COVER DETECTIVE

BY
LENA DIAZ

First Published in Great Britain 2016
By Mills & Boon, an imprint of HarperCollins*Publishers*
1 London Bridge Street, London, SE1 9GF

© 2016 Lena Diaz

ISBN: 978-0-263-91914-1

46-0816

Our policy is to use papers that are natural, renewable and recyclable products and made from wood grown in sustainable forests. The logging and manufacturing processes conform to the legal environmental regulations of the country of origin.

Printed and bound in Spain
by CPI, Barcelona

Lena Diaz was born in Kentucky and has also lived in California, Louisiana and Florida, where she now resides with her husband and two children. Before becoming a romantic suspense author, she was a computer programmer. A former Romance Writers of America Golden Heart® Award finalist, she has won a prestigious Daphne du Maurier Award for Excellence in mystery and suspense. To get the latest news about Lena, please visit her website, www.lenadiaz.com.

This story is dedicated to Sean and Jennifer Diaz. My greatest, most rewarding accomplishment in life is having amazing children like you. I'm so proud of you both.

Thank you, Amy, Diana, Gwen, Krista, Manda, Rachel, Sarah and Sharon. KaTs rule.

Thank you, Angi Morgan and Alison DeLaine, for daily laughs and the magic room.

And, as always, a sincere thank-you to my editor and agent, Allison Lyons and Nalini Akolekar, for their constant support.

Chapter One

Colton shook his head in disgust and thumped the nav screen on his Mustang's dashboard. It had to be broken. Either that or the GPS tracker he'd tucked under Eddie Rafferty's bumper in Naples was on the fritz. Because if the screen was to be believed, the budding young criminal had driven his car off the highway and directly into south Florida's million-and-a-half-acre swamp known as the Everglades.

Driving a car into the saw grass marsh and twisted islands of mangrove and cypress trees was impossible unless the car was sitting on pontoons. And Eddie's rusted-out vintage Cadillac boasted bald tires just aching for a blowout. Not a pontoon in sight.

Colton pulled to the shoulder of I-75 near mile marker eighty-four, just past a low bridge over a culvert. This was the last location where the navigation unit showed Eddie's car before it had taken the turn toward the swamp. So much for using technology to follow the suspect. He should have stayed closer, keeping Eddie in sight instead of relying on the GPS tracker. But when the kid had taken the ramp onto the interstate, Colton had worried that Eddie might get spooked seeing the same black Mustang in his rearview mirror the whole time he was on the highway. So Colton had dropped back a few miles.

Where was the juvenile delinquent now? Certainly not on the highway, and not on the shoulder. Heck, even if the GPS was right and he *had* pulled off the road here, there was nowhere else to go. Eight-foot-high chain-link fencing bordered this east-west section of I-75 known as Alligator Alley. The fence kept the wildlife from running out onto the road and causing accidents. And yet the dot on the dashboard screen still showed Colton's prey continuing south, *past* the fence.

He eyed the tight, solid-looking chain-link mesh twenty feet away. No holes, no skid marks on the asphalt to indicate that a vehicle had lost control. The safety cable along the bottom was intact. But he supposed that could be misleading.

Twice now, that he knew of, vehicles had managed to go airborne after clipping a guardrail and had sailed over the cables and slid under the chain links—without triggering the cable alarms that would automatically notify the police and the department of transportation to send help. Had the same thing happened to his burglary suspect? If it had, the GPS would show him as stationary. And yet that dot just kept moving. Had a gator swallowed the tracker on Eddie's bumper and was swimming down one of the canals?

Determined to figure out exactly what was going on, Colton got out of the car and stepped to the edge of the road. And that was when he saw it. *Another* road. Single lane and parallel to the highway, it was set at a slightly lower elevation than I-75, making it nearly impossible to see when driving past unless someone was specifically looking for it. The road turned a sharp right before the fence, heading back in the direction that

Colton had just come from. It went down an incline, toward the culvert beneath the bridge where wildlife could cross to the other side of the highway without interfering with traffic.

The culvert, of course.

That must be where Eddie had gone. Maybe Colton hadn't been as subtle as he thought he'd been when following the kid back in town and Eddie realized he had a tail. So he'd hidden out down there, waiting for Colton to pass him by.

An even better scenario would be that Eddie *didn't* know he was being followed, and he'd just accidentally led Colton to his secret hiding place for his stash of stolen goods. This could be the break Colton had been looking for. If he caught Eddie red-handed, he would have the leverage to coerce him into revealing the identity of the burglary ring's leader. The case could be wrapped up in a matter of days. And then Colton could go back to his normal life for a while, at least until the next big assignment came along and he had to go undercover again.

Excitement coursed through his veins as he ran back to his car. He hopped inside and yanked his pistol out of his ankle holster, automatically checking the loading before placing it in the console. He didn't think Eddie had crossed the line yet to becoming a gun-toting criminal, but he wasn't betting his life on it. Be Prepared might be the Boy Scouts' motto, but it was Colton's, as well. He had no desire to end up on the wrong side of a nervous, pimply-faced teenager's gun without firepower of his own at the ready.

He wheeled the car around and followed the mysterious road that he must have passed a hundred times over the years and never known was there. But after reaching the bottom of the hill, instead of continuing, the road turned a sharp left and dead-ended at the chain-link barrier with a line of tall bushes directly behind it. And the culvert on the other side was clearly empty. No sign of Eddie or his car.

Colton's earlier excitement plummeted as he pulled to where the road stopped so he could turn around. But before he could back up, a section of the fence started rolling to the right, along with the bushes, which he now realized had been cleverly attached to what was actually a gate. The bushes must be fake, since they weren't planted in the ground. And they were obviously someone's attempt to obscure the view, so others wouldn't realize what Colton could now clearly see—that the road did indeed continue south into the Glades.

It was narrow, and mostly gravel, but it was dry and elevated a few feet above the marsh that bordered it on both sides. It curved into the saw grass, probably by design to help hide it. But a section of it was just visible about fifty yards away, where it headed into the pine and live oak that began a thick, woodsy part of the Glades.

Figuring the gate might close on him while he pondered his next move, he pulled forward to block the opening. Then he called his friend and supervisor in the Collier County Sheriff's Office, Lieutenant Drew Shlafer. After bringing Drew up-to-date on the investigation and the discovery of the hidden road, Colton was disappointed in Drew's lack of surprise.

"You know this road?" Colton asked. "You know where it leads?"

"You said it's just past mile marker eighty-four, right? Opposite a culvert?"

"Yeah. So?"

"Ever heard of Mystic Glades?"

"Rings a vague bell. Isn't that where some billionaire crashed his plane a few months ago?"

"Dex Lassiter. He ended up smack-dab in the middle of a murder investigation, too. But that's a story for another day. Mystic Glades is the small town at the end of the road that you found, the same town where Lassiter ended up, a few miles south of the highway. The residents are a bit...eccentric...but mostly harmless. From what I hear."

"Mostly? From what you hear? You've never been there?" Colton accelerated through the gate. Just as he'd expected, it slid closed behind him as he drove down the winding road.

"Never needed to. It's rare for the police to get a call from a Mystic Glades resident. They tend to take care of whatever problems they have on their own. There have been a few hiccups recently, like with Lassiter. But other than that, the place is usually quiet."

"There's no permanent police presence?" Colton glanced at the nav screen as he headed around another curve. The screen blinked off and on. He frowned and tapped it again.

"The people of Mystic Glades don't really cotton to outsiders, or police. Although I hear they're starting to cater a bit to tourists that have heard about the place because of Lassiter's case. Still, I wouldn't expect them to exactly welcome anyone unless they bring the almighty dollar with them and plan to leave without it. But don't worry. You're in an unmarked car and you've gone grunge, so I doubt they'll even look twice at you. They might even think you're one of them."

Colton rolled his eyes and glanced at his reflection in the rearview mirror. Grunge wasn't his thing, but the description wasn't too far off for how he looked right now. Since going undercover, he'd let his dark hair grow almost to his shoulders and worked diligently every morning to achieve a haven't-shaved-in-days look without letting it get out of control and become an itchy beard. His usual military-short hair and clean-shaven jaw would be a red flag to the types of thugs he'd been hanging with lately. They'd smell "cop" the second he walked through the door, thus the unkempt look. His new look did have the advantage of making getting dressed every morning a no-brainer. A pair of jeans and a T-shirt and he was good to go. Not like his usual fare of business suits that he wore as a detective.

"Just how far off the interstate is this place? I've gone about three miles and all I see are trees and saw grass." A black shadow leaped from the ditch on the right side of the road just a few feet in front of his car. He swore and slammed his brakes, sliding to a stop. But whatever he'd seen had already crossed to the other side and disappeared behind some bushes.

"You okay?" Drew asked.

"Yeah. Something ran out in front of me. I'd swear it was a black panther, but that doesn't seem likely. They're pretty rare around here."

"Nothing would surprise me in Mystic Glades. But I'd be more worried about the boa constrictors people let loose out there once they get too big and eat the family dog. And gators, of course. Watch your step when you get out of the car."

Colton could hear the laughter in Drew's voice. He could just imagine the ribbing he'd get at their next poker game if he *did* manage to tangle with a snake or gator. Assuming that he lived to tell about it.

"You sure you don't want to trade places?" Colton

asked. "You sound as if you're having way too much fun at my expense."

Drew didn't bother hiding his laughter this time. When he quit chuckling, he said, "You couldn't get me out there if you held a gun to my head. There's a reason I traded undercover work long ago for an office. I like my snake-free, air-conditioned, pest-free zone. Did I mention how big the palmetto bugs are in the Glades? It's like they're on steroids or something."

"Don't remind me. That's why my last girlfriend left me. She couldn't handle the humidity or the giant bugs here in Florida."

"Serves you right for dating a Yankee. And for picking up a woman while on vacation at Disney World. What did you expect? Wedding bells?"

Colton grinned and started forward again, keeping his speed low so he wouldn't accidentally veer off the narrow path into the water-clogged canals now bordering each side. He didn't mind Drew teasing him about Camilla. Dating her had been a wild whirlwind of fun. Exactly what each of them had wanted. Neither of them had expected it to last. He had no intention of ever leaving Florida and offered no apologies for his modest, blue-collar roots. And Camilla's perfectly manicured toes were firmly planted in the upper-crust society back in Boston.

It had been a hot, sweet, exceptionally pleasurable three weeks and they'd parted friends, but with no plans to reconnect in the future. With the kind of life he led, that was for the best. Disappearing for months at a time while undercover didn't create a foundation for an enduring relationship. And he loved his job far too much to consider giving it up, at least not for a few more years.

"Another thing to look out for," Drew said. "I've heard that electronics go kind of wacky around there."

Colton thumped his GPS screen, which alternated between showing a moving dot and blacking out every other second. "Yeah, I see that."

"Cell phones are especially unreliable out there. Except maybe in a few choice spots. You might not be able to get a call out for backup if something goes wrong. Keep that in mind before jumping into anything. When you check back in with me, you'll probably have to head outside Mystic Glades to do it."

"Understood." He drove around another curve and then pulled to a stop. Directly in front of him on an archway over the road was an alligator-shaped sign announcing the entrance to Mystic Glades.

He inched forward, then stopped again just beneath the archway, blinking at what seemed like a mirage. "You're not going to believe this," he said into the phone. "Mystic Glades looks like someone took an 1800s spaghetti Western town and plopped it right into the middle of the Everglades. I'm at the end of a long dirt-and-gravel road with a line of wooden buildings on either side. Instead of sidewalks, they've got honest-to-goodness boardwalks out front. Like in horse-and-buggy days."

The phone remained silent. Colton pulled it away and looked at the screen. No bars. No signal. The call had been dropped. Great. He put the phone away and checked the GPS. That screen was dark now, too. Useless, just as Drew had warned.

He debated his next move. Going in blind didn't appeal to him, with no way to let his boss know if he needed help. But working undercover often put him in situations where he couldn't call for days or even weeks at a time. So this wasn't exactly new territory. Plus, the kid he was after was just a few days past his eighteenth birthday and still had the lanky, gangly body of a teenager. Physically, he wasn't a threat to Colton's six-foot-three frame, and probably had half his muscle mass, if that. But if Colton discovered the other members in the burglary ring out here—and their leader—he could be at a huge disadvantage by sheer numbers alone, not to mention whatever firepower the group had.

His undercover persona so far hadn't managed to get him inside the ring, but he'd been living on the streets in Naples where most of the burglaries had occurred, developing contacts. And he'd heard enough through those contacts, along with his team's detective work back at the station, to put the burglary ring at around fifteen strong, possibly more. He even knew the identities of a handful of them. But without being sure who their leader was, and having evidence to use against him, Colton needed some kind of key to break the case open. Right now that key appeared to be the group's weakest link, Eddie Rafferty. A small fish in the big pond, Eddie would be the perfect bait to draw the others out. But to use him as bait, first Colton had to catch him.

Even though he didn't see the rust-bucket Caddy anywhere, he might have caught the break he needed. Because little Eddie Rafferty had just stepped out of a business called Callahan's Watering Hole and was sauntering toward the far end of the street.

Time to go fishing.

Chapter Two

Silver stood in the front yard, shading her eyes from the sun as she faced the whitewashed two-story—her pride and joy, the first bed-and-breakfast ever to grace Mystic Glades. Thanks to the recent success of Buddy Johnson's airboat venture that was bringing in tourists and the dollars that went with them, all but one of her eight bedrooms was booked for the next three months, starting tomorrow, opening day.

Bright and early, Tippy Davis and her boyfriend, Bobby Jenks, would be here to help Silver after Buddy's airboats brought the B and B's first guests. Everything was ready—except for attaching the large sign to the part of the roof that jutted out over the covered front porch with its gleaming white railings.

"A tad to the left, Danny," she called out to one of the two men on ladders beside the front steps, holding either end of the creamy yellow, bed-shaped sign that announced Sweet Dreams Bed & Breakfast, proprietor Silver Westbrook.

"Looks perfect where it is, if you ask me."

She smiled at skinny Eddie Rafferty, who'd just walked up. The beat-up junker that he was so proud of was nowhere to be seen. Since he lived several miles away, deep in the Glades, she figured maybe he'd parked his car in the lot behind the building next door, Mystic Glades's answer to Walmart, Bubba's Take or Trade.

"You think it's centered?" she asked.

"Yep."

"Stop right there," she called out. "Eddie said the sign's perfect."

Danny gave them both a thumbs-up, and the sound of hammers soon shattered the early-morning quiet. Snowy egrets flushed from a nearby copse of trees and the razor-sharp palmetto bushes that separated her little piece of town from Bubba's and the rest of the Main Street businesses. On the other side of her B and B, more trees and lush, perpetually wet undergrowth formed a thick barrier between the inn and Last Chance Church. Beyond that, there was only the new airboat dock and the swamp with its ribbons of lily-pad-clogged canals.

She loved the illusion of privacy and serenity that the greenery provided, along with the natural beauty that her artist's soul craved. Being this close to nature, instead of seeing concrete and steel skyscrapers out her attic-bedroom window every day, was one of the reasons she'd returned to her hometown after being gone for so many years. *But not the only reason.*

"You're right, Eddie. It's perfect. You have a good eye."

He flushed a light red and awkwardly cleared his throat. It practically broke Silver's heart knowing how much her compliments meant to Eddie. He was like a stray cat. Once offered a meal or, in her case, friendship and encouragement, he'd made a regular habit of making excuses to visit her.

Unlike a stray, he wasn't homeless. But since he'd turned eighteen a few weeks ago and was technically an adult, he *would* be homeless soon. His foster parents, Tony and Elisa Jones, were anxious for him to move out so they could put another foster kid in his bedroom and continue to receive their monthly stipend from the state. Eddie was supposed to be looking for a job every day in Naples, but Silver suspected he was up to something else entirely. Probably hanging out with the wrong crowd, like Ron Dukes or Charlie Tate, the two little hoodlums she blamed for half the trouble that Eddie got into.

In spite of their friendship, Silver didn't know all that much about him except that, unlike her, he hadn't grown up here. She knew he didn't have any blood relatives. But whenever she'd tried to get him to open up about his past, he would shut down and disappear for days. So she'd stopped asking.

Town gossip, assuming it could be trusted, said that Eddie had spent over half his life in the foster system. And for some reason, even though there had been interest off and on, no one had ever adopted him.

It was a chicken-and-egg kind of thing. Did he continually get into trouble because he didn't have a family, or did he not have a family because he kept getting into trouble? Either way, he was too young to be thrown away like a piece of garbage. He had potential, and she fervently hoped he would turn his life around one day, before it was too late.

Danny Thompson and his friend exchanged a wave with her as they folded their ladders and headed back to Callahan's. Buddy was probably champing at the bit for Danny's return. The morning airboat tours couldn't start without him to pilot one of the three boats. But Danny had insisted there was plenty of time to help her hang the sign before the boats were due to push off. After all, the tourists were enjoying the "free" breakfast portion of the tour package right now at Callahan's.

It was a point of contention between Fredericka "Freddie" Callahan and Labron Williams, the owner of Gators and Taters, the only official restaurant in town. Callahan's was a bar, and had added the "grill" part of their service only after Buddy decided to add breakfast as a stop on his daily tours. Labron felt the tours should have breakfast at his place and was furious with Freddie for undercutting his bid. But, secretly, Silver believed that Labron—who'd always run a lunch-and-dinner-only place anyway—just wanted an excuse to see Freddie every day, thus the melodramatic feud going on between them.

"I brought something else that I think will look good in your inn," Eddie said.

She noted the brown bag tucked under his left arm and had to fight to hold on to her smile. *Please don't let that be another expensive piece of art that I know you can't afford.*

He pulled a short, thick, cobalt-blue vase out of the bag.

Oh, Eddie. What have you done now?

Unable to resist the urge to touch the beautiful piece, she reverently took it and held it up to watch the sunlight sparkle through it. The color was exquisite, so deep and pure it almost hurt to look at it. She'd never seen anything like it and was quite sure she never would again. It was a one-of-a-kind creation. And probably worth more than she'd earn in a month. She carefully lowered it and handed it back to him.

"It's gorgeous. Where do you manage to find such incredible pieces?"

"Here and there," he answered with a vague wave

of his free hand while he hefted the vase in the other, making her heart clutch in her chest at the thought of him dropping it. "Do you want it or not?"

Yes. *Desperately.* She absolutely adored all things blue. Opening her eyes every morning to the sun filtering through that thick glass and reflecting the color on the walls of her bedroom would be like waking up in heaven. But she could never afford it. Still, letting it go wasn't an option, either. No telling where the vase might end up, and whether its new owner would realize how precious it was or be careful to keep it from harm.

Once again, she'd have to become the temporary caretaker of a priceless piece of art to keep it from falling into someone else's hands, at least until she could figure out how to return it to its rightful owner—along with several other pieces Eddie had brought to her over the past few months. If he ever suspected what she knew about him, and her ulterior motives for coming back to Mystic Glades, he'd disappear faster than a sandbar in high tide. And then she'd have no way to protect him or help him out of the mess he was making of his life.

"How much?" she asked, careful not to let her disappointment in him show in her voice.

He chewed his bottom lip, clearly debating how much he thought he could get. "Fifty dollars?"

She blinked in genuine surprise. He had no clue what that vase was worth. Add a couple more zeroes to the end of his fifty-dollar price and it would be much closer to the true value.

"Forty-five?" he countered, probably thinking she was shocked because the price he'd asked was too *high.*

Knowing that he'd expect her to bargain with him, she shook her head and played the game. "I can't afford that, not with all the expenses of opening the inn.

I just spent a small fortune at the Take or Trade to get a shipment of fresh fruit and vegetables for my guests tomorrow." She eyed the blue vase in his hand again. "Will you take…thirty?"

The rumble of an engine had them both looking up the street to see a black muscle car of some kind heading toward them. Silver didn't recognize it, so she assumed it was probably a tourist. But even that seemed odd, since most tourists didn't drive here—they came by airboat, courtesy of Buddy's new tour company. Almost no one but the residents of Mystic Glades could even find the access road off Alligator Alley.

"Thirty's fine." Eddie's gaze darted between Silver and the approaching car. He tended to be shy and nervous, even around people he knew. So she could understand his trepidation around a stranger. But was there something more to it this time? He seemed more nervous than usual.

"You can pay me later. I'll put the vase inside." He jogged to the steps and rushed into the B and B, letting one of the stained-glass double doors slam closed behind him.

Silver winced, half-expecting the glass inset to shatter. When it didn't, she let out a breath of relief. It had taken her weeks to design and painstakingly put together the glass in those doors. And she didn't have the money to fix anything until her first paying customers arrived tomorrow.

Or until payment for her *other* job was deposited into her banking account.

She turned around as the black car pulled into one of the new parking spots she'd had paved just last week— with real asphalt instead of the dirt and gravel that dominated the rest of the town. Just one more thing to set her inn apart, a diamond in a sea of charcoal. Not that she minded charcoal. She'd made many a sketch with paper and charcoal pencil, some of which were hanging on the walls inside. But she wanted her place to sparkle, to be different, special. She'd paid, and was still paying, a hefty price for the inn. She needed everything to be perfect.

As she watched the sporty car, the driver's door popped open and a cool-drink-of-water of a man stepped out. Silver's concerns about Eddie faded as she appraised the driver, studying every line, every angle, appreciating every nuance the same way she would any fine piece of art. Because he was definitely a work of art.

Graphite. If she sketched him, that was what she'd use—a graphite pencil across a dazzlingly white sheet of paper. The waves in his shoulder-length, midnight-black hair would look amazing against a bright background. And that stubble that stretched up his deeply tanned jaw? She could capture that with a pointillism technique, then shade it ever so carefully to emphasize his strong bone structure.

Her fingers itched with the desire to slide over his sculpted biceps not covered by his ebony, chest-hugging T-shirt. The curves of those muscles were perfect, gorgeous, the way God meant them to be. And his lips... they were sensual, yet strong, and far too serious. She would want to draw them smiling. Otherwise, the black-and-white sketch would be too severe, intimidating. Yes, definitely smiling.

She tapped her chin and studied the narrowing of his waist where his dark T-shirt hung over his jeans. Did he have one of those sexy V's where the abdominal muscles tapered past his hips? She'd bet he did. And his thick, muscular thighs filled out his faded jeans as if they'd been tailored—which maybe they had. A man like him, so tall and perfectly proportioned, probably couldn't buy off-the-rack.

Scuffed brown boots peeked out from the ragged hem of his pants, making her smile. A cowboy in the Glades. That might be a fun way to draw him, maybe with a lasso thrown around that big stuffed gator Buddy had recently put in his store, Swamp Buggy Outfitters, to draw in tourists. She'd have to add a hat, of course. Or she could change those boots to snakeskin and draw him—

"Ma'am? Hello?"

She blinked and focused on his face. He must have been talking to her for a moment, but she hadn't heard him. No surprise there. Happened all the time. He stood a few feet away, his thumbs hooked in his jeans pockets, watching her with a curious expression.

As she fully met his gaze for the first time, something inside her shifted beneath an avalanche of shock and pleasure. His eyes…they were the exact shade of cobalt blue as the vase. They were, quite simply, amazing. Beautiful. Incredibly intriguing. Her fingers twitched against her palms as if she were already grasping a pencil. Or maybe a paintbrush.

His eyes widened, and she realized she still hadn't said anything. "Sorry, hello," she said. "I tend to stare at people or things and zone out."

The almost-grin that curved his sensual lips seemed to be a mix of amusement and confusion—an unfortunate combination of emotions that she was quite used to people feeling around her. When she was a child, it had hurt her feelings. As an adult, she felt like telling people to just grow up and deal with it. So she was different. So what? Everyone was different in one way or another. That was what made the world interesting.

He motioned toward the inn. "Yours?"

"Yep. You looking for a place to stay?"

"What makes you think I'm not a local?"

She laughed. "Not only are you not a local, you've never been here before or you'd know that was a silly question. There are only a few hundred residents in Mystic Glades. And there's not a stranger in the bunch. We all know each other."

"What about that young man I saw go inside a minute ago? You know him, too?"

Her smile faded. Was this one of the men Eddie was mixed up with? This man, as ruggedly gorgeous as he was—looked like the wrong crowd, dangerous even. She crossed her arms. "Why do you ask?"

He shrugged. "Just testing your theory—that you know everyone. Maybe he's a tourist like me. Doesn't matter." He held out his hand. "I'm Colton Graham. And if you've got a room available tonight, I'd appreciate a place to stay."

She reluctantly shook his hand, not quite ready to trust his claim of being a tourist. "Silver Westbrook."

Still, if he *was* a tourist, then his interest in Eddie was probably just harmless curiosity, nothing she really needed to worry about. And that meant that she didn't have to feel guilty for wanting to enjoy the play of light across the interesting planes of his face. She rarely painted anymore, preferring to sketch with pencil or charcoal, sometimes pen, without all the mess or work involved with setting up her paints and then cleaning up afterward. But the best way to capture him might be with paint, perhaps watercolors.

"Ma'am?"

She blinked. "Sorry. Spaced out again, didn't I?"

The almost-grin was back. "Yeah, you did. Is something wrong? You seem preoccupied."

"No, no. Everything's fine." She waved her hand impatiently, tired of having to explain her unfortunate quirks to everyone she met.

At his uncertain look she sighed. "I get lost in shapes, textures, colors. I can't help it."

"Ah. You're an artist. I know the type. My sister does that a lot." He smiled, a full-out grin this time that reached his incredible blue eyes. And completely transformed him, just as she'd thought it would. Smiling, he looked approachable, warm, *perfect*. She *had* to put him on canvas. It would be a sin not to. And she wouldn't use watercolors. They were too muted for this vibrant man. No, acrylics...that was what she'd use to capture every detail in vivid color.

Her gaze dropped to his narrow waist. "Have you ever modeled?" she asked. "I'd love to paint you nude. I would pay a sitting fee, of course. I'm a bit strapped for cash right now, but I could let you stay a night without charge and call it even."

He made a strangled sound in his throat and coughed. "Um, no, thanks. That's not really my thing." He waved toward the inn again. "But I *would* like to rent a room for the night, if you have a vacancy."

Swallowing her disappointment, she glanced around, suddenly very much aware of how alone the two of them were and how separated the inn was from the other businesses. The street was deserted, with most of the residents out of town at their day jobs or inside the local businesses. The idea of taking this man, this complete stranger, into her home had her feeling unsettled.

"You don't have any vacancies, then," he said, interpreting her silence as a no.

"It's not that. Actually, the grand opening is tomorrow. I hadn't really planned on renting out any rooms tonight."

He waited, quietly watching her.

Why was she hesitating? This wariness was silly. If she was going to run a bed-and-breakfast, she'd have to get used to renting rooms to people she didn't know. And drop-ins were bound to happen. It certainly wouldn't be nice to turn him away when she was fully capable of offering him a place for the night. And the extra income was always welcome.

"Okay, why not?" she said. "But don't expect me to cook for you today. That starts tomorrow, when my help arrives."

"I'm sure I'll figure something out so I don't starve."

His smile was infectious, and she couldn't help smiling, too. "Just one night, then?"

He glanced toward the front doors, then in the direction of the airboat dock about fifty yards away, which was barely visible from here. Or maybe he was looking at the church with its old-fashioned steeple and bell that the ushers rang by pulling on a rope every Sunday morning at precisely nine o'clock.

"Just tonight," he said.

His rich baritone sent a shiver of pleasure up her spine. He really was an exquisite specimen of male. And she really, *really* wanted to paint him. Maybe she could ask him again later to model for her and he might change his mind. And if she could convince him to stay longer than one night, she'd have more chances to try to sway him into modeling for her. Plus, starting tomorrow, the place would be full of other people. Any concerns about being alone with a man she didn't know wouldn't matter at that point. When it came down to it, more important than the painting was the *money*. A fully rented inn was far better than a partially rented one.

"If you want to stay just one night, that's okay," she said. "But there are only eight rooms and seven are booked solid for the season. I expect the last one will get snatched up pretty fast once the first group of guests begins to spread the word about their stay here. If you don't take it now, it might not be available later in the week."

"You're quite the saleswoman. Okay, I'll book a week. Might as well. Never been in the Everglades before and this looks like a great spot."

Yes! That put her at 100 percent occupancy. She couldn't ask for a better start to the business she'd been saving her whole life to start. And her other job would be over soon, God willing, so that income wasn't something she could rely on indefinitely. Every penny counted now.

"Aren't you even going to ask the price?" She crunched down the gravel path toward the front doors with him keeping pace beside her.

"That was going to be my next question."

She gave him the particulars and he handed her a credit card before holding one of the doors open for her.

"Sounds more than reasonable," he said.

"Great. And thanks," she said as she stepped through the door he was holding. She led him to the check-in desk beside the staircase. She took an impression of his credit card on an old-fashioned carbon paper machine and set it on the counter for him to sign.

"Haven't seen one of those since I was a little kid,"

he said as he took the pen from her and scrawled his signature across the bottom.

"Yeah, well. You do what you have to do without reliable internet and phone service. Don't worry, though. There are hundreds of movies in the bookshelves in the great room for you to choose from if you want to watch something while you're here. I've got the classics along with tons of newer titles in all genres. And each guest room has its own TV and DVD player."

"Sounds good." He pocketed his credit card and scanned the lobby as if he was looking for someone. Then he suddenly grew very still, his gaze settling on something behind her.

Fearing that a wild animal had somehow managed to sneak inside, Silver whirled around. No furry attacker was waiting to jump at her. But what Colton was staring at was just as dangerous...*for Eddie.*

The network of cubbies on the homemade bookshelf that spanned the wall behind the desk held the blue vase prominently in the middle where Eddie must have placed it. And that was where Colton's gaze was currently riveted. A shiver shot up Silver's spine at the intensity of that look. And this time it wasn't a good shiver.

Without asking her permission, he rounded the desk and hefted the vase in his right hand. "This is...beautiful. Where did you get it?"

Beautiful? She'd bet her last sketch pad that he'd been about to say something else and stopped himself. Did he recognize that piece? Suspect that it was stolen?

After taking the priceless vase from him, she set it back in the cubby. "I bought it from a friend. I'd appreciate it if you wouldn't pick up any pieces of art that you see around here. Some of them have been in my family for generations."

"But not that one." He eyed it as if he was itching to grab it again.

"You seem quite interested in that." She waved toward the cubby. "Do you have one like it back home, wherever home is?"

"Atlanta, Georgia. And no, I don't. But I'd like to. This…friend you bought it from. Do you think I could meet him? Maybe see if he has another one for sale?"

"What makes you think my friend isn't a woman?"

He shrugged. "Him. Her. Doesn't matter. My sister recently bought a new house and I've been meaning to pick her up a housewarming gift. I know she'd love something like that." He pointed to the vase. "She adores bright colors. Like I said earlier, she's an artist, too."

Sure she was. Silver doubted the man even had a sister, or that he lived in Atlanta. His story sounded too pat, as if he'd quickly made it up to cover his unusual interest in the vase and his sudden appearance in Mystic Glades—just a few minutes after Eddie had approached her. Coincidence? Maybe. Maybe not.

"How did you happen to find the entrance to our little town?" she asked as she recorded his name in the registration book. "It's unusual for anyone but residents to know that exit."

He shrugged. "Honestly, it was an accident. I ran over some debris on the highway and pulled to the shoulder to check my tires. That's when I saw the exit. Figured I might as well take it and see where it led. After all, I'm on vacation. Have all the time in the world."

His story was plausible, she supposed. But the timing of his arrival, along with his interest in the vase, still bothered her. Did he have a hidden agenda for being here? He seemed like a man with a purpose, not the kind who'd randomly pull off a highway and take a gravel road that seemed to lead nowhere. She sorely regretted having rented him a room for the night, let alone the whole week.

"About that vase—"

"Sorry. Can't help you." She snapped the registration book closed and grabbed a key from the drawer underneath the counter. "The person I bought it from isn't around right now. Here's your key, Mr. Graham." She plopped it in his hand. "Your room is upstairs, room number eight, last one on the right."

Unfortunately, his room was right beneath *her* room in the converted attic, with the door to the attic stairs right next to his door. That was far too close for comfort. But all the rooms were decorated with specific themes, and the guests chose the themes they wanted when they made their reservations. She couldn't reassign them.

Maybe she should drop into Bubba's Take or Trade and buy a lock for her bedroom door. If Colton ended up snooping while he was here, he might discover the other items that Eddie had brought her, including several in the attic. Until she could be certain *why* he was so curious, and whether he was a threat, she'd have to be very careful.

"As I mentioned earlier, there aren't any formal meals planned for today," she continued. "But you're welcome to make full use of the kitchen." She waved toward the swinging door to the left of the entry. "I'm sure that you'll find everything there you could possibly need. You certainly won't starve. And there are toiletries in the bathroom attached to your room—shampoo, soap, even a toothbrush and toothpaste in case you didn't think to bring them. Do you have any luggage you'd like me to get for you?"

His eyebrows rose. "I'll get my bag myself in a few minutes. Thanks. I'll just go up and check out the room first." He headed toward the stairs to the right of the desk.

Silver hesitated as he disappeared down the upstairs hallway. She worried about the attic and whether he'd snoop. But she had a more important errand to do right now than babysit her first guest.

She hurried to the front door, determined to find Eddie.

And warn him.

Chapter Three

Colton leaned back against the wall upstairs, just past the open banister, waiting. Sure enough, the inn's front door quietly opened below, then clicked closed, just as he'd expected. He jogged to the stairs and caught a glimpse of Silver Westbrook through one of the front windows as he headed down to the first floor. Her shoulder-length bob of reddish-brown hair swished back and forth, a testament to how fast she was going as she turned right.

She looked like a little warrior, ready to do battle as she marched up the street—except that he couldn't quite picture her holding a weapon while wearing a tie-dyed purple-and-lime-green poncho with bright blue fringe brushing against her tight jeans. And the flash of her orange tennis shoes would be like a beacon to the enemy on a battlefield, just as it was a beacon to him.

The woman certainly wasn't subtle about her love of color. The fact that the outside of the B and B was white was the real surprise, because the inside was just as colorful as Silver's outfit—a mix of purple, blue and yellow hues on every wall, and even on the furniture. But instead of being garish as he'd expect of an inn decorated with that palette, somehow everything combined to work together to make the place feel warm, inviting.

She really did remind him of his artistic sister. Too bad the two would never meet.

Because Silver Westbrook would probably end up in prison when this was all over.

Once she was a few buildings up the street, he headed out the door after her. But instead of skirting around the backs of buildings to follow his prey, he forced himself to walk up the street in plain sight. He didn't want anyone looking out a window to think he was anything but an interested tourist exploring the town. And all the while he fervently hoped that Silver wouldn't turn around and realize he was following her.

The concern in her eyes, and the wariness when he'd foolishly grabbed that vase, had put him on alert that she knew far more about its origins than she was letting on. And he'd figured she would want to go warn whoever had sold it to her as soon as he was out of the way. That was why he'd gone upstairs. And sure enough, she'd bolted like a rabbit.

He regretted that he'd shown his interest in the piece. He'd just been so stunned to see it that he hadn't managed to hide his surprise. That blue vase was at the top of his stolen goods sheet and worth several thousand dollars. The owners were anxious to get it back. And Colton was anxious to catch whoever had stolen it.

The fact that the vase had been taken two nights ago in Naples and ended up here today, along with Eddie, couldn't be a coincidence. He really, really wanted to get that little hoodlum in an interrogation room and get him to roll over on his thug friends. But now there was another wrinkle in the investigation.

Whether Silver Westbrook was part of the burglary ring.

He would hate to think that a woman as intriguing

and beautiful, and smart enough to run her own business, would get involved in illegal activities. But how else could he explain how defensive she'd gotten when he'd asked about Eddie and, later, the vase, unless she knew she'd accepted stolen property?

From the moment he'd met her and had been the recipient of such a brazen evaluation of his…assets…and then propositioned to pose nude so she could draw him, she'd fascinated him. Her tendency to space out and get lost in her own little artist's world was as adorable as it was frustrating. He'd love to get to know her better, find out what other unique quirks she was hiding, and how her fascinating artist's mind worked—which wasn't going to happen if he ended up arresting her.

And that was what made this whole trip so frustrating. Because he was pretty sure that if things turned out the way it looked as though they would, he'd end this day by hauling both Eddie and Silver to jail.

Near the end of the street, almost all the way to the archway that marked the beginning of Mystic Glades, she turned right, jogged up the steps to the wooden boardwalk and went inside one of the businesses. The same business where Eddie had been earlier, Callahan's Watering Hole. Coincidence? Not a chance. Silver was definitely going there to find the kid, probably to warn him that a stranger seemed far too interested in his whereabouts and the stolen goods he'd brought with him.

Colton increased his stride and hurried to the same building, which appeared to be a bar, based on the name and the tangy smell of whiskey that seemed to permeate the wooden siding. He couldn't worry about stealth now. He had to hurry to catch both of his suspects before they managed to disappear completely.

His boots rang hollowly across the wooden board-walk. He pushed the swinging doors open, bracing him-self for something like a line of saloon dancing girls and drunken patrons lined up at the bar, even though it was still morning. After what his boss had told him about Mystic Glades, and what little he'd seen for him-self, nothing could surprise him.

He stopped just past the opening. Okay, wrong. He *was* surprised, surprised that everything seemed so *normal*.

The mouthwatering, sweet smell of sugar-cured bacon hit him as his eyes adjusted to the dark interior and more details came into focus. There weren't any saloon girls or patrons at the bar guzzling whiskey. But the place *was* packed, and from the looks of the cheap, souvenir-shop types of Florida T-shirts on most of the people sitting at little round tables throughout the room, they were mostly tourists. This must be why the street out front was so deserted. Everyone was in here, eat-ing breakfast.

There was no sign of Silver, though.

"Are you part of the airboat tour group?" a well-en-dowed young woman in a tight T-shirt and short shorts asked as she stopped in front of him, a tray of drinks balanced on her shoulder and right hand.

"No. I'm alone."

"Okay, well, there are a couple empty seats over there." She waved toward a pair of vacant tables near the bar. "I'll take your order as soon as I give these air-boat peeps their refills."

"Thanks."

"Thank me with your pocketbook, sugar." She winked and bounced off to a table on the far side of the room, her long blond ponytail swishing along with her hips.

Good grief. She didn't look old enough to serve alcohol, let alone dress like that or flirt with him. He looked away, feeling like a perv for even noticing the sway of her hips. Hopefully she was older than she seemed. But one thing was for sure—*he* felt far older than his thirty-one years right now.

He scanned the tables again, more slowly this time, the booths along the right wall, the short hallway on the left side of the room, just past the bar. But there was no sign of Silver. And no sign of Eddie, either. He eyed the set of stairs directly in front of him that ran up the far wall. A red velvet rope hung across the bottom with a sign on it—Employees Only. Was that where she'd gone? If not, she had to be in the kitchen, or in one of the rooms down the hallway.

Maybe he was too late and she'd already ducked out a back door. He decided to check the hallway first, to see if that was where the door was. But all he found were the restrooms, which he presumed had no exits. He did a quick circuit of the men's room and then paused outside the ladies' room, debating whether he should check it, as well.

"Something wrong with the men's room?"

He turned, surprised and also relieved to see Silver standing about ten feet away, at the opening to the hallway. *She hadn't gotten away.* Her eyes, which he'd already realized were a fascinating shade of gray, a *silvery* gray—her namesake perhaps?—narrowed suspiciously and her hands were on her hips. Or maybe Silver was a nickname because of her taste in jewelry. Right now she had on silver hoop earrings and a long silver necklace.

A peacock. Her unique, colorful ensemble—topped off with purple laces on her left shoe and neon green laces on her right—reminded him of a beautiful peacock with its feathers spread in all their glory. That made him want to smile, which only made him irritated. *She's a suspect, Colton. Get a grip.*

"Just checking the place out," he said, seeing no benefit in giving up his cover just yet, not without knowing where Eddie was and whether she'd warned him. "I was curious what was down this way."

"Right. Was there a problem with your room at the inn? Is that why you followed me?"

The accusation in her tone, in every line of her body, swept away his earlier amusement. *She* was the one accepting stolen property *at best*; in league with the robbery ring at worst. And she was acting as if *he* was in the wrong? He was tempted to take his handcuffs out of his back pocket and put an end to this charade right now. But there was too much on the line to let his anger, justifiable or not, rule his actions. He needed to play it cool, try to calm her fears and, if possible, make her trust him.

He stopped directly in front of her. "Okay, you caught me. I didn't actually go into my room. I changed my mind and thought I'd explore the area first. And when I noticed you going in here, I figured—" he smiled sheepishly "—I *hoped*, maybe I could catch you and convince you to have breakfast with me." He braced an arm on the wall beside her and grinned. "After all, you did ask me to take off my clothes. Sharing a meal is nothing compared to that."

Her eyes widened and her face flushed. Good. He'd knocked her off balance. And hopefully deflected her suspicions. If he could get her to believe he was interested in her, then maybe she'd think his earlier questions had been an excuse just to talk to her.

It wasn't as if he really had to pretend. He *was* interested in her. If he wasn't on the job right now, and didn't believe she was mixed up in criminal activity, there'd be no question about his intentions—he'd pursue her like a randy high school teenager after his first crush. Because Silver Westbrook was exactly the kind of woman he liked—beautiful and smart. And unlike his last fling, Camilla, Silver was a Florida native. And she was blue-collar, like him. On the surface, there didn't seem to be any reason to keep them apart.

Except for a little thing called grand theft.

"That *is* why you came in here, right?" he said. "To eat?"

Now *she* was the one looking as though she was worried that he'd caught her in a lie.

"Of course," she said. "Yes, I'm here for breakfast. Starving. Let's find a table."

She practically ran to one of the empty tables near the bar, and Colton followed at a more sedate pace, trying not to let it bother him that she seemed so anxious to get away from him. Man, he really needed to focus here—on the case, not on the way she made his blood heat as he sat across from her.

They quickly ordered. Just a few minutes later, a brawny man in his mid- to late-thirties helped the overworked waitress by bringing Colton and Silver's food to their table. Faded tattoos decorated his massive arms, intricate patterns of loops and swirls that meant nothing to Colton. But the ink did—it looked homemade, like the kind convicts used in prison.

Colton nodded his thanks while he studied the man's face, automatically comparing it to the wanted posters back at the station. The cook nodded in acknowledgment, his dark eyes hooded and unreadable as he returned to the kitchen through a doorway behind the bar without saying a word.

"Who is that guy?" Colton asked.

Silver shrugged. "Can't say I've ever talked to him. I think his name's Cato. He's one of the new guys from out of town that Freddie hired to help out with our little tourist boom."

"Freddie?"

"Fredericka Callahan. She owns the place." She waved toward one of the larger tables on the opposite side of the room. "She's the elderly redhead arguing with the elderly bald guy."

"Arguing with a customer doesn't seem good for business."

"Labron Williams isn't a customer. He owns Gators and Taters on the other side of the street, a little farther down toward the B and B. I'm pretty sure he came in here just to gripe with Freddie."

"Gators and Taters?"

"Uh-huh. They like each other."

"The gators?"

She rolled her eyes. "Freddie and Labron."

He glanced toward the rather odd-looking pair. Freddie was built like a linebacker. Labron would probably blow away in a stiff wind and was a foot shorter than her. And while Freddie's unnaturally bright shock of red hair was rather loud, it had to compete with Labron's bald pate that reflected like a headlight beneath the bright fluorescents overhead, as if he'd just applied a thick coat of wax and polished it until it shone.

"But they look like they want to kill each other," Colton said.

"That's because they like each other."

She casually took a sip of water as if nothing about

their conversation seemed strange. Then again, maybe to her it didn't.

"Why did you ask about Cato?" She set her water glass down and pinned him with her silvery gaze.

Colton was still trying to figure out why two mature adults who "liked" each other would face off like a pair of pit bulls over a bone. But Silver's question about the cook had him focusing on what was important—not blowing his cover as a tourist.

"No reason. I was just curious. He doesn't seem to fit in with everyone else around here." He waved toward the waitress. "Neither does she. Too young. Did Freddie hire her from out of town, too?"

"No. That's J.J., Jennifer junior. She's lived here all her life. She's J.S.'s daughter, on summer break from college. She graduates next semester from the University of Florida. A year late, unfortunately, but at least she hung in there."

The young waitress was old enough to have already graduated from UF? *Thank God.* Now he didn't feel *quite* as bad for noticing her figure. "J.S. Jennifer... senior?"

"No, silly. Jennifer *Sooner.* She used to live closer to town but just built a cabin about five miles southwest of here, not too far from Croc Landing."

Croc Landing. Why would someone name a place Croc Landing around here when there were only a few hundred crocodiles in south Florida and probably a million alligators? He decided not to ask. No telling where that conversation might lead.

He took a bite of eggs, and was pleasantly surprised at how fluffy and delicious they were. Maybe ex-con Cato had learned some cooking skills while he was in prison.

As the two of them ate, the silence between them grew more and more uncomfortable. For his part, he kept thinking about the case and was annoyed that the intriguing, sexy woman across from him chose to be a criminal. For her part, he supposed, she was trying to figure out why he was here and who he really was.

By the time J.J. arrived with the bill, they were both so desperate to end the stalemate that they grabbed for the check at the same time.

Colton plucked it out of Silver's hand. "I've got this."

"Thank you," she snapped.

"You're welcome," he bit out.

J.J.'s eyes got big and round as she glanced from one of them to the other. As soon as Colton handed her his credit card, she scurried off like a puppy afraid it was about to be kicked.

An older man who'd been making the rounds from table to table, talking to each group of tourists, stopped beside Silver and gave her a warm smile. "Who's your new friend, young lady?"

Colton didn't figure he needed an introduction. It was pretty hard to miss the man's name, since it was written in big white letters across his dark brown T-shirt.

"Hey, Buddy," Silver said. "He's a guest at the inn. Colton Graham, meet Buddy Johnson, owner of Swamp Buggy Outfitters next door, the airboat operation down the street, and a handful of other businesses. He practically runs the town."

He puffed up with self-importance, reminding Colton of that peacock he'd likened Silver to earlier, but minus all the colorful plumage. This man had arrogance stamped all over him. But he must have some redeeming qualities, too, because Silver appeared to like him.

"I wouldn't say that," he corrected Silver as he shook Colton's hand. "But I'm definitely vested in our little piece of the Glades." He put his hand on the back of Silver's chair. "I thought the inn didn't open until tomorrow."

"It doesn't. Not officially. But Mr. Graham needed a place to stay so…" She shrugged.

Buddy eyed him speculatively. "Decided to come see the Everglades, have you? First time in Florida?"

"No. I've come here every summer since I was a kid." And fall and spring and winter, too.

"Ever been on an airboat tour, Mr. Graham?"

"Can't say that I have." Another lie. Normally, hiding the truth wasn't a big deal. It was part of his job. But for some reason, lying to this white-haired man was making him uncomfortable. It was like lying to his grandfather.

"Well, then. I insist that you take a tour." He waved toward the other tables. "I run airboat tours daily. Picked this passel up this morning at the main dock twenty miles south of here. We're heading out in a few minutes. Three boats, plenty of room. Come along. I'll give you ten percent off for being a guest at the inn. Silver and I offer cross-promo discounts, since I bring guests to her inn, starting tomorrow, that is. But I'll give you a discount a day early."

"That sounds like a *great* idea." Silver sounded way too enthusiastic as she smiled at Colton. "The airboats are the best way to see the Everglades. You should go."

The reason behind her eagerness to get rid of him was pathetically obvious. While he was gone, she'd probably rush to have a powwow with her criminal friends. His fingers itched to grab her shoulders to shake some sense into her and ask her why she was so foolishly throwing her life away.

"I'll think about it." He had no intention of going on a tour. He planned to keep Silver in his sights.

"Now, son. There's no time for thinking. The tour is going to take off in a few minutes. And you won't want to miss out. You're going." Buddy nodded as if it was a done deal. "And, Silver, since he's your guest, you can both sit together on the same boat."

Her eyes widened. "Ah, no. I'm not going to—"

"I've been trying to get you on one of my tours for weeks," he interrupted. "This might be your only chance this season, since the inn opens tomorrow and you'll be busy after that. You'll come, right?"

"I really don't think that I can…"

His face fell with disappointment.

Silver's shoulders slumped in defeat. "Okay. I'll take the tour today. But I'm sure that Colton has other plans."

"I wouldn't miss it for the world."

Her narrowed eyes told Colton exactly what she thought of his sudden change of heart.

"Excellent," Buddy said, grinning with triumph. "You can both pay the cashier at the dock. Make sure you tell her about the discount." He waved his hand in the air and headed toward another table.

Silver frowned after him.

"He basically forced you into taking a tour," Colton said. "And he's still going to charge you for it."

"Yeah. I noticed." Her voice sounded grumpy. "I'll have to return the favor if he ever wants to stay at the inn."

Colton grinned. And, surprisingly, Silver smiled back. For a moment, they were simply a man and a woman enjoying each other's company, sharing their amusement at Buddy Johnson's tunnel-vision focus on making a buck, even at a friend's expense—quite literally. But then Buddy's voice boomed through the room, telling the tour group it was time to go. Silver's smile faded and she looked away. The magic of the moment was lost.

"Let's go, let's go, ladies and gents," Buddy called out. "We need to get going before the skeeters and no-see-ums start biting."

Chairs scraped across the wooden floor and the buzz of voices echoed through the room. The tourists headed toward the front door like a herd of elephants, waved on by three men dressed in khaki shorts and brown T-shirts the same color as Buddy's, but instead of their names across the front, there were logos of airboats with the company name, Buddy's Boats.

The last of the tourists headed out. Silver mumbled something and hurried after them. She and Buddy were out the swinging doors before Colton could stop her. He had to wait for the waitress, who was heading his way with his credit card and one of those ridiculous carbon papers for him to sign. This place really was stuck in a different decade.

After taking care of the bill and thanking J.J., he hurried outside. The tourists were already halfway down the street. Buddy had Silver by the arm and was talking animatedly about something while she nodded.

Good, she hadn't managed to escape.

Chapter Four

In spite of Buddy's promise to ensure that Silver and Colton could sit together on one of the three boats, Silver did her best to thwart that plan. Since the boat that Danny Thompson was captaining was the most full, she hopped on it and almost squealed with triumph when she got a seat without any empty ones close by. But, at the last minute, the man beside her got up and hurried to a different boat. And who should plop down in his place but Colton Graham.

As he settled beside her, his broad shoulders rubbing against hers, she glanced toward the man who'd just left and saw him shoving one of his hands into his pocket. The flash of green paper left no question as to what had just happened.

"You bribed that man to let you sit here," she accused.

His very blue eyes widened innocently. "Why would I do something like that?"

Since she couldn't answer that without voicing her suspicions about the vase and Eddie, she didn't bother to reply. Instead, she looked out over the glades as the boat pushed away from the dock, and she did her best to ignore her unwanted neighbor.

Once out in the middle of the waterway, the giant

fan on the back of the boat kicked on. Any questions Colton might have planned on asking her would be difficult at best to ask now. She gave him a smug smile before turning away.

When they reached an intersection of canals, the boats split up, each going down a different waterway. Buddy grinned and waved at her from one of the other boats and she returned his wave, unable to fault or even resent him for pressuring her into this trip.

He'd been asking her all summer to take one of the tours so she could recommend them when her B and B guests asked about the airboat rides. Today really was the last realistic chance this season for her to take the tour. And without him bringing a boat of B and B guests every morning as agreed, the chance of her inn flourishing, or even surviving, was practically zero. She owed Buddy a debt of gratitude that he'd come up with the idea once she mentioned her desire to start the B and B.

She glanced at Colton, who was studying the passengers rather than the twisted, knobby-kneed cypress trees they were passing. Everything about him seemed... off. He wasn't acting like a tourist. A feeling of alarm spread through her every time he looked at another one of the handful of men and women on their boat, as if he was memorizing their faces or looking for something. Or someone.

Who *was* he? An insurance investigator trying to save his company money by finding that vase? A family friend of the vase's rightful owner? Or, worse, one of Eddie's so-called friends who was looking to settle some kind of debt? Her fingers curled around the edge of the seat cushion beneath her as her mind swirled with even worse possibilities, including the very worst—that he might be a cop.

That would ruin everything.

He turned and caught her staring at him. And just then, Danny cut the engine, dramatically dropping the decibel level as the loud fan sputtered and slowed and then fell silent. Great. Just great.

"We'll drift here for a few minutes so you can catch some gator action or maybe see some cranes fishing for an early lunch," Danny announced. "We'll tour the salt marsh after that."

A low buzz of excited conversation started up around them as the others took out their cameras and phones and began pointing and clicking.

"About that vase—" Colton began.

"Don't you want to take some pictures?" she interrupted. "There's a gator sunning himself on the bank over there. You'll probably never get another chance to take a picture this close without getting your arm bitten off."

"Seen one gator, you've seen them all."

"I thought you've never been to the Everglades before."

"There's this thing called a zoo," he said drily.

"Don't you live in Georgia?"

"I do."

"Atlanta, right? Like your sister?"

He frowned at her. "I'm pretty sure that I already told you that. Why?"

"I've been to Zoo Atlanta. They don't have gators."

He gave her a smug smile. "Then you haven't been there lately. They brought in four from Saint Augustine this past year."

She had no clue whether he'd made that up or not. But she had a feeling he was telling the truth. Which meant…what? That he really was from Atlanta?

"About the vase—"

"Where in Atlanta? I have friends there. Which subdivision?"

He let out an impatient breath. "No subdivision, just some land outside town."

"Where?"

One of his eyelids drooped. "Where what?"

"Where's your land?"

He cleared his throat. "Peachtree. Can we get back to my question about—"

"Peachtree." She laughed. "Seriously? Everything in Atlanta is on Peachtree. Which Peachtree?"

He stared at her, his dark, brooding eyes and serious expression making no secret that he was frustrated with her evasion of his questions. Finally, he let out a deep breath and opened his mouth to say something else.

Silver quickly turned to the woman sitting on the other side of her and tapped her shoulder. "Look." She pointed toward the bank. "There's a snowy egret. Ever seen one of those before?"

The woman's eyes widened and she grabbed her camera. "It's so pretty!"

As the woman snapped pictures, Silver told her everything she knew about egrets, which turned out to be a lot, since she'd grown up in the area. On her other side, she heard another one of Colton's deep sighs, and when she carefully turned ever so slightly a few minutes later to see what he was doing, he was staring out at the bank on his side of the boat. Good, maybe he'd finally give up trying to ask her questions. She could keep up her conversation with the other woman and maybe even some of the other tourists if she had to in order to survive the boat ride. But what was she going to do once they got back to the inn?

She'd figure *something* out.

Maybe she should invent some kind of disaster—like a burst pipe in a wall—to get him to leave. No, that would cause real harm to the inn and she couldn't afford that. The air conditioner? She could take a fuse out or something to get it to quit cooling. That would make the place miserably hot as the sun got higher in the sky this afternoon. Yes, maybe that would work.

Danny used a long paddle to edge them closer to the bank on Colton's side and pointed out several different species of plants to his picture-snapping audience.

"What the…" Suddenly Colton raised his left arm in front of her and angled his body so that his back was to her.

"Stop the boat against the bank," someone yelled. The voice sounded as though it came from the shore. And it sounded…familiar.

Someone in the boat screamed.

Silver leaned over to see what was happening.

On the bank about ten feet away, beneath a twisted cypress tree, a man stood with a bandanna tied across his face with holes cut out for the eyes. On his head was a Miami Marlins baseball cap. And in his hand, pointed directly at Danny, was a gun.

Excited chattering erupted all around as the tourists began to realize what was going on. Danny did as he was told, poking his guide pole beneath the water into the mud to push the boat toward the bank. A low grinding noise sounded as the bottom of the hull scraped across weeds and mud, then stuck and held.

The gunman rushed over to the boat but didn't try to board. He aimed his pistol at Danny and pitched a large burlap bag into the boat. "Jewelry and cash," he said. "Fill it up. Hurry."

Oh, no. She suddenly recognized the voice. *Eddie, what are you doing?* She groaned and shook her head.

Colton moved his left hand down between them, the back of his fingers skimming her calf as he slid the leg of his jeans up his boot.

Silver blinked with horror when she saw why. He had a gun. It was strapped in a holster against the side of his boot.

She grabbed his arm just as his fingers closed around the gun. "What are you doing?" she whispered.

He jerked his head around and frowned at her. "I'm a cop," he whispered. "I'm an undercover detective with the Collier County Sheriff's Office. Don't worry. It's okay."

A cop? Her stomach sank. Everything had just gotten a whole lot more complicated. And dangerous. *He was about to ruin everything.* She had to stop him. She shook her head back and forth. "Too dangerous," she whispered back. "Someone could get hurt."

"Someone could get hurt or *killed* by that kid holding the pistol. Now stay down." He pushed her hand off his arm.

Silver clenched her fists. Danny was passing around the burlap bag while Colton slowly pulled his gun out of the holster, his gaze never leaving Eddie.

This was a disaster waiting to happen. She *had* to protect Eddie. The gun in Eddie's hand was shaking so hard Silver was afraid he was going to shoot someone by accident. And Colton had his gun completely out of the holster now.

Silver leaned back and raised her right hand as if swatting away a bug. The movement caught Eddie's attention, as intended. His head swiveled her way, and his eyes widened. Silver made a gun signal with her pointer finger and thumb and pointed at Colton's back. It didn't seem possible, but the gun in Eddie's hand started to shake even more. He nodded, and Colton snapped his head around to look at her suspiciously.

She dropped her hand from behind his back and gave him a nervous smile.

His eyebrows slashed down and he whipped his head back toward Eddie.

"Your jewelry, Silver," Danny said, pushing the bag toward her.

She hesitated, glancing from Colton to Eddie. They were staring at each other like two gunmen about to have a shoot-out.

Do something. You have to stop this before someone gets hurt.

Silver started to pull her necklace over her head.

Eddie turned his gun away from Danny and toward Colton.

Colton started to bring his gun up.

Silver dropped her necklace and it clattered against the floor of the boat in front of Colton. "Oh, darn it. Sorry." She braced her right hand on his shoulder and leaned across him.

"Out of the way," he snapped.

"Sorry, sorry, oops." She fell across his lap, slamming her right arm on top of his gun arm and trapping it between her breasts and his lap.

She jerked her head up and looked at Eddie. *Go,* she silently mouthed to him.

He whipped around and ran for the trees.

Colton swore and tried to yank his gun out from beneath her, but she clung to him like pine sap on a brand-new paint job. He looked toward the bank, then shook his head and looked back at her. His glare was so fierce she was surprised she didn't turn into a human torch on the spot.

"I should arrest you right now," he growled. "You let him get away on purpose."

"I fell." She blinked innocently and braced her hands on his thighs, pushing herself upright.

He swore viciously and let his gun slide back into the holster, then yanked his pants leg down over it. No one seemed to have even noticed his gun. The rest of the passengers were all chattering excitedly. And Danny had turned away to try to comfort a loudly crying woman.

Colton leaned down toward Silver, his face a menacing mask of anger. "Until I figure out my next step, you keep quiet. Not a word to anyone about me being a cop or I *will* arrest you. Got that?"

Bristling at his tone but understanding his anger, she decided to comply—for now—and gave him a curt nod.

He crossed his arms and looked away, as if he couldn't stand the sight of her anymore.

A hand touched her left shoulder. The woman who'd been so excited by the egrets earlier looked ready to pass out. Her eyes were like round moons brimming with tears about to spill down her cheeks.

Her lips trembled as she whispered, "I can't believe we were almost robbed. We could have been killed."

Silver's heart tugged at the poor woman's fear. Her own anger at Eddie probably rivaled Colton's anger with her. Thank God, no one had gotten shot, but that didn't mean they hadn't been hurt. This poor woman, and others, would probably have nightmares and no telling what other lasting effects because of Eddie's stupid stunt. Silver squeezed the woman's hand and pulled her into a hug, rocking her and patting her back as she tried to soothe her.

"You'll want to take the boat to the main dock where everyone's cars are parked." Colton's deep voice cut through the conversations around them as he addressed Danny. "We'll have cell phone coverage there and can call the police to report the gunman."

Danny hesitated, then nodded. "Right. Of course. Um, ladies and gentlemen, my apologies for the fright you just had. The tour is over. We're returning to the south dock." He gave Colton another curious look before using the pole to push the boat off the mud.

Chapter Five

Colton switched his cell phone to his other ear and leaned against the police cruiser as he and his boss debated his next move. The airboat captain had brought the tourists to this main dock near the Interstate. This was where the tourists had parked their cars earlier this morning before being taken in the boats to Mystic Glades for breakfast.

Half a parking lot away, on the mini-boardwalk outside Buddy's Boats Boutique, a team of four Collier County Sheriff's deputies were interviewing the few remaining airboat riders. Most of them had already given their statements and had been allowed to go. Only Silver, Danny Thompson and a couple of others were left.

A different group of deputies had taken one of the department's airboats out earlier, with Danny as their guide, to the spot where the gunman had been, in order to search for clues. But other than some muddy footprints that the soggy marsh had rendered useless as evidence, there wasn't much to find. And no trace of the gunman. They'd brought Danny back and now those deputies were already on their way back to Naples.

As Colton listened to Drew, some of the store's staff members came outside on another one of their rounds, checking on everyone and passing out bottles of water—at four bucks a pop. Colton supposed that was entrepreneur Buddy Johnson's brand of Southern hospitality.

"Okay," Drew said. "Since the B and B owner interfered and it's unlikely the perp even saw your gun, what do you think had him spooked?"

"Miss Westbrook must have signaled him, warned him, just before she threw herself on me so I couldn't draw my gun."

"You think she interfered on purpose?"

"Yes. But I can't prove it. When I drove into Mystic Glades and saw Eddie talking to her, I should have confronted her then and there. Instead, before I continued to the B and B, I waited to see what they would do. Eddie disappeared. And Miss Westbrook's been playing cat and mouse with me ever since. Did she interfere on purpose? I'd bet my next raise on it."

"All right. Then how do you want to play this?" Drew asked.

He'd already given it some thought and knew exactly what he wanted to do. Namely, get out of Mystic Glades. "Once all the passengers have been interviewed, the airboat captain is going to take Miss Westbrook and me back to the dock in Mystic Glades. Once there, I'll arrest her and drive her to the station for an interrogation. And while I'm working on getting her confession, one of our guys can get a search warrant for the inn. My statement that I saw that blue vase should be good enough to get a judge's signature."

He kept an eye on Silver while his boss considered his recommendation. She seemed to have made it her personal mission to help the mostly older crowd of tourists after each one of them was interviewed by the police. She hugged them as if they were old friends, put her arms around their shoulders and helped them to their cars. Anyone watching her would think she was a saint and that she really cared about those people. And yet she was covering for the man who'd pointed a gun at them. It didn't make sense.

"What about Rafferty?" Drew asked. "Can you peg him as the gunman?"

Colton thought about it. "My gut tells me it was him. But he had his entire face covered, and since he wore a ball cap, I couldn't even tell you his hair color. No way could I swear in court that it was him. A defense attorney would hear me describe the guy as Caucasian, average height and build, and then he'd remind the jury that half the people in the country could be described that way."

"All right. Then, basically, this is where I think we stand. Your cover as a tourist is still intact with everyone except Miss Westbrook. If we can ensure her silence, you can still hang around Mystic Glades and try to get in with the town gossips, or maybe listen in at the bar you mentioned. Someone is bound to know where Rafferty's hiding and give him up. Then you can confront him, lie, tell him we've got his prints at one of the burglarized homes or something. Get him to roll over on the ringleader."

Colton straightened away from the police car. "Hold it. What are you saying? There's no way we can trust Westbrook."

"Maybe, maybe not. You told her not to tell the other tourists that you were a cop. From what you've said, she's kept her word."

"Only because either I or one of the other deputies has been with her the whole time. She hasn't had an opportunity to spill the truth. We have no way of knowing whether she'll continue to keep quiet."

"Then you'll have to stay with her. Don't let her out of your sight."

"Drew—"

"It's not a request, Colton. You've spent months and plenty of resources on this case. Other than pegging a few minor players that we agreed wouldn't have access to the man at the top of the food chain, we've got nothing. We were putting all our chips on Rafferty because he seemed knee-deep in this thing and might lead us to the higher-ups. But if he was the gunman today, then it's a safe bet that he's going to lie low for a while. I want you to try to flush him out, but we have to consider that the ship may have sailed. Which leaves us with Westbrook as our only link to the whole ring. That's the angle you need to work."

"I can *work* it by hauling her to the station and interrogating her."

"Or you can go back to the bed-and-breakfast, threaten to arrest her for interfering with a police investigation if she doesn't cooperate, then step back and see what happens. If she thinks the jig is up, she'll want to warn the other members of the burglary ring. My guess is she'll do that after she thinks you're asleep. So follow her. See where she goes."

Colton shook his head in frustration. Drew's plan was too risky. Rafferty had already gotten away and might not be seen again. What if Silver slipped away, too? It would be far safer to take her into custody right now. And although he'd never admit it out loud to Drew, in spite of everything that had happened, he was worried about her.

He knew her type, how her creative mind worked,

from growing up with a sister much like her. To Silver, the world was a fascinating, enchanting place full of interesting people and things to study and capture in some kind of medium. She judged people based on their faces, voices, maybe even the colors they wore. She put faith and trust where it wasn't always warranted. To someone like her, "bad guys" could be hard-luck cases and she felt sorry for them. He doubted she saw true evil in anyone. And that made her particularly vulnerable.

In spite of how angry she'd made him by risking her life and throwing herself on him when he was pulling out his gun, he was also shaken that he could have hurt her. And damn it, he didn't want her hurt. Even though she frustrated the heck out of him, and was likely involved with the criminals he was after, she didn't strike him as a "bad" person. His instincts, honed from years of working with some of the worst excuses for humanity out there, told him that by most people's measures she was probably a "good" person who'd gotten caught up in something and didn't know how to get out of it.

But that didn't mean he'd go easy on her. She needed a wake-up call before she got hurt or her misplaced loyalties got someone else hurt.

"Colton? You still there?" Drew asked.

"Unfortunately. I still think that bringing her in is the better plan, the safer one."

"When you're the boss, you can make that decision. Until then, give our B and B owner enough rope to hang herself. Let her lead you to the burglary ring leader and end this thing once and for all."

SILVER SPENT THE airboat ride back to Mystic Glades trying to think of some way to get rid of Colton Graham. Since throwing him overboard would likely get her arrested or force her to jump into the gator-infested swamp to save him, she discarded that notion, no matter how tempting. And she couldn't think of a reasonable excuse to toss him out of the B and B, nothing that wouldn't raise his suspicions even more than they already were.

She'd expected him to barrage her with questions the whole trip back, but instead he'd stared out over the water and occasional spans of saw grass and trees, as if he were deep in thought. Even the scores of alligators they passed, lying on the banks sunning themselves, didn't shake him from his silence.

A few minutes later, Danny cut the noisy engine and steered the boat toward the landing. As soon as it bumped against the dock, Silver was out of her seat. But before she could hop out and leave her unwanted guest behind, his right hand clamped around her left wrist like an iron band.

She shook her arm, trying to make him let go. "What are you doing?"

"We need to talk." He stepped onto the dock and helped her out, but then his hand was around her wrist again, an unbreakable vise.

"Silver?" Danny eyed Colton's hand on her wrist as he stepped onto the dock and tied off the boat. "Everything okay here?"

Colton aimed a warning look her way. It wasn't necessary. She hadn't forgotten his vow to arrest her if she told any civilians that he was a police officer. And even though he'd shown her no ID to prove his claim, the deputy who'd interviewed her back at the south dock had assured her—in answer to her whispered question—that Colton was definitely a Collier County deputy. Which meant his threat to arrest her was probably quite real.

She forced a smile, appreciating that the boat captain was always so nice to her, even though they'd only met a few months ago when Buddy hired him for his latest venture. "No worries, Danny. Colton is…an old friend. Everything's fine." She leaned against Colton and patted his chest when she would rather have punched him.

He played along, letting her wrist go and anchoring his arm around her shoulders, pulling her close and *very* tightly against him. "We have a lot of catching up to do."

She subtly pressed the heel of her sneaker on top of the toe of his left boot and shifted all her weight onto it while smiling at Danny as if nothing were going on. Colton grunted and eased the pressure of his arm around her. She rewarded him by moving her foot.

Danny's eyebrows climbed into his hairline. "Oh, okay. I didn't know." He slowly grinned and gave Silver a wink. "I thought there might be something going on between you two. You were whispering quite a bit on the boat earlier. Y'all have fun, um, catching up." He winked again and tipped his baseball cap. Then he headed into the little shack at the entrance to the dock, probably to lock up for the day, since the other boats were already tied up, having long ago ended their tours.

Silver stared at the closed door. Great. Danny had obviously jumped to the conclusion that she and Colton were lovers. By tomorrow the whole town would think the same thing. But what was the alternative? Telling him the truth? That wouldn't do.

"Come on." Colton grabbed her hand and tugged her away from the building. They headed through the edge of the woods and a few minutes later emerged onto the street near the church.

After being towed along like a child's toy, Silver couldn't stand it anymore. She stopped and pushed at his hand. "Let me go. I'm not yours to pull around and manhandle no matter what threats you throw around."

He immediately dropped her hand and faced her. "Are you going to try to run away again?"

"Again? I never tried to run away."

"Oh? When you hightailed it out of the restaurant this morning, you weren't trying to get away from me?"

"I, uh, needed to talk to Buddy."

"Right. And you wanted to get on a different boat than me."

She frowned at him. "So? It's not like we knew each other."

"We know each other now. And you still tried to hop out of the boat and take off before I could catch up. If you don't like me, that's one thing. You're entitled. But let's set the record straight between us. I'm a police officer and I believe you know something about that attempted robbery today, among other things. You may have been interviewed once already, but you're about to be interviewed again. By me. And you'd better not lie anymore. I won't stand for it." He leaned down toward her, obviously using his size to try to intimidate her.

And it was working, but not the way he thought. Instead of scaring her, he was pissing her off.

"We also need to discuss that lovely blue vase sitting behind the desk at your inn," he continued, oblivious of the war going on inside her. "Because you and I both know you didn't buy it, not the honest way at least."

Shoot. "I don't know what you're talking about."

"What we're talking about is you receiving stolen property. And make no mistake, that vase is definitely stolen. That's just a fact. The who and why are what I'm going to find out. If you don't want me holding your hand, then you'd better not do anything to make me think you're trying to get away. One wrong step and I'll slap a pair of handcuffs on you."

"Oh, good grief. That's quite enough with the caveman routine." She put her hands on her hips. "If you're going to make threats, at least make ones I'll believe. Taking out handcuffs would ruin your plan to not let anyone else know your—" she did air quotes "—*super-secret* occupation. After all, we're on a public street. Someone is bound to look out a window and notice."

"You'd make a lousy cop."

She blinked up at him, thrown off by the amusement in his voice and the sudden change of subject. "What are you talking about?"

He waved toward the other businesses up the street. "You're not very observant. No one has to look out any windows when they're standing in the open watching us, and talking about us."

She looked up the street, then gasped and pressed her hand to her chest. Danny must have circled around them through the woods and had already blabbed his gossip. And his timing couldn't be worse—after rush hour, when most of the residents were back in town and doing their evening shopping.

Half the businesses had people out on the boardwalk in front, chatting with one another and not trying all that successfully to pretend that they weren't watching her and Colton. The grins and hands held over their mouths as they glanced at the two of them were a dead giveaway. As was the fact that Danny stood in the middle of one of those groups looking embarrassed when his gaze caught hers.

"I'm going to kill Danny Thompson," she muttered.

"I'll keep that in mind if something happens to him." Colton's mouth twitched suspiciously.

"Don't you dare laugh at me."

He cleared his throat. "It was the furthest thing from my mind."

She crossed her arms and gave him a smug look. "Well, one good thing has come out of this. You definitely won't be pulling out your handcuffs. Everyone will know you're a cop. Your cover would be blown."

"Honey, if I cuff you right now, I'll throw in a kiss and put you over my shoulder. My hand on your pretty little bottom will convince everyone those handcuffs have nothing to do with my occupation and everything to do with our relationship. They'll think we're into kink."

She pressed her hand against her mouth, her face warming more from his "bottom" comment than from the one about "kink."

He grinned, enjoying her discomfort far too much. "Want me to prove it?" He reached behind him as if to pull out the promised handcuffs.

"Don't you dare," she whispered harshly.

He laughed and held his hand out for hers, waiting expectantly.

She slapped her hand in his, forcing a smile that was more a baring of her teeth. "Don't expect me to hold your hand once we're inside the inn."

His smile faded and he pulled her hand to his chest, clasping it over his heart in a gesture obviously designed for their audience but that had her suddenly feeling... unfocused.

"All I plan to do once we get there is talk," he assured her. "Promise."

The kindness in his eyes, in his voice, was as unexpected as it was confusing. It was as if he realized how embarrassed she was and he felt bad about it. Maybe the show he was putting on really was just to keep his cover from being blown, and not to humiliate her.

And if she was being honest with herself, this predicament really was her fault. She never should have put her hand on Colton's rather impressively muscled chest that his snug T-shirt did nothing to conceal and told Danny they were old friends. She should have come up with a better story than that. Colton was simply continuing the fiction that she'd created.

Dang, she hated that she couldn't be mad at him about that.

She turned toward the B and B, forcing him to lower her hand or wrench her shoulder from its socket. And as she strode toward the steps with him practically glued to her side, it occurred to her that heading into the B and B would give the gossips even more fodder. But the alternative was to head uptown and face everyone's questions.

The inn was the safer choice.

She pushed the front door open and stepped inside.

He gave her a disapproving look. "You should keep that door locked when you're not here."

"Why? Everyone knows everyone around here. We're all a big family."

"Which family member pointed the gun at us when we were on the airboat?"

She hesitated, then continued toward the great room to the right of the stairs. "I already told you that I don't know who the gunman was. And, honestly, I don't see what else you could possibly ask me that I didn't already answer when that other detective interviewed me. As I explained to him, I don't—"

"Where's the vase?"

"What?" She turned around.

He stood in front of the registration desk and gestured toward the middle cubby where the gorgeous blue vase had sat this morning. But now the spot was empty. And there was only one person she could think of who'd have taken it. *Eddie.* Probably to protect her in case the police went to her inn to question her after the botched holdup attempt.

"Did you call someone and tell them to hide it?" he asked.

"Of course not. Why would I? Assuming I could even get a call to work around here. Trust me, this inn is right in the middle of an electronics dead zone."

"Maybe you called from the south dock, after you found out that I was a cop, and you remembered my interest in that vase. You were worried that you'd get into trouble for accepting stolen property. So you asked a friend to move it somewhere else."

She crossed her arms. "Or maybe, like you said, I should have kept my front door locked."

His mouth twitched. "I guess I deserved that one."

The man really shouldn't smile like that. It made her notice those incredible blue eyes again and it was killing her concentration.

"What does a vase that may or may not be stolen have to do with you interviewing me about the gunman anyway?"

He leaned against the registration desk and crossed his long legs at the ankles. "Fair question. How about we start over? I'm Collier County Deputy Colton Graham. I'm working undercover to bring down a burglary ring that's been operating in Naples for the past six months. This morning I followed one of the suspects here to Mystic Glades. The same man who held up that blue vase in front of your inn and then went inside—

Eddie Rafferty. The same man who I believe pointed a gun at a boat full of people this morning when he tried to rob them, when he tried to rob you and me. Does that clear it up?"

She raised her chin a notch. "I suppose it does. What's *clear* is that you've made a terrible mistake. The vase you believe to be stolen obviously looks like some other vase. You've confused the two."

"Oh, I have, have I?"

"You most certainly have. And since I can't tell you who that gunman was, there's no point in even continuing this conversation."

"Can't? Or won't?"

She let out an impatient breath. "In case you've forgotten, I have a grand opening tomorrow. And although most everything is ready, I'd like to take advantage of the last few hours of daylight that we have left to double-check all the rooms and menus. And I also need to confirm that my two helpers are still set to arrive in the morning. Which means I have to run an errand, to go visit them."

"Them? Just who are these helpers?"

"Not that you really need to know, but I've hired a friend's daughter, Tippy, to help me run the inn all summer, starting tomorrow. The work will look good on her résumé, since she's pursuing a degree in hospitality."

"You said *them*. Who else is coming?"

"Her boyfriend, Jenks. He'll do the chores around here." She waved her hand impatiently. "None of that matters. Like I said, I need to make sure everything is set. You're of course welcome to stay in your room, free of charge, as long as you don't interfere with my work. It's the least I can do for a police officer. I'll cancel the charge against your credit card."

"Very kind of you," he said, his voice dry.

"If that's all, then, I'll just go—"

"There was a small painting displayed here earlier. It's missing, too." He gestured toward the wall of cubbies behind the registration desk.

She noted the empty square and let out a cry of dismay. "That was one of my favorite pieces."

"Eddie sold you that one, too, huh?"

Her stomach sank with dread. No, he hadn't *sold* it to her. "Why did you remember that particular painting?" she whispered.

"You know why." His voice was soft this time, kind even, without its accusatory edge. As if he realized she'd just had a shock, even if he didn't understand why.

She could do without his pity. She certainly didn't deserve it. *Stupid, stupid, stupid.* How could she have been so gullible? Even though she considered herself a temporary caretaker of the vase and other items that Eddie had sold her, she'd never once suspected that the painting was stolen, too.

It had been a gift, no money exchanged between them. He'd brought it to her after she helped him study for an algebra final exam. He'd been close to tears, telling her he wouldn't have graduated if she hadn't helped him. The painting was his way of saying thank-you and had supposedly been purchased with money from mowing lawns and other odd jobs he'd worked last summer. She'd treasured it, not for its beauty, but for the sentiment behind it. And now to find out that it was just like everything else he'd brought broke her heart.

She sank onto the nearest chair, a ladder-back she'd restrung herself, after painting the wood a cozy, happy yellow. But even her favorite chair couldn't make her smile now.

A few weeks ago, she'd thought she had everything under control. Things were going as planned. And she'd believed—foolishly, she now realized—that she could cover for Eddie, at least until she managed to extricate him from the mire he was caught up in. And then, once that was taken care of, she'd planned to have a heart-to-heart talk with him and insist all the stolen items be returned. She'd be his advocate in court. She'd explain everything that had been going on in the hopes that the court would be understanding and would be lenient with him. She'd hoped to *save* him. But now, thanks to this irritating, nosy cop, it was clear that she might have done more harm than good.

Colton sighed and crouched down in front of her, his face a study in compassion. He took her hands between his, surprising her so much that she didn't try to pull back. She stared into his cobalt-blue eyes and was rather shocked at the zing of awareness that shot through her. Before now she'd thought of him only as a potential model for one of her projects, or the irritating police officer who was interfering with her life. But now, seeing that gentle, concerned look on his face, with those incredible eyes seeming to delve into her very soul, she was noticing him in an entirely different way. A way that made her body melt from the inside out.

Good grief. She was attracted to him.

She yanked her hands from his and pressed back against the chair. This was even more of a disaster than she'd feared. There was no room, and no time in her life for a relationship. Not now. And certainly not with a man who was, in many ways, her enemy.

He sighed and stood, looking mildly disappointed in her. And for some reason, that stung.

"We can rule out that a stranger came in here and

robbed you," he said, "unlocked door or not. Whoever took the vase and that painting was specifically here for those items."

"Why do you say that?"

"If a typical burglar had come in here, he wouldn't have left behind the other valuables." He waved toward the network of shelves.

Not sure what he was talking about, she looked at the mixture of plants, books and other knickknacks decorating each cubby. "I don't understand what you mean. Everything of value *was* taken."

He gave her an incredulous look and pointed at a small five-by-seven painting on the third shelf down. "That has to be worth several hundred dollars." He pointed to another one on the far right. "And that one? I can't even guess. But I've had a crash course in art valuation on various assignments this past year and I know that painting would fetch an exorbitant price at auction."

She blinked, wondering just what he meant by exorbitant. "You think those pieces are...valuable?"

"Of course." He searched her gaze. "You don't?"

Her face flushed with heat and she shrugged. "I suppose so. Maybe." Since she was the one who'd created those particular pieces to decorate the inn, she'd never thought about their monetary value. It was...nice, unexpected...to have someone besides her look at them and think they held more than just sentimental value. Although art, and making art, had always been important to her, she'd never felt confident enough to try to sell any of her pieces. They never seemed good enough.

His look turned suspicious, as if he thought she was lying about the paintings. Maybe he believed they were stolen, too, but that they hadn't popped onto his radar yet. She'd like to put his mind at ease, but telling him that he'd just complimented her own work felt far too… intimate…to share with him after all the lies she'd told. And the threats he'd made.

Intimate? Who was she kidding? She'd asked him to pose nude for her. It didn't get much more intimate than that. But that was all about her art. Now, knowing he was a cop and that she'd asked him to pose for her, she was mortified.

He stepped closer to study one of her canvases, a depiction of the Glades at dawn, with fields of golden saw grass bending in the breeze while a whooping crane searched for its next meal. Colton was probably looking for the artist's signature to see if it was listed with the other stolen goods he was investigating. Before he could find her initials hidden in the intricate details of a wildflower near the bottom right corner, she rose from her chair, drawing his attention.

"Are we finished here?" she asked.

"Are you ready to finally tell the truth?"

If only it were that simple. But the truth would bring more policemen, scouring through the woods, putting all the residents on high alert. And *that* would be a disaster.

"What else do you want to know?" she asked, beginning to fear that this was a losing battle. The man just didn't know when to quit.

"Where's Eddie Rafferty?"

Hopefully lying low, staying out of harm's way until she could get to him.

"I don't know."

"And you wouldn't tell me if you did, would you?"

She braced her hand on the edge of the registration

desk, her fingers curling against the wood. "He's not the bad person that you think he is. He's just a kid—"

"He's *eighteen*, legally an adult. Old enough to vote, old enough to die for his country. Which means he's plenty old enough to know right from wrong, and he should pay the consequences for the choices he's made. Where is he?"

She wasn't sure, but she knew who his friends were. And even though *Eddie* didn't know that she knew, she also knew his favorite hiding places. Finding him wouldn't be all that difficult. And she *needed* to find him. Because that attempted holdup had changed everything. She'd bring him into the police station herself if she could just get this relentless detective to give her a break so she could slip away and bring Eddie in *safely*.

"Silver, this is your chance to do the right thing. Tell me where he is."

Again, his voice was soft, understanding. Too bad they were on opposite sides. He was exactly the sort of man she could like, respect, admire. But his timing couldn't be worse.

"And if I don't *do the right thing*, you're going to arrest me?"

He frowned, his dark eyebrows lowering. "I don't want to. But if you force my hand, I will."

She considered her options, her plans. But there was really only one option that she could think of that would end this stalemate without sacrificing Eddie. Even if it meant sacrificing the inn, and everything that she'd worked for.

She held her hands out, palms up. "I guess I'm forcing your hand."

Chapter Six

"What the Fourth of July were you thinking, Detective?"

Colton would have laughed at his boss's die-hard commitment to avoid cursing, but his ears were ringing from the shouting. He belatedly wished he *hadn't* closed the office door. Then maybe some of the sound waves would have swept through the open doorway into the squad room, reducing the shouts to a bearable decibel level. Then again, with the door *open*, what few peers of his were still around, owing to the late hour, would hear the dressing-down he was being given. So maybe the closed door was a good thing. It was a toss-up.

He rested his forearms on his knees and leaned forward in his chair. Drew glared at him from behind his desk, his face so red he looked as if he was about to have a stroke. Colton was doing his best to calm him down, but nothing he'd said so far was working. He supposed he was just going to have to weather the storm.

"What else was I supposed to do?" he said, keeping his voice as calm and nonconfrontational as possible. "She basically told me to arrest her."

"Well, I wouldn't have expected you to actually do it." Drew shoved a folder out of his way, frowned, then picked it up and put it on a stack of folders, carefully aligning all the edges.

Again, Colton wanted to laugh. Or knock the stack askew just to see Drew straighten it again. But he rather enjoyed his job—most of the time—and didn't relish the idea of being fired.

"I can just see this in social media," Drew practically growled. "Collier County Deputy Manhandles Woman Who Witnessed Attempted Holdup."

"*Witnessed*, my…" His boss's warning glare made Colton stop before he broke the golden no-cursing rule that Drew had instituted after taking over the leadership from the former lieutenant. Trying to clean up the department's poor image in the press was a worthy goal, certainly. But the no cursing, even when civilians weren't present, seemed a bit extreme—especially to guys like Colton who spent much of their time under-cover. Criminals didn't go around saying *darn* and *shoot*, and neither did Colton when he was pretending to be one of them. Which just made it all that much harder when he was in the office. Like now.

He drew a bracing breath and tried again. "What I'm saying is that Miss Westbrook isn't simply a witness. And you know it. She's a part of whatever's going on in Mystic Glades."

Drew flattened his palms on the desk. "You do realize that any rent-by-the-hour attorney will get her out within minutes. And they'll just make us look heavy-handed to the press. Officer Scott told me she's already contacted a lawyer. Heck, he's probably already in the interrogation room with her by now. We're going to have our heads handed to us on a platter."

Colton rose to his feet. There was only so much he could take, and he'd about reached his limit. "Drew—"

"Don't call me that. I'm too ticked off to be your friend right now."

"Fine, *Lieutenant Shlafer*. But keep in mind that I've been deep undercover on this case for months. Rafferty is the closest to a true lead that I've gotten. And I don't know where he is. And now he's pulled a gun on someone, graduating from burglary to armed robbery. In case you haven't noticed, this is escalating, fast. Someone's going to get hurt or killed if I don't get a jump on this. And right now my only chance is to interrogate and intimidate his guardian angel into spilling the beans on him. I don't know about you, but I don't want to sit around on my...butt...waiting for something worse to happen. What if I hadn't been on that boat? What if that kid hadn't gotten scared off? Someone could have been killed."

A knock sounded on the door.

Drew glared at Colton, letting him know just what he thought of his little speech. "Come in."

The door opened and one of the uniformed officers stepped in. "Miss Westbrook's lawyer spoke to the judge and the charges were dropped."

"Perfect," Drew muttered. "Now we look even more inept. All right. Put the paperwork through to release her."

"Already done."

Drew gave Colton a hard look. "At least someone around here is efficient and on the ball."

Colton gave him the best comeback he could think of. He smiled.

Drew narrowed his eyes.

"Lieutenant?" the officer at the door called out again.

"What?" Drew yelled, then reddened. He cleared his throat. "Sorry. What else can I help you with?"

"Miss Westbrook wants to speak to you before she leaves."

"Well, of course she does. And I'll just bet her lawyer tags along with her, so they can tell us together that they're suing for false arrest."

Colton couldn't help it. He rolled his eyes.

Drew jabbed his finger in the air, pointing at him. "As for you, Detective. I'm going to—"

"Sir," the officer called out again. "Miss Westbrook is here, right now, to see you."

"All right, all right." Drew pulled on his suit jacket with quick, jerky movements. "Send her in."

The officer moved back and Silver stepped through the doorway.

Colton and Drew rose to their feet just as two men in dark suits stepped in behind Silver.

"She needed two lawyers?" Colton grumbled beneath his breath.

He must not have been as quiet as he'd thought, because one of the men gave him a sharp look.

"No," the man said, directing his comment to Colton. "She only has one lawyer—Mr. Stanton." He waved toward the other man.

"Then who are you?" Colton asked.

"He's my boss," Silver said, drawing everyone's attention back to her. "Lieutenant Shlafer, Detective Graham, meet Special Agent Eduardo Garcia. DEA."

EVERYONE STARTED TALKING at once.

Silver tried to intervene, but her boss, Colton's boss, and even the lawyer her boss had brought with him to supposedly ensure cooperation and make sure any charges against her were dropped, were all so busy arguing with one another that she couldn't get their attention.

"I think this is where the art of a stealthy retreat comes in," Colton whispered as he passed by her on his way to the door. He held it open in invitation.

After casting another irritated look at the other men who were steadfastly ignoring her, even though this whole situation was *about* her, she followed Colton into the squad room.

He led her to an empty desk well away from the few desks that still had detectives on phones or typing up reports. Most of the room was deserted, probably because it was well after seven in the evening and everyone else had gone home to their families.

Since she'd been sitting for over two hours—counting the trip from Mystic Glades, handcuffed, in Colton's car—she turned down his offer of a seat and chose instead to lean back against the desk.

He joined her, leaning back beside her, arms crossed and his long legs spread out in front of him. They both stared at the far wall for a minute, a depressing gray decorated with an even more depressing collection of plaques. Above them were two simple, but poignant words. *Our Fallen*. She shivered and rubbed her hands up and down her arms.

"So," Colton finally said. "DEA, huh?"

"Yep."

"How long?"

"Eight years. What about you?"

He thumped his fingers against the edge of the desk. "About the same, I reckon, come October."

The silence stretched out between them again. Or, rather, it would have been silent if it weren't for the thankfully muted sound of yelling coming through the walls of Lieutenant Shlafer's office behind them. It sounded like a war going on.

"Don't let it bother you," Colton said, jerking his head toward the office. "They're probably trying to figure out whose is bigger."

"Is that supposed to be funny?"

He sighed. "Apparently not. I was just trying to cut through some of the tension in here. You want a soda or something?"

She shook her head. "No, but feel free to leave. I don't need a babysitter."

"Yeah. I kind of figured that once you introduced your boss. DEA, huh? Why didn't you tell me?"

"I was undercover, just like you."

"But after you found out that I was a cop, you should have told me."

"Really? Just like that, I should have trusted you?"

"Of course."

She glanced around the room to make sure no one was paying them any attention before she replied, "Tell me, Detective."

"Call me Colton. I've been calling you Silver all this time. The least you can do is use my first name, too, so I don't feel like quite as much of an idiot for being in the dark."

She couldn't help smiling at that. He was obviously feeling put out that he hadn't guessed she was in law enforcement. "All right. Colton. If you'd spent months deep undercover and you met an undercover police officer who could *blow* your cover if he didn't believe your story, would you have leveled with him and risked everything?"

"No way."

"Thank you."

He frowned. "Okay, so you moved to Mystic Glades, what, a few months ago?"

"Six."

"Only six?"

"Yep. Why does that surprise you?"

He tapped the desk again. "In that bar, you seemed pretty cozy with everyone, like you belonged there. And you knew all about that Freddie woman and the guy she liked."

"Labron. And that's because I do belong there. It's where I grew up. I left to go to college, and then to start my career. Mostly I worked out of the office down in the Keys. But I always went back every summer, kept up on everything going on. Since I couldn't risk word getting out that I was DEA since I mostly work undercover, I told everyone I paid the bills with my art. They always knew me as that flighty daydreamer who'd rather paint than go shoe shopping anyway." She shrugged. "The ruse worked. And when tourism finally came to Mystic Glades, I thought it was a sign that it was finally time to take all the money I'd saved over the years and chase my dream."

"The bed-and-breakfast? It's your dream?"

She nodded. "I put in notice at my job and hired a contractor to start the work on that plot of land my grandfather had passed down to me."

"You said you put in notice. Obviously you didn't end up quitting. What happened?"

"Eddie Rafferty."

He gave her a curious look. "What do you mean?"

She tried not to let it distract her that his shoulder kept brushing against hers whenever he talked, or that he smelled so clean and masculine—probably his soap. Whether they'd said it out loud or not, the minute he found out that she was a fellow law-enforcement officer, his demeanor toward her had changed. He was now treating her like an equal, a comrade in arms.

And without the hostility bubbling between them, she could finally let her guard down. But that seemed to have been a green light for her hormones, too. Because she kept getting distracted by little things about him— like the sexy rumble of his deep voice in his chest, or the way he'd held the door open for her earlier, or that he was asking her questions instead of making more accusations. He was all good *hot* cop now. And she was more than relieved to say a permanent goodbye to *bad* cop.

"Silver? You were going to explain about Rafferty?"

She looked away, focusing on a painting—a poster, really—hanging on another wall, just outside of a conference room. It wasn't to her taste. The colors were too muted. But she couldn't seem to pull a coherent thought together when he turned the full attention of those gorgeous baby blues her way.

"Eddie was busing tables at Gators and Taters last summer when I was staying with some friends who run the Moon and Star."

"Moon and Star? I think I remember that. It's across the street from Callahan's?"

She nodded. "Faye Star, well, Faye *Young* now that she and Jake got married, owns the shop. It's a mystical kind of thing with potions, fragrances, even some clothing you wouldn't find anywhere else." She waved her hand in the air. "Anyway, I was staying in their guest room above the shop while on vacation. When I was having lunch at G&T, I met Eddie. I guess I…noticed a kindred spirit, saw the way others treated him, like he was invisible. Like just because he didn't have a family, and didn't fit in, that he wasn't worthy of their time. So

I made time, made the effort to offer him friendship. I even helped him with his homework."

She could feel his stare, but she didn't turn to face him.

"Kindred spirit," he said. "Because you focus so much on your art? Because people can't understand your world so they don't go out of their way to welcome you into their circles?"

This time, she *did* look at him. "Most people would say I'm *unfocused*."

"They'd be wrong. I've always thought of artists as having a sixth sense, the ability to see another dimension, another plane of existence that others don't. That ability, to see, *really* see, and to find joy in everything and everyone around you is your superpower, while the rest of us are handicapped."

She blinked back the unexpected hot burn of tears at the backs of her eyes. "What an amazing thing to say."

"Yeah, well." He cleared his throat, suddenly looking uncomfortable. "Just calling it like I see it."

"You really do have a sister who's an artist, don't you?"

"Yep."

"And she lives in Atlanta?"

"Right again. I'm not the one who told a passel of lies since meeting you. Most of what I said was the truth."

"Ouch." Those tears weren't burning to be shed anymore.

He lightly bumped her shoulder with his in a show of camaraderie. "No worries. I get it. I'd have done the same thing. To some extent."

A moment of awkward silence passed between them. She didn't need him to tell her exactly how she'd bungled her job. She was well aware of that.

"Finish your story," he said. "How did meeting Eddie change your plans to quit the DEA?"

"I saw him arguing at the edge of the woods with a couple of other guys—one of his foster brothers—Charlie Tate—who's Eddie's age, and Ron Dukes, a troublemaker in his midtwenties who has no business hanging out with high school kids. And their argument didn't strike me as typical, either. They were far too serious, and they kept glancing around, like they were looking for someone, or maybe worried that someone might see them. A few seconds later, Ron led the other two of them into the woods."

He stiffened beside her. "You followed them?"

"I did."

"Even though your instincts told you that something was off?"

She crossed her arms. "It's not like I was out of my element. I know every inch of Mystic Glades. And I'm an officer of the law. It's my job to investigate things that don't look right."

"Tell me you at least had your sidearm."

"Are you going to let me finish this or not?"

He crossed his arms in an echo of her pose and gave her a curt nod.

"Okay, no, I didn't have my gun with me. But it was because I was on vacation, in my hometown. I didn't have any reason to expect something like that would happen."

"Something like what, exactly?"

"I followed Ron, Charlie and Eddie about a mile in. Then Ron pulled a brick of cocaine out of a hollowed-out tree."

He cursed beneath his breath.

"No one got hurt," she said, knowing he was still

upset that she hadn't had her gun with her that day. "I knew a bad scene when I saw it. I didn't confront any of them. Instead, I backtracked to town and then high-tailed it out of the Glades so I could call my boss."

"You should always, always, have your sidearm. Hell, I even take mine into the bathroom. And I sleep with it under my pillow. Even when I'm undercover I carry a gun. Hell, especially undercover. You should, too."

"Yeah, well. Maybe I just suck at being a cop." She echoed his earlier words back at him.

"No. You don't suck at being a cop. You're just too close to this, because you know Eddie, and Mystic Glades is your hometown. Your boss thought that would be an asset after you told him about that kilo, didn't he?" He didn't wait for her response. "He sent you in there to track down the supply of drugs. And then, what, you discovered Eddie was in deeper than you thought? And you found out he was involved in the burglary ring, too?"

She pursed her lips and stared at the opposite wall again.

"You don't have to answer," he said. "I can guess the rest, based on my own observations from earlier today. Instead of hauling Eddie in and getting him to roll on his friends, you covered for him and tried to figure out how to keep him out of jail and still catch the bad guys. But that's where you went wrong. Because Eddie is one of those bad guys. You let your friendship with him cloud your judgment. That's why you lied to me today about the holdup."

The more he spoke, the angrier he sounded. It was as if all the pieces were falling into place and destroying any fellow law-enforcement empathy he'd had for her just moments ago.

She didn't try to defend herself. What would be the point? Everything he was saying was true. She'd screwed up.

"You weren't worried that I'd blow your cover like you probably told your boss," Colton continued, sounding disgusted. "You were worried that if you told me the truth, I'd tell you that you're too close to this. You had every opportunity to come clean. When the other officers interviewed you outside Mystic Glades, where we all had cell phone coverage and could have verified your story with one call to the DEA, you continued to lie. And the *reason* that you lied wasn't so you could protect your case. The reason you lied was to protect Eddie Rafferty. Everything that you've done was to keep me from hauling that kid to jail. Admit it."

She stared into a pair of stormy blue eyes that had darkened with anger, not sure what to say, or even whether she *should* say anything. After experiencing his support, and his thoughtful insight into something she'd struggled with all her life—the way she viewed the world through her artist's lens—she found it so much worse now to be the object of such hostility from him. As if she'd discovered a friend, or something…deeper, only to have it whisked away.

"Is all of that true, Agent Westbrook?" a voice demanded.

Her heart stuttered in her chest as she turned to see her boss standing beside a stunned-looking Lieutenant Shlafer. There could be no doubt. They'd heard every word, every accusation that Colton had just made. But what made her humiliation worse was that Colton had to have known they were standing there. He'd been half turned toward her, and her back had been to Shlafer's office. He'd known they were there, the whole time, and he'd kept going, spouting off things that could very well destroy her career.

"Well?" Garcia demanded, his voice so sharp it could have cut glass.

She pushed away from the desk and stood ramrod straight, refusing to look at Colton. She fervently hoped that after today, she'd never have to see him again.

"I was trying to figure out the best way to extricate Rafferty from the trouble he was in, yes. But, as we previously discussed, I was also using him and his contacts to discover who was heading up the drug-running operation, and how they were bringing the drugs in and out of the Everglades."

"Conference. Now." Garcia whirled around and marched back toward Shlafer's office.

Colton raised his hand toward her, regret mirrored in the tiny lines of tension around the corners of his eyes. "Silver, I'm sorry. I didn't mean to—"

She pushed his hand away and straightened her shoulders. "My *name* is Special Agent Westbrook." After making a wide berth around him, she followed her boss into the office and shut the door.

COLTON DROPPED HIS hand to his side, hating that he'd caused that hurt that had flashed across Silver's face after his tirade. His anger had bled out as soon as he saw that look and realized what he'd done. But he'd been so upset that she'd made so many poor choices, mainly because she could have gotten herself hurt, or worse. As to *why* the idea of her getting hurt bothered him so much, well, he didn't even want to go there. It didn't make sense that he'd care so much, not after knowing her for less than a day.

Now who was losing focus?

He shook his head in disgust. "I made a royal mess out of that."

"Yeah, you did," Drew said. "But you were right. And you didn't say anything that her boss didn't already guess. He was planning on confronting her after we shared everything about our cases."

"Shared?" Colton snorted. "Is that what you call all that yelling?" He glanced around. "And what did you do with the lawyer? Is he back in your office?"

Drew grinned. "We gave him a headache. I think he went downstairs for an aspirin." He plopped down in the chair that Silver had refused earlier. "Special Agent Garcia has been worried about her working alone on this case but wasn't sure how to help her without blowing her cover. People in the Glades aren't quick to trust outsiders."

"So what's he going to do now?"

"Pull her. He'll send a team into the marsh to see if they can salvage any evidence, maybe get lucky. But most likely they'll have to start a new investigation to stop the flow of drugs moving through there, from outside of Mystic Glades."

"That's a shame. From what she said, she was close to a break in the case."

"You thought the same thing, and look where we are on that."

He winced. "Point taken. What do you want me to do? Find Rafferty and bring him in?"

"I think that's about the only thing we *can* do at this point. Cut our losses. We'll coordinate with Garcia, help him salvage as much as possible from Westbrook's investigation. Then we all start over." He pushed the chair back from the desk and stood.

"All right," Colton said. "The kid's gone to ground right now. I think we should give him a couple of days to start feeling secure before we go looking for him. Then I'll get a couple of guys to go with me up through the canals and we'll sneak in the back way. We'll catch him as soon as he pops his head up somewhere."

Drew nodded. "Sounds like a good plan. I'll see if Garcia wants to—"

"Lieutenant." Another detective several desks away held up one of the landline phones. "There's a call for you, from the Miccosukee."

"Miccosukee? Their resort's almost two hours away. Why aren't they calling Broward County or Miami-Dade if they need help?"

"Not the resort. Alligator Alley. The Miccosukee police out on their section of I-75 said they've had some kind of incident that you need to know about."

Drew took the call. From the way his jaw tightened, Colton knew the news was bad. The detective who'd notified him about the call grabbed a piece of paper off the printer on his desk and handed that to Drew as well. The lieutenant read it while he spoke on the phone, then shook his head and tucked the paper into his suit jacket pocket. By the time Drew ended the call, Silver and her boss had finished their meeting and joined Colton in front of the desk.

Silver's face was pale and she wouldn't meet Colton's gaze. He was about to demand that Garcia tell him what he'd said to her when Drew joined them. He nodded at Silver and Garcia, before his weary gaze met Colton's.

"What happened?" Colton asked.

"The Miccosukee police had heard about the attempted holdup earlier and that we were interested in interviewing Rafferty." He glanced at Silver before continuing. "There was a 911 call a few hours ago around mile marker fifty-two on I-75, in their jurisdiction, and they just briefed me on their initial findings." He cleared his throat and looked at Silver again.

She sucked in a breath and fisted her hands at her sides.

"Please," she said, her voice so tight and hoarse that she couldn't finish her sentence.

Garcia gave her an odd look, as if he didn't understand what the rest of them had already guessed.

Colton circled around him and stood behind Silver. He put his hands lightly on her shoulders, as a show of support and to let her know that even if her boss was being a jerk, she wasn't in this alone. Instead of pushing him away, as he'd half feared, she took the support he offered and subtly shifted so that her back was pressed against his chest. Colton nodded at Drew to continue.

His face was a mask of misery and sympathy as he broke the news. "I'm sorry, Agent Westbrook. Eddie Rafferty is dead."

Her body started to shake and she wobbled against him as if she was about to collapse.

Colton reacted on instinct, wrapping his arms around her waist and holding her tight. He didn't care one whit that Garcia frowned at him or that Drew raised an eyebrow. She'd fought for that kid, had allowed herself to be arrested and risked losing her inn for him. Maybe Colton didn't agree with her choices, but he admired her just the same for fighting for a troubled young man whom everyone else had thrown away—including Colton. He couldn't help feeling guilty about that now.

When Silver didn't say anything, Colton asked the

questions that needed to be asked, the questions that he knew she'd want the answers to, later, when she could move past her shock and process them.

"How?" he asked. "What happened?"

Drew hesitated and shot an uncertain look at Silver.

"Say it," Colton told him. "She needs to know."

Drew looked to Silver's boss for guidance, but Garcia shrugged as if he didn't have a clue how to handle Silver's silence.

"A motorist called it in a couple of hours ago," Drew said. "A body lying in the grass beside the highway. The coroner still has to perform an autopsy, of course, but the cause of death is probably internal injuries. He was beaten, and…" He looked at Silver again. "I don't think the medical details are pertinent at the moment. Suffice it to say, he was murdered. And the evidence suggests it was the primary site. He was killed right there on the side of the highway."

Silver drew a sharp breath and started pushing at Colton's arms around her waist. He let her go and she shoved away from him, wobbling like a drunk on her feet.

Colton reached for her, but she scrambled back out of his way. "Silver, let me help—"

"No, don't," she whispered, her voice full of anguish. "I have to…I need to go to the ladies' room."

The stubborn woman looked as though she was about to pass out, but Colton didn't argue. He could tell she was about to break down and she desperately wanted some privacy before that happened. "Down that hallway, first door on the right." He waved toward the right side of the room.

"Thank you," she whispered, then made her way unsteadily out of the room.

Garcia frowned after her. "She shouldn't be that upset. She's too softhearted, too weak for this job. I should have recognized that years ago. And now she's obviously crossed the line even more than I'd realized, made this personal."

Colton swore. "You do realize she knew Rafferty before your case started, right? He was in high school. A kid. She even helped him with his homework. But she still did her job, let you know that he was mixed up with a drug-running operation. And she was working to bring that operation down in spite of that personal connection to Rafferty. If she's choked up over his death, it's understandable, expected. From where I stand, you're the one with the problem. You aren't making this personal enough. You should be offering her support and understanding instead of criticizing her."

Garcia took a step toward him, his dark eyes flashing with anger. "Watch your tongue, Detective."

Colton matched his step. "Why don't you—"

"Hey, hey, hey." Drew moved between them, pushing his hands against them to keep them apart. "Back off, gentlemen. This has been a stressful day for all of us. Let's leave our opinions and our egos at the door and focus on our cases."

"What cases?" Garcia sneered. "Rafferty was the link to the robbery ring and the drug ring. There *aren't* any cases anymore. We have to start over. This is a complete cluster from beginning to end." He glared at Colton. "Since you're so cozy with Westbrook, you can give her a message for me when she comes back. She's fired."

Colton shoved Drew's hand out of his way so he could reach Garcia, but the agent whirled around and strode toward the exit.

"Let it go," Drew ordered.

"He's a colossal jerk who doesn't even support his own agents," Colton ground out.

"Agreed. But it's his call. She'd given notice that she was quitting after this case anyway. It's not like he destroyed her career."

"Maybe not, but once she works through her grief, she'll want to catch Eddie's killer. And without the DEA's support, she's lost her vehicle for doing that. You know good and well the Miccosukee police aren't going to know what to do with this one. And we sure don't want them trouncing over our burglary ring while trying to solve the murder. It's part of our case. We should take it and find Eddie's killer. And if there are drugs flowing through Mystic Glades, we can't turn a blind eye just because Garcia does. Someone needs to stop it."

"I'm well aware of that. But if this wasn't political before, it just got political. I'll have to smooth Garcia's ruffled feathers and see if we can't come up with a joint plan, maybe even a task force. Obviously if Rafferty was involved in both cases, it makes sense to work together. It's a pretty safe bet that the guy at the top is running both the drugs and the burglary ring. I'll have to think on this and figure out how to handle it without putting my job on the line. First things first, we need to notify Rafferty's family."

"He didn't have a family. He was in the foster system, never adopted."

"Oh, man. Poor kid."

"Yeah. Poor kid." Colton shook his head. "From what I can tell, Silver's all he had. But I can ask her about it. We can do the notification together if there's anyone to notify. Or I can do it alone once I get the details from her."

"Works for me." Drew pulled the piece of paper out of his suit jacket pocket that the other detective had given him while he was on the phone. "I was going to tell the others about this, but obviously Miss Westbrook is in no shape to read it right now."

"What is it?"

"A copy of a letter from Rafferty, addressed to Miss Westbrook. The original was found in his jeans pocket in an envelope, so the responding officer emailed us a picture of it that he took with his phone. Looks like Eddie had planned on mailing it to her when he got to wherever he was going. I assume he avoided text or email, since the coverage is unreliable in Mystic Glades. Unfortunately he never got the chance to send it." He handed it to Colton. "Take her home. Watch over her for a few days and then check back in with me. I'll put you on paid administrative leave until I get together with Garcia and we decide where to go from here. If he won't do what he should—support his agent when she's in crisis—then we'll have to do his damn job for him."

Colton stared in shock at his boss. "Did you just say—"

"Do you like your job, Detective?" Drew practically growled.

He choked back a laugh. "Yes, sir. I do. Which means I never heard you break your own cursing rule."

"Good answer." Drew headed toward his office.

Chapter Seven

Colton glanced at Silver in the passenger seat of his Mustang as he drove under the archway into Mystic Glades. But she was just as silent, just as withdrawn as she'd been since Drew announced that Eddie was dead. She hadn't even reacted when Colton told her that her boss had fired her.

She was definitely in shock, and probably blaming herself, second-guessing everything and replaying the investigation over and over in her mind to see if she could have done something differently. He hated that she was going through this, but at least she wasn't pushing him away. No one should have to face grief like that alone.

As he pulled into a parking space in front of the B and B, he frowned at the lack of lights outside. At a minimum, the porch light should be on to help dispel the darkness. A streetlight would be better, something that would cast a glow across the entire front yard, especially since the inn was a bit isolated from the other businesses. There were streetlights farther up the street, but they stopped short of the B and B.

It was only a little past ten, but with all the businesses closed except for Callahan's Watering Hole, which was a good distance away, it seemed even later. And too quiet.

Silver's inn seemed far too vulnerable for his liking. He'd have to talk to her about the lighting and maybe even a high privacy fence, at least on the sides of the property. That would remove a burglar's ability to hide in the bushes and trees. Anyone intending harm to the inn or its inhabitants would be forced to come out on the street in full view or approach from the back. He'd take a tour of the property tomorrow in daylight and see just how bad the security setup was.

Glancing over at Silver, who seemed to be lost in her own little world at the moment looking out at the dark sky, he was glad he'd brought her home and that he'd be there tonight to watch over her. Because right now he wasn't sure she could protect herself if it came to that.

He took his pistol out of his ankle holster and slid it into his waistband so he'd have it at the ready. He'd been thinking about Eddie's murder the whole way here and had come to a conclusion. If the burglary or drug ringleader was behind Eddie's murder—which seemed the logical conclusion—then the only reason to kill Eddie and leave his body in a public place was that the killer wanted him found. Which meant the killing was a message. Eddie had to have done something that put the killer at risk, and his murder was to warn others not to do anything similar.

But the only true risk to a drug boss would be exposure to law enforcement. And since Silver was the only law-enforcement officer in Mystic Glades and she had established a friendship with Eddie, then putting those together added up to one thing—Colton was convinced that the killer knew that Silver was DEA and that Eddie was her contact. The kid might not have realized he was being used, but his "boss" would have figured it out if Eddie mentioned anything about Silver and then the boss did some research. If he had the right contacts, he might have figured out that Silver was a threat.

Which meant Colton needed to stay extra vigilant, at least for the next few days until his boss soothed Garcia and figured out a new game plan.

"Silver," he whispered, not wanting to startle her in the quiet of the car. "Hey, Silver?"

She shook herself as if waking up. "Oh. We're here. Sorry."

She popped the door, but Colton leaned across her and pulled it shut. She looked at him in question.

He patted the gun at his waist. "I'd rather you wait until I get out and open your door. It's dark out here, and we don't know what Eddie may have told his killer, and what they may have deduced. We have to assume we're being watched. And since you don't have a gun—"

"I have a gun. Garcia gave it to me before, well, before everything went south at the station." She yanked her pant leg up to reveal an ankle holster much like his, with a Ruger 9 mm snapped into place. She let her pant leg drop. "I'm just keeping it hidden. You know, because B and B owners don't typically walk around with guns at their waists. It's bad for business."

He smiled. "You had me worried earlier. But you're going to be okay, aren't you?"

Tears suddenly brightened her eyes, but she blinked them back. "I'm okay."

"Wait here." He hated that he'd managed to bring her out of her stupor one moment and then had her ready to weep the next. She was still fragile, and he needed to keep a close eye on her. He hopped out and moved quickly around to the passenger door, keeping a watchful eye on the woods to the left and right of the property before opening her door.

A hurried walk down the path through the middle of the front lawn, with him looking left and right every few seconds, his right hand on the butt of his gun at his waist, found them at the front door.

She turned the knob, then turned it again. "I don't understand. Why won't it open?"

Colton shook the keys in his left hand. "Because I made you lock it when we left. You don't remember?" He put the key in the lock and opened the door.

"Now I remember."

She started to step inside first, but he moved past and pulled her in behind him, tucking her back against the wall as he locked the door. He flipped the entrance hall light switch and pulled out his gun, still blocking her with his body as he scanned their surroundings.

"Stay here while I do a security sweep. Stay alert. And don't hesitate to use your gun if someone other than me comes back. I'll announce myself before I step back into the foyer."

"No." She pulled her gun from its holster and held it down by her side, pointing at the floor. "We'll both clear the house."

"Silver, I don't think that's a—"

"Good idea?" she finished for him. "I'm grieving. And I feel guilty as hell for what happened to Eddie. But I'm not helpless. I'll deal with this. And just because Garcia fired me doesn't mean I'm suddenly not capable of using my training." She motioned toward the doorway to their left. "You can start with the kitchen and dining room, and circle around to the hallway that runs across the back of the house. I'll go right and clear the gathering room, the bathroom under the stairs, and circle around to the same hallway."

He agreed reluctantly, and they each headed off in

a different direction. They ended up meeting halfway down the hallway she'd mentioned, after he'd cleared the two rooms.

"What else is down there?" he asked, waving toward the other end of the hall.

"Bathroom, office and a sunroom. I cleared all three."

"Does this place have a back door? I didn't see one."

"Through the sunroom. And before you ask, yes, I locked it. Let's hurry and check upstairs so you'll stop worrying. I'm tired and I want to go to bed."

Together they searched all eight bedrooms and attached bathrooms, plus an additional bathroom accessible from the hall.

"This place is a lot bigger than it looks from the front." Colton shoved his gun in his waistband as he met up with Silver outside the stand-alone bathroom.

"Yeah, I wanted the straight, two-story farmhouse look on the front, so it's not very wide. The two short wings on each side form a U in back, which is perfect for the courtyard and outdoor eating area that I set up."

"Your design?"

She nodded absently and rubbed the back of her neck, and he suddenly realized just how exhausted she looked. The emotions of the day had taken their toll.

"Which room is yours?" he asked.

"Room number nine."

"Nine? I only saw eight bedrooms."

"That's because you didn't look in the attic. Come on. I'll show you." She led the way to the end of the hall, where a reading chair and small table and lamp sat in an alcove. Behind them was a decorative fireplace and a chunky oak mantel. She reached underneath the right end of the mantel and a wall panel slid open be-hind the chair, revealing a dark opening. "Cool, huh?"

He leaned in, his hand resting on his gun, ready to pull it out if necessary. A steep flight of stairs ran along the wall up to the left. A dim light at the top revealed a closed door. "Who all knows about this?"

She shrugged. "Anyone who helped with construc-tion, which is a lot of people around here. They pretty much all pitched in. It was a town project, really, even though I had professional crews. It's not supposed to be a secret or anything. I didn't want the stairs to mar the look of the upstairs hallways and thought this would be fun. It's a cool room, with a large dormer window that overlooks a gorgeous century-old oak tree in the back-yard. I'm told it's a good climbing tree, lots of hand-holds and branches."

"Where's the light switch up there?"

"On the right as you open the door, pretty much where you'd expect it to be. Come on, I'll show you since you obviously want to search my room, too."

"No. Wait here." He ignored her exasperated look as he headed up the stairs. At the top, he pulled out his gun, eased the door open and felt for the light switch. He flipped it on and rushed inside, sweeping his gun back and forth as he made a quick circuit of the rather large room.

The wide window off the back drew him forward. During the day, it would let a lot of light in. He imag-ined that was the reason the window was so large, so Silver could do her art projects up here. And through the window was the huge oak tree she'd mentioned, framed like a picture, which again he supposed was on purpose. Its thick branches reached out toward the attic window like giant hands, dripping with thick vines. What she thought was beautiful, he thought was a little creepy. And her comment about it being a good climbing tree had him worried. But after seeing how far away from the structure it was, he was reassured that even if someone did climb that tree, they'd never be able to use it as a way to get into the attic window. They'd end up falling to the ground below and breaking their neck.

Even though he was satisfied that no one could break into her room through that window, he still checked the locks to make sure it was secure.

The creak of a board behind him had him whirling around.

Silver stood in the door opening, her eyes wide as she held her hands out. "It's just me."

He swore and put his gun away. "I told you to wait."

"I don't take orders very well. And you're totally overreacting. The place is empty."

"And locked up tight now. Keep it that way."

She rolled her eyes and plopped down on the king-size bed that dominated the room. "Good night, Colton."

He smiled. "I guess that means you're kicking me out."

"Yes. I am. Your room is—"

"Right below this one. I know. If you need me, just—"

"Tap on the floor?"

"Yeah. That'll work." He crouched down in front of her and gently swept her bangs out of her eyes. "I'm really sorry for your loss. I know that Eddie meant a lot to you."

She winced when he said Eddie's name, and her eyes took on a haunted look. "Thank you."

He debated giving her the note that Eddie had left her, then decided against it. She was too tired, too…

fragile looking. Her insistence on helping him search the house had given her an excuse to push back the pain, to focus on something else if only for a few minutes. And probably her way of feeling that she had some kind of control over her life again. He just hoped she could manage to get some sleep without dwelling all night on the tragedy that had happened.

"Try to get some sleep," he said, giving her hand a squeeze.

"If you ever leave, I will," she grumbled.

He laughed. "I guess I've overstayed my welcome. Good night, then."

"Night."

He rose and headed to the door.

"Colton?"

He paused in the opening and looked back in question.

"I know what…what you did for me, with Garcia. When you were bringing your car around to take me home, your boss told me that you stood up to him, that you took up for me. I just wanted you to know that I appreciate it. After all the lies that I told you, I wouldn't have expected that. So, well, thanks."

He must be going insane, because all he wanted to do was cross the room and pull her into his arms. He was a sucker for a woman in trouble, and that little catch in her voice, the little wobble of her chin as she'd thanked him told him how close she was to losing her composure again. How could he go from being furious with her to wanting to hold her in the span of one day? It made no sense. As soon as they notified Eddie's friends or foster family or whoever needed to be told about his death tomorrow, he was going to get in touch with Drew and tell him to assign someone else to watch over Silver.

Because if he hung around her much longer, he wasn't sure that he *could* leave.

"You're welcome," he said, and hurriedly made his escape while he still could.

As soon as the door closed behind Colton, Silver rolled onto her side and buried her face against the sheets. The dam she'd been holding back finally burst and her entire body was racked with sobs. She cried for the pain and fear that Eddie must have endured in his final moments. She cried for a life lost far too soon, for a young man who had never really lived.

By the time she ran out of tears, the moon was hanging low in the sky out her bedroom window and she fell into an exhausted sleep.

Bam!

Silver jerked upright in her bed and clawed for her gun, still holstered to her ankle. She yanked the gun out, sweeping it in an arc around the bedroom. But no one was there.

Bam! Bam!

What was that? She slowly lowered her gun. The sound was coming from downstairs. Along with… voices…and…laughter? She drew in a sharp breath and looked out the window. The sun was fully up. And she suddenly realized what had woken her. The sound of doors slamming.

Oh, no. Her guests were here. Grand opening day. It hadn't even occurred to her last night to cancel the guests' reservations. What was she going to do? She couldn't deal with this right now. But someone had to go downstairs and greet them, tell them the inn was closed.

She ran into the adjacent bathroom to take care of her near-to-bursting bladder and quickly brush her teeth.

More noises sounded belowstairs as she thrust her legs into a pair of jeans and threw on a fresh top. A quick run of the brush through her hair and she was groaning at her reflection in the bathroom mirror. Her makeup from yesterday was a smeared mess, but she didn't have time to do much more than rub some of it off with a tissue before running out of her room.

The guests had to be fuming by now that no one was there to greet them. Tippy and Jenks weren't due to arrive until around noon. She'd planned it that way so she could greet all the guests herself and soak in the fun of being her own proprietor. But now everything was a total disaster.

She burst out of the attic doorway onto the second floor.

"Whoa, whoa, whoa."

She saw Colton a split second before she barreled into him. He grunted from the impact but wrapped his arms around her, saving her from a nasty fall. He steadied her with his hands on her shoulders.

"You okay?"

"Yes, fine. Sorry. Let me go. I have to—"

"Hold it. Wait a minute."

She frowned up at him. "The guests are here. I have to—"

"I know the guests are here. But no, you don't have to run down there like the inn is on fire. It isn't. Everything is under control." His gaze dropped down and he cleared his throat before meeting her gaze again. "And as lovely, and I do mean lovely, as you look without a bra, it might not present the professional image you're going for."

She looked down and then drew in a sharp breath and crossed her arms over her chest. The shirt she'd thrown on was white and left nothing to the imagination. "Oh, no," she groaned.

"Don't worry."

The laughter in his voice had her flushing hot.

"Like I said, everything is fine. Tippy and Jenks are here and they've corralled everyone into the dining room and are busily serving an excellent breakfast, or so I've heard. I was just coming up to check on you and see if you wanted some."

She blinked and glanced toward the stairs. "Tippy's here? And Jenks? But I don't understand. They weren't supposed to be here until—"

"Noon. I know. When I checked on you early this morning, you were zonked. Knowing your guests would be arriving soon, I went up to Callahan's Watering Hole—which seems to be the neighborhood hangout around here—and sure enough, it was open. I asked if anyone there knew Tippy, and like you said, everyone knows everyone around here."

"Wait, you're saying the grand opening is a—"

"Success. Yes." His smile faded and he gently brushed her hair out of her face. "Tippy and Jenks know about Eddie, and they were more than happy to come early and take care of things. Freddie said she'd send J.J. over in another hour, just as soon as she finished with the morning rush at Callahan's. You don't have to worry about the inn. Not today."

She searched his gaze, amazed at everything he'd just said. "You did all that, for me?"

He suddenly looked uncomfortable and cleared his throat. "I did all that for both of us. We have to notify Eddie's foster family. I told Tippy and Jenks not to say anything to anyone about what happened until we take care of that. And we can't do that while you're worrying about the inn."

She backed away from him, still holding her arms across her chest. The tears she'd thought she was out of last night pricked the backs of her eyes again. She swallowed hard and held them back. "Well, thank you. I mean, of course you're right. We need to notify his foster parents and foster brothers. Wait, what time is it?"

He pulled his phone out of the holder on his belt. "About nine-thirty. Why?"

"And it's the first of the month, isn't it?"

"Yes. Why?"

"We're too late."

"For?"

"Eddie's foster parents."

He leaned back against the wall. "You've lost me."

"Tony Jones, Eddie's foster dad, works in Naples. He would have left around seven. The kids are all at school. And the mom, Elisa, always goes into Naples on the first of the month, bright and early, to spend their foster program stipend. She won't be back until the kids come home from school."

"Do you have any contact information for them? Or know where the father works?"

She shook her head. "Unfortunately, no."

"Well, waiting is less than ideal. But I don't see where we have a choice." He pushed off the wall and straightened. "Maybe this is a good thing. You can greet your guests and get your mind off everything else for a few hours."

"No. I'm going to take a quick shower. And then we're getting out of here. I can't deal with happy people on vacation right now. And we have something far more important to do while we wait for the Joneses to get home."

"Oh? And what would that be?"

"We're going to find Eddie's killer."

Chapter Eight

Colton paced the upstairs hall for what seemed like forever before he finally heard Silver coming down the attic stairs. As soon as she emerged from the hidden panel, he grabbed her arm and spun her around to face him.

"You don't just say something like that and take off. We need to talk about this."

She shook off his hand and smoothed the dark blue blouse she was now wearing over her jeans. "What is there to talk about? We both know the odds are that whoever killed Eddie is in this town, one of the thugs behind the robberies and the drugs. And I'm going to find out who that is. I'm through being subtle, taking my time. Because you know what? People get killed while you're dotting all the *i*'s and crossing all the *t*'s. The waiting, the slow, methodical investigating so I can make sure that any evidence I gather will hold up in court, is over. I'm going to figure out who's behind everything. And I'm starting right now."

She headed toward the stairs. He swore and caught up to her, but this time he didn't try to stop her.

"So, what's your plan?" he demanded as they both headed down the stairs.

"My plan is to shake things up and make people nervous. I'm going to flush out the bad guys."

The sound of laughter and the clink of dishes came from the doorway off the foyer that led into the kitchen and dining room. But Silver didn't even pause to look in on her first-ever guests at the inn, or even to talk to Tippy and Jenks. She flung open one of the front glass doors and marched outside.

Colton shook his head and hurried to catch up to her. She crossed the yard and headed up the street as if she were trying to win a race.

"Where's the fire?" Colton demanded. "Slow down. At least tell me what you mean by 'shake things up.'"

She stopped and faced him, right beside the beginning of the boardwalk at the business next to the B and B. "Look. I appreciate everything you've done for me. I really do. But you're not going to talk me out of this."

"Who said anything about talking you out of it?"

Her look of surprise had him gritting his teeth.

"You're not going to try to stop me?" she asked.

"Last I checked, you're a grown woman with a mind of your own. It's not my place to stop you. But I'd be a terrible friend, and an even worse police officer, if I didn't at least try to discuss this with you so you don't get hurt. You're too close to this. Your emotions could cloud your judgment. You know that. Let me help you. Let's figure this out together."

She blinked up at him. "Friend?"

"What?"

"You said 'friend.' You consider me a friend?" Her unique silver-gray eyes stared up at him in wonder.

"You don't want to be friends?" he asked, completely baffled by her change in subjects. Talking to her was like riding on a runaway train with a switch-happy con-

ductor. He never knew which track the train would take
next or whether the train was going to jump the tracks
completely.

She slid her arms around his waist, hugging him
close. He promptly forgot how to breathe. Good grief,
she felt good, her soft curves pressed against him. The
tantalizing scent of her shampoo or maybe perfume—
he didn't know which—filled his senses. Lust slammed
into him so hard and unexpectedly that he had to clench
his hands into fists against the urge to slide his fingers through that sexy, short bob of reddish-brown hair
and slam his mouth down on hers. Which was crazy.
They barely knew each other. How could he want her
so much?

"Silver." His voice came out in a hoarse rasp. He
cleared his throat. "Silver," he tried again, relieved that
he was able to speak coherently. "What are you doing?"

"Hugging you."

He awkwardly patted her back. "I, uh, see that. *Why*
are you hugging me?"

"Because we're friends, of course."

"You hug all your friends?"

She sighed and let go of him. "No, Colton. At least,
not all the time. I just really needed a hug and you surprised me. Please forgive me. It won't happen again."
She whirled around and stepped up onto the boardwalk.

"Oh no, you don't," he growled. He swung her off
the boardwalk back down in front of him and pulled
her against him, circling her with his arms and resting
his cheek on the top of her head. When she just stood
there, stiff, unyielding, he said, "In case you can't tell,
I'm trying to hug you. I think it's customary for the
huggee to put their arms around the hugger. Tit for tat.
Or something."

She laughed and hugged him back, resting her cheek against his chest.

Holding her felt so good that he decided not to worry that strangers across the street at one of the businesses were whispering behind their hands. It had been a long time since he'd held a woman, just for friends' sake. Then again, maybe he never had. And even though he still wanted her, just holding her, offering her his support without expecting anything in return, was an entirely new kind of closeness. And he liked it. Maybe she was onto something with this hugging thing.

All too soon, she pushed back and he had to release her.

"Thank you, Colton. I really needed that. And now I feel that I can tackle anything. You're a good hugger, by the way."

He was about to reply when she took off again, hurrying up the boardwalk, forcing him to jog to catch up to her.

"Where are you going?"

"To the heart of Mystic Glades." She pushed through the swinging saloon doors at Callahan's Watering Hole and went inside.

SILVER SCANNED THE dimly lit interior, marking each person that she wanted to interview—and Cato Green was at the very top of her list. She made a beeline toward the bar, which was empty, since the patrons were having breakfast at the round tables. And that suited her just fine.

She climbed onto one of the tall stools that faced the kitchen doorway, barely registering that Colton sat beside her as she waited.

"You're not going to do anything foolish, are you?" Colton asked, keeping his voice low.

"I guess that all depends on your definition of foolish."

"Anything that could make you a target if word gets around to the big fish we're after."

"Big fish, huh? I guess that fits. Whoever's behind Eddie's death is definitely slimy. But to catch a fish, you need bait. And I'm about to bait the hook."

"Maybe we should go somewhere and talk this out first."

"Too late."

The door swung open. Silver reached into her front jeans' pocket.

Cato stopped right in front of her, balancing a tray of breakfast dishes. He looked from her to Colton and back again.

Silver slapped her DEA badge on top of the bar. "Good morning, Mr. Green. When you're finished with those dishes, I'd like a moment of your time."

Cato stared at the badge, and his Adam's apple bobbed in his throat. "I ain't done nothin'."

"I'm sure your parole officer will be happy to hear that. I'll just wait right here while you deliver that yummy-looking breakfast to Freddie's customers."

Cato eyed Colton as though he was sizing him up, then gave Silver a crisp nod and rounded the end of the bar, carrying the tray to one of the tables.

"Mr. Green?" Colton whispered harshly. "Parole officer? The other day you said you thought his name was Cato. But you knew his name, his full name, all along. Are there any other secrets you haven't told me?"

"Probably."

A muscle developed a tic in the side of his jaw. "I

wonder what the penalty for impersonating a federal officer is these days. I should have searched your room and taken that badge when I brought you to the inn last night. You do remember that Garcia fired you, right?"

She shrugged. "I remember you telling me he fired me. But since he didn't tell me himself, how am I to know if you can be trusted?"

He swore.

"You can be mad at me later," she said. "Right now I need your help. Get ready."

"Ready for what?"

"To duck." She gestured toward the mirror above the bar.

Colton followed the direction of her hand. "Ah, hell."

"Duck!"

They both dove to the floor as Cato slammed a chair across the top of the bar, obliterating the chair and sending sawdust and chunks of wood flying around the room. He let out a war cry and whirled around just as Colton leaped to his feet and slammed his fist against the side of Cato's jaw, spinning the larger man around.

Silver scrambled out of the way and grabbed her gun from her ankle holster. "Hands up, Cato," she yelled, aiming her gun off to the side so she wouldn't hit Colton if she had to shoot. Behind her she heard scrambling feet and shouts as the customers hurriedly moved out of the way of the two circling men.

"Cato Green, hands up," she repeated.

Cato let out another yell and charged Colton. Colton slammed his fist into the other man's jaw again. Cato grunted with pain but didn't stop. He barreled forward, wrapping his huge arms around Colton and slammed into a table and chairs.

They fell in a tangle of arms and legs, fists flying, biceps bulging as they each grappled for control.

Silver winced as one of Cato's fists drove into Colton's belly. She glanced around for someone to help, their wide-eyed audience consisting of mostly senior citizens, including Freddie, who was glaring at her from her spot by the far wall.

"You started this, Silver. You're going to pay for everything they break!"

"Sorry," she called out as she shoved her gun into her waistband. She frantically looked around for something to use to help Colton. There, one of the legs of the chair that Cato had busted. She ran across the room and swiped it off the floor.

A loud whack and the sound of shattering glass pinging onto the wooden floor had her whirling around with her makeshift weapon raised. Cato lay unconscious, the remnants of a broken beer mug scattered all around him, except for the handle, which was in Colton's hand as he glared up at her from his crouch on the floor. He tossed the handle into the puddle of soda from whoever's drink he'd grabbed and wiped his hands on his jeans as he stood.

Silver dropped the chair leg and ran to him. "Are you okay? Did he break anything?" She didn't see any blood on him anywhere, but his left cheek was beginning to swell. "We need to put some ice on your face." She reached up, but he glared at her and shoved her hand away.

Without a word, he headed toward the swinging doors.

"Colton, wait." She hurried after him. "Where are you going?"

He waved toward Cato lying on the floor. "This is

your mess. You clean it up." And then his brilliant blue eyes met hers, looking darker, angrier than she'd ever seen them. "You can take care of notifying Eddie's foster parents on your own. I'm done."

"Wait, what do you mean you're done? I can fix this. I can—"

Whump. The saloon doors swung in her face. Colton's boots rang on the boardwalk outside as he strode back toward the inn.

Silver's shoulders slumped and she shot an annoyed look at Cato, who was groaning and holding his head as he struggled to sit up.

"Somebody get him a towel," Freddie called out. "And some ice for the lump on his head that I'm sure he's got." When no one moved, she clapped her hands. "Go. Move."

Two of the men hurried over to Cato and crouched down to talk to him while another from their group rushed into the kitchen, presumably to get a towel.

Freddie stopped in front of Silver with her hands on her hips and her flaming red hair looking as if it might actually catch on fire from the red-hot flush on her angry face. "Silver Westbrook, if Jake Young wasn't out of town right now I'd have him arrest you for startin' a bar fight. And it's not even noon. Most people need to get drunk first to do the kind of damage you've done."

"Jake couldn't arrest me, Freddie. He's not a cop anymore."

She leaned down close. "Neither are you, but I saw the flash of the badge you slammed on the bar all the way from my seat over there."

"You knew?"

"Sugar, everyone around here knows you're DEA and that you got fired last night."

She blinked and looked around. Every single person there nodded to let her know they knew. "Oh, my gosh. All this time, I thought I kept it a secret. How? How did you know?"

"Oh, don't get your panties in a wad. It's just us old-timers that figured it out. We keep up with all our chicks when they leave the nest, knew you'd gone to college to be some kind of lawman. But when you came back to start an inn, well, we might have made a few calls. Your folks mentioned you was working undercover in the Keys just a few months before you showed up here. We figured you were taking a vacation, but after seeing you snooping around so much we figured you was workin' a case."

Silver put a hand to her head, feeling dizzy from all the revelations. Cato let out a loud curse when one of the women pressed a plastic Baggie full of ice water against his head. He glared at Silver and staggered to a chair they offered him.

"My folks left Mystic Glades years ago," she said. "I didn't think they even kept in touch with anyone back here."

"You figured wrong."

"They wouldn't have known about last night."

"No. But we have friends in the department. Word gets around."

"Wow. It gets around fast."

Freddie hooked a chair with her leg and scooted it over. "Sit down, Silver. We're gonna talk this through and figure it out together." She waved at her circle of friends. "Come on. Pull up a chair. Silver's been on her own long enough worrying about whatever case she's working on. We're gonna help her put the pieces together."

Silver's mouth dropped open as the people she'd always taken for granted as being too oblivious to pay her any attention all pulled up chairs around her like cowboys circling the wagons, only they were circling them for her.

"I don't…I don't know that this is a good idea," she said. "The case I'm working on is dangerous."

"Aren't they all?" Freddie waved her hand again. "This ain't our first rodeo, dear. We helped Jake and Faye sort out their troubles. And Buddy and me helped Amber and Dex solve a murder."

"I didn't think you helped with that," one of the men closest to Freddie said. "I heard Dex did that pretty much on his own."

Freddie narrowed her eyes. "I don't recall asking for your opinion, Dwight."

He swallowed hard and balanced both his gnarled hands on the top of his cane.

"Now," Freddie said. "Where were we? I think, Silver, that you were about to tell us about the case you've been working on. And then you're going to explain what that tall, sexy Colton Graham meant when he said you could notify Eddie's foster parents on your own."

Silver waved toward Cato, who was slowly hobbling toward the kitchen with the help of the two men Freddie had assigned to help him.

"Don't worry about him," Freddie said. "He's not part of whatever you're looking into. He's harmless."

"Harmless? He's an ex-con. I looked into him when I first arrived. He's done time for armed robbery. He's my most promising suspect."

"Sometimes innocent people go to jail. We think Cato didn't get good enough lawyering. He was in the wrong place at the wrong time. That's the only reason he went to jail."

Cato grumbled his agreement as he headed through the kitchen doorway.

"He tried to kill Colton and me because I showed him my DEA badge."

Freddie clucked her tongue and shook her head. "This young generation. You jump to all sorts of conclusions without thinking things through or knowing all the facts. No, Cato wasn't trying to kill anyone. He probably figured he could rough you two up so he could hightail it out the back. You got him riled up on account of mentioning his parole officer. He doesn't want to go back to jail."

Silver slumped in the chair. "If Cato isn't involved, then who is?"

Freddie leaned toward her. "That's what we're gonna help you figure out. But first, what's this about notifying Eddie's foster parents?"

Chapter Nine

Colton held his phone and leaned back against the side of his car on the shoulder of I-75 near mile marker fifty-two. A semi blasted past, blowing hot air in his face and swirling some of his hair in his eyes. He shoved it back impatiently.

"When I get back to Naples, the first thing I'm going to do is get a dang haircut."

"What's stopping you?" Drew said over the phone. "You said Miss Westbrook doesn't want your help."

"That might not be the most accurate slant to what happened," he admitted. "Pretty much she's just not a team player. Instead of letting Homicide investigate Eddie's murder, she decided to amp up the drug investigation, figuring if she found the top guy she'd find the killer. But she went about it all wrong and I, well…" He waggled his jaw where Cato had thrown a particularly hard punch. "I guess I lost my patience with her and told her I was done."

"Huh. That doesn't sound like you."

No, it didn't. He was known for his patience, which was one of the reasons he was so often chosen for undercover work, which tended to move at a snail's pace when he was trying to get in with a bad group of people. It took a lot of time to convince them he was just as bad as them and could be trusted, inasmuch as that type of crowd trusted anyone, even each other. So why was it that he got so frustrated and impatient around Silver?

"Regardless," Colton said, "I just checked out the area around where they found Eddie's body. I was hoping to see some tire tracks or something the forensics guys missed, but there's nothing here."

"Maybe not nothing, exactly," Drew said. "The homicide guys sent me an update on their investigation a little while ago. Hang on a sec." The sound of papers rustling was followed by a thumping noise. "Okay, got it. Yada, yada, yada, yeah, here, second page in. Officers interviewed some morning commuters at one of the rest stops on Alligator Alley and it looks like two different people remembered seeing a car parked on the side of the road in the general area where Eddie was killed, during the time frame we're concerned about. While they didn't see anyone in the car or on the side of the road, they remembered the car itself because of the bright sky blue color and because it was belching out black smoke from the exhaust pipe."

"Sounds like an old diesel maybe?"

"You guessed it. From their descriptions, looks like a Mercedes from the early eighties. Basically an antique. The witnesses said it appeared to be in pristine condition, except for the smoke, of course."

"So our killer likes old cars, and keeps them up. Good to know. And that kind of car would really stand out if I see it somewhere. Anything else in that report?" He idly watched the cars go by as he listened to Drew give him the details, most of which sounded useless for finding the killer, at least now. Sometimes it took one solid piece of evidence to make all the other evidence make sense. "What about Eddie's foster parents? Silver seems to think they're in it for the money, which seems crazy, since there's not a ton of money in taking care of foster kids. Not exactly a get-rich-quick scheme."

"You got that right. I've got friends who foster kids and they spend way more than the state allots them. It's a labor of love for sure, at least with the people I know who do it. Let's see here. The guys are still looking into the Joneses. Found out the father works at a chemical plant here in town, but he's in Alabama at some conference. They did confirm that he bought a car recently."

"You sure he's at the conference?"

"The guys are contacting police in Alabama to do a wellness check. We should know in a few hours if he's really there. You're thinking he killed his own foster kid?"

Colton drummed his fingers against the quarter panel on his Mustang before opening the door and getting in. He started the engine and pulled out onto the highway heading west. He'd have to take the next exit to turn back east toward home. "Just fishing. I have no idea if he's that kind of guy or not. I'm assuming he doesn't have a criminal record, since you didn't mention one. How new is the car he bought? How expensive?"

"Bingo on no criminal record. The wife's clean, too. And the car is about five years old, a Ford Taurus."

The disappointment in his boss's voice mirrored Colton's. Drug dealers or robbery ring runners didn't buy five-year-old cars.

"Doesn't sound like the Joneses are rolling in money," Colton said.

"No. It doesn't. That, unfortunately, is all I have."

"There's an ex-con working in Mystic Glades. He's the cook and maybe bartender, too. Not sure about that.

His name's Cato Green. Can you do a quick search on him, see what comes up?"

"Cato Green. Doesn't ring any bells." The tapping sound of Drew's fingers across his computer keyboard echoed through the phone. "Huh, yeah, okay. Looks like he did a few years for robbery. He was the getaway car driver. Claimed he didn't know the guy he was with was robbing the store. Swore he was innocent."

"Don't they all?"

"You got that right. Did a few years. He's on parole. Could be involved. I'll get the guys to dig a little deeper. Any other suspects you want me to add to the list?"

Colton rattled off all the names he knew of people in Mystic Glades, which weren't many. "I really haven't had much of a chance to dig in."

"You weren't supposed to be investigating anyway. Just come on back. Use the rest of the day to get that haircut you've been wanting and spend the night in your own bed for a change. Miss Westbrook can handle the notification to Mrs. Jones this evening. But I'll send a patrol unit out tomorrow to ensure that she's been noti- fied, just in case. I'd hate for his name to get out to the press before everyone who knows him has been told."

"Is the press an issue?" Colton asked.

"Not so far. There was a minor mention of a body found on the highway, but since it's not in the heart of town, there's no big uproar or anything. Still, better to be safe. Mrs. Jones deserves that after taking care of him for however long she did."

"Agreed." He exited the highway and then looped back onto I-75 west this time, toward Naples. Soon he'd pass the hidden turnoff to Mystic Glades, but on the op- posite side of the road. The only way to get there from here would be to go to another exit a lot farther down the road and turn around. Or he could just take one of the turnabouts in the median reserved for law enforcement and emergency vehicles. But he wouldn't, of course. There was no reason to return to Mystic Glades.

"Colton? You coming to Naples?"

About a quarter of a mile ahead was a turnabout. He slowed the car, then swore. No, there wasn't any point in going back. Silver didn't want his help. He checked his mirrors, clutched the wheel until his knuckles ached.

"Colton? Hey, man. Should I wait around for you or not?"

The turnabout was coming up fast. Colton hit the brakes, then jerked the wheel, making the turn.

"Apparently not," he said. "Looks like I've got sucker written all over my forehead."

Drew laughed. "I think it's something else entirely, but I won't go there. She sure is pretty, though."

"That's got absolutely nothing to do with it. I'm just worried…about the case."

"Yeah, keep telling yourself that. Talk to you later."

The call clicked off. Colton tossed the phone into the console.

It was just past noon when he made his way underneath the archway with its alligator-shaped sign. He was a fool for coming back. Silver might need him, but she'd never admit it. She wasn't a team player. And her kind of play was more likely to get him, or herself, hurt or killed than solve a crime.

So why had he come back? He told himself it was out of respect for Eddie's foster mom, that it was his duty to make sure she was told about Eddie's murder. But he very much feared the real reason was a sexy little redhead who was slowly but surely giving him an ulcer.

After he'd parked in front of the inn and checked

in with Tippy and Jenks, they told him that Silver had come back almost an hour earlier to get her sketch pad and pencils. But she hadn't told them where she was going. Just to be sure that she hadn't come back and they were busy with guests and didn't notice, he went up to her attic room. But it was empty, and his quick search of the main floor confirmed that she hadn't secluded herself in the office or sunroom either, let alone any of the public areas of the inn. He waved good-bye to Tippy and headed uptown.

He checked out every inch of Main Street. He ducked inside Swamp Buggy Outfitters, which was basically a camping and hunting supply store with an enormous swamp buggy sitting in the front window. But after walking up and down the aisles to make sure Silver wasn't there, he tried Locked and Loaded—a gun store, then Bubba's Take or Trade, and a taxidermy shop called Stuffed to the Gills. He even looked inside Last Chance Church, but he couldn't find Silver anywhere, or any-one who'd seen her since the debacle with Cato earlier.

He'd just passed Callahan's again on his way back to the B and B to search it one more time when a group of about twelve gray-haired citizens descended on him like a horde of slowly moving locusts. The woman in front of the group waved her cane at him and yelled at him to wait for them, so he did, leaning against one of the posts on the boardwalk in front of the saloon while their canes and walkers clicked and clacked on the wooden slats of whatever store they'd come out of.

Good grief. What in the world is this all about?

"See, I told you he'd come back," one of the men in front said as they circled him like a pack of geriatric wolves. "He's sweet on her. He likes Silver."

Colton blinked in surprise. "What? Hey, I'm not *sweet* on her, whatever that means."

"Then why did you come back?"

"It's my job."

"Hey, Freddie," the elderly man called toward the back of their little gathering. "Didn't your friend at the station say that Colton was voluntold to go on vacation for a few days?"

"Yep, he sure did," she called back.

"Then he's not technically working right now. So if he came back to help Silver, it sure looks to me like he's sweet on her."

"Oh, for the love of…stop it. Just stop it." Colton gave them all a look that should have had them running to get out of his way. Instead, if anything, they crowded closer, as if to ensure that he knew they weren't intimidated.

He was really losing his touch.

He held his hands up in surrender. "Okay. How about I admit that I like her? A little. Will that make you tell me where she is?"

Freddie pushed to the front of the senior squad and crossed her arms over her ample bosom. "Define…a little."

He threw his hands in the air in frustration. "I don't know. I…like I said, I like her. She's interesting. And funny. And smart. And she's kind of adorable when she spaces out and goes off somewhere in her artistic little world that the rest of us don't understand. But she's also frustrating and stubborn and in trouble if she's out there on her own somewhere working on the case. So, please. If you care about her at all, *please* tell me where she is so I can protect her."

Freddie glanced around at her mini-mob. "Well? What do you think? Should we tell him?"

Labron squeezed in between two of the others and took up a stance beside Freddie. "He didn't even mention how pretty she is. I reckon that says a whole lot about how much he likes her, 'cause he likes her for who she is, not for her looks. I'm officially giving my stamp of approval to their relationship."

Colton blinked. Twice. This conversation had gotten so bizarre he didn't even know what to say.

"All in favor of telling him where Silver is?" Freddie asked.

"Aye."

"Aye."

"Tell him."

Cheers went up from all around and Freddie held up her hand so Labron could give her a high five. He grinned and tried, but he couldn't reach it. Freddie laughed and lowered her hand and they slapped palms.

Colton counted silently to five, trying to keep a rein on his temper. "Would someone please tell me where I can find Silver, before she gets hurt?"

"Oh, she's plenty safe. I can see her from here." Freddie pointed across the street to the second story over the shop called the Moon and Star. "With Faye and Jake out of town, she decided to use their apartment upstairs to noodle over everything we told her. She's sittin' in the living room right now trying to figure out who dunnit."

Colton fisted his hands at his sides. Good grief. To think that if he'd just turned around and looked, he'd have seen her silhouetted in the upstairs window by the desk lamp where she was sitting, apparently deep in thought, because she didn't seem to notice her admirers and champions gathered on the street below.

Freddie waved her hand and the senior squad parted like Moses parting the Red Sea, leaving him a clear path across the street.

"Thank you," he managed to say in a civil voice, somehow not shouting even though he wanted to.

"Anytime," Freddie called after him as he strode across the dirt-and-gravel road and then jogged up the steps to the boardwalk in front of the Moon and Star.

The store was dark and a sign in the glass door said Closed. He was about to knock when he decided to just try the knob to see what would happen. Sure enough, it turned easily in his hand.

"Doesn't anyone lock their doors around here?" he grumbled beneath his breath as he stepped inside.

After shutting the door behind him, he threw the dead bolt, relieved that at least the door had a lock on it. He'd half expected that it wouldn't. Now he could be relieved that he didn't have to worry about Freddie's little warriors coming in uninvited to see what was going on.

He wasn't sure what he was going to say to Silver, but for some reason it seemed urgent that he see her. She'd had over an hour and a half since he left to cook up some other crazy scheme. He was already sweating just wondering what fool thing she might want to try next.

He wove his way between tables of what appeared to be exotic potions and perfumes in velvet pouches on various displays. There was jewelry, too, and a few racks of rather interesting clothing that consisted of short, midriff-baring tops and matching skirts that were more silk scarves than anything that would remotely retain anyone's modesty. Just thinking about how Silver might look in a getup like that had his mouth watering and had him cursing himself for a fool. He had to get this attraction to her under control and focus on the danger around them. Because Silver sure as heck wasn't focusing on it and he needed to keep both of them safe.

A quick tour of the bottom floor brought him full circle. Most of the place was the main, open front room that was the shop. There was a small office in the back with a bathroom beside it, and a few other little rooms that looked to be more for inventory and storage than anything else. There was a back door, too, also un-locked. He shook his head in disbelief and decided to open it and check out back, just to make sure things looked okay. He pushed the door open and something big and black hissed at him from just past the left side of the doorway. He shut the door and bolted it even as his mind struggled to tell him what he already knew.

He'd just been hissed at by a black panther.

Probably the same one that had jumped in front of his car earlier. Great, just one more thing to worry about. He was going to have to warn people that there was a wildcat roaming these woods. Maybe even alert the Florida Panther National Wildlife Refuge southwest of here, back toward Naples. Maybe one of their cats had escaped, or at the least, they might be able to hunt this one down and trap it.

He strode to the opening to the narrow stairs that he'd spotted earlier that led to the second floor. "Ready or not, Silver," he said beneath his breath, "here I come."

Chapter Ten

Stiff from sitting at the desk by the window in her friend's apartment, Silver closed the blinds and then worked off her bra from underneath her shirt. She pitched it onto the desk, kicked off her shoes and then carried all her drawings into the center of the living room.

She lay on her belly on the carpet, fanning the sketches out around her like a dealer in Vegas. She'd come here hoping the quiet and isolation would help her get her creative energy flowing and she'd finally be able to make all the pieces form the big picture she was searching for. But as she looked at everything, tapping her pencil against her bottom lip, she couldn't seem to make the pieces fit. There was a key somewhere, something she was missing.

One of the people she'd drawn *had* to be the killer, had to be the man or woman at the top of the criminal food chain who had taken up residence in her hometown. But none of them were leaping out at her as the culprit. And her boss's insistence on slow, methodical approaches meant she had little to show for the months she'd been here—other than setting up her B and B, which she barely even cared about anymore.

She rubbed her tired eyes. What she needed was a

break, something that would really take her mind in a new direction. Then she could come back to the notes she'd written on each sketch and make it all make sense.

"Tell me I didn't just get hissed at by a black panther outside."

She jerked up, sitting on the backs of her legs as she clutched her pencil and pressed her hand across her galloping heart. Of all people to be standing in the middle of the living room of her friend's upstairs apartment, Colton Graham was the last person she'd have expected.

His gaze dipped to her chest, reminding her that she'd taken off her bra. Heat flashed through her, and her pulse began to race as she stared up at him. He seemed to drag his gaze up with visible effort and cleared his throat.

"That was probably Sampson," she said. "Faye's pet."

"Someone has a panther as a pet?"

"More or less. He shows up every few days, looking for food. Amy feeds him ground-up meat when Faye's not here to take care of it."

He swore beneath his breath. "I don't care how tame he may seem to your friends. He's still a wild animal, and dangerous."

"He doesn't have any teeth. He can't hurt anyone."

"Does he still have claws?"

"Hmm. Good point." She looked past him to the door. It was closed, and he'd locked it, had even thrown the chain in place. "I thought you'd left for good. What are you doing here? And how did you find me?"

He looked at the floor, at her drawings. "Freddie told me where you were." He moved around the end of the couch and knelt down beside her, looking at each of her pictures. "You drew Cato? And Buddy? Why? Who are all these other people?" He shuffled through them and picked up the picture of Danny, the boat captain.

He was trying to act as if nothing were happening between them, but the tension was so thick she felt she would die if she didn't touch him soon. Her hand shaking with anticipation, she placed it on his forearm.

His gaze snapped to hers, and a bead of sweat made its way down his temple, even though the air-conditioning was on, keeping the heat and humidity at bay.

"Why are you here?" she asked.

His gaze dropped to her lips, briefly, like a butterfly's touch, making her pulse leap even more. But then he frowned and looked down at the pictures again. "I was worried…about the case. And I want to help. That is, if you'll listen. If you want my help."

She wanted *him*. And, yes, she wanted his help, too. Needed it. But why couldn't he have been worried about *her*? But then again, she'd given him no cause to see what she'd only come to see herself after he'd stormed out of Callahan's.

She was hooked on him.

She wouldn't call it a crush, although to anyone else it probably would look that way. After all, they'd only met, what, yesterday? But it felt like something so much deeper. And it seemed as if they'd known each other much longer than that. She couldn't get him out of her thoughts, no matter how hard she tried.

"Silver?" His rich, deep voice stroked over her nerve endings, sending delicious shivers straight to the core of her. "Do you want my help?"

She took a chance, and dove into the deep end. "I want *you*." She waited for it to sink in, her face flushing with heat. If he turned her down, she'd feel like a fool, humiliated. But she'd learned long ago, if something was worth having, it was worth fighting for. And that waiting for something to happen might mean it never would. The timing sucked. She should be focusing on the case. They both should. But she also knew how her mind worked, how flustered and unfocused she became the more she tried to concentrate. She needed this. She needed him, to make her world right again. To focus, and to have something, someone, wonderful to hold on to, someone who would be there when all this was over—hopefully. She needed Colton.

He straightened, looking like a nervous stallion scenting a mare, wanting to grab her and flee from her at the same time. His eyes had darkened like a stormy night as his warring needs fought inside him. He didn't bolt. But he made no move toward her, either. Instead, his hands fisted at his sides. A slight hitch in his breathing told her that she had a chance to win this battle.

She rose to her feet, keeping her eyes locked on his the whole time. Slowly, she padded across the thick carpet to stand in front of him, with only a few inches and the heat from both their bodies between them.

"Colton," she whispered. "I want you."

He swallowed, his Adam's apple bobbing in his throat. "We're working on a case. We don't have time—"

"We do have time. Hours to kill before we can go talk to Mrs. Jones." She slid her hands up the front of his chest, delighting in the feel of his muscles bunching beneath the thin fabric of his T-shirt. "And I've got the perfect way to spend at least one of those hours."

"Silver…" His voice came out a harsh rasp. He cleared his throat and tried again, still not touching her, hands at his sides. "I'm not what you're looking for."

"Now, that's where you're wrong, Colton." She slid her hands higher, higher, her fingertips brushing against the heated skin of his neck, tangling with the wild ends of his dark overly long hair where it brushed his collar. He shivered in response, his pupils dilating as he stared down at her like a hungry wolf, ready to devour her. And, oh, how she wanted to be devoured.

She stood on tiptoe, angling her mouth up toward his and pressing herself full against him for the first time. She could feel every thud of his heart where her breasts were flattened against him. "You're exactly what I'm looking for," she whispered. "And you're far too tall. I'm going to need some help here." She tugged the ends of his hair. "Kiss me."

He groaned his surrender deep in his throat a second before he grabbed her and lifted her up, clasping her tightly against him as he captured her mouth in a sweltering kiss. The moment his lips touched hers, everything became right in her world. He kissed away her fears, her confusion, making everything clear in a sparkling, shocking moment of clarity. It was as if she'd spent her whole life in a fog and he was melting that away, revealing the world to be far more beautiful than even her artist's soul had ever dared to dream.

Rainbows of color burst behind her eyelids as she soaked in his ravenous hunger, answering every clever stroke of his tongue with one of her own, moaning at the exquisite pleasure that just being held by him in this way sent surging through her entire body. She was like a match, bursting into flame as he turned with her and set her bottom on the back of the couch, freeing one of his hands to roam over her body.

He broke the kiss, and she whimpered in disappointment. But then he moved to her neck, lightly sucking her heated skin, nibbling his way across the sensitive cords and then pulling her earlobe into his mouth. She arched against him, gasping with pleasure as her fingers dug into his shoulders.

Everything in her was melting, softening, readying for him. And she couldn't wait another minute. She fumbled with his belt and quickly unzipped his jeans. He sucked in a sharp breath when she found him, hard and ready for her.

"For the love of...slow down, Silver."

"I don't want to. We can go slow the next time. Please, please tell me you have a condom."

He laughed against the side of her neck. "If not, your friends had better have some around here or I'm going to have to kill somebody. In my wallet, there should be—"

"Don't stop." He'd started to step back to take out his wallet, but she pulled him back to her. "Don't stop."

He framed her face in his hands and captured her mouth again in a kiss that was even hotter, wetter, wilder than the one before. Hello, Dolly, could the man kiss!

She shoved her hands in his back pockets, searching for his wallet, and nearly died of pleasure at the delicious feel of his perfect bottom beneath her searching fingertips. He jerked against her very core, hard, ready. Her fingers frantically plucked at his pocket. A piece of paper crumpled in her hand and she dropped it to the floor. Other pocket, there, his wallet. She hungrily drank in his kiss as she fumbled with his wallet behind his back. As soon as she found the foil packet, she dropped the wallet and pulled back, breaking the kiss.

She shoved his jeans down his hips, then reached for his boxers.

He tipped her chin up, forcing her to look at him. "Silver, I want you, more than anything. But this is so soon. Are you sure that you—"

She pushed his underwear down, freeing him. He

swore and jerked against her in all his glory. Her breath left her in an unsteady rush. "Oh, I'm sure. Am I ever! You're beautiful, perfect." She rolled the condom onto him and gave him a powerful, long stroke, worshipping him with her hands.

He whispered sexy words in her ear, telling her exactly what he wanted to do to her while his fingers made quick work of her jeans and panties, lifting her bottom off the couch while he raked them away. And then he was poised at her entrance, and they stared into each other's eyes.

His hands shook as he slid one hand around her back and adjusted himself with the other. "It's not too late to say no. It will probably kill me to stop, but I will."

"You *see* me, Colton. The real me." She feathered her fingers down the side of his face. "You understand me like no one else ever has. This is what I want. You're what I want." She pressed a soft kiss against his lips and pulled back to look at him again. *"Don't. Stop."*

His entire body shook with need as he clasped her tightly to him and surged forward. Pleasure zinged through her unlike anything she'd ever felt. He was made for her. And she was made for him. Every thrust of his body, every maddeningly clever stroke of his fingers against her most sensitive spot as he made love to her had her arching against him and matching his rhythm with hers.

Every drawing she'd ever done, every painting she'd ever created in her search to show the true beauty of life seemed to culminate in this moment. Instead of painting him on canvas, capturing his likeness with pencil or pen, she drew him inside her, his every stroke like a master artist wringing out the beauty of this moment, creating the most incredible, eloquent masterpiece ever imagined.

And then he lifted her in his arms, turning with her, staggering down the short hallway to the sparse bedroom that was obviously the guest room on the right. Without breaking away from her, he gently laid her down, his strokes slower now, more delicious, his body shaking as he obviously made every effort to hold himself back, to make this last.

Her shirt was suddenly gone over her head, and his hot breath washed over her as he clasped one of her nipples into his mouth and sucked.

"Colton!" She arched off the bed, drawing her knees up as she came apart in his arms, soaring to planes she'd never known existed as the colors burst behind her eyelids.

He lavished her other breast with the same attention, his strokes coming harder and faster as he rode her through her climax. And then his hands were on her again, rebuilding the delicious tension inside her, impossibly bringing her higher than she'd been before.

As she catapulted into another wave of pleasure, her name burst from his lips and he joined her, clasping her tightly against him as he spent himself in her arms.

EVEN BEFORE COLTON opened his eyes, he knew he'd made a mistake. Well, not a mistake exactly. Making love to Silver had probably been the highlight of his existence and he wouldn't want to undo it, even if he could. There were no words in his vocabulary equal to the task of describing how right it had felt being with her. After this, he couldn't imagine ever being with another woman. Ever.

That was the problem.

What was he supposed to do now? Go down on bended knee and ask a woman he'd just met to marry him? She'd think he was crazy. Hell, he thought he was crazy. And it wasn't as though he wanted to get married. The thought had never even crossed his mind. His career always came first. And while he adored women, he'd never loved one. Never planned on loving one. And since he didn't believe in love at first sight, what, exactly, had happened to him?

All he knew for sure was that he needed distance—from this case, from Silver, from the disaster his life had just become. He needed to think and figure out what he was going to do. Giving up his career, months of being undercover where there was no room or time for a family, wasn't an option. Which meant after this investigation was over, he'd go his way and Silver would go hers. That was the only way this could end. But when he tried to conjure a picture of his future without Silver Westbrook, all he could see was a big, black void.

Man, was he in trouble!

"Wake up, sleepyhead." Silver's warm, soft hand patted his abdomen. "We have work to do, a case to figure out."

That one, simple touch awakened his body again, making his pulse leap through his veins and hardening him almost instantly. He gritted his teeth and willed his body back under control.

"Colton? Are you okay?"

Nope. Not under control. Even her voice had lust crashing through him. What he needed was a stiff drink. Maybe that would take care of his…stiff problem. He groaned at his own pun and forced his eyes open.

The bed dipped and Silver braced her hands on the mattress on either side of him, her face a mirror of concern. "Did you hit your head on the headboard or something?"

Since his body had become invaded by some kind of emotional wreck of a man whom he didn't recognize, he went with it, dragging her down for a kiss, all the while hoping he'd been wrong and that kissing her wasn't nearly as incredible as he remembered.

Nope. It wasn't like what he'd remembered. It was better.

He groaned and ended the soul-shattering kiss that had him hard and aching beneath the comforter. She'd ruined him. And he didn't have a clue what he was going to do about it.

She blinked down at him. "Wow. I don't even want to know how many women you've kissed to become that great at it. The jealousy would kill me. Now get up and get dressed. I'm all focused again now—thank you for that, by the way—and ready to solve this case."

She hopped off him and sashayed into the living room, already dressed and acting as if their lovemaking hadn't knocked her off her axis as it had him. What had she said? She was *focused* again, thank you? He frowned. Did she have sex with near strangers often, to focus her thoughts?

That dark thought had a little green monster poking him in the vicinity of his heart. And he didn't like it one bit. A drink. Yeah. He definitely needed something to take the edge off. And he didn't care that it wasn't five o'clock yet. It was five o'clock somewhere.

He rolled onto his side and looked for his clothes before remembering they were on the living room floor. And he was lying here with a hard, aching erection. Going out there and waving that around was a recipe for disaster. If she even looked at him as though she might want another roll in the hay, he'd probably tackle her to the floor and do all the things he desperately wanted to do to her that he hadn't done yet. No. He couldn't go out there naked. In that way lay danger. He'd just have to wrap the comforter around himself and go get them.

He slid his legs out of bed and held the comforter over his lap, about to get up, when Silver came back in carrying his things.

"Oh, hey." She smiled. "I just remembered you didn't have your clothes with you." She waved at the adjacent bathroom. "Want me to put them in there in case you want to wash up?"

He smiled tightly, or tried to. But he wasn't in a smiling mood and rather doubted he'd succeeded by the way her gorgeous silver-gray eyes widened.

"Sure, thanks," he said.

"O…kay." She set his things on the counter. "Oh, I almost forgot." She stepped back to him. "I accidentally pulled this out of your pocket earlier when I was, well, you know, looking for your wallet." She held her hand out toward him, holding a folded sheet of paper.

The paper that Drew had given him at the station.

He'd completely forgotten about it.

"Colton?" She continued to hold the paper out. "Is something wrong? If this is private, no worries. I didn't read it."

"It's yours."

"What?"

He grabbed her empty hand and tugged her to the bed. "Sit. Please."

She sat beside him and waited, the paper still in her hand. He set it aside and took both her hands in his, half-turning to face her, with one leg folded beneath him on the bed.

"Remember back at the station, when you left the room after finding out about Eddie?"

She stiffened, a shuttered look entering her eyes. "Yes. Of course I remember."

"That piece of paper is an email the Miccosukee police sent to Drew. It's a copy of a letter. The original was found in an envelope at the crime scene." He picked it up and unfolded it, then held it out toward her. "The envelope was addressed to you. And this is the letter that was inside. I'm sorry it's taken me this long to give it to you. At first, I was worried how you'd take it. And later, it slipped my mind. I know that's not an excuse. I really am sorry."

Her eyes filled with tears and she quickly wiped them away. "You read it. I can't."

"Silver—"

"Please. Just read it out loud." She closed her eyes, her hands fisting against the sheets.

Colton sighed and began to read.

"Dear Miss Westbrook. Can I call you Silver? I always wanted to, but it didn't seem respectful enough. But since this is goodbye, maybe you'll forgive me this one time.

"You were always a really good friend to me, and the only adult who really, truly seemed to care what happened to me, and whether I studied or ditched class. Because you wanted me to make something out of my life.

"I'm sorry to say that I let you down.

"Me and some of the guys got into some things that we shouldn't have. That blue vase? It was stolen, and some of the other things I brought you. Stupid, I know. It started out as a onetime thing, a dare. But it grew from there. And other stuff happened, stuff I'm too ashamed to talk about in this letter. And once I was in, I couldn't get out. That stupid attempted holdup? Yeah, I could tell you knew it was me. And I was so ashamed because you just wanted to help me, protect me, and I was there to take money, jewelry, anything I could get—I would have taken yours, too. Please know that I had good intentions. To help some friends. I can't say anything else because I don't want them to get into trouble."

"He was talking about the drug ring, wasn't he?" she asked.

"I think so," he said. "That's what Drew thinks, too."

She nodded. "Please, go on."

Colton searched for where he'd left off in the letter, then continued.

"Well, I've found a way out. I'm turning the thefts into something good and helping some people, some friends. But I can't stick around, because what I've done will send me to jail once it's out. And I could never survive a place like that. But at least I'll have done some good by helping others out. You should be proud of me for that."

She squeezed her eyes tightly shut, but tears rolled down her cheeks.

"Want me to stop?" he asked. "We can finish this later."

"No. I want to hear all of it. Go on."

"I'm sorry I left without saying goodbye. I'm starting a new life somewhere else. I don't want to go to jail, so I had to do it this way. I promise I won't get into trouble again.

"Goodbye, Silver.

"Your friend,

"Eddie."

He folded the paper and handed it to her. She took it between both hands and shook her head. "I told you that he was a good kid. He made mistakes, and he wanted out. He tried to fix things. He was a good kid," she repeated.

Colton wasn't so sure he agreed, but it obviously meant a lot to her that he believe her. He put his arm around her shoulders and held her close. "He was a good kid." He kissed the top of her head and rubbed her arm, gently rocking her against him as she absorbed the contents of the letter.

Finally, she sniffed, wiped her face and pushed away from him. "When you first got here, you asked if I needed your help. I do. Very much. Help me find Eddie's killer?"

"Of course."

"Thank you. I'll wait in the living room." She got up and hurried toward the door.

"Silver?"

She paused and turned, looking at him expectantly.

"I'm not going to stop until we find the creep who killed him. You have my word."

Her jaw trembled and her eyes shone overbright with more unshed tears. She nodded her thanks and pulled the door shut.

Colton groaned and collapsed back onto the bed. He knew better than to promise something he couldn't really control. He knew from experience that no matter how hard he might want to crack a case, sometimes the evidence just wasn't there.

Chapter Eleven

Silver sat down on the carpet in the living room again. But this time she was fully dressed—bra and all—and there was a deep, burning thirst for justice inside her belly that she hadn't felt in a long time. Yes, she'd wanted to catch Eddie's killer before she'd read that letter, or rather before Colton had read it to her. But knowing that Eddie had finally gotten it, that he'd realized he needed to turn his life around, and then that he'd had that life snatched away so brutally, had focused all her emotions into a deep-seated need to do this last thing for her friend—to bring down whoever had taken his future away from him.

And now that she had Colton to help her do it, she finally believed that this case could be solved, that together they would find justice, and Eddie Rafferty could rest in peace—God rest his soul.

Colton came out of the room and sat down beside her. He picked up a couple of the drawings. "Catch me up to speed. What is all this?"

"Suspects," she said, thumping the picture of Cato with her pencil. "Or potential suspects, I suppose. After you left earlier this morning, Freddie and her friends helped me brainstorm who could be the real bad guy. And these are the people we came up with. I added a few of my own, but mostly this is from the group, uh, meeting that we had." She shrugged. "Drawing anything that's bothering me helps clarify things in my head. Normally. No luck today, though. At least, not earlier. I'm hopeful that together we can figure it out."

His jaw tightened, as if he wasn't so sure. But he nodded his agreement. "I see you drew Buddy. Why not Freddie, too?"

"She's harmless."

"But Buddy isn't? They're a lot alike, about the same age, feisty, strong, stubborn. I wouldn't peg either of them as being able to hurt a physically fit eighteen-year-old. But ordering someone else to do it? Yeah. I can totally see that."

"Hmm. I'm not sure that I agree. I certainly can't picture Freddie doing anything like that. She might be a Brillo Pad on the outside, but inside she's a squishy sponge. Buddy's a lot like her, a really nice guy at heart."

He shook his head. "Yeah. I saw that nice heart when he charged you for an airboat ride that he pressured you to take. And when his staff charged crime victims four bucks for bottles of water at the south dock."

"Okay, okay. So he takes making a profit a bit to the extreme." At his incredulous look, she said, "A *lot* to the extreme. Agreed. But that doesn't make him a killer. And if you were down-and-out, he'd be one of the first in line to step up and help."

"If you say so. But if you believe that, why did you draw him?"

She picked up Buddy's picture and pointed to the notes written on the bottom. "*Organizer, leader, tends to be arrogant.* Those characteristics made me include him. He does love money, and he's driven to make as much as he can, even though he doesn't ever spend much. It's the thrill of it. He's competitive. I can totally see him as a guy in charge, organizing, making things happen. But even if he was the guy at the top, I seriously doubt he'd do it if he knew anyone was stealing or there were drugs involved. Someone could be taking advantage of him, stroking his ego, using his resources and knowledge of the area to run the operation without him even realizing what's really going on."

He took the picture from her and read the rest of the notes that she'd written, dates and times when she'd seen him with Eddie and other young teenagers, or in conference with Cato and others. "He does run those airboat tours. Airboats would be a perfect way to get goods into Mystic Glades, up through the canals. But he'd need another way to distribute them from there, onto the streets, without making anyone suspicious." He handed the picture back to her. "There may be something to your theory about someone using him without him knowing it. So who would use the airboats—when they're not running tours? How many boats are there?"

"Three. But if someone takes them out after the tours, they'd be noisy. We'd hear that."

"I remember seeing that captain on our boat—"

"Danny."

He nodded. "During the holdup, he used a pole to push the boat to shore. Looked fairly easy and didn't make any noise. If he or the other boat captains are in on this, they could push the boats away, or even pull them out into a canal using a canoe or kayak before turning that noisy engine on."

"I'd hate to think that Danny or the other boat pilots were involved. He seems so nice."

"How long have you known him?"

"Not long. He's one of the men Buddy hired just this summer. He doesn't live around here."

"We should look into his background, then. And keep him on our suspect list. When I spoke to Drew earlier, I listed Danny, along with everyone else whose name I could remember. He's having the team run background checks on everyone. We'll check back with him tomorrow and see if they've found anything useful."

"Drew, your boss? You spoke to him?"

"When I left Callahan's, I drove out to Alligator Alley and called him. The homicide team found some witnesses who saw a rather unique car near the crime scene at the right time—a nineteen-eighties sky blue Mercedes. It belches black smoke, so I figure it's probably one of the early diesels. Seen anything like that around here?"

"Honestly, it's so rare that I see cars around here. And I'm not much of a car person. I can hardly tell one model from the next."

"What kind of car do *I* drive?" he asked.

"A black Mustang GT."

He smiled. "Seems to me like you *do* pay attention to cars."

She waved her hand. "No, that's just because it's *your* car. Of course I remember what kind you drive."

His eyes widened and her face heated. Just because they'd made love didn't mean that he felt about her the way she'd already accepted that she felt about him. She was getting way too comfortable around him, letting things slip that she'd rather not share. If she wasn't careful, he'd realize how much she craved being around him. Which would be nothing short of humiliating if he didn't share the same affliction.

Even when he was mad at her, she wanted to see his

handsome face, listen to that rich baritone soothe her troubled spirit. That was it really, the reason she was so drawn to him, and why he seemed like the yin to her yang. It was because he *understood* her and made her feel comfortable in her own skin. That was such a rare gift, and she'd never experienced it with anyone else.

And, of course, after that practically out-of-body experience of making love with him, she couldn't exactly discount the physical part of their attraction. It was almost as though her soul recognized a kindred spirit in him, and her body recognized it, as well. Making love with Colton had changed her forever. She just wished she knew whether he felt the same.

"You mentioned you don't see many cars," he said, apparently deciding to let her Mustang comment go. "Why is that?"

"There aren't many cars around here to see. The residents who live in apartments above the businesses on Main Street generally walk to get where they need to go. Others walk if their homes aren't too far back in the woods. Cars are for those who work outside town, so they don't tend to drive down the main street. They go down a side road that heads into the trees. The few who do drive cars into town tend to park them behind the businesses that have parking lots, like Swamp Buggy Outfitters. And still more use canoes, kayaks or ATVs to get around."

She pitched her pencil down. "Maybe there's no point in even looking at these. Maybe Garcia's right and I suck at being an agent. I was going to quit anyway, start a new career as a bed-and-breakfast owner. So I must have known, subconsciously, that there wasn't much point in my continuing as an agent."

He stood and pulled her to her feet and then gently

tilted her chin up. "Whatever Garcia said is irrelevant. That man couldn't find his own socks if they were sitting right in front of him. Forget him."

She laughed, some of the tightness easing in her chest. "I think you have him pegged."

He stepped back and bent down, scooping up the pictures. "Let's see if we can't figure this thing out before we go notify Mrs. Jones this evening."

He held the drawings up and motioned toward the table in the eat-in kitchen that was really just an alcove off the main room. "We might be more comfortable in there."

"Good idea. Have you eaten lunch? It's getting closer to the dinner hour than lunch but still too early for me to wait that long. I'm starving. I could check the fridge and see what Jake and Faye have in there. I'm sure I can whip up something decent."

"I could eat. Maybe sandwiches or something light. We can work on them together. And while we do, you can tell me who Jake and Faye are—and why you're in their apartment."

While they worked in assembly-line fashion putting together two rather impressive ham-and-cheese subs with all the fixings, she told him about the owners of the Moon and Star, Jake and Faye, and how they were out of town on a second honeymoon trip along with friends of theirs, Dex and Amber. Dex was paying for the trip because Jake and Faye had cut their honeymoon short to help him when he was in trouble.

"Sounds like you like Faye and her husband very much. I can hear it in your voice." He set their plates on the table. "Chips? I saw some in the pantry when I got the bread out."

"Sure." She opened the refrigerator. "Want a soda? Or beer?"

"Water. Beer would be my preference, but I want a clear head for the case." He stepped into the walk-in pantry. "You were going to explain why you're in this apartment instead of in your room at the B and B."

"Isn't it obvious? There are a ton of people over there right now. I needed peace and quiet to concentrate." She grabbed two cold water bottles.

"Tell me about it. I was over there earlier looking for you."

He moved her drawings to the counter before setting a bag of chips on the table. The almost reverent way he treated her work, even if it was just quick, throwaway-quality sketches, had her feeling all funny inside. She might not know squat about his past, but everything he'd done from the moment he met her had been designed to protect her and others. And he always treated her with respect, never looking at her as if she were crazy or flighty, the way so many people in her life did. Instead, whenever she spaced out, he found it amusing. So many people had gotten exasperated with her, or had mocked her for what she really couldn't help.

If her boss had seen her sketching suspects, he'd have told her to stop wasting time. But Colton respected her methods even if he didn't understand them. He hadn't even batted an eye at her drawings. And his questions were spoken with genuine curiosity, not disdain.

"Earth to Silver," he teased, waving a hand in front of her face. "Where did you go there?"

She shrugged. "Nowhere important. Let's eat, and try to narrow our list of suspects."

She hadn't realized how hungry she was until she

took the first bite of her ham-and-cheese sandwich. Then she practically inhaled it.

"Hungry much?" Colton grinned, with over half his sandwich still left.

Her face heated. "I didn't have breakfast."

"And I did. Totally understandable." He leaned to the side and pulled a knife out of a drawer without having to get up in the tiny kitchen. After cutting off the part of his sandwich that he'd eaten from, he set the rest of it on her plate. "Be my guest."

The half sandwich did look tempting. But she couldn't possibly eat it when the incredible male specimen in front of her had barely eaten anything. She'd be embarrassed.

He tilted her chin up again. "Hey. I can tell you're still hungry. So eat. As tiny as you are, it's not like you have anything to prove."

Her stomach chose that moment to growl.

Colton laughed and shoved her plate closer to her. "Go on. You eat while I ask a few more questions."

"About what?" she said, holding a hand up in front of her mouth, since she'd already taken a bite.

"Charlie Tate and Ron Dukes, the young men you first saw with Eddie the day you found that kilo. I noticed you didn't draw them."

She chased her bite of sandwich with a quick drink from her bottle of water. "That's because they aren't around anymore. Charlie's family had been going to therapy and jumping through hoops with the Department of Children and Families and were finally approved to take him home. So they did, in Naples. And I haven't seen Ron in a couple of weeks."

"Doesn't that strike you as odd?"

"That Charlie moved, no. Ron? Yeah. I wondered if

something had happened to him. I followed up as best I could, but he didn't really have any friends in town. And nothing came up in any missing persons databases. No crimes or unsolved homicides that involved anyone fitting his description. My boss told me to keep my focus on our most promising—and remaining—suspect, Eddie. Even before Ron disappeared, I pretty much spent every free moment when I wasn't working on the B and B keeping tabs on Eddie. But I was limited in what I could do because of using the B and B as my cover. There were big gaps in the day when I was stuck at the inn and couldn't say where Eddie was. But as to where Ron is right now, I couldn't tell you."

He sat back in his chair, seemingly lost in thought as he looked past her.

She quickly finished the rest of her sandwich, giving him the time he needed to think things through. But when she started clearing the dishes, he got up and helped her. They worked together in a comfortable silence until everything was put back the way it should be. And then they attacked the guest room, changing the sheets and putting everything to rights. Silver couldn't bear the teasing if her friend somehow figured out that she'd slept there with Colton. Faye would be thrilled for her, of course, but Silver was more private than Faye and preferred to keep things, well, private.

They returned to the living room and straightened up in there, too, before Silver headed back into the kitchen.

"I'll have to remember to take out the garbage when we leave," she said. "Faye and Jake get back in about a week. I wouldn't want them to come back to a smelly kitchen."

He braced his shoulder against the kitchen wall.

"What do residents of Mystic Glades do, just set the garbage out back and someone picks it up?"

"No, there's a collection of Dumpsters a quarter mile back in the trees, northeast of the entrance. Everyone hauls their trash there. It's picked up three times a week so it won't smell too bad."

"It's hard to imagine a garbage truck making that tight U-turn on I-75 to go down the road by the culvert to get here, let alone drive the five or six miles past the fence. And three times a week? We don't even get that kind of service back in Naples."

"It's more like eight miles from I-75," she said absently as she leaned back against the counter. "And you're right, the county doesn't send a truck. Our town purchased its own special truck years ago that we keep parked in the woods. The truck is used to unload the Dumpsters and carries everything to a garbage-processing facility several miles out of town, way back in the woods." She stared up at him. "It all goes out on a small barge every week, down the canals to a collection point. The county takes it from there."

He grew still and returned her stare. "A barge. Every week."

She slowly nodded. "Are you thinking what I'm thinking?"

"That our drug dealer doesn't need the airboats to deliver his drugs? Yeah. That's what I'm thinking. Who owns the barge operation?"

"The same person who runs everything else around here. Buddy Johnson."

"No surprise there. He probably charges everyone here for trash collection, and gets a check from the city, too."

"I think so, yes."

"And who does all the work?"

"High school kids take turns running the truck from the Dumpsters to the facility. It's a quick trip, probably takes no more than an hour to empty the Dumpsters, haul the contents to the site, then park the truck back by the Dumpsters. A different kid does it each time so it doesn't infringe on their homework time. And Buddy pays them pretty well. It's quick, easy work. The truck takes care of all the lifting."

"I'm guessing Eddie was one of the kids doing that."

She nodded. "Yes. And Charlie, and several others."

"What about the processing of all that garbage into bales and loading it onto the barge once a week? Who oversees that?"

"It used to be Ron Dukes. But after he disappeared, someone else took over."

He braced his arm on the countertop. "Who?"

"Cato Green. It's his weekend job now, to supplement the money he makes at Callahan's during the week. Colton, I think you need to make another call to your boss. We need to find out where Ron Dukes went, and see if Drew has found out anything else about Cato."

He arched an eyebrow. "I think we both know where Dukes probably ended up."

She swallowed against the bile rising in her throat. "The county dump, after taking an involuntary ride on a barge full of garbage."

"It's a perfect setup. Anyone who crosses the boss, or makes a mistake, can be hauled out with the trash. No one would have any reason to search through a barge full of bundled-up garbage thinking there'd be a dead body. And what do you want to bet that the kilos are in one of those bundles, and they get off-loaded onto another boat right before the barge reaches the collection point? Mystic Glades could be a distribution point for all of south Florida. But if that's the case, why kill Eddie on the side of the highway and leave him there for others to find when they could have just taken him out on the barge? You think the killer was sending a message?"

"I do. Unfortunately, in my job—or former job—investigating drug dealers," she said, "that's not uncommon. Whoever killed Eddie wanted him to be found. It was a message, maybe a warning to others who knew Eddie, others who were working with the same boss, not to cross him. Drug dealers are known for sending messages like that. But where does the burglary ring fit in with all this?"

"It doesn't, not at first blush," he said. "I can't imagine a drug dealer running a ring like that out of the same place as his base of operations, his distribution point. Why risk bringing any scrutiny that could destroy his whole operation? The drugs have to be raking in hundreds of thousands of dollars, if not millions, depending on how many kilos he's funneling through here. Burglary, even from wealthy homes, isn't nearly as profitable. At least, not based on the lists of stolen goods I've been working with. And the logistics, the location of buyers and the risks are completely different."

"Maybe the two aren't related?"

He shook his head. "What would be the odds of two major crime hubs in one tiny town that aren't related? There has to be something else that explains the link. The note that Eddie left certainly made it sound like the burglary ring and drug ring were connected. I didn't have the kind of proof to go to court and build a case against Eddie yet for the thefts, but I had enough to know he was deep into it, even before we read his pseudo-confession. That's why I wanted to use him, to get him to turn against his boss and make a deal. But I never got the chance. As for the drug part, you saw him with a kilo. Even if that was the first, it obviously wasn't the last." He pulled his keys out of his pocket. "We can speculate on that later. You said the barge won't run until the weekend. What about the Dumpster pickup? When is the next day that's scheduled?"

"Tomorrow night."

"Good. We can check it all out now while there's no one around, and look into that barge operation, see if it really makes sense that it could work the way we're thinking. If our suspicions seem feasible, then we'll head out to Alligator Alley, where I can get cell phone coverage and call Drew."

"Right," she said, fisting her hands at her sides. "So he can investigate Cato. And send someone out to the county dump, with cadaver dogs."

Chapter Twelve

Silver wrinkled her nose as Colton drove his Mustang down the narrow dirt road past the Dumpsters and toward the barge operation. "I can see why they have this place so far away from town. No one wants to smell this every day."

"Yeah, I can't imagine Buddy wanting the aroma to interfere with his tourism plans for the town." The trees opened up ahead, revealing patches of blue sky. "Let's assume someone could be here even though we think it's deserted."

"My pistol's loaded." She patted her jeans over her ankle holster. "And I don't ever intend to leave home without it again."

He pulled the car over into a patch of gravel that appeared to be for parking and cut the engine.

They both got out and surveyed the huge clearing. There wasn't a lot to it. Just a metal building on the right with enormous containers hooked to the outside of it— probably where the teenagers emptied the trucks. And there was a steel conveyor belt coming out of the building leading toward the swamp. It looked a lot like what she'd seen at airports, the metal rollers she pushed her suitcase on, along with the plastic containers that held her shoes, so it could feed the X-ray scanners.

"Looks fairly automated," Colton said as they crunched through the dirt and gravel to where the conveyor ended.

A small barge, a miniature version of what would normally be seen on a river carrying boxcars to a dock, was tied up to a bulkhead. It appeared to be designed to keep the swamp from encroaching on the land, ensuring deep enough water for a heavily loaded barge to not get stuck.

"There's a small crane on the barge," she pointed out. "I guess they dump the garbage into the large containers, and then the trash feeds into the building to be bundled. All they have to do is run the bundles down the conveyor and use the crane to load it. What do you think? A two-man operation?"

"Easily. One person could do it if he had to. And it wouldn't require anyone with much skill."

"That explains why Cato was hired. He's not the brightest bulb in the box." She put her hands on her hips and scanned the area again. "It looks amazingly clean around here. Far more kept up than I'd expect of a garbage facility."

"I was thinking the same thing. Stay alert. Let's check out the building."

He drew his pistol and she did the same. Better safe than sorry. They kept their weapons pointed down toward the ground as they approached the opening. There was no door. The building was more like a small aircraft hangar, open on one side. The smell was worse inside than out by the containers. But underlying the familiar odor of garbage was…something else. She sniffed, trying to identify the smell. It was familiar, too, and not unpleasant, just…not what she'd expect here.

They performed a quick search of the building, but it

was clearly empty except for the baling machine hooked up to chutes on the container side of the facility.

"What *is* that?" she asked, sniffing again. "It seems like it's coming from—"

"Over here." He crouched beside the baling machine and picked up a piece of gravel from the ground. He sniffed it and jerked back, holding it away from his nose. "This is the source, for sure." He pitched the rock down and stood, pointing at the base of the machine. "Someone splashed it all over the ground here, and the bottom of the machine. See how the paint's peeling there?"

When she reached him, she nodded in agreement. "Bleach."

"Yep. And what do criminals use bleach for? Especially this large an amount?"

"To destroy blood evidence."

He kept his back to the walls, his gun at the ready as he scanned the clearing, visible through the opening to the building. "Let's get out of here."

Her mouth went dry as she followed him to the entrance. Living in a remote area like Mystic Glades, being surrounded by woods and trees and hemmed in by acres of saw grass and marsh had always seemed like a mecca, a blessing. It was like living inside an extraordinary painting that one of the masters had left for lesser artists like her to soak in and enjoy. But right now, realizing how far away from town she and Colton were, isolated—and suspecting that someone could have been murdered in the building behind them—had her hands going clammy and her heart racing as if she'd just run a marathon.

He waved her to stop at the opening as he looked outside. It was a long, quiet minute before he motioned her forward, and she followed him around the corner. They hurried to his car and hopped inside. The wheels spit up gravel as he took off toward town. It wasn't until they were back at the archway that announced the entrance to Main Street that she finally relaxed against the seat and holstered her gun. Colton hesitated, idling the car.

Silver pushed her hair out of her face with a hand that was embarrassingly shaky. "What are you doing? Don't you want to head out to the highway to call Drew?"

He nodded and checked his phone. "Yeah, and I will. But between the time we spent at your friend's apartment and the time that it took to look over that garbage facility, it's already past six."

"Mrs. Jones. I completely forgot. And Freddie and her close circle of friends know about Eddie. We really do need to officially notify her before she finds out from someone else."

"I was thinking the same thing. How far away is her house?"

"If you turn left here instead of going down Main Street, and circle around behind that first business, there's a little road that heads east to several different homes. The Joneses' house is pretty much at the end, about five miles or so down."

"All right. Let's get that taken care of. Then we'll circle back to the B and B and get you an overnight bag. I'd like to sit with Drew and the other detectives and talk all this through. If he thinks our theory is worth looking into, he can send that team to the dump, and we'll plan on bringing a CSI team back here in the morning to go over the garbage facility to see if the cleanup missed anything. We can try to get a warrant, but our best bet will probably be just to get Buddy Johnson's permission. If neither of those happens, we'll surround the facility and sit on it until we get something that can convince a judge to issue the warrant. But I don't want to do anything tonight that will alert someone to go out there and scrub that place any more than it's been scrubbed."

"Sounds like a plan. You mentioned an overnight bag. Is there a hotel close to the station where I can stay?"

"Yes. But you're not staying there. You're staying with me, at my apartment." He glanced over at her, his expression unreadable. "You okay with that?"

She expected him to explain his reasons, like that he wanted to keep her nearby so they could discuss the case. But when he didn't say anything, she realized what this was—his way of saying, finally, hopefully, that making love to her hadn't been a onetime thing. That maybe there was a future here. That he was interested in a relationship with her. And she wasn't about to say no to that.

"I think it's a great idea," she said.

He gave her a curt nod. "Good." He shifted gears and sent the Mustang down the road toward the Joneses'.

LEAVING THE COMFORTING of Mrs. Jones to Silver, now that they'd broken the news about Eddie to her, Colton—with Mrs. Jones's permission—walked through their one-story house, looking for clues, anything that Eddie might have left behind that could help them figure out who he'd associated with and which one of them might be the one pulling the strings.

The house was a typical ranch house, but built on four-foot-high stilts to keep it high and dry whenever storms or late-afternoon summer rains caused the swamp to encroach on the property. Colton had noticed that all the houses they'd glimpsed back in the trees when driving here were built on stilts. She'd told him that there were only a few that weren't, like a mansion down a different road that the founder of Mystic Glades had built. It was on a solid foundation but high up off the ground and had never flooded until last summer, the summer when Dex and Amber were here. Both of them had nearly lost their lives in that flood, but thankfully they were okay.

Bunk beds were in three of the bedrooms. He counted six beds. But he also counted six names on the doors. Apparently the Joneses assigned each bed and put the boys' names on the doors. He rather sourly wondered if that was so they'd remember the kids' names as they funneled child after child through here. From what Silver had told him, Eddie had never felt loved here.

But then again, Eddie was probably hard to love because he got into so much trouble. So maybe it wasn't fair to just assume the foster parents didn't care about the kids in their care. After all, once he and Silver had broken the news about Eddie to Mrs. Jones, she'd broken down. And she'd sent the other boys to a neighbor's house down the road until she could compose herself. She didn't want them seeing her cry and worrying, or at least that was what she'd said.

Still, what he was seeing with the bedrooms, and the number of kids he'd counted when they arrived, had him heading back into the living room to ask a question.

Mrs. Jones kept staring straight in front of her as if preoccupied with her sad thoughts, but she'd dried her tears by now and was quietly talking to Silver. They sat beside each other on the couch, holding hands like old friends. He paused in the doorway, admiring Silver once again for the way she seemed to truly care about others and want to help them, even if they didn't deserve it. He knew she didn't like the woman she was comforting, and yet he could see the compassion in her expression, in the way she held the other woman's hand and spoke to her. Silver was a truly special woman, and he was getting deeper and deeper in this. What had he been thinking to offer to take her to his apartment tonight?

She glanced up at him and gave him a watery smile. She must have cried right along with Mrs. Jones.

He returned her smile and headed into the room, taking a seat across from them on a brown leather recliner. "Mrs. Jones, I noticed there are six boys here and six bunk beds. Where did Eddie sleep?"

She glanced off into space before waving her hand, the wadded-up tissue in it flopping as she did. "Oh, he moved out on his birthday. I mean, he still came home for dinner and such. But he wanted his own space. He couldn't afford anything yet, so we let him move into the tree house out back."

"Tree house?"

She had the grace to blush. "Yes. I know it sounds bad, but honestly, the tree house is just about as nice as this house inside. Tony built it years ago when we realized we were going to end up taking in middle-school-aged kids. He thought it would be fun to have a big tree house for them and even hooked up a bathroom of sorts, with real running water and a pipe that connects to the septic system." She patted the corners of her eyes. "Eddie loved that tree house. He spent a lot of time there. I couldn't tell him no when he begged to move out there."

"If it's okay, I'd like to see it," he said.

She looked off into space again. "Of course, of course. You do whatever you need to do, Officer. And if there's something I can do to help your investigation, let me know. Tony will be devastated when he hears about Eddie."

Silver exchanged a startled glance with Colton, who only shrugged. What Mrs. Jones had just said didn't jibe at all with the way that Eddie had portrayed his foster parents. But where Silver probably believed everything Eddie had ever told her, Colton was more inclined to think that maybe Eddie had exaggerated. There certainly wasn't anything about this house, or in how the other foster kids had acted when they got here, to make him think they weren't well taken care of or that the Joneses didn't care about them.

Eddie had been a teenager, and life through the eyes of a teenager, especially a troubled one, could often be very different from the reality of those around them.

Silver rose from the couch along with Mrs. Jones. "Will you be okay if I go with Detective Graham to look at the tree house?"

"Of course, of course. I'm going to head on up to Betty's to see the boys. You've been very sweet to me this evening, Silver. You didn't have to be, either, so I want you to know that I appreciate it. You and I have never said more than a few words to each other, but I've always admired you."

Silver blinked in obvious surprise. "You do?"

She nodded. "You went to college and worked hard for everything that you have. And you've never been anything but nice to me. I appreciate that. Thank you for being Eddie's friend, too. I know you tutored him and helped him out. Not that Eddie ever said anything about it. I heard from others what was going on." She swiped at her wet eyes again. "Eddie and I didn't always see eye to eye. It does my heart good to know he had you as a friend when I couldn't be that for him."

Silver hugged the other woman, and the three of them left the house, with Elisa Jones hurrying up the road toward the house where she'd sent the boys and Colton and Silver heading around to the back of the property.

"You okay?" Colton asked.

"I guess I'm...confused." She shrugged. "Maybe I misjudged her all this time."

He didn't know what to say to that, so he didn't say anything. She'd have to work through this one on her own.

In spite of what Mrs. Jones had said about the tree house being nice, Colton hadn't expected it to be *this* nice. A good fifty yards from the house, it was about fifteen feet off the ground, with a massive deck circling around it, snugged up against the tree trunk. A system of steel supports beneath it went all the way to the ground, preserving the health of the tree by not impaling it, but also providing the strength needed to keep the heavy contraption from falling down.

Arched over a split in the main trunk, the actual "house" part of it was about the size of a bedroom, with windows on two sides and a full-sized door on the front. Silver and Colton climbed the steel ladder and he helped her step out onto the deck.

"This is one heck of a tree house," he said. "But I suppose it makes sense. Drew said that Mr. Jones is an engineer. This was probably a pet project, to use his skills from work in addition to making something the boys would enjoy."

Silver ran her hand along the railing, her face a mask of awe and pleasure. "It's beautiful. I love that he used real branches to build the railing system. And the forest is gorgeous up here. What a view."

Colton couldn't help smiling to see her joy in something as simple as a view. He loved how she appreciated the simple things that most people missed. The view was amazing, even though most of it was of other trees, too thick to reveal much of the surrounding canals and swamps. But he was more interested right now in the heavy vines hanging down on all sides from the branches above. Instead of twining around the tree trunk, they'd been cut free to swing like thick ropes. He reached out and grabbed one of them and yanked. Solid, sturdy, easy to hold on to because of the offshoots and holes nature automatically built into the vine. He looked down at the railing in front of him. And then at the next tree over, which also had thick vines hanging down.

"Huh. I'll be."

"What? Did you find something?" Silver rushed over to him, her eyebrows drawn down.

He held up the vine and pointed to the railing. "See how that top rail is scuffed and scarred? And how that tree over there has more vines hanging down?"

Her eyes widened. "What are you thinking? Surely Eddie didn't stand on the railing and swing on that vine as if he were Tarzan or something."

"I'd be willing to bet that he did. And from the way this railing is scarred up, he did it a lot."

She shaded her eyes from the setting sun that was peeking through the branches. "That's a scary thought. We're a long ways up. One wrong step or one mistimed grab and it would be all over."

"Yeah, but it's also genius. If someone was after you and you could get up in the trees without them seeing you, boom, you're gone. A quiet getaway with no one the wiser."

"I suppose so. But that gives me hives just thinking

about it. Someone could have been killed." She grimaced and exchanged a solemn look with him, silently acknowledging that someone *had* been killed—Eddie. Just not while he was swinging from the vines.

He squeezed her shoulder. "Wait here. I'll go in first, make sure there aren't any critters inside."

She shivered. "Be my guest. I don't want to come face-to-face with a raccoon or, worse, a bat."

He swung open the door. A guttural shout sounded from just inside.

"Colton, look out!" Silver yelled.

He swore and threw his arms up to block the man lunging at him with a knife.

Chapter Thirteen

Silver clawed for her gun. Colton twisted his attacker's wrist, and the knife clattered to the deck. Colton pivoted and rolled, throwing the other man against the railing. He let out a cry of pain just as Silver brought her gun up.

That blond hair. That youthful face. Oh, no.

Colton drew his fist back.

"No, stop!" Silver yelled as she holstered her gun. "It's Charlie."

Colton hesitated, his fist still raised. Charlie jerked to the side, rolled out from under him and ran for the railing.

"Oh no, you don't," Colton growled as he jumped to his feet. He ran and dove for Charlie just as the boy grabbed a vine and shoved off the top railing.

Silver gasped and covered her mouth in horror as the young man fell several feet. Then the vine jerked as he caught a good handhold, and it swung him toward the other tree. A flash of white tennis shoes as Charlie grabbed another vine and pushed off the other side of the tree and he was gone.

Colton grabbed the vine by the tree house and looked as though he was considering going after him. Silver jumped between him and the railing and held her hands out to stop him.

"Wait. It's too dangerous. You could fall. And besides, we don't know why Charlie was here or what he was doing. As much as I hate to admit it, it could be a trap."

His jaw muscle worked as he stared at the other tree. He'd climbed more than a few in his day and even swung from a few, courtesy of a well-hewn rope. Vines couldn't be that much harder and might even be easier to use because of so many handholds. But if Charlie had been watching them and scrambled up into the tree house to lure him into chasing him, it could very well be a trap.

He dropped the vine and stepped back. "Okay, you're right." He scooped up the knife Charlie had left behind, a six-inch blade with a serrated edge. "This is a heck of a knife. He meant business. I don't think we have to wonder whose side he's on. Definitely not ours." He hiked his leg up on the railing and yanked back his jeans, then carefully secured the knife inside his boot.

"You're right," Silver said. "I shouldn't have interfered. It's just that he's so young, and I was afraid you'd hurt him. But *you* could have been hurt, or worse. I'm so, so sorry."

His face softened as he straightened. "Your idiot former boss is right about one thing—you're softhearted. But he's wrong to think that's a weakness." He cupped her face and pressed a gentle kiss against her lips. "Don't ever change, Silver Westbrook."

She stood there in shock as he drew his pistol, then made a textbook entrance into the tree house, searching for intruders of the two-foot variety even though he'd teased her about the four-foot kind. He was doing his job, exactly as he should, while she'd failed miserably in that department.

Distracting him while he was fighting someone was inexcusable and went against her training. But seeing that young face had reminded her of Eddie, and the horrible way that he'd died, beaten to death. And she'd just…reacted.

She shivered and rubbed her hands up and down her arms. Crying out for Colton to stop was wrong, and dangerous. And yet he wasn't even upset with her. That kind of understanding and forgiveness was so foreign to her she wasn't sure that she understood it. And she certainly didn't deserve it.

"Clear," he called out from inside the tree house. "You can come in."

Determined to do better—for Colton's sake, and hers—she scanned the trees around them. Then she looked below, from every angle. When she didn't see any signs of intruders, she headed inside.

The tree trunk came up through the middle of the room, making it a doughnut shape with more than three feet of clearance all around the tree. A tiny sink and full-size toilet sat on one side. A microwave and dorm-sized refrigerator formed a kitchen. And an air mattress with a pillow and quilt thrown on top must have been where Eddie slept when he was here.

"I wonder what Charlie was doing in here," she said.

He was currently kneeling on the floor, looking at an old trunk beside the air mattress. He waved at a trash can off to the side, full of plastic wrappers from candy bars and the kinds of sandwiches that came from a machine, along with a mound of empty water bottles. "Looks like he was camping out. He was supposed to have left with his parents, right? Maybe he ran away?"

"He must have. I wonder why. I hope they weren't abusing him or something. Sad."

"I suppose it's possible, but he didn't look abused. No bruises or cuts. Then again, I know that stuff doesn't always show, especially if it's psychological abuse."

"No," she said softly. "And that can be the worst kind." She hugged her arms around her middle.

Colton's head shot up. "You sound like you speak from personal experience."

She thought about denying it, but this was Colton. And although she'd never talked about her troubled past with anyone, she knew she could talk to him about it. He wouldn't judge her or make her feel ashamed. "Yes. I speak from personal experience."

He started to rise, but she waved him back down.

"I'm fine. No reason to go over that, certainly not now. But thank you for caring. I can see it in your eyes."

"Silver, if you want to talk—"

"I know. Thank you. Not now."

He hesitated, looking uncertain.

She knelt beside him and kissed him, then waved at the trunk. "What are you doing?"

He searched her eyes, as if undecided.

"Colton, it was a very long time ago. I'm fine. The trunk?"

He frowned at her, and she loved that he was so concerned. But he finally turned back to the trunk. "It's the only thing in here that's locked up and I want to know why. I couldn't find a key anywhere." He pulled his knife from his boot and went to work on the wood surrounding the lock. It popped off and the top sprang open. "Looks mostly like clothes. And books."

Silver helped him sort through everything, smiling sadly when she found the algebra book with notes in it that she'd made while helping Eddie pass his final.

"Aha." Colton held up a small key. "This looks promising. If we can figure out what it goes to." He ran his hands along the bottom underneath the clothes, then sat back. "I don't think there's anything else in here, though. So the key must be what he wanted to keep safe."

"It kind of looks like a padlock key, or maybe it's to another trunk," she said. "I suppose we could ask Mrs. Jones where he might keep more belongings, in case there's a trunk there."

He helped her to her feet and soon they were back on solid ground. She'd just turned toward the path that led to the house when he tugged her hand.

"I'm pretty sure there isn't anything in that house where the key would fit. I searched it pretty thoroughly earlier. But we can check out that path over there." He pointed off into the trees. "If you'll notice, it follows the direction where Charlie went, and it appears well-worn, like maybe Eddie went there a lot. I for one would like to know where it goes. And the sun is going down. I'd rather do it while we have daylight left, especially if there's some evidence out here that Charlie might be in the process of making disappear. I'd hate to come out here tomorrow with Drew and a team and find out we'd just missed a big score that would crack the case wide open. Are you game?"

"You bet I am. Let's go."

After a good fifteen-minute walk, the path abruptly ended in a clearing, not all that far from the tree house— maybe about a few hundred yards. And in the middle was a dilapidated-looking wooden shed that was about twenty-by-twenty, with rotting boards. It would have looked abandoned and unused if it weren't for the shiny metal door affixed to the front, and what was hanging off the metal loop. A padlock.

"Do you see what I see?" Colton asked.

"A place for our key."

They searched the woods in the immediate vicinity of the shed, but it was all clear, so they headed back to the shed, key in hand.

Silver took out her gun, scanning the clearing while he tried the key.

Click.

"Bingo," he said. He took the lock off, flipped back the latch and pulled out his pistol. "Wait until I give the all clear."

She nodded, keeping guard while he went inside. A few seconds later, a low whistle sounded from inside.

"Jackpot," he said. "You'll want to see this."

When she stepped through the doorway, Colton held up his phone, using the flashlight app to show her what he'd found. Nearly every inch of space along the walls was taken up with three-foot-high stacks of something beneath heavy green tarps. And since Colton had flipped back the tarp closest to the door, she didn't have to guess what was underneath.

Bricks of cocaine. Dozens of them. No, hundreds based on the number of stacks.

"This is worse than anything I ever imagined. If Eddie did anything to make the dealer feel threatened, no wonder he killed him. This is worth millions on the street."

He flipped off the light on his phone and tried to make a call. "No signal. No surprise." He shoved the phone into the holder on this waist. "We're getting out of here. Now."

They turned around, but suddenly Colton put his hand over her mouth and hauled her back inside. "We're too late," he whispered next to her ear. "Listen."

Voices, two men and a woman, sounded from outside, approaching fast.

He moved his hand and pulled out his knife.

"What are you doing?" she whispered. "We have to get out of the shed."

"Nowhere to go without them hearing us. Hurry, get under that tarp at the far end."

"Should I close the door?"

"No. We can't lock it from inside." He threw a tarp up near the door, pulled out his knife, and slashed and tore several jagged holes inside the top brick, spilling white powder all over the floor.

He shoved the knife back into his boot and grabbed her hand. "Hurry."

Shouts sounded from outside in the clearing as she and Colton scrambled over one of the stacks and slid into the tight space next to the wall. He threw the tarp over the top of both of them and they both pulled their guns out, waiting, listening, barely breathing for fear of making any sound.

She wanted to ask him why he'd cut open that brick of cocaine, but she couldn't for fear of someone hearing. Because the sound of footsteps told her that whoever was outside had just stepped into the shed.

"What the hell?" a man's voice shouted. "You didn't lock the door?"

"Of course I locked it," another man said. "Someone must have busted in."

"Yeah, I'll tell you who got in. A rat, or maybe a raccoon. Because you forgot to lock the place. Look at that mess. It tore open one of the bricks."

"For the last time, I didn't forget."

"Tell that to Cato and see what he says."

Silver drew in a sharp breath. Colton put a hand on

her shoulder in warning. She hoped they hadn't heard her, but she was so surprised to hear them say Cato's name. So he was involved. But how deep? Could he be the leader they'd been looking for? Somehow she couldn't picture him as the head of a multimillion-dollar operation.

Footsteps crossed farther into the shed. The sound of vinyl sliding against vinyl came from just a few feet of their hiding place. One of the men had thrown back a tarp. "Everything else looks untouched."

"Of course it does," the first man's voice said, sounding as though he thought the other man was an idiot. "The rodent got high and went off to die somewhere. If a person had done this, he wouldn't have wasted anything. He'd have made off with our stash."

Another tarp was flipped up, the air whispering against the one where she and Colton were hiding. She tightened both hands around her gun. Colton's left hand touched her right wrist, applying gentle, steady pressure, forcing her to lower the gun just a few inches. It was his silent way of letting her know not to panic. She swallowed hard and focused on her breathing, in, out, in, out, all through the mouth. No noise.

"Bring her in here," the first man ordered.

The man who'd flipped back the tarps covered the stacks again, or at least that was what Silver guessed he was doing based on the vinyl sounds.

Her mind raced, wondering who "her" was. Did they have a hostage?

"Mrs. Jones," the first man said. "You been in the shed?"

Mrs. Jones? Silver's hands tightened on her gun again. How could she? Eddie had died, and she'd been a part of this all along.

"No, no, no, sir. I don't even have a key. Eddie had the key."

"See?" the man said. "I told you, raccoon. 'Cause Eddie sure ain't comin' in here anymore." He laughed at his own joke.

"That's a terrible thing to say," Mrs. Jones said, her voice shaking with fear and anger both. "Why would you kill that boy? We've done everything you asked us to do."

What was she talking about? Had she made some kind of deal?

"I'm not the one who killed him. But I tell you what, I can take you to the boss, let you ask him directly if you want."

The cruelty in his voice had bile rising in Silver's throat. Colton's shoulder brushed against hers, and she could feel the tension in his body. He was just as angry as she was. And there was more to Mrs. Jones's situation than Silver had guessed. She definitely didn't seem to be a willing participant in the drug operation.

"What about my Tony? You said you'd let him go. Where is he?"

"Hold your horses. He's fine, just like we promised. As long as you ain't told no one about us?"

"No, no, like I said. We've done everything you asked."

"You did just fine, Mrs. Jones. Now, we've heard there might be a couple of cops in town, a man and a woman. You know anything about that?"

There was a pause, then, "Yes, they were at my house. They told me about Eddie. But I didn't tell them anything. I sent them away."

"You sure about that? You sure you didn't tell them anything?" His voice sounded menacing again.

"I swear, as God is my witness. Please, you're hurting my arm."

"Well, I'm sorry about that, Mrs. Jones. There, now, all better?"

"I'm fine," she said. "I always do what you ask. I meet you here every night to check in."

"And we appreciate that, don't we, Jack?"

A noncommittal grunt was the only sign that the other man was still there.

"Tell you what," the obvious leader of the duo said. "You don't even have to meet us out here tomorrow. We'll give you a night off, for good behavior. But we'll still be watching you, to make sure you aren't talking to anyone that you shouldn't."

"I don't need a night off. I need to see Tony. It's time to let him and the others go. Like you promised. You were supposed to let them go after the last shipment."

"We're running behind schedule. *This* is the last shipment. We have to wait until the weekend to bring the barge around or we'll attract attention. Just a few more days and this will all be over." His voice sounded placating now. "You run on back to the house and keep those cops out of our hair. And just as soon as that barge is loaded, we'll let Mr. Jones and the others go."

"You promise?" she said. "You give me your word? You won't hurt Tony?"

"You have my word, Mrs. Jones. As long as I have yours that you aren't going to tell anyone."

"I haven't told a soul. And I won't."

"Good, good. Now run along."

The sound of her hurrying out of the shed and into the clearing gradually faded.

"What were you talking about?" the second man said. "This is our last shipment?"

He laughed. "Not even close. This place has been a gold mine for us. Not a single lost kilo, until that stupid critter got in here. No, we're going to be here for a long time to come. We just have to clean up a few messes, and make sure all the leaks are plugged. Starting with Tony. Once that's all taken care of, and the shipment is on its way, then we'll have to arrange some kind of accident for Mrs. Jones. And next time you have to go, go in your pants, dude. No leaving your post until it's time for the next guard. We'll be lucky if Cato or the boss doesn't take the price of that ruined kilo out of our take as it is. Now keep an eye on the place. Can you do that?"

They stepped out of the shed arguing and the door slammed shut. The padlock clicked, and the sound of footsteps moved away, but only one set. The man who'd gotten in trouble for leaving the shed was still outside, standing guard.

"We're trapped," Silver whispered next to Colton's ear.

"Not for long. Stay here."

"But—"

"Wait for me. Don't come out until I tell you." He threw back the tarp and climbed over the stack of cocaine bricks they'd hidden behind, then flipped it back over her.

She fisted her hands, hating that he hadn't given her a chance to even discuss whatever plan he had.

A light shuffling noise sounded near the door, then a scratching sound like claws on wood. Oh, no. Was there a rat in here?

The shuffling and scratching started again, and the door rattled in its frame as though something was pushing against it. Silver shivered with revulsion, thinking about the animal doing that. And where was Colton? What was he doing?

Scratch. Thump.

Cursing sounded from outside. The padlock rattled against the door and then the door flew open.

"All right, you little rodent. Where are you hiding?"

Another loud thump sound. Then a crack. A loud groan. Then nothing.

"You can come out now," Colton called out.

Silver threw the tarp off and blinked in surprise. A man lay facedown on the dirt, eyes closed.

"Well, I'll be," she said. "I guess the rodent's name was Colton. Pretty slick."

"We'll tie him up and leave him in here. Mind pulling his shoelaces out of his shoes? We can tie his hands behind his back with those and save my handcuffs in case we need them later."

While she did as he'd asked, he used his knife to cut long strips from the man's shirt and then gagged and bound him so he couldn't cry out.

When they were done, he was trussed up like a turkey for Thanksgiving, still unconscious on the floor.

Last, Colton took the man's gun, then waved Silver out of the shed so he could lock it again.

"We don't have any way of knowing what time another guard will come to relieve him. We need to get out of here."

They hurried into the cover of trees. Silver stopped when she realized Colton wasn't following her. He stood staring back at the clearing and the trees surrounding it.

Her stomach dropped with dread. "Is another guard coming already?"

"I don't think so." They both kept their voices low so they wouldn't carry. His intense gaze bored into her.

"What did you make out of their conversation with Mrs. Jones? That they've got hostages, right? Tony is Mr. Jones. And she mentioned others."

"You're thinking we should try to free them, aren't you? Instead of going for help?"

He shook his head. "No. I'm thinking *I* should try to free them, and *you* should go for help."

She put her hands on her hips. "If you think for one minute that I'm going to leave you to face them alone, you're seriously deluded. No way. Where you go, I go. I'm your wingman. I've got your back."

His jaw tightened and he strode toward her. If she hadn't already met him and known how kind and honorable he was, she'd have been intimidated by his deep scowl and flashing blue eyes. As it was, he was still a bit intimidating as he glared down at her.

"I'm all about equal rights and respect for women and not trying to impose false limitations on them," he said, "but this is one time when I'm going to be a complete chauvinist. You are *not* going with me."

"I'm an officer of the law, just like you. We've got the same training. I'm armed and a pretty good shot. Why *wouldn't* I go with you?"

He backed her up against a tree and tilted her chin up. "I can't risk something happening to you. And besides, it makes more sense for one of us to go for help. You can head to the interstate, call Drew, have him send the cavalry. Once I locate where they've got the hostages, I'll do some kind of diversion, hold them off until you bring help. It's a good plan."

She rolled her eyes. "It's a terrible plan. Two guns are better than one any day. And the idea of a diversion is to have one person create the diversion while the other does whatever needs to be done. It doesn't make sense for you to try to do both."

He started to say something else, but she pressed her fingers against his lips, stopping him. "I appreciate that you care about me. Trust me. The feeling is mutual. I don't want anything to happen to you any more than you want something happening to me. But I'm just as stubborn as you, maybe more so, and there's no way you're going to make me abandon you. Standing here arguing about it is just wasting time. If you want to try to save the hostages, then you'll have to accept my help, or keep looking over your shoulder the whole time. Because that's where I'll be, behind you, watching out for you, covering you. We're partners in this. And that's what partners do."

He pulled her hand down from his mouth. "You are the most frustrating female I've ever met."

She slid her hands up behind his neck and pressed her body against his. "Shut up and kiss me so we can get on with this."

His mouth swooped down and covered hers in a wild, almost savage kiss that had her toes curling in her shoes. And then, before she could even catch her breath, he grabbed her hand and tugged her behind him in an all-out run in the same direction where they'd heard the gunman go earlier.

Chapter Fourteen

Their light was fading fast. Silver was amazed that Colton had been able to track the second gunman at all with what little light they'd had. He was obviously an experienced tracker, which opened up all kinds of interesting questions to ask him someday about his past—if she ever got that opportunity. But even Colton didn't seem to know which way their prey had gone now.

He knelt on the trail they'd been following, pressing his fingers against the soil, feeling for the ridges that would indicate a footprint.

"What about using your flashlight app?" Silver asked. "I can cup my hands around it to try to keep anyone from seeing the light while you get a quick look and try to find more shoe prints."

He considered it, then shook his head. "Too risky. One flash of light seen by the wrong person and suddenly we're surrounded." He stood and brushed off his hands on his jeans. "We'll have to make an educated guess. We know they went this way. From here, there are only two places where the brush is thin enough and the ground firm enough to make for easy travel—that northeast area up by that big oak, and this more westerly turn near that fallen log."

"So we split up?"

"No way. We choose one or the other, together, and see where it goes. If, after a few minutes, we can't pick up the trail again, we'll backtrack and try the other one."

"You're taking this chauvinist thing really far."

"You knew how I felt before we started out. You ready to turn back and ride for help?"

"If I thought I could get help in time to really help, I would. But you and I both know that by the time we could get someone out here, whatever plans those gunmen had for the hostages could be over. No, our only chance to save them is to work together and keep going forward."

He scrubbed his jaw and studied both potential paths. "Northeast?"

"That's the way I'd go. Seems firmer, drier. I'm surprised we haven't seen anyone else out here. Leaving one man to guard a shed full of merchandise doesn't seem very smart."

"I agree. But you heard what they said about the hostages and cleaning up messes. Maybe whoever else is out here is helping with whatever is planned for the hostages."

"Then we need to find them, fast. Let's go."

They continued along the path, looking out for bent or broken branches, or footprints, in the dirt. But with the sun almost completely set, their only light was from the rising moon. And it wasn't even a full moon.

He suddenly held up a hand, signaling for her to stop, then pressed his finger against his mouth for her to be quiet. She paused beside him, listening, trying to hear whatever he'd heard. And then she heard it—the low murmur of voices, muted, as if coming from far away. It was hard to tell in the woods just how far because of the way sound carried out here.

He motioned again for silence, then crept forward. She followed, and together they made their way, getting closer and closer to the sounds they were hearing. After they had maneuvered around a particularly thick mass of fallen limbs and soggy ground to find solid ground again, the glow of lights had them ducking down. But the lights weren't moving. They were steady, and coming from what appeared to be a large clearing at least half a football field away.

Colton reached back for her hand and tugged her with him behind an enormous, twisted cypress, its knobby knees pushing up out of the brackish water of the encroaching swamp on its southern side. She and Colton crouched behind the opposite side, blocking them from the light.

"There could be guards out here in the woods," Colton whispered. "I'll circle around, try to pinpoint how many there are and where they're stationed. If I see the hostages, I'll get a count and the lay of the land, see what we're up against. Then we'll brainstorm the best way to proceed."

She grabbed his hand as he started to turn away. "Promise me you won't try to take on these guys all by yourself. Promise me you'll come back and we'll do this, whatever we decide to do, *together*."

He framed her face in his hands and pressed a fierce kiss against her lips. "Together," he whispered.

And then he was gone.

COLTON CREPT THROUGH the woods, skirting around thick mud bogs and sharp palmettos, carefully making his way in a circle around the source of the light, which he presumed to be the drug dealers' base camp.

He hated lying to Silver, but if the situation was as

dangerous as he expected, no way was he going to come back and bring her with him. Not because he didn't think she was capable. She was DEA and had probably faced worse before. But he'd bet everything he owned that she'd faced it with a team of agents at her side. Because no one in their right mind would try to take on a group of heavily armed mercenary types and thugs that typically made up drug-running operations. And that included him, at any other time. But tonight everything was different.

Because of Silver.

She was one of those rare people who believed in the inherent good in people, in spite of the job she had and the evil she must have seen on a nearly daily basis just as he did. And she'd already suffered such incredible loss when Eddie was killed. He couldn't bear to see her hurting like that again if more innocents were killed. So, knowing it was virtually impossible for Drew to round up the troops to save the hostages in time, here he was, risking everything to try to do the impossible himself.

As he made his way around a large group of palmettos to finally get a clear view of what he was up against, his only real hope was that it wasn't as bad as he'd feared.

Nope. It was worse, far worse.

A large tent sat at one side of the clearing, with at least ten feet of cleared space between it and any foliage, making it nearly impossible to approach without being seen. As Colton watched, three armed men stepped out of the woods and went into the tent. Four armed guards walked the perimeter of the clearing, each with a semiautomatic rifle strapped over his shoulder. And lighting all of it up were three clusters of bright lights, powered by generators.

At the other end of the clearing sat two combat-style heavy-duty Jeeps, their drivers armed with the same type of semiautomatic rifles. Arms crossed and looking bored, they appeared to be waiting for someone or something. Silver had been right. Something was definitely going on.

And he was pretty sure that "something" had to do with the four men bound and gagged in the middle of the clearing, inside a cage. Correction, *one man*, and three *boys*—Eddie's age, around nineteen or twenty. Counting the drivers in the Jeeps, the hostages were guarded by at least nine heavily armed men, ten if he counted the other guard back at the shed, who could come running if needed.

Yeah, this was way worse than he'd hoped.

A whisper of sound from above had him diving to the side and whipping out his knife just as a man leaped down at him from a tree branch. He scrambled to roll away. Colton tackled him and jumped on his back, shoving the man's face into the mud so he couldn't cry out. He held his knife at the ready, grabbed a fistful of the man's hair and yanked his head up to draw his knife across his throat. He'd just reached his blade around to end it when he heard a whimper.

Like what a child might make. *Or a terrified teenager.*

Colton held the knife against the man's throat and leaned down to get a good look at his face. *Charlie.* Ah, hell. He lightened the pressure of the blade. "Give me one good reason not to kill you right now."

"We…we could have…we could have killed *you*," he blubbered, barely able to get coherent words past his lips. "But we didn't."

"We?" He pressed the knife harder against Charlie's throat.

Charlie thumped one of his hands against the ground. Branches crackled overhead. Colton swore and yanked Charlie up out of the mud, pulling him in front of him as he scooted back against a tree, knife still held to the teenager's throat. He whipped out his pistol, aiming it at the six other young men who'd just dropped from the sky and now crouched in front of him as if ready to pounce. But, in spite of Charlie's claims about them killing him, the boys had no weapons, at least none that Colton saw.

"Back up, or he dies," Colton ordered, leveling his pistol at the nearest boy while holding the knife steady against Charlie's throat.

"Do as he says," Charlie whispered, his voice hoarse, barely audible.

The boys slowly raised their hands in the air and backed up several steps. Moonlight slanted down through the branches overhead, illuminating some of their faces. And that was when Colton recognized them. They were the foster kids whom Mrs. Jones had sent to a neighbor's house when he and Silver arrived to break the news about Eddie's death. But how had they ended up here?

A quick glance up confirmed that there were vines hanging from the trees above, the vines these boys had used to swing from tree to tree and sneak up on him, then drop down like ninjas. He couldn't help being impressed.

He slowly lowered his gun, pointing it at the ground, and eased the knife a few inches away from Charlie's throat.

"All right." He kept his voice low so the gunmen back by the tents wouldn't hear him. "You've got my attention. Start talking."

THERE SHOULD HAVE been a trench in the dirt by now for all the pacing that Silver had done. She strode back and forth between the same two trees with her pistol out, hanging down by her thigh toward the ground. How long had it been since Colton had left? Twenty minutes? Thirty? More? Certainly enough for him to have performed reconnaissance and returned.

Unless he'd lied about coming back for her and them rescuing the hostages together.

A whisper of air stirred her hair against her neck. But there didn't seem to be a breeze. She lifted her gun, panning it back and forth, but she didn't see anything.

"Colton?" she whispered. "Is that you?"

"Silver, put your gun away."

She frowned. "Colton?" She turned around. "Where are you?"

"Look up."

She lifted her head, and her mouth fell open in shock. "What are you...how did you—"

"The gun?"

"Oh, sorry." She shoved it into her waistband and moved back.

He let go of the vine he was hanging from and dropped to the ground, rolled and then jumped to his feet. Before she could ask him what was going on, he grabbed her and pulled her back against the trunk of a tree.

Thump, thump, thump. Several more men dropped from the sky near where Colton had been a moment before. By the time he let her go, she counted six, no, seven young men, *young* being the operative word, standing there staring at her. She frowned as she studied their faces, and then it dawned on her who they were.

"You're all Mrs. Jones's kids. And...is that you, Charlie?"

The blond boy moved from the rear of the group to the front. "Yes, ma'am. I hope we didn't scare you. We're on your side. I mean, you and Detective Graham's side."

She pressed her hand against her chest where her heart seemed to want to burst through her ribs. She'd had quite a fright and wasn't sure what to think. Obviously, these boys weren't a threat or Colton wouldn't have led them here. And he didn't have his gun out. But, then, why were they here? And what did they want?

"Colton, what's going on? Were these young men taken hostage?" She put her hands on her hips. "Did you risk your life and rescue them all on your own? You promised me you wouldn't—"

"Whoa, whoa, now." He held out his hands in a placating gesture. "One question at a time. No, I didn't rescue anyone. And no, these young men weren't hostages—not this week anyway."

She frowned. "What do you mean, this week?"

"Charlie, tell her what you told me."

She listened with growing horror as he recounted his tale, explaining how it had all started because Eddie and some others were being bullied by a kid at school who acted as if the fact that his parents were rich meant he was important and they were beneath him. One of the boys got a hold of some liquor from his older brother and passed it around as they griped about the snobby boy. Then, on a drunken dare, Eddie and some of the others decided to break into the kid's house when no one was home and trash the place.

And that was exactly what they did. But they also found something at the house, a kilo of cocaine and a stash of money, thousands of dollars. If they'd been sober, they'd have thought it through. But they were high and mad and took the drugs and the money.

"Wait," Silver said. "Are you saying the man you stole from was a drug dealer?"

"Yes, ma'am. But we didn't realize it. I mean, we were kind of wasted or we'd have known that we should have hightailed it out of there as soon as we found the drugs."

"Let me guess. He had you on surveillance video? And knew you were local high school kids?"

Charlie nodded. "He threatened to tell the police, show them the video of us breaking in. He said no one would believe us about the drugs being his. That our only chance was to do some favors for him."

"The burglary ring," she said, finally understanding how it had started.

"No," Colton corrected her. "The robberies came later. The man they crossed was a low guy on the totem pole in the drug world. A lowlife who's already been arrested on other charges. I recognized his name when Charlie gave me the details. But before his arrest, he told his boss about the break-in, and his boss sent some thugs to rough up the kids and said they had to work off their debt."

She nodded. "Debt meaning they owed the dealer for double-crossing his organization, even though they didn't realize they were doing it."

"Yes, ma'am," Charlie said. "We gave him the kilo

and cash, but he still said we owed him. He threatened to kill us, or the Joneses, if we didn't do what he said."

"Which was what? Running drugs for him?"

"Basically. He needed a location where the cops wouldn't be looking for a drug operation and thought he could use Mystic Glades with us guiding them through the canals and covering for him, warning him if things got hot."

Another boy stepped forward. "We didn't know what to do, so we told Mr. Jones. But we were being watched and didn't know it. Two men busted in the door and took him away, along with me and Todd." He waved at the boy beside him.

"But, what, you escaped? Both of you? But Mr. Jones is still a hostage?"

"No, ma'am. They knew social services might get involved if we went missing. So he let us go but kept Mr. Jones. But then Eddie got the idea that he could buy us out of this mess. That's when he started the burglary ring. We were trying to get enough money that the dealer would leave us alone and let Mr. Jones go."

"Remember Ron Dukes?" Colton asked her.

She nodded.

"He was the brains of that operation, a genius with security alarms. So they enlisted him to help."

"Wait, then Ron was…he wasn't working with the dealer?"

"No. He wanted to help Eddie and the others buy their freedom."

"Oh, my God. And he paid for it with his life."

"No, ma'am. Ron is one of the hostages."

She blinked in confusion.

Colton took her hands in his and gave her a sympathetic grin. "It's a lot to take in all at once. That bleach we saw at the garbage facility was just that, bleach. It had nothing to do with Ron or anyone else, as far we know. But, basically, what happened is that Eddie and the others got mixed up in the drugs by accident. And they tried to buy their way out of it by stealing things and selling them on the black market. What they didn't realize was that once you're in—"

"There's no way out," she said. "Believe me, I've seen that lesson over and over in my years as a DEA agent. So then Eddie, what, took the proceeds and tried to buy everyone's freedom?"

Colton nodded. "And he paid for it with his life."

She nodded, fighting back tears. "And the hostages are, what, insurance to make sure no one else pulls a stunt like Eddie did?"

"Yes, ma'am."

"Who killed him? I have to know."

"To answer that, we have to know who's running the whole operation."

She looked at Charlie. "I don't understand. All of you have to know who's calling the shots here."

"Cato's the head guy's right hand. We think he's the one who killed Eddie, too. But only because his boss told him to."

"Then who's his boss?"

Colton looked at the other boys and they all shrugged.

"We don't know. We've never seen him."

Silver shook her head in frustration.

"Silver," Colton said, "The hostages are in a small camp not far from here. It looks like they're about to be taken somewhere else. There's no reason to move them unless—"

"They're cleaning up," she whispered.

He nodded. "We can't wait any longer. We have to get them out of there."

"You said there was a camp. There are other gunmen there?"

"Ten, or more. With semiautomatic weapons."

She looked down at her pistol shoved into her waistband. Two guns, hers and Colton's—no, three, counting the handgun that Colton had taken off the guy in the shed. But that wasn't enough to take down ten armed men.

His hand gently pushed her chin up to look at him. "Hey. Don't give up already. This isn't over." He grinned and held up the key to the padlock. "The boys and I have a plan."

Chapter Fifteen

Colton held the keys to his Mustang out to Charlie, then hesitated. "Are you sure you know how to drive a stick?"

"Grew up on one. But I've never driven a 'Stang. That's gonna be sweet."

"Colton, we don't have time for this," Silver reminded him.

He winced as he dropped the keys in Charlie's hand. "All right, go. Be as quiet as you can. Assume Cato or his boss could have someone else out here in the woods looking for you. Don't take any chances. Once you get back to town, don't stop. We need real backup, cops, a SWAT team, not Freddie and her senior squad heading up here and getting themselves killed." He handed Charlie his phone. "Get to the interstate and press Send. The call is ready to go through to my boss. Tell him to send the cavalry."

"Got it."

"Go."

Charlie whirled around and disappeared into the woods.

"All right, to the shed. Come on." Colton took off at a run, with Silver and the boys trying to keep up with his long stride.

When they reached the shed, everyone stopped and Colton waved two of the boys forward.

"Okay, Ned—you're the one with the cigarette lighter, right?"

"Yes, sir."

"Good. You and Robert know what to do. Wait fifteen minutes to give us enough time to get in position. Then light it up. And, Ned? After this, you're giving up smoking. It's bad for you. Understood?"

Ned grinned and gave Colton a salute. "Yes, sir."

"As soon as the fire catches, you climb a tree and make like Tarzan and get out of here. Got it?"

"Got it," they said in unison.

Colton returned Ned's salute and then eyed the rest of the group. "Okay, which of you juvenile delinquents has a pocketknife?"

Silver lightly punched him in the arm and he winked at her.

All three remaining boys raised their hands.

Colton cocked an eyebrow at Silver.

She rolled her eyes.

"All right. Special Agent Westbrook and I will do our part. Remember, only slash the tires on the rear Jeep. We'll need the other one to transport the hostages. Everyone ready?"

At their eager nods, he leaned down close to Silver. "Are *you* ready? If this doesn't go as planned, we'll be in a firefight for our lives, not to mention *their* lives." He motioned toward the boys.

"Let's do this."

They headed off in single file through the woods, following Colton's lead, stepping where he stepped. He really seemed to know what he was doing to not make much noise, avoiding twigs and anything that might alert the camp that they were coming.

When they reached the perimeter, they quietly made their way to the far side, where the Jeeps were parked.

Colton waved the boys over to a bush close to the first Jeep and gave them the thumbs-up signal. Then he and Silver circled through the woods toward the back middle of the camp and crouched down, opposite the cage where the hostages were sitting. Colton pulled out his knife. Silver drew her gun.

And then they waited.

And waited.

Colton was just about to suggest they go back to the shed to check on the boys when a flash of light speared through the night from that direction. Sparks rose in the air. The distant crackle of flames had the hostages turning to see what was happening.

One of the perimeter guards shouted, "Fire! It's coming from the direction of the shed. Come on."

To a man, the guards surged forward, including the ones in the tent and even the drivers, and ran toward the shed. Colton had based his plan on what would be more important to the head honcho and therefore to his men—the hostages or millions of dollars of cocaine. Money won every time.

But he was all too aware that it wouldn't take ten men to put out one little fire. They only had a few minutes, at best.

"Cover me," he told Silver.

She held her gun up, watching the other side of the camp for any returning guards.

Colton ran to the cage, his knife drawn. He hacked at the twine holding the door closed and then yanked it open.

"Hurry," Silver said. "I saw some kind of movement."

He ran inside and sliced the bindings on the hostages' legs but didn't bother with the hands.

"Come on," he said. "To the first Jeep. Run." He guided them out the door, but one of the boys had a hurt leg with a nasty cut. He winced when he tried to put weight on it. The boy was as tall as Colton and too heavy for him to carry. He pulled the boy's arm over his shoulder and helped him hobble to the Jeep.

When they got there, he settled him into the back. All the hostages were accounted for. And his prize tire slashers had done their job. The second Jeep's tires were all flat.

"Get in. Start the engine."

Shouts sounded behind him. He turned around to see two of the guards sprinting toward the encampment, guns drawn. He looked back at the Jeep, expecting Silver to be in it. She wasn't. He whirled around again. Silver wasn't by the tent. She wasn't in the Jeep. She wasn't anywhere.

"Silver?" he called out. "Silver?"

The crack of a bullet echoed through the woods. Colton dove down and brought up his gun, firing at the guard who'd shot at him. The guard catapulted back in a heap on the ground. The second guard took aim. Colton squeezed off two quick shots. The guard dove behind some bushes.

Colton thumped the back of the Jeep. "Go, go, go. Get out of here."

The man who Colton assumed was Mr. Jones hopped into the driver's seat. "Come on," he called out. "Get in."

"Not without Silver. Go. We'll catch up with you. Hurry before the rest of them come back."

Another bullet whined past him.

The Jeep took off, spitting up dirt and leaves as it barreled away.

Colton whirled around, ducking behind a tree as he looked everywhere for Silver. Where could she be? She should have been right behind him.

A scream sounded from off to his right somewhere, galvanizing him into action. He fired two quick cover shots and took off, running as fast as he'd ever run in his life. *Please be okay, please be okay.*

Another scream.

Colton swore every curse word he knew.

Then he started praying.

His foot sank into a muddy bog and he fell hard, splashing face-first into some brackish water. He pushed himself upright and took off again. The sound of a powerful engine started up. He knew that sound. An airboat. He sprinted faster, pumping his legs up and down.

Moonlight flashed off the white hull of a boat, an airboat just up ahead. And on it he could see two figures, Silver and a tall, brawny man he'd fought with once before.

Cato.

The boat took off, speeding away from the make-shift dock.

There was no other boat.

Panic sent a burst of adrenaline straight through Colton. He put on a fresh burst of speed and leaped off the dock toward the airboat. He splashed into the marsh, then jerked forward. He managed to get one hand on the back of the boat, wedged in between the metal cage around the fan and the hull. The boat skipped and hopped over the shallows, slapping him around like a rag doll.

He struggled to hold on and finally got his other hand on the back of the boat. With the fan between him and the rest of the boat, Cato hadn't realized he was there. Silver sat on the floor of the boat at his feet, with Cato's gun pointed at her while he steered.

Colton gritted his teeth and fought inch over inch as he painstakingly clung to the boat and made his way up the side to get around the fan. The boat bumped across a mudflat, bouncing him up in the air. By some miracle he was flipped into the boat instead of into the marsh. He landed with a bone-jarring thud on the metal floor.

Cato and Silver both jerked their heads and looked at him.

His gun was long gone, lying somewhere on the bottom of the marsh. And he figured Silver's must have been taken, as well, or she'd already have figured out a way to shoot Cato.

He watched, seemingly in slow motion, as his fate played out in front of his eyes. Cato's gun began to swivel toward him. He knew the bullet would rip through him, killing him. It was impossible to miss at this range. He braced himself, feeling at peace, believing his sacrifice would give Silver the distraction she needed to save herself—to either push Cato overboard or jump over herself. She would survive. And that was all that mattered.

"No," he heard her scream.

Cato's gun jerked back toward her.

Colton launched himself at him, slamming his shoe against the other man's knee with a sickening crack as he delivered an uppercut to the underside of his arm, shoving the gun up toward the sky. The gun fired but then flew out of the boat, into the black marsh rushing by them at a dizzying speed.

Cato roared with rage, clutching his bad knee even as he struggled to remain upright by holding on to the wheel well.

Colton was about to punch him again when he looked past him and saw a black void rushing toward them. He shouted a warning and dove toward Silver, grabbing her around the waist and yanking her with him over the side of the boat. They plunged into the water, bottoming out on the muddy shallows.

A dull sound reverberated through the water and a fireball flashed its light above them. They broke the surface, bobbing like corks in the water as they stared at what was left of the airboat. It had run full speed into the upended roots of an enormous dead tree and had exploded on impact.

Colton grabbed Silver and hauled her to him, giving her a fierce hug. "I died inside when I couldn't find you back at the camp. And then I heard you scream."

"I'm sorry. I'm so sorry. He snuck up behind me."

He pulled her back and framed her face in his hands. "Are you okay?"

"I'm…" She looked down and wrinkled her nose in disgust. "Very dirty. And smelly. But yes, I'm fine."

"You smell wonderful to me." He kissed her until they were both breathless. Then they held hands, laughing as they struggled to find their footing in the shallow water and climb out onto the muddy bank.

Once they were on semidry land, they stood arm in arm watching the greedy fire licking at the wreckage and scorching the roots of the tree. Something white flashed in the water near the fire. A white shirt. Cato. He lay facedown in the water, his clothing ripped and burned.

Silver shivered against Colton and hugged him

around the waist. "Please tell me the boys are okay. The hostages."

"Last I saw they were bouncing around in the back of the Jeep with Mr. Jones driving like his pants were on fire. And they were laughing, having the time of their lives. They should all be fine."

"Thank God." She let out a relieved breath. "Too bad we don't have a Jeep. Or a boat. I don't suppose you have a canoe hidden around here somewhere, do you?"

"Fresh out. How far do you suppose we are from town?"

"Let me put it this way. It's going to be a long night."

A loud hiss sounded from some tall grasses behind them. They jerked around.

"What was that?" Colton demanded.

"I think it was an alligator."

"You *think*?"

"Okay, *definitely* an alligator."

Another loud hiss sounded, along with what sounded like a low roar, closer, from their left.

Colton pulled her back toward the water. A splash sounded behind them, then another.

"Okay. This isn't looking good." A pair of green lights reflected at them from the water—alligator eyes lit by the light of the fire devouring the airboat and tree.

"How fast do alligators run?" he asked.

"Not as fast as they swim. But in a straight line, they can easily outrun a human in short bursts of speed."

"Okay. So we avoid the water, zigzag through the grass, pray we make it to the burning tree and hope that will keep them at bay until we figure something else out. That's my plan. I'm hoping you have a better one."

A beautiful smile lit up her whole face. "Ask and you shall receive. Listen. Do you hear that?"

He listened, and then he heard. The jet-engine whir of an airboat fan. Seconds later, powerful searchlights flickered over them.

"Silver? Is that you?" Buddy Johnson's gravelly voice called out.

She waved her hand in the air, grinning like a kid.

"I never thought I'd be happy to see another airboat," Colton said.

Less than a minute later they were on the boat, laughing and shaking hands with their rescuers—Buddy Johnson and three other men whom Colton had seen at Callahan's before but whose names he didn't remember, with Danny Thompson at the wheel.

As Danny turned the boat back toward Mystic Glades, Buddy handed bottles of water to Colton and Silver from a cooler. "That'll be four dollars. Each."

"Put it on my tab," Colton growled.

Buddy laughed and slapped his shoulder. "It's on me. I'm just glad we could help, that Charlie stopped in at Callahan's and—"

"Wait, he didn't go to the interstate to call the police like I told him?"

"Didn't have to. He said he kept checking for bars on the phone as he headed into Mystic Glades and voilà, bars. He made the call and swung over to Callahan's. So your boss is on his way. Oh, he said he'd meet you there, at the bar. But he put a call out to get some state troopers out here and some kind of rescue team or other. I imagine they're already out looking for those fellas from that camp. They won't get away."

"Once they're all rounded up," Colton said, "they'll start falling like dominoes all over each other to squeal on their boss in return for a lighter sentence. We'll have the head of the drug operation, and Eddie's killer, in no time. Hopefully some of the cocaine in that shed we torched survived the fire to be used as evidence." He shrugged. "But if not, I'm sure there's enough residue and eyewitnesses to overcome that."

"And the robbery ring will be stopped, too," Silver said.

Colton grimaced. "I suppose you'll want me to speak for the boys and try to get any charges against them dropped in return for their testimony against the drug dealers."

She patted his chest. "Of course."

He kissed her. "I suppose I could do that for you."

The airboat slowed, then bumped gently against the dock.

"We're home," Danny announced, and tied off the boat.

Silver hugged him and smiled. "Thank you. And thank you, Buddy. Thank you all. Colton and I weren't looking forward to a night with the gators."

They headed through the path to the street, talking about everything that had happened. When the group reached the street in front of the B and B, Silver tugged Colton to the side.

"I'm filthy. I'm going to get a shower. And I want to check on Tippy and Jenks. They're probably pulling their hair out by now. Neither of them ever expected to have to run everything completely on their own. You go on ahead to Callahan's to meet up with Drew and I'll join you in a few minutes."

He hesitated, and looked toward the inn, which was all lit up, with the lights on throughout the bottom floor and some of the rooms on the second. He reminded himself that there were tons of people—eight bedrooms' worth—in the B and B. She wouldn't be alone. He had nothing to worry about.

Buddy turned toward him. "You coming, Colton? That boss of yours is probably already waitin' on you by now."

"Go," Silver said. "I'll be fine." She didn't wait for his response. She hurried down the walkway and up the steps, then waved before heading inside. She pulled back the curtains from one of the front windows, blowing him a kiss before ducking back inside.

Buddy patted Colton on the back, urging him toward Callahan's. "You can wash up at the bar. Why don't you go ahead and tell me how you and Silver met? The grapevine says you're friends from way back. But I don't remember her mentioning you before."

Not wanting to go into the details about being undercover, Colton steered the conversation to questions about Buddy's mini-empire in Mystic Glades. Once he got Buddy talking about how to make money, he didn't stop. Which suited Colton just fine.

He noted his Mustang was parked in front of Callahan's and, thankfully, didn't look the worse for wear— not that he could see in the dark anyway. Daylight might show another story altogether.

Once he stepped inside the bar, he was surprised by how full it was. Nearly every table was taken. And J.J. was running around with heavy trays of food and beer, laughing and flirting with all the customers. He noticed Charlie at a table in the far corner, laughing with some girls. He was probably bragging about his exploits and no doubt embellishing them considerably.

Freddie hurried up to him and looked as though she was going to hug him, which was a scary thought in itself, but she wrinkled her nose and stopped a few feet away. "There's a utility sink in the back of the kitchen. You might want to rinse off some of that mud in there. Here, I'll show you."

She tugged him through the swinging kitchen doorway, which he didn't mind, since Buddy was left with his friends, extolling his genius and how to take advantage of the current tourist market.

Two cooks were running around at full speed, slapping burgers on the grill and throwing nachos in a pizza oven. When they stopped near the back door, Freddie waved him to the big, square sink with a hose hooked up to the faucet, which he eagerly took advantage of. There was a drain in the floor back here, so he washed off while she leaned against the far wall by the back door.

"Heard you and Silver had a busy night. Where is she?"

"At the B and B, washing up." He grabbed the bar of soap sitting on the top of the sink and lathered up his hands. "You're having a busy night, too. I don't think I've ever seen the place so full."

"Yeah, well, Tippy and Jenks about reached their limit trying to feed and take care of all those people at the inn, so I told 'em to bring them on up here for dinner."

Colton hesitated with his hands under the running water. He nodded at one of the cooks who hurried through and headed out the back door. "You're saying all the guests are here?"

"That's what I'm sayin'."

He grabbed some paper towels and dried his hands. "What about Tippy and Jenks? Are they at the B and B?"

"Nah, they're in the bar. Is there a problem?"

He shrugged. Maybe, maybe not. He didn't like the

idea of Silver being alone, not with the boss of the drug-running operation still at large. He hurriedly dried off as best he could.

A knock sounded on the back door. Freddie propped the door open for the cook to bring in a large box that he must have gotten from a storage area outside.

Colton stepped past the door to go through the kitchen, then froze. Sitting in the parking lot behind the bar was a sky blue Mercedes, an old-fashioned one, from the eighties. And he'd just bet it was a diesel. "Freddie, whose car is that?"

She leaned around the door. "Cato drives it mostly."

"Mostly? Who else drives it?"

"Danny, sometimes. As a matter of fact, I think he drove it tonight."

Danny, the airboat captain. One of the new people Buddy had hired for the summer, right around the time the robbery and drug rings started up. And he knew these canals and waterways. He also knew every new person who came or went, courtesy of his role as boat captain bringing tourists to and from Mystic Glades. Hanging out while waiting for the tourists to have their "free" meal before a tour, he'd hear any gossip from the townspeople. He'd know everything going on.

And he'd been in the boat tonight, hearing Colton and Silver talk about the operation being over, about men testifying against their boss. He'd also heard them talk about destroying the cache of drugs. Which meant he knew it was over, that he had nothing to lose.

And every reason to hate him and Silver.

"Where is he?" He hurried through the kitchen to-ward the bar.

"Who?" Freddie called out after him.

"Danny."

"In the bar as far as I know."

He shoved the swinging door open and it slammed back on its hinges, making J.J. jump in surprise as she approached the door.

"Whoa, slow down there, Mr. Graham. What's the hurry?"

"Danny," he said. "The boat captain. Where is he?" He scanned the bar, searching the groups of people around the room.

"I don't know. Look around. I'm sure he's here somewhere. Everyone else seems to be." She laughed and headed into the kitchen.

Buddy turned from a conversation with someone sitting on a bar stool. "You lookin' for Danny?"

"You know where he is?"

"Didn't you notice? He stayed with the boat. Said he had to refuel it and get it ready for the morning tour."

The swinging doors at the front banged against the wall as a man ran inside, gasping for breath. "Fire!" he choked. "The B and B's on fire!"

The crack of a gunshot boomed like thunder from outside.

Silver! Colton almost knocked the man over as he ran through the doors and leaped off the boardwalk. He pumped his arms and legs, sprinting as fast as he could toward the inn and praying all the way.

Let her be okay. Please, please, God, let her be okay.

Chapter Sixteen

Colton slid to a halt, shielding his face from the heat of the flames. The entire bottom floor was already engulfed. And the heat was so intense he couldn't get closer than about twenty feet from the structure.

"Silver! Where are you? Silver!" He ran around the perimeter, looking up at the second floor, which was belching smoke. The windows had already exploded from the heat.

He was vaguely aware that men were running around him and that Buddy was barking orders about some kind of pump system and hoses, something about running them to the marsh for a water supply.

"Silver!" Colton yelled again, desperately looking for a way inside. He ran to the back, dodging men who were running hoses to the rear of the property. He cupped his hands around his mouth. "Silver!"

"Here! Colton! I'm here!"

Silver. He frantically spun around, trying to figure out where her voice was coming from.

"Up here!"

He shaded his eyes from the glow of the fire and looked up. Silver leaned out the attic window, and even from that distance he could see she was covered in blood.

"Hold on!" He ran along the back, desperately looking for any way to climb up to her. He grabbed Buddy as he and Charlie ran by with what looked to be a fire hose, although no water was coming out of it. "Buddy, a ladder. Do you have a ladder?"

"Why?"

He pointed at Silver.

"Dear God. No, nothing I have would reach that high. The whole bottom floor is engulfed. We couldn't use a ladder even if we had one tall enough."

A hair-raising roar had them whirling around.

Charlie pointed to the enormous oak tree in the middle of the yard. "Is that a panther up there?"

The same black panther that Colton had seen twice before sat on a thick limb, halfway up the tree. But it wasn't the panther that caught Colton's attention. It was the thick vines hanging down beside the large cat that had hope bursting inside his chest. He took off and leaped up for the bottom branch, hauling himself up into the tree.

"What are you doing?" Buddy called up. "That tree's too far from the house to do you any good."

Colton ignored him and scrambled up the tree, a good climbing tree as Silver had said, with thick, sturdy branches. The panther hissed at him when he got near it, but he paid it no mind, climbing higher and higher, until he was a good ten feet higher than the attic window. Below him, he saw Charlie climbing up, as well.

A burst of heat flared out from the house as the greedy flames began to consume the second floor. Black smoke started billowing out the attic window. Silver clung to the sill, leaning out with a towel over her face to filter out the smoke.

"I'll be right there!" he yelled. The vines that had

been hanging below by the panther were too short to reach the house. He selected another vine and pulled his knife out of his boot, using it to hack the lower part of the vine free.

"No, that one's too thick. You won't have a good handhold." Charlie had just reached a branch below his. "This one. Use this one."

Colton immediately cut the vine loose that Charlie had pointed to and yanked on it. It seemed strong and well anchored. He looped his hand through one of the knots formed by the vine's intricate stem.

"Over there." Charlie pointed. "You need a good running start. Climb to that branch there, then run and jump."

Colton leaped to the other branch. It was thinner than the others and bowed beneath him. He cartwheeled his arms, to regain his balance.

"Colton! Be careful!" Silver yelled, her voice hoarse and raspy.

"Get ready!" He moved as far out on the branch as he dared, got a good hold on the vine, then took off running toward the other side of the tree.

"Now!" Charlie yelled. "Jump!"

He dove off the branch. The vine jerked and held and swung him toward the attic at a dizzying speed. He lifted his feet to clear the window and suddenly he was inside, falling onto the floor. But before he could stop it, the vine slipped from his grasp and jerked back toward the opening.

"Silver, the vine!" He lunged toward the window as she made a grab for the vine.

She lost her balance and started to fall. "Colton!"

He grabbed her legs just before she could plummet down below and hauled her back in.

"I've got it. I've got it!" She held up the vine and gifted him with the most amazing smile he'd ever seen.

"You're incredible," he said, giving her a quick kiss. He wanted to check her injuries, stanch the bleeding, but there was no time. The floor beneath them was bowing from the heat on the second floor and could collapse any second.

"We have to jump."

Her face turned pale and she coughed. "I know."

He picked her up in his arms. "Wrap your legs around my waist and your arms around my neck. And hold on. Don't let go."

She tucked her face against his neck. "I won't let go."

He looped his hands through the vine and climbed onto the sill.

An explosion sounded behind them and searing heat blasted out at them.

"Now!" He leaped out of the window.

The vine jerked, and then they were swinging toward the tree. Charlie reached out for them, grabbing the vine as they came close and helping Colton haul them both onto the branch.

"Oh, my God," Silver whispered. "Oh, my God. I can't believe we just did that."

Another explosion sounded behind them and they looked back. Flames shot through the attic window where they'd just been standing.

"Ever heard the expression in the nick of time?" Silver teased.

Colton laughed and hugged her close.

She coughed and he pulled back to look at her.

"The blood—"

"Is mostly Danny's, but some of it's mine. I'll explain later. Can we get out of this tree, please?"

But some of it's mine. Those words sent a chill deep inside Colton. He clasped her close. "Charlie, we need another vine."

"Already planned on that." He held out a vine that hung all the way to the ground.

Colton grabbed it and wrapped his legs around the bottom to use as a brake. With Silver holding on, he shimmied them down to the ground. Charlie did the same and landed right beside them on another vine.

Colton scooped Silver up in his arms. "Charlie, we need a ride to the hospital."

"You got it, boss."

Charlie took off toward the front and Colton carried his precious cargo in his arms as he made his way through the gauntlet of makeshift firefighters pumping swamp water onto the B and B.

Silver coughed again, black soot staining her skin beneath her nose, and closed her eyes.

"Hold on, sweetheart," Colton said. "Hold on."

Chapter Seventeen

Silver hated hospitals, and this one in Naples was no different. Actually, it was worse. Because in addition to being poked, prodded and fussed over for the better part of two days, she'd been interviewed over and over and over again. Not just by the police, but also by DEA agents and the FBI, all hoping that they'd be able to close several open investigations that all centered on Danny Thompson. They wanted to know everything that he'd done. And how he'd died.

"I've told you this several times already," she said to the investigator sitting on the left side of her hospital bed.

A warm hand gently feathered down the right side of her face. Colton. He leaned over the bed and kissed her. "I promise this is the last question you have to answer today. Just tell Special Agent Williams what you already told me about Thompson."

She let out an impatient breath and relayed how she'd started upstairs for a shower when she smelled some kind of fuel, which turned out to be the boat fuel that Thompson had spread around the foundation of the inn. He'd started the fire, and she ran for the front door to get out. But he'd stopped her and they'd fought. He'd blocked her way out but hadn't anticipated how quickly the fire would consume everything. He ended up trapped just like her.

"We ran from the fire, up the stairs. I knew I had a gun in my room in the attic, so when I fought my way free of him, I ran up there. He followed me and I shot him."

"In self-defense?" Williams asked.

"Of course it was." Silver frowned at the other woman. "Are we done here?"

"Just a few more questions."

Silver groaned and thumped her head back on the pillow.

"Tomorrow," Colton said, ushering the agent out of the room. "Come back tomorrow to finish your interview."

Williams sputtered and protested, but Colton was determined, and soon it was just the two of them left in the room. Which Silver belatedly realized wasn't necessarily a good thing. Because from the way he'd been doting on her, since finishing all his interviews, she knew he wasn't going to like anything she had to say.

He sat in the seat Williams had vacated and took her hand. "You're breathing better."

"Yep. All the smoke is gone."

He gently smoothed her bangs back. "Your stitches look good. I bet you won't even have a scar from where that jerk hit you. If Thompson were still alive, I'd pay him back for that."

"Well, he's not. So that's one less thing you have to do for me." She tugged her hand free from his.

He frowned. "What's wrong? And don't say 'nothing.' I know you. Something's definitely bothering you."

She let out a long breath. "You don't know me, Colton. *That's* what's bothering me. You should be getting on with your life instead of camping out in my hospital room."

The smile faded from his face and he searched her eyes. "What's this about?"

"I'm just…we've only known each other for a few days. And all of it was under extraordinary circumstances. Neither of us really knows each other."

"Well, of course we do. Extraordinary circumstances means we experienced a lot in a short amount of time. I care about you, Silver. Very much. And I…why are you shaking your head? You think I don't care?"

She twisted her fingers in the blanket covering her, hating what she had to do. Nothing had ever seemed this hard, because she cared far too much for him, so much that her heart was breaking. But she knew this was the right thing.

She had to let him go.

"Silver—"

"I think you should leave."

He froze. "What?"

"You heard me. Colton, I owe you my life. I owe the future of my hometown to you. You saved us, the Jones family, those kids, and we all owe you a debt of gratitude. But you and I, well, there's no future for us. We need to call it like it is."

"Call it like it is? What's wrong? Are you upset that I haven't said that I love you? I thought it was obvious, but I'll say it. I—"

"No. Don't say it."

He frowned. "What's really going on here?"

She blinked back the moisture in her eyes. "Don't you see? You think you…care about me…because of everything that has happened. But two people can't fall in love after only a few days. I don't know anything about you. And you know little about me. I've never met your family, know nothing about how you grew up, who your friends are, what you do for fun. None of it's real."

He waved his hand in the air. "All those things—our pasts, our families, how we grew up—they made us who we are today, who we are right now. And we do know each other. I know that you're creative, and smart, and care deeply about people, especially young people. I suspect you love babies and I bet you want a houseful someday."

"You suspect, but you don't know that."

"If you're worried that we're going too fast—"

"I am."

His frown smoothed out with relief. "If that's all you're worried about, no problem. When you get out of here we'll date. I'll take you to movies and restaurants, learn your favorite foods. And we can go visit our families."

"Colton. You work undercover, for months at a time. And you love it. I don't want to be the cause of you giving that up. You aren't ready to settle down, or even start a family."

"How would you know that?"

"Because when your boss, Drew, interviewed me, we talked about you, too. And he told me what a fine detective you are, and how much you love your job. That you planned to work undercover for at least several more years."

His eyebrows dipped down. "He had no business discussing my career decisions or my future plans with you. He doesn't know what I want."

"What do you want? To sit at a desk? You'd miss all the excitement of going undercover, of living a secret life, of trying to trick the bad guys and make that big score when you bring down an operation. I know. I've been there. I know the rush and how exciting it can be. But I'm done with all that. I'm ready to settle down, which is why I started the B and B." She grimaced. "Which I'll now have to rebuild. But my point is, you're not at that place. You aren't ready to settle down."

"You said we don't know each other. But you claim to know what I want, or don't want?"

She sighed. "You're right. I don't know. But I do know this. You never talked to your boss about getting out of undercover work until after you met me. I've been through this before. I've been that girl with a guy who changed his life, who gave up his dreams, so they could be together after a whirlwind romance. I married him, Colton."

He blanched. "You're married?"

"What? Oh, no, no, no. Of course not. Not anymore. We got married right out of high school. And within a few months, he was already resenting me, hating me, for everything he gave up to be with me. He'd lost a football scholarship in another state because he knew I didn't want to live there. And then he held that against me. It was horrible. That psychological abuse I mentioned? That's what I was talking about. We were divorced after six months. And I don't ever want to do that again. I do care about you, very much. But we have different dreams. And I don't want you giving yours up for me, and then hating me for it."

"I could never hate you," he said softly.

"You don't know that."

An awkward silence filled the room.

He stared across the bed, out the window. "You've given this a lot of thought, haven't you?"

"I have. Yes." And it was killing her inside to let him

go. But she could never live with herself knowing she'd destroyed his dreams. Even if it destroyed hers by telling him goodbye.

He finally rose and leaned down and kissed her on the top of the head. His incredible blue eyes were unreadable as he looked down at her. His mouth worked, as if he was trying to come up with the perfect words to change her mind. But then he gave her a stiff nod and turned away.

And walked right out of her life.

"A TAD TO the left, Charlie," Silver called out as Charlie and Ned stood on ladders beside the front steps, holding either end of the blue, bed-shaped sign that announced, Under the Covers Bed & Breakfast, proprietor Silver Westbrook.

"Looks perfect where it is, if you ask me."

She smiled at Tippy standing beside her. "You think so?"

"I do."

"That's it," she called out. "Perfect."

Charlie gave her a thumbs-up, and soon the sound of hammers once again echoed through Mystic Glades. It had taken four long months to rebuild, but finally the inn was ready again.

"They're here." Tippy pointed up the road.

Silver turned to see a string of cars heading down Main Street. She checked her watch. "They're early. The Larson family must be in an awful hurry to start their reunion."

"I think it's so exciting that one family booked the whole inn for two weeks. This is going to be fun."

Silver gave her a hug. "And since you have your degree now, you're totally prepared if I ditch you again and you're stuck taking care of everyone, right?" At the look of panic on Tippy's face, Silver laughed. "Don't worry. J.J. will be here soon. I promised I'd get you some real help this time, and I have. And I don't plan on going anywhere."

A flash of pain shot through her as a memory of Colton floated through her mind, but she held on to her smile to face her arriving guests. "Tippy, hurry inside. You'll need to register everyone."

"Yes, ma'am." She grinned and hurried down the walkway.

"Miss Westbrook?" A beautiful young woman with striking blue eyes stopped in front of her and held out her hands.

"Please, call me Silver. You must be Celia?"

A smile lit the woman's eyes, painfully reminding Silver of another pair of blue eyes.

"That's right, Celia Larson." She suddenly wrapped Silver in a tight hug. "I'm so glad to meet you."

Silver stiffened, then laughed and hugged the woman back. "Nice to meet you, too. Please go on inside. Tippy will help you find your room."

Celia pulled back, squeezed her hand, then hurried off with the others, who were lugging their suitcases into the inn. When everyone was inside, and Charlie and Ned had folded up their ladders and headed up the street to return them to Buddy's store, Silver remained in front of the inn. She wanted a few more minutes to compose herself before facing the lovely, happy family inside.

To a person, every single one of them had smiled and waved at her as they went into the inn. She'd adored them all on the spot and looked forward to getting to know them. But first, she had to tamp down the melancholy that always overcame her whenever something reminded her of Colton, as young Celia's eyes had done. He was never far from her thoughts. And the feelings she'd had for him, that she hadn't trusted because they'd come too hard, too fast? They'd only grown stronger in his absence. She now knew that she was hopelessly in love with him. And although she'd go on with her life and find joy in other things—like getting to know the Larson family—she knew she'd always have a hollow place in her heart for the only man she'd ever really loved.

The throaty sound of an engine roared from up the street. She turned, and her heart gave a little lurch when she saw a black Mustang GT coming down the road toward her.

It couldn't be. Could it?

The car pulled into the only free spot, two spaces away. The engine cut off. The door opened. And out stepped Colton Graham.

Silver pressed her hand against her thundering heart and took a step toward him, before she caught herself. Just because she now knew she'd made a mistake in letting him go didn't mean it was a mistake for him. She'd given him his dream back or, rather, she hadn't taken it away. He was doing what he wanted with his life. And she shouldn't read anything into the fact that he was here. They'd been friends once, briefly. So maybe that was what he was doing, just checking up on an old friend.

She just hoped she could survive seeing him again without breaking down into a puddle at his feet.

He got out of the car and literally took her breath away. His wavy, shoulder-length hair had been cut short, but not too short. And although she'd loved his wild hair, the new cut fit his personality better and emphasized the gorgeous angles of his face. Yes, she liked him like this. Loved him.

He took off his dark sunglasses and tossed them through the open window of the car, never taking his eyes off her. The cooler weather now had him wearing a leather jacket over his black T-shirt and black jeans. And his boots, shined to a high gloss, echoed on the pavement as he strode toward her, stopping so close she could feel the heat of him and had to crane her neck back to meet his gaze.

"Hello, Silver." His deep voice stroked goose bumps across her skin.

"Colton. You look…good."

He grinned. "You look amazing."

She couldn't help smiling. "And you're just as charming as ever."

He gestured toward the sign. "You changed the name. And the color."

"I wanted a fresh start."

His smile faded and he turned to face her. "Me, too." He held out his hand. "I don't think we've been correctly introduced. Colton Graham was my undercover name. My real name is Cole."

She shook his hand, feeling a bit stunned. "Cole. And your last name?"

He hesitated, and in that moment she suddenly knew.

"Larson," he said. "My name is Cole Larson."

She blinked. "Your…your family…they're…"

"Inside your inn right now. Yep. Pretty much every last one of them. Well, there are some aunts and uncles back in Jacksonville who didn't make the trip down, but my three brothers, sister, mom and dad, plus a few nieces and nephews made it. I imagine you remember

Celia. She wouldn't have passed up the opportunity to meet you. And I'm told we look a lot alike."

She blinked again, still reeling. "Celia. Her eyes, that dark hair. Twins?"

He nodded.

"Then she's—"

"The artist. Yes. I didn't lie about that."

"I see." She shook her head. "No, no, I don't see. Colton… Cole…what are you doing here? And why is your family here?"

His hands shook as he reached for her, but then he stopped and dropped them to his side. "I tried to stay away, to forget you, since it was what *you* wanted. But it was never what *I* wanted. I went back undercover and hated it. I quit my job."

She drew in a sharp breath. "You quit? You're not a police officer anymore?"

"Oh, I'm still a detective. I'm just not doing undercover work anymore. Which means I have fairly regular hours, except for the occasional callout. And I've discovered that I like that. No, actually, I love it. I was ready to make that change, Silver. I was wearing myself down undercover all the time. Now I'm discovering the life that was passing me by." He waved toward the inn. "And rediscovering my family. I've spent a lot of time with them over the past few months."

He raised a hand, and this time he didn't stop. He cupped the side of her face, his fingers shaking as they feathered across her skin. "I've talked of little else but you to them, and they got pretty sick and tired of it. They told me I was a fool if I didn't go after you, beg you if I had to, to give us a chance. Because you haven't taken my dreams away, Silver. You've given me a new dream, of a future with a wonderful, beautiful woman who takes such pleasure from the simplest things, and makes me see the world through her artist's eyes."

He cupped her face with his hands. "I. Love. You. It wasn't a fluke, or an infatuation because we shared some intense experiences. It's stronger, brighter, than it was the day I left the hospital. All I'm asking is that you give us a chance. Date me. Get to know me, my past." He waved toward the inn again. "My family. And if you still don't feel the way that I feel, it will probably kill me, but I'll go. I'll walk away if that's what you want. Because your happiness is what matters most to me. I love you. You're everything to me."

A sob burst from her lips and she wrapped her arms around his waist. "Colton…Cole…oh, good grief, I'll never get that right."

He laughed and tightened his arms around her. "Call me anything you want if it makes you happy."

She pulled back and slid her hands up around his neck. "You…you make me happy. I was an idiot for making you go away. I've been miserable ever since."

His eyes bored into hers with an intensity that took her breath away. "What are you saying?"

Tears tracked down her face now, unchecked. She smiled and threaded her fingers through the gently curling wisps of hair at the nape of his neck. "I'm saying that I love you, Colton Cole Graham Larson. I have from the moment I looked into those incredible blue eyes of yours. And I'd love nothing more than to meet your family, learn about your past. But it doesn't really matter." She flattened her palm over his chest. "What matters is what's in here, the person you are today, and that you love me, too."

The smile that lit his face, his eyes, was like sunlight

rising over a beautiful field of flowers, painting happiness and joy across the land and across Silver's heart.

"I love you, Silver." His voice was thick with emotion. "I love you."

"Shut up and kiss me."

He laughed, and then he was kissing her and making her toes curl inside her shoes, melting her from the inside out. All too soon he pulled back. She sighed with disappointment.

He glanced at the inn, his face falling. "Damn."

"What?" She followed his gaze, but she didn't see anything alarming. "Is something wrong?"

"My family. My *mom* and *dad* are here. And all I want to do is make love to you."

She beamed up at him and grabbed his hand in hers, tugging him toward the B and B. "There'll be time for that later. Promise. Come on. Introduce me to your family."

He grinned and scooped her up in his arms. She laughed the whole way to the door. And then he carried her across the threshold.

* * * * *

"Don't leave me!"

Every muscle that had been ready to spring to action hardened. Jonathan turned back to Kate. She wasn't crying, but the way her beautiful dark eyes reached out to him let him know that she was close.

"Please, stay with me."

It was in that moment that he knew there was no other place he wanted to be.

"It'll be okay," he said. "I promise."

Sirens could be heard in the distance. The crying and yelling still sounded around them. For the first time since the car had nearly run them down, he realized the silver case hadn't left Kate's side.

She'd kept it with her through it all. What was in it?

And why was it worth killing for?

BE ON THE LOOKOUT: BODYGUARD

BY
TYLER ANNE SNELL

First Published in Great Britain 2016
By Mills & Boon, an imprint of HarperCollins*Publishers*
1 London Bridge Street, London, SE1 9GF

© 2016 Tyler Anne Snell

ISBN: 978-0-263-91914-1

46-0816

Our policy is to use papers that are natural, renewable and recyclable products and made from wood grown in sustainable forests. The logging and manufacturing processes conform to the legal environmental regulations of the country of origin.

Printed and bound in Spain
by CPI, Barcelona

Tyler Anne Snell genuinely loves all genres of the written word. However, she's realized that she loves books filled with sexual tension and mysteries a little more than the rest. Her stories have a good dose of both. Tyler lives in Florida with her same-named husband and their mini "lions." When she isn't reading or writing, she's playing video games and working on her blog, *Almost There*. To follow her shenanigans, visit www.tylerannesnell.com.

This book is for Virginia Spears.

You're a beautiful, brilliant, hilarious sunflower. I hope we grow old together and can still make fun of all the silly things we did when we were younger. You're one of the best humans I know and, for that, you deserve much more than a dedication in a book. However, that's all I'm working with for now, so I hope this will do, you exotic, sparkling unicorn, you.

Chapter One

He wouldn't tell anyone this, but the fight almost ended much differently.

The punch that landed squarely against his jaw almost knocked him out. Pain, bright and bold, exploded along the bone as the blow connected. It made him stagger to the side, and for a moment he struggled with fighting the urge to cradle the pain and seek refuge.

Or pass out. Blackness fringed the edges of his vision.

But Jonathan Carmichael wasn't that easy to take down.

He dropped low into a crouch and swung his leg around. His attacker wasn't fast enough to move out of the way. His legs were swept out from under him and he hit the ground hard. The wheeze of someone who had lost their breath escaped from his lips.

Jonathan wasn't where he needed to be physically—the punch really had done a number on him—but he knew the hired thug wasn't just going to lie down and take it. Plus, he still had someone to protect.

Out of his periphery, Jonathan saw the door behind him and to the left was still closed. Fleetingly, he wondered if Martin actually locked the door like he had been told.

"You—gonna—gonna pay," the thug started to wheeze out, but Jonathan didn't have time for a speech. He turned on his heel and leveled the man with his own knockout punch. The muscle-clad baddie didn't wage an internal war of whether or not he was going to slip into unconsciousness. Or, if he did, he didn't win the battle.

His head clunked against the hardwood while the rest of his body relaxed.

"I'm *gonna* have a tall beer tonight," Jonathan said, tenderly touching his chin. He winced. "That's what I'm gonna do, all right."

He nudged the guy's foot with his work boot before feeling comfortable enough to walk back to the door his client was behind. Trying the doorknob, he cursed beneath his breath.

"Martin, I told you to lock this."

His client, an older man who was five feet three inches of scatterbrain, didn't offer an apology for not listening to his bodyguard. Instead his eyes widened at Jonathan's appearance.

"You're bleeding," Martin exclaimed. He pointed to his eyebrow and then his lip.

"Don't worry," he hedged, temporarily forgetting he had other injuries. "It's the jaw that hurts the worst."

"And the bad man?" Martin didn't try to see out into the other room. To him the hired gun was his own personal hell. An evil man who had threatened him, stalked him and attacked him. All in an attempt to exact revenge for sending his boss to prison. Jonathan remembered when the man had come into Orion Security Group's front doors begging for protection, for a bodyguard to keep him safe. The police hadn't believed he was being targeted, but Jonathan's boss had.

A call Jonathan was grateful for and so was Martin.

"He won't hurt you anymore."

Martin's entire body sagged in relief.

"Thank you, son. Thank you."

Jonathan nodded, ignoring how the endearment struck a sore chord. Before he could stop it, the invisible wall that he had built for thirty-three years sprang up. He cleared his throat.

"Tell me you at least called nine-one-one," he deadpanned. Martin's eyes widened again, guilt written clearly across his face.

Jonathan let out a long breath.

"Call them while I go tie up our friend," he ordered, pulling the zip ties from one of his cargo pants' pockets. Martin nodded and for once listened.

The thug, a man around the same age as Jonathan but who had obviously had a much harder life, stayed unconscious while Jonathan tied his wrists together in front of his stomach. Just to be safe, he patted him down, revealing a wicked pocketknife and a wad of cash. There was no ID, but Jonathan didn't need it. He felt as if he knew the man on some level. Fiercely loyal to his boss.

Hardened by life from the streets with scars that bore testament to that theory.

Determination unwavering.

Was he that different?

Would this have been Jonathan's life had he not run into his current boss all those years ago?

Jonathan shook his head. He'd learned at a young age that *what-ifs* did more harm than they ever did good.

"I called them—they're on their way and a little confused," Martin said from the doorway, eyes staying away from the man who had tormented him for months.

"But then this man called?" He held Jonathan's phone away from him with a shrug.

The bodyguard quickly took the phone, confused, as well.

"Carmichael here."

"Why does the client have your phone?"

Jonathan cut a grin as the voice of one of Orion's finest—and his closest friend—filled his ear.

"Well, look who it is! Mark Tranton, back from vacation."

A chuckle came through the airwaves.

"Well, you couldn't expect me to pass on a free weeklong stay at a beachside bungalow, could you?" Mark exclaimed.

"The old Mark would have," Jonathan reminded his friend. "But the new Mark is a lot more fun, so I guess it's understandable."

"The new Mark also has two ladies who would never let him pass on a former client's generosity like that," the other man added with another laugh. Jonathan had known Mark for almost a decade and was glad to see his friend happy with his girlfriend and her young daughter. "Now, why did the client answer your phone?"

Jonathan gave his fellow bodyguard a rundown of the exchange from the moment the man picked the front door lock to the knockout minutes before Mark called. He could hear the concern in Mark's voice as he questioned Jonathan's injuries, but Jonathan's walls were still up. He brushed the concerns off.

"The cops should be here soon, so I need to go," he started. "Wait, did you need something?"

"Yeah, but it can wait. Give me a call when you land in Dallas and I'll meet you at Orion."

Jonathan agreed to that and they ended the call.

The bodyguard slid his phone back into his pocket and took another long look at the man on the ground.

I could have been you.

TWO DAYS LATER Jonathan was cruising through Dallas, Texas, in the familiar comfort of his old, worn Range Rover. It was raining, but not enough to spoil his homecoming or Mark's insistence that he come straight to Orion's office. He wondered what all the fuss was about but didn't think on it too much as he puttered his way through afternoon traffic.

Before Orion he'd been an agent with Redstone Solutions, an elite and very private security agency. With more funding than they knew what to do with—and very little care for those who couldn't afford basic safety—he'd had contracts that had taken him all over the world. Orion, operating on a smaller financial but higher moral scale, still made him travel the nation. Through all of his travels, though, he could safely come to one concrete conclusion: traffic anywhere was horribly annoying.

There were some things he missed about his hometown, but this wasn't one of them.

The rain let up by the time he reached the one-story building with its Orion Security Group sign blaring atop the front doors. Steam rose from the parking lot asphalt as he stretched. Unlike Mark or even Oliver, another close friend and Orion employee, Jonathan had a wide wingspan and stood taller than the two at six-three. Growing up, his long limbs had made him self-conscious—catching names like "String Bean" and "Stretch"—but being a bodyguard had taught him how to use his lean body to his advantage.

Strength and speed were two traits he trained hard to keep.

Orion's lobby had long windows tinted to keep the Texas sun at bay. It kept the lobby cool as Jonathan passed by the desk where their cyber-techy secretary, a young woman named Jillian, sat. At her absence, he felt a sort of alertness flare. Just because she wasn't in the lobby didn't mean he should think something ominous was going on.

Yet, as he walked through the door and down the hallway that led to the common area for employees, Jonathan couldn't shake the growing feeling of unease. Especially since he had passed empty offices belonging to Mark and Thomas, another Orion agent.

"Hello?" he said, rounding the corner to the grazing area, as he liked to call the open-area lounge for employees between the boss's office and the training room. Normally it was a comfortable space to relax or play a way-too-competitive game of Ping-Pong, never too much action going on. So when he found it filled with people who yelled, "Surprise," when he was in view, while a brightly colored banner that said Congratulations hung above him, Jonathan was wholly taken aback.

His eyes roamed over the many people bunched together. Among them he found Mark, his boss, in-house Orion employees and a few people he'd never met. He was sure he looked like a jackass standing there gaping.

"I don't understand?" he asked when the cheers had died down.

An attractive woman with short, dark red hair laughed. She was Nikki Waters, founder and main boss at Orion, as well as one of his three closest friends.

"To be honest, this—" she motioned to the banner

and then to the people next to her "—isn't really for you, but we couldn't resist trying to surprise you. Though, I guess it could count if we said, 'Congratulations for a supremely well-done job of handling yourself this week!'" She held up a champagne flute—something he realized the other partygoers also held—and lifted it in the air. "To Jonathan Carmichael for an excellent job well-done!"

A chorus of "hear, hear" sounded.

"Thanks," he said, still uncertain. "But who is this all really for?"

Nikki looked at Mark, who stepped to the side. Kelli, Mark's girlfriend, showed herself.

"Us," she answered before holding up her left hand. A ring graced her finger, but it was the smile on Mark's face that really sold it.

"You're kidding me," Jonathan exclaimed, a smile as pure as they came pulling up the corners of his lips. "You two are getting hitched?"

They laughed in unison.

"You better believe it, best man!"

Jonathan's happiness for his best friend pushed him forward and he gave the many-muscled man a big hug. Mark, knowing Jonathan wasn't big on shows of affection, knew not to comment. Instead he returned it before passing the second embrace on to his future wife. The rest of the party went back to their own mingling as Jonathan took a step back to congratulate the two of them again.

"I wanted to wait to tell everyone after I'd told you, but this one here got a little too chatty." Mark looked at Kelli, who just laughed. A woman Jonathan didn't recognize pulled Nikki's and her attention away, leaving Mark and Jonathan alone.

"So should we talk about your face?" the bodyguard asked. Jonathan knew how it looked—a cut above his right lip, a bandage on his eyebrow and a gnarly bruise across his jawline—but he was happy that no one else had brought it up while he was in front of everyone.

"Don't worry, it feels worse than it looks," he joked. "So, best man, really?" Jonathan didn't want to keep talking about his previous job when he'd just been extended an honor that could be taken as the epitome of male friendship. Mark clapped him on the shoulder.

"Who else would I pick? Now go put your stuff away and we'll talk bachelor party ideas." Mark wiggled his eyebrows. Once again it reminded Jonathan of how much happier his friend had become in the past year of being with Kelli and her daughter. Life, according to him, had become more enjoyable than even he had imagined.

A mixture of longing, sadness and regret exploded in Jonathan's chest as he set his pack down behind his desk. From the open door he could see Kelli take Mark's hand even though the two were in separate conversations.

Looking back Jonathan would realize that it was in that moment that he made his next decision, but while he was still in the moment he would think it was when Nikki walked into the room to give him a new client file.

"I don't want to be a field agent anymore," he responded, surprising the two of them. "I'm missing out on life, Nikki, and I don't want to anymore." She took a seat. Jonathan continued, "Mark's getting married and already has a little family. Oliver has a kid on the way. I—" He struggled to find the words.

"Want to grow roots," she supplied.

"Yes, but I can't do that if I'm never in one spot for long."

"So you want a desk job," she added.

He nodded.

Nikki Waters wasn't an easy woman to ruffle. She pursed her lips but didn't try to sway his decision.

"Okay," she said instead.

"Okay?" He'd half expected her to be angry. Other than Mark he was the highest-ranking field agent.

"When I started Orion, I knew it would be a lot of work, and you've been an integral part in helping me carry that workload. That's included sacrificing your personal life, I've noticed. If you want to stay in one place, we can make that happen."

"So...that's it?"

Nikki held up her index finger.

"Now, I didn't say *that*."

Chapter Two

Kate Spears sighed as she looked down at the letter covered in blood. It, like the handful of others before it, was folded and had been placed squarely on the middle of her doormat.

Her father, Deacon, a man who was made of worry more than anything else, was lagging behind her, talking on his phone. His current worry that his wife, her stepmother, was having a less than good day at work rated low on the stress totem pole. But like his ability to worry, he took pride in being a good husband. So there he paced across the sidewalk next to Kate's mailbox, listening to his wife's woes as his daughter tried to figure out how to handle the bloody stationery.

"If this isn't a true case of the Mondays, I don't know what is," she muttered as she riffled through her larger-than-life purse. Unable to distinguish or adhere to the line between work and home, she found the pack of latex gloves within seconds and pulled one on. In another pocket of her purse she found a clean baggie. Being a scientist had its perks.

"Okay, honey, love you, too," Deacon said, suddenly closer. Kate panicked and stuffed the note into the plastic bag along with her latex glove as quickly as she could. The bag was then stuffed into the purse. All within seconds. It made Kate momentarily feel like she'd gotten away with something. Though, in hindsight, she would realize there were few things you could get past Deacon Spears. "Are we going to pretend that I didn't just see you shove several things into your purse?"

Kate let out another long breath. While she didn't always leave work at work, she didn't want to bring this conversation home. Especially not during lunch with her father.

"I don't know what you mean," she lied, finally opening the front door.

"And there's the higher pitch to your voice," he pressed, following her into the entryway of her town house. Normally she would place her purse beneath the table next to the front door, but she kept it close to her side this time. Or else her father would already be going through it.

"Can you stop analyzing me? I'm not data, you know," she said, grinning. While Deacon owned a hardware store, Kate still insisted on cheesy jokes from her field of work. He usually laughed at them. Not now. The fake mirth didn't dissuade Deacon's determination. He crossed his arms over his chest and used the voice reserved only to scold his daughter. Never mind that she was twenty-nine, had a mortgage and had just completed a five-year project that could save countless lives.

"Kathryn Gaye Spears, I don't know why you're lying to me, but I do know you better cut the crap now."

Kate physically shied away from the accusation by moving down the hallway and into the kitchen. Her hand clung to the strap of her purse as if the contact would somehow help it magically know it needed to hide until lunch was over.

"Dad, do you want some coffee?" she hedged. "I *really* need some." Deacon followed silently and stood like a statue next to the refrigerator. From growing up with him, Kate knew it was a matter of minutes before his steely resolve broke hers, but Kate was also stubborn. She met her father's blue-eyed stare with her own brown-eyed one and was reminded in full how the two of them looked nothing alike.

Short yet solid, Deacon had been blessed with a hereditary tan from his half-Hispanic mother, but had his father's once blond-white hair—even though it was sparse at the crown around an almost shiny bald spot. Besides his overall look that just cried "retiring in Florida," the fifty-six-year-old had a young, slightly rounded face. One that was partially hidden by another sun-bleached mustache he said his wife Donna thought made him look regal.

Kate, on the other hand, was the spitting image of her mother. Before her death, Cassandra Spears had been taller than her husband when she wore high heels—though she never did—and much leaner. In the same respect that was true for Kate. At five-nine, she could see over Deacon's head with heels—though she also wasn't a fan—and was lean but without the muscles that had been a necessary part of Cassandra's job in law enforcement. Kate also shared the rich brown hair her mother had once sported, waving to her shoulders with thick bangs across her forehead, and her mother's teardrop face and full lips. The only way she differed from either parent was the less than active tan that graced her skin. In the last five years Kate had resided in labs or over her computer screen during almost all waking hours. There was no time to go outside and play in the sun for her.

Though, as her father's stare bored holes into her own, Kate thought a break for the park might be better than what was about to happen.

"It's really not that big of a deal," Kate finally conceded. "Can't you just let me deal with it?"

Her father shook his head with a firm no.

Defeated, she put her purse on the counter and pulled out the baggie and its contents.

Alarmed wasn't a strong enough word for Deacon's reaction.

"Is that blood?" he asked, voice a mile past concerned. Careful not to rumple the letter inside, he took the bag and set it on the counter.

"It's made to look like it, but if it's like the last one it's synthetic." His eyes widened.

"The last one? You mean you've gotten one before this?"

Kate gave one more sigh. She'd hoped to avoid this conversation with her father until after her trip, when she was sure the letters would stop altogether. Sitting on one of the bar stools opposite him, she explained.

"Over the last few months I've received a handful of letters here and at the office," she admitted. "Only this one and the last one were covered in what *looks* like human blood, but we tested and confirmed it to be fake. Though, I still wouldn't touch that without gloves on." She pulled another set out of her purse and passed them to her father—a man curious enough to want to pull the letter out. Silently he slipped them on and did just that. Kate quickly put down a paper towel so the blood—fake or not—wouldn't touch the granite.

"It's covered front and back with writing," he observed, squinting at the handwritten letters. It was identical to all of the other notes she'd received. "But it's only one word, repeated. *Zastavit*." He kept saying the word, as if tasting it to figure out its root.

"I think it's Czech," she said after a moment.

"Are you sure?"

She shrugged. "No, but I can guarantee it means 'stop.'"

His eyebrows rose in question.

She held up her index finger and made a quick trip to her bedroom. There she picked up a small box and brought it back to her father. Sitting back down, she waited for him to open it and extract the bundle of letters.

"Only a handful of letters? How many hands are you talking about in this scenario?" The letters numbered eighteen in total. Each had a single word repeated over the paper's entirety.

"They are all in different languages, but they all roughly translate to the word *stop*," she explained. "Plus, the first one was in English. I suppose to help me out just in case I didn't understand…or, you know, use a translator or the internet."

"Stop…stop what?" Realization lit his features before Kate had time to answer. "Your research."

She shrugged. "I suppose so. That's the only thing I really have going on in my life. Unless they want me to stop drinking coffee. Which, I'll be frank, isn't going to happen anytime soon."

"Dammit, Kate!" Her father slammed his free hand down on the counter, making her jump. "Stop joking about this!" He waved the note closest to him—the Hungarian one—in the air. "These are *threats*, not some love letters. Someone obviously invested a lot of thought and time into these."

"But they aren't threats, Dad," she insisted. "They

are simply eclectic suggestions. No threat of harm has been given in any of them."

"But they've been delivered to your *home*, Kate!"

"And that's what I told the cops after the second one I received."

He was surprised at that.

"What did they say?"

"Exactly what I just said. They aren't really threats and nothing else has happened. They suggested putting a camera on the front porch, but..." She quieted.

"But what?"

"But I've been so busy preparing for the convention that I keep forgetting." Her father seemed to be trying very hard to keep his anger at his daughter's apparent lack of concern under control. He placed the letters back in the box and the newest one back into its bag. He slid that one over when done.

"You will test this as soon as possible to make sure it is in fact fake. I am calling in to the store and taking off the rest of the day. Make me that coffee you mentioned." He picked the box up and walked to the eat-in table. "I'm going to look through all of these in silence while I try to figure out what I did to deserve such a stressful child."

KATE PINCHED THE bridge of her nose and hoped the pain behind her dark brown eyes was a tease and not the beginnings of a headache. Sprawled out on her bed, amid her suitcase and carry-on, she called upon every entity there was and begged that the headache would stay far, far away.

She didn't need any more complications than she was already dealing with.

"Having a bodyguard is not that big a deal," her father said from the doorway. Since learning about the notes a week ago, she'd had constant supervision and parental advice. "Stop being such a baby!"

Kate, often referred to as brilliant by her supervisor, stuck out her tongue before responding.

"I'm not being a baby," she retorted, trying to keep the whine from her voice. "I think I'm reacting normally given the circumstances."

"Most daughters would be grateful, you know."

She laughed.

"Most daughters don't have their fathers go behind their backs and hire *bodyguards* to supervise their trips to life-changing work functions!"

He managed to look momentarily guilty before shooting back with a response. "Well, most daughters don't—" He held up his hand, stopping himself. "Listen, we can sit here and fight about this all day while you lie next to your empty luggage, or you can just take the gesture with graciousness and understand that I only have one baby girl and that's you." His voice took on an edge that Kate recognized as vulnerability from the almost always strong man. It killed the less-than-nice reply she'd had waiting on the tip of her tongue. He walked over and took a seat next to her. She sat up to look him in the eyes.

"It's because of that fact that I can say this without getting into trouble," he started. Kate swallowed, unsure whether or not she was about to get into more trouble. However, when he continued, his voice was kind. "You've spent most of your life fighting to help people you'll never meet by doing research and working tirelessly in labs. Along the way you've achieved a level of greatness I never could have, and for that I'll be forever proud... But your drive—your dedication—often puts blinders up, making it hard for you to see the big picture. While your research is important, *you* are, too. You've tried to keep your work a secret, but what have I told you about secrets?"

"They don't exist."

He smiled.

"Someone will always tell someone else. It's the law of the land. And one that your mother tried to teach us. Someone obviously knows something, and whether or not it's the truth or some half-baked version of it, they have set their sights on you. Now, you've told me this convention will change everything. Well, I want to make sure you're there to see that through and continue to see it through long after it's over. Because even though you won't see the big picture—and its danger— I'll tell you right now that it's there." He patted her knee. "So, please, accept this protection, if only to give your old man some peace of mind."

Kate watched as a range of emotions played across her father's face. It reminded her of all the sacrifices he'd had to make to raise her on his own since she was nine. Never once asking anything of her.

Until now.

"Because I love you and can see your point, I'll make a deal with you," she offered. "I will humor you by accepting the protection of only *one* bodyguard. Any more than that will bring unwanted attention and, well, freak me out a little. So one and that's it, okay?"

He looked like he was ready to fight her again, but after a moment he nodded.

"Okay." He stuck out his hand to shake. "Deal."

They shook and she rolled her eyes. Their tender moment dissipated as he stood and stretched.

"Now, I have to ask, how exactly are you *paying* for

this bodyguard service?" Like Kate, her father wasn't particularly wealthy. He worked at the hardware store he and his wife of five years owned.

"I was lucky enough to get connected to a place that works for free on cases they believe need it. One of my customers worked a news story for them when he lived in Dallas and was kind enough to give me a reference." He grinned.

"Oh, so they're amateurs, then."

"Definitely not. Their track record is impressive, to say the least," he answered. "Don't worry, I vetted them pretty well."

"So why exactly are they doing it for free?" she asked, perplexed. Deacon smiled wide.

"I guess that's a question you'll just have to ask your bodyguard."

Chapter Three

Traffic.

Here it was again.

Jonathan looked out his rental's window and snorted.

"Welcome to New York City," he said to himself.

He'd been stuck in standstill traffic for the last half hour thanks to a fender bender that had escalated to the point of the cops being called. It had made the two lanes of traffic that had been moving along nicely stop dead.

Unnecessary. Annoying. Unpleasant.

It probably didn't help that he could use all three descriptors for his current client, Kathryn Spears. Instead of waiting for him at the airport like Nikki and the woman's father had agreed on the night before, Jonathan had landed to a voice mail from her saying she'd gone ahead to the hotel.

Because, in her words, "I really need some better coffee."

After ten more minutes of waiting, traffic finally started to pick up again. Jonathan had spent the time while he waited going over the route to the hotel in an attempt to not get lost. He'd been to New York before and he knew the frustration of getting turned around this close to Times Square. Thankfully he avoided any misdirection, a feat considering if he had missed the turn into the hotel's parking garage—an almost hidden entrance due to the sidewalk that was barely sloped for a car to drive up—he would have had to take a series of left turns until he made his way back. Costing him more time away from fulfilling Orion's end of the contract.

He parked, sent a text to Nikki to let her know he'd finally gotten in and collected his bag. It contained a suit, pressed and folded, along with a myriad of pristine yet flexible clothing. It was light but had everything he needed for the Friday-through-Tuesday stay—not the longest contract he'd done nor the shortest. But, as he'd told Nikki, it would be his last. In his mind he went over the layout of the building as he rode up in the elevator. Above the parking garage, there were four floors. A lounge area branched off the lobby on the first floor with guests having access to a twenty-four-hour gym. There were two sets of stairs on opposite sides of the building with two elevators positioned next to them, diagonal from the lobby front desk. The front entrance led directly to the sidewalk that ran along the street.

Jonathan hadn't stayed at the dismal pink-painted hotel before, but Jillian had walked him through its layout before he'd left. It was nice to know what he was going into versus going in blind. Orion agents prided themselves on being prepared—though that wasn't always easy, considering people often did surprising things—and since Orion's expansion three years ago they'd gotten better at it. Even when a contract changed at the last second.

He looked at his reflection in the elevator door and let out a grunt. Not getting the best sleep the night before and catching an early flight, he hoped the client didn't notice the dark circles beneath his eyes. He blamed the chatty man who'd had the aisle seat next to him. It made him wonder if Kathryn was like that, recalling what he had been told initially by Nikki at Mark's engagement party.

"I wouldn't ask you to take this one, since, for one, you just got back, and, two, you just asked for a desk job. But the man requesting our services was so concerned...I could almost feel it myself." Nikki's eyes had traveled to the wall at that. It was a blank space, but he knew on the other side was her real target. A single picture of a young woman. The reason behind Orion's origin. The woman who had changed their lives, whom Nikki, Oliver, Mark and Jonathan couldn't have been what they were now without. The woman they hadn't saved. "He lives in Florida but heard about us through one of Thomas's recent clients. His daughter has been receiving some really troubling letters."

"His daughter?"

"Yes, a scientist—book smart but maybe not exactly up to par on the common sense. Her father, Deacon—what a name—says she's pretty nonchalant about the whole thing, but he's completely freaked. She's due to present her research at a convention in New York City on Sunday and he's worried the person or persons sending her the letters—to her home, I might add—might try to cause her harm before she can make it there."

"And that's where we come in."

"Hopefully that's where you come in."

Jonathan respected his boss and friend too much to turn the request down on the spot. Though he had been on the fence about it until the next day.

When she'd shown him the pictures of the letters Deacon had faxed over, they'd made a chill run up his spine despite his calm.

"Okay, I'm in."

And he'd stayed in even after the call had come in that said scientist refused to have more than one body-guard around. Never mind her safety was in question.

The doors slid open and Jonathan made his way to check in with a suddenly sour mood hanging over his head at the thought of Kathryn Spears. Other than the basic information about her, he really didn't have much to go on, but he had already formed an opinion about her.

She was controlling, apathetic and had an ego. There were no doubts about it.

"Welcome, and how may I help you?" chirped the front desk attendant. He looked to be in his early twen-ties. His name tag read Jett.

Jonathan set down his bag and started to take out his ID.

"Check-in for Jonathan Carmichael." He passed his driver's license over as well as the company credit card, having done the hotel check-in dance many times be-fore. Another part of this routine was his next question.

"Can you tell me if my friend has checked in yet? The name's Kathryn Spears."

The man looked back up and without missing a beat nodded.

"About an hour ago."

That surprised Jonathan.

"You remember her?" he asked.

"Yeah, the first thing she did was ask for coffee that was actually good." Jett didn't seem to be offended by the question. "I sent her to a café a block over." His eyes went over Jonathan's shoulder. "I guess she found some."

Jonathan didn't have to follow the man's gaze too far. Walking through the front doors, Kathryn had a cup between her hands and no trace of a smile across her lips. She met his stare with recognition he didn't expect and made a beeline for him.

"Mr. Carmichael," she said, stretching out her free hand. There was no question in the greeting. "Glad to see you finally made it."

Despite himself he grinned.

"Miss Spears, glad to see you were able to get that coffee that was so important." They shook and he was once again surprised by the woman. Not only was her grip firm, but she held it longer than necessary, squeezing tight as she answered.

"Two coffees, actually."

They dropped hands but his grin stayed. Even though he'd been shown her picture before he'd left Orion, the still of the woman sitting behind a desk covered in papers didn't do the woman before him justice. She was attractive, sure, but there was something else there that caught and held his attention. An unspoken element that he couldn't yet place or define.

Suddenly, Jonathan Carmichael was intrigued by his client.

"I would have waited for you," she continued, voice notably cool, "but I'll be honest, I think you being here is a bit unnecessary."

Jonathan let out a laugh at that, considering earlier he had thought the same about her.

"Don't you want to play it safe rather than be sorry?" he asked.

Kathryn's lip quirked up at the corner. Her smile wasn't humorous.

"I'd rather not have to worry about a bodyguard following me around everywhere, watching my every move while I get ready for one of the largest career moves of my life." She popped her hip out to the side a fraction, he noticed. "That would be my choice if I'd been given one."

Jonathan couldn't decide if the way she spoke was born out of ego or frustration, but he definitely felt a chill wafting from each word. Part of him instantly felt the need to defend his skills and the company that was more than just his employer but an important part of his life. However, Jett was obviously still listening in, so the bodyguard went a more judicious route.

"The Orion Security Group doesn't force clients to hire them," he pointed out. "It was your father who did that, and you consented. As for watching your every move while I'm on the job, I can assure you that—if I'm doing said job correctly—my eyes won't be on *you* but on your surroundings, trying to keep you safe. So if you have a problem with this arrangement, it's your father—and really, yourself—you'll need to be speaking with."

Kathryn didn't immediately respond. When she did it was clipped, definitely chilly.

"Noted. Now, if you'll excuse me, I need to do some work up in my room."

She started to turn to go—already testing the boundaries of his job as her bodyguard—when Jonathan smiled once again.

"Hey, I'll walk with you on the way to mine." She gave him a questioning look. "Oh, didn't your dad tell you? He requested we have adjoining rooms."

Jonathan might not have known the scientist long, but he knew he'd struck a nerve with that comment.

It was going to be an interesting few days.

KATE DIDN'T WANT to wait for the bodyguard. No matter how attractive he'd turned out to be. The picture she'd been forwarded from her father and Orion's Nikki Waters had shown her a lightly tanned man who looked like a stock image a website might use to show an everyman, not a bodyguard. He had seemed flat, one-dimensional. Someone who would easily blend into the background and, hopefully, not bother her.

However, in person she'd been surprised to see that maybe she'd misjudged him in that department. His dark blue eyes had depth, his facial features were sharp and his goatee was trimmed and neat, matching the jet-black hair that stood an inch or two high. He wore a gray tee and jeans and he wore them well. When he turned back to the desk attendant, she even spotted the bottom of a tattoo on the back of his upper arm, peeking out under his sleeve.

Maybe Jonathan Carmichael wasn't the type of man to blend.

"This is a massive invasion of privacy," Kate commented as she led them into the elevator. Like the hotel, it was dated. She pressed the second-floor button and hoped above all hopes that it didn't get stuck. Her nerves had been rubbed the wrong way, annoyed at her father and the man next to her. Getting trapped in the small space with him would most likely incite a flurry of rudeness from her. She was already having a hard time being polite without the added close proximity.

"Again, I'll remind you that your father hired Orion and you agreed," he said, not looking at her but obviously surveying the elevator. He was tall enough to reach up and push against the ceiling—trying to do what, she wasn't sure.

"I meant the adjoining-room situation," she corrected.

Jonathan stopped his inspection and gave her a dry smile.

"Just because there's a door there doesn't mean I'm going to use it. I don't even have a key. We just wanted the rooms to be close, and since it's an older hotel they just happen to share a door." His eyebrow rose. "Unless you want me to get *you* a key?"

Kate felt heat crawl up her neck.

"No," she said quickly. "I don't need or want one."

"Good. Then there shouldn't be a problem."

The elevator doors slid open and Kate hurried with her coffee to her room down the hall. Jonathan was right behind her with his bags.

"I'm going to look in your room, okay?" he said as she pulled out her key card. "I'd like to know the layout, just in case."

Kate wanted to argue, but was trying to channel her inner Spears' manners. She still rolled her eyes.

"Sure, why not?" She opened the door and swung it wide for the bodyguard. "Knock yourself out."

He moved past her, bags still in hand, into the room. For a moment she worried about her more intimate things being left out in the open, but it was a baseless fear. She was meticulous, a trait that had bled over from her professional life into her personal one. She'd already unpacked and sorted her things.

"To be honest, I expected something different," Jonathan said, apparently okay with his inspection.

"Something different?" she repeated. "Like a man in a mask lying in wait?"

The corner of his lips pulled up a fraction.

"I meant I expected to see, I don't know, test tubes and beakers on the nightstands. Aren't you a scientist?"

Kate walked over to the small desk in the corner and

leaned against it. She felt a twitch try to pull her own lips into a small smile, but she tamped it down.

"Generally labeled, yes, I suppose." She took a sip of her coffee. "What else do you know about my work?"

If Jonathan knew about her project, she was sure she'd have seen some kind of reaction to her question. However, the man simply shrugged.

"If you're asking do I know what you're currently working on—why you're here for the convention—I don't. Orion tries to look into a client's life without being intrusive. Our analysts dip into your past and present to try to find potential threats, but we don't overstep. Your father and Nikki made it clear that, as far as your work goes, the only person who can tell me about it is you." He paused, tilting his head slightly. "And I suspect that that information is something you won't be sharing with me."

Before Kate could stop it, the image of a bloodied woman tied to a chair flashed across her vision. Head bent over, body beaten. Her last breath having already left her body hours before.

The image was something she'd had to confront for a long time. It twisted the very core of her heart.

"No," she said, voice turned to ice. "I won't."

Chapter Four

Jonathan wasn't invited to stay past the woman's answer. He didn't want to, either. Kathryn's voice had gone steely, her eyes almost to slits, and even from his spot across the room he'd been able to see her breathing change. Whatever she'd just experienced, it pulled his curiosity to the forefront, but he kept his mouth shut. What was behind her dark eyes was something darker. Something he had no business seeking out.

His room was to the right and was an exact replica of hers. The adjoining door was placed between the desk and the dresser with its TV on top, locked tight with a key card swipe on the handle. It was true he didn't have the key to it, but he doubted he'd be able to get one if he wanted it. Kathryn Spears wasn't hiding the fact that his presence was something she neither wanted nor thought she needed.

"Hey, Nikki, this is Jonathan," he said into his phone after he'd unpacked, leaving a message after the beep. "Just made first contact with Miss Scientist. Let me say, you picked one hell of a last contract for me."

Jonathan unpacked quickly, not as neatly as he'd noticed said scientist's room to be, and reflected on what he knew about the woman next door. He hadn't been lying—it wasn't much. Nikki had received the reports from the analysts and made the decision to only tell him what he needed to know in an effort to preserve some of Kathryn's privacy. What Jonathan knew was that the scientist was dedicated to her work and that work was a secret.

But that didn't mean he wasn't curious as hell as to what it entailed.

A quick knock on his door pulled him from his thoughts. He was surprised to see Kathryn standing on the other side. Her expression had softened, but only slightly.

"I want to apologize for being *frosty*," she greeted him. "I just, well, my work is a sensitive topic and this convention is very, very important for my career. My father tells me that sometimes I tend to get a little too into the zone and can lose sight of my manners." Jonathan hadn't expected an apology. "So, why don't you come with me to the Chinese restaurant a few blocks down and we can get reacquainted?"

"I appreciate the offer, but you know as part of my job I'd go anyway," he pointed out. Kathryn gave him a wry smile.

"I'm inviting you to eat *with* me," she corrected. "Not sit creepily behind me like a weird stalker."

Jonathan stepped back to retrieve his wallet and walked out into the hall. As she shut the door, he snorted.

"You apologize and then call me a stalker. I feel like you don't often apologize to people."

Kathryn crossed her arms over her chest, smile gone. "I don't."

The walk down to the lobby and out to the street was silent. Their conversation hadn't stalled. It had stopped completely. Jonathan walked at her side but kept his eyes in a constant sweeping motion of their surroundings. It was late afternoon and the streets were packed even tighter than when he'd first driven in. Gaggles of pedestrians crowded the corners of blocks and only half waited for the Walk sign to flash green before darting across the street. Jonathan wondered if Kathryn had been to the city before. She walked with purpose and little doubt. Jonathan followed without question or comment.

Two blocks from the hotel, they hung a left into a small, one-room Chinese restaurant. It was dark and surprisingly quiet despite the street noise. The handful of patrons paid them no mind as they slid into a booth against the wall. Before they could settle in, a man took their drink orders. Jonathan checked his sight line to the door again and then decided to break his client's quiet.

"So you've been here before?" he asked, motioning around them. "Which means you've been to New York before?"

"Yes, to both. An associate who is based in Buffalo frequents a lab here and commutes just to eat the chicken fried rice when in the city." She shrugged. "Not the healthiest traveling diet, but I had to admit I was impressed the last time we ate here." Kathryn paused before smirking. "And I'm somewhat of a fast-food queen back home, so take my word for it as a weighty stamp of approval."

"Noted." The timing couldn't have been better for the waiter. He came for their orders and Jonathan decided to test out the scientist's theory. He ordered the chicken fried rice.

"So home, that's in Florida?" he asked, eyes scanning the new couple who'd just entered.

"Yes, where the humidity is king. I've lived there almost all of my life, with the exception of school."

"You moved back when finished, then?"

She nodded.

"Out of graduate school I was offered a somewhat rare job at a lab that was located near my father." She shrugged. "At the risk of sounding like a child who can't crack it without their parent nearby, I couldn't have hoped for a better setup. I love my father dearly, so back to Florida and its god-awful heat I went."

Though it was out of sight, Jonathan felt the burn of the tattoo on the back of his arm. Not a physical pain, but a memory that often flared to life when the past swarmed him.

"There's nothing wrong with staying close to family," he said, truth in each word but no experience within them.

"And what about you, Mr. Bodyguard? Where's your home?"

A simple question and one he had fielded time and time again.

"I moved around a lot growing up. Never in one place for too long." He shrugged. "When Orion started up in Dallas, I decided that I liked that city best. As someone who's traveled the world for the job, you can take my word for it 'as a weighty stamp of approval.'"

She smiled. Jonathan wondered how often she used that expression.

"Noted. You know, I've done some research of my own on Orion Security, and I must say that as a service of bodyguards, it has a fascinating track record," she began, lacing her fingers atop the table. Jonathan had wondered when she'd bring up Orion's history. He'd had no doubt that a woman whose life was so poised in research would do her own. He sat up straighter and nodded.

"We've had a few interesting cases."

"Ha! Interesting? If I recall correctly, last year one of your fellow bodyguards was instrumental in bringing down an underground drug-running organization that the police had no idea existed." Jonathan shrugged but couldn't stop the smile that sprung to his lips. The bodyguard to whom she was referring was none other than Mark Tranton. What she didn't know was that the media had been forced to keep the identity of his equal partner in crime, his now-fiancée, Kelli, and her daughter out of the public eye.

"Each case—each client—is always interesting. It's just part of the job." Kathryn seemed put off that he hadn't divulged more, but she clearly wasn't done with the topic.

"I also found a newspaper article about a woman named Morgan Avery," she said after a moment. Her expression softened just as Jonathan felt his body tense. At the moment he realized maybe he shouldn't underestimate the woman sitting across from him. While Morgan Avery was in no way a secret, it was a truth rarely connected to the agency. When he didn't respond, Kathryn took it as a sign to continue. "You used to work for Redstone Solutions, elite bodyguards, if I read their bio correctly. Morgan came to Redstone for protection but was turned away." Jonathan felt his hand start to fist. He moved it to his lap. "You quit a few weeks after she was killed."

He didn't know if it was her lack of questions that put him so suddenly on edge or if it was hearing the history of Morgan made so brief. Especially when her death had created an inexplicably vast chain of events that had so completely altered his life, as well as the lives of those he cared about most. Kathryn's eyes had narrowed a fraction. A researcher studying a subject. A scientist seeking answers. If he didn't answer in some part, he was sure she wouldn't let it go. Plus, how long had it been since he'd talked about Morgan?

"I was on a team of three. We were in the office, just having come off two back-to-back contracts, when she first came in," he started. "Young, beautiful and utterly brilliant. She was an astronomer in training who had won a spot in a prestigious program in England. It was a pretty cutthroat competition, and after she won it, she started getting threats. So bad, in fact, that she contacted us. Like you said, Redstone was viewed as a security service for the elite."

"Which translates to money, and I'm guessing she didn't have any," Kathryn supplied.

"She was a student—she had nothing to give. So she was turned down multiple times. Even when our office's secretary went to the higher-ups on her behalf. She didn't have the money. So we didn't protect her." An image of Morgan's body in a ditch, beaten almost beyond recognition, flared in his memory. Guilt and anger followed. "She was killed on the way to the airport by a man who wanted her spot. It was her original fear, and it came true."

"And then Nikki Waters founded Orion?"

It took a moment, but the chill of the past slowly heated. They'd made it to the part of the story that was no longer dripping with regret. He nodded.

"Nikki was the secretary at Redstone. After Morgan's death, she refused to work for a company that valued money over people and decided to use her contacts to create an agency that never would make that mistake again. She approached me and the team I was on and asked us to come with her." He shrugged. "So Mark, Oliver and I did. We've been there ever since."

The tattoo on the back of his arm came to the forefront of his mind. His dark mood was gone.

"You know, my mother once told me that some of the most noble pursuits begin with some of the most senseless tragedies," Kathryn said after a moment had passed. "While I don't feel I need Orion Security's protection, I see the value and heart behind what you're doing." She gave him another rarely used smile just as their food came out. Jonathan was stunned by the absolute sincerity that seemed to be behind her words. One moment she was calculated, somewhat tactless, and the next she was insightful and empathetic. Certainly one of the most interesting clients he'd had in a while.

THEY ATE THEIR food quickly and, soon after finishing, they were singing its praises.

"I'll have to let Greg know the food is still fantastic," she said. "This fast-food queen will be coming back here before I leave."

"Greg?" Jonathan asked.

"Oh, sorry. Greg is the work associate I was telling you about. If you insist on following me around the entire trip then you'll get the chance to tell him, too. I have a meeting with him tomorrow morning."

Jonathan's brows drew together.

"There was no mention in your itinerary about a meeting tomorrow," he said, most likely trying to recall the schedule she'd sent to her father, who had sent it on to Orion. Kate couldn't help it. Tension rose fast and fierce, straightening her shoulders. She pursed her lips. For a moment she'd forgotten her annoyance at the bodyguard's presence.

"That's because I didn't include it in my itinerary."

She stood and left the table to pay at the podium near the door. His next question was going to be why, and the only answer she could give would create more questions. Ones she couldn't answer.

Jonathan didn't berate her as they left the restaurant and made their way back to the hotel. In fact, he had gone silent as he trailed the space beside her, yet kept his distance. It gave her a sense of being alone. One that was shattered when he moved close with a whisper that nearly tickled her ear.

"Let's pause for a second, please."

Kate did as she was told and turned to the man, confused.

"I can see the hotel from here," she pointed out.

Jonathan grabbed her arm and pulled her backward with him. Not ready for the contact, she started to pull away when he spoke again. "I think we're being followed." His gaze cut behind her. Kate allowed him to position her so she could see the people behind them on the sidewalk. Her eyes hopscotched across each of them quickly and, she hoped, covertly. She understood the concept that if someone was following them, they would be spooked if they noticed their target noticing them.

But, then again, Kate didn't think she was being followed at all.

"The couple in the green and black jackets," he added when she was coming up empty. She turned to look for the couple in question. A dark-haired man and a dark blond-haired woman, arm in arm. Kate let out a loud sigh and turned back to Jonathan.

"You mean Mr. And Mrs. All Over Each Other?"

She snorted. "I don't think their interest lies anywhere other than with each other."

"They were in the restaurant and left when we did, even though their food wasn't finished."

Although Jonathan's eyes were on hers, she could tell his attention was still tracking the upcoming couple. His intensity was almost surprising and, perhaps, the reason why she did what she did next.

"You know, you're right," she said, looking back at the couple that was nearly upon them. "They might be following us." She grabbed Jonathan's hand, abruptly breaking his focus, and smiled. "So, why don't we lose them?" Without another word from her bodyguard, Kate began moving. "Let's take a detour."

Chapter Five

The scientist pulled Jonathan to the nearest crosswalk and together they surged across the road in a cloud of pedestrians. Kathryn's grip was firm while the rest of her body seemed surprisingly loose. When she looked back at him, she even had a smile across her lips. One that, again, looked odd there, but also right.

As they hit the sidewalk she kept straight, angling them down a block with a chain clothing store and a twenty-four-hour bakery. Jonathan had studied the layout of the surrounding blocks from their hotel on the plane. It would be hard to get lost unless you intended to do just that. He was comfortable with their small detour. However, his attention was still sharp, frequently looking back over his shoulder at where the couple had been.

They stayed across the road, passing over their own crosswalk to get to the next stretch of sidewalk. Maybe he had been overreacting. The man in the green jacket turned his head and met Jonathan's stare.

Maybe not.

"Mr. Bodyguard?" Kathryn said. Jonathan didn't turn until the man dropped his gaze, laughing at whatever the woman beside him had said. "Staring isn't polite."

Jonathan refocused his attention on Kate. She had

slowed her clip but kept holding his hand, steering him through foot traffic. Jonathan felt her warm skin against his. It was soft in his rugged hands, which were hardened by his time with the punching bag and weights. He briefly wondered what she thought of his rough skin before quickly killing the thought. While he knew the woman wasn't thinking about the intimacy that came with holding hands, he found his focus was starting to break because of it. Instead of shaking the hand free, however, he cleared his throat and used his training to get back to what was important.

His job.

"Let's hang a right up here. If we cross the road we'll hit construction," he said.

Kathryn snorted.

"If we're being followed, we won't lose our tail that easily," she said back, dropping her voice as if the two were conspiring. "Don't tell me I've been assigned a *lazy* bodyguard."

She looked ahead with a smirk trailing her lips. She was being difficult and she knew it, teasing him while simultaneously goading him. Jonathan didn't know if he thought the attempt was amusing, considering her earlier mood covered in frost, or annoying. Either way, he wasn't about to be labeled as lazy on his last field assignment. Even if it was by a woman he was starting to guess would never be happy with his job performance.

"You're absolutely right," he said with enthusiasm. "I really need to step up my game."

Kathryn started to loosen her grip, probably feeling her sarcasm backfiring, but Jonathan held it firm. Instead of trailing behind her, he took two long strides ahead.

Now he was leading her.

Looking both ways, Jonathan tugged her across the street to the left, in between a lag in traffic. Had they both not run, they might not have made it. Despite Kate's gasp of concern, Jonathan continued parallel to the block they'd just left before coming to the intersection. He blew through it within another pocket of pedestrians until they were at the opening of a preppy clothing store. He didn't waste any time and ducked through its double doors, passing through an invisible cloud of loud cologne and expensively dressed mannequins. One thin, very tan sales associate was on them within seconds.

"Can I help you two find anything?" the young woman said, eyes dropping to their clasped hands. She raised her expertly styled eyebrow as Jonathan kept moving.

"We're just browsing."

The associate backed off, but not without a huff.

Jonathan scanned the tops of clothing racks and display tables for an exit. While he was familiar with the shops and buildings around their hotel, he didn't know their layouts once inside. This particular store was the first of several housed in a much larger mall. Another set of double doors could be seen in the back corner, leading to what looked to be a common area between the other stores.

Jonathan slowed, hesitating in his next decision. Playing into Kathryn's teasing was fun, but pulling her into a busy area just to show he wasn't a wet blanket? That was starting to toe the line that separated fun and responsibility.

However, Kathryn didn't seem to care or to be currently struggling with his internal dilemma. She took advantage of his pause to untangle her hand from his.

"Come on, Mr. Bodyguard, let's see if you can multitask."

Then she darted toward the back corner of the store and was at the common area doors before he'd even had time to process how the absence of her hand left his cold.

KATE WASN'T SURE what had come over her. Maybe it was belated excitement at being so close to the convention, a giant step toward realizing a goal she'd striven toward for as long as she could remember. Or maybe it was years of being cooped up in a lab finally catching up to her that had created the sudden desire to be playful. Or maybe it was the handsome, dark-haired man who had a backstory that tugged at her heartstrings, taking him from a man who was annoying to surprisingly human. Like his picture, the man definitely wasn't of the stock variety.

Kate pushed into the common area of the minimall with a grin from ear to ear. Whatever had made this mood crop up, she was still enjoying it.

"Kathryn," Jonathan called from behind. She cast him a quick glance, noting he wasn't sharing in her mirth, but kept going.

The common area had a good number of people bustling down the hall before turning into different chain stores. Kate passed a shoe store and an electronics boutique before hitting a pocket of air that smelled so delicious it grabbed her full attention. She whipped her head upward to look at the second story. Her full stomach batted the thoughts of cookies out of her head, but the escalator leading up to them made her turn on the spot. She gave her bodyguard another grin that she felt in her bones was as mischievous as she could muster and didn't stop as she walked up the escalator.

"Kathryn," he said again, warning her. But, really, what was he going to do? He wasn't her father. He wasn't her boss. He wasn't her funder.

He definitely wasn't her husband or boyfriend.

With another weird thrill of amusement, she let out a giggle that carried her along to the second story. Heavy footfalls sounded against the metal behind her as she hit the tile. Jonathan was now quickening his pace. So, what was a girl to do?

Kate matched and then added some speed of her own. Walking fast turned into sprinting, weaving through the shoppers with nothing more than a few nasty faces and words thrown her way. She didn't care. Now she had a mission. She was going to lose her bodyguard to prove to him that, even if his intentions were good, they weren't needed.

She could lose her imaginary tail.

She could outsmart a man trained in surveillance.

She could take care of herself.

The humor she'd been feeling hardened into determination.

Kate spotted an opportunity to slip out of Jonathan's view when a group of laughing teen girls exited a coffee shop. She cut to the right of them and immediately ducked behind their group, moving toward the second escalator that led to the first floor. When she righted herself, already descending downward, she looked over her shoulder at the bodyguard.

It worked!

Jonathan kept going straight, slowing but not stopping as he tried to get his eyes on her. The flush of success at evading her guard narrowed her focus as she hurried down the last of the escalator. Sure, she'd just proven she could get away, but how far could she go?

Instead of hurrying to the first-floor main entrance that deposited shoppers back to the sidewalk, Kate saw a second opportunity she couldn't pass up. Past the public bathrooms at the end of a short hall at the corner of the building were two large metal doors that must have been primarily used for bringing in merchandise. A rubber doorstop kept the door ajar. Beyond that she could see a strip of daylight. Kate booked it as fast as she could without her shoes slapping the tile too loudly, straight to and through the door.

It was the end of the mall, the building and the one next to it separated by the small walkway that ran the width of both. A set of industrial Dumpsters and their stench filled the small space, making her escape less ideal than she'd hoped it would be. But, then again, Kate didn't much care.

She'd just outsmarted her bodyguard and his tailored knowledge of keeping tabs on people.

Kate finally slowed and walked at a leisurely pace down the small alley and back to the sidewalk that ran in front of the mall's entrance. She half expected to see Jonathan blocking her path, huffing and ready to call her father, but as she scanned the faces she didn't find his.

Kate froze.

Her muscles seized, her breath held.

While she'd expected to see the bodyguard, she hadn't expected to see another face she recognized. In fact, two faces she recognized.

The couple that had originally spooked Jonathan, starting Kate's fun little exercise, were not only walking out of the mall, but doing so quickly. Like they too were in a hurry. This need seemed to intensify as the man looked to the left and the woman looked to the right, also seemingly scanning faces in the crowd.

And then the woman stopped when she locked on to a familiar face.

Hers.

Suddenly Kate cursed her game of cat and mouse with the bodyguard. The woman turned back to the man, but Kate didn't wait to see what happened next. She backtracked in record time to the alley and hurried down its length as the sound of pounding drew nearer.

Was the couple really running after her?

Why?

Was she just overreacting?

Or had Jonathan been right about the couple all along?

Kate reached the metal door that led back into the mall and started to second-guess herself. It was a coincidence. That was all. It was perfectly normal for a couple to eat and then go shopping. It was New York City, after all. She nodded to herself, trying to ignore the fear that had cropped up. She took a step back and looked toward the mouth of the alley.

Seconds later the woman and her green jacket came into view. Kate's blood ran cold but her feet stayed warm. She grabbed the door handle, ready to fling it open and make a mad dash inside, when it swung wide so fast that she gave a little scream.

"Whoa, it's me," said Jonathan. He grabbed her shoulders, steadying her. Relief didn't just pool within her, it flooded. "What's wrong?"

Kate turned back to the mouth of the alley. The woman and her counterpart were nowhere to be seen.

"She was just there," Kate whispered.

"Who?" Jonathan's grip tightened. He moved her around behind him, looking where she had.

Maybe Kate *had* imagined it.

"Who?" he asked again. "Kathryn?"

"Call me Kate," she whispered. She shook her head and looked up at him. Embarrassment at acting like such a carefree child washed over her. While trying to avoid the bodyguard and what she believed to be a service she didn't need, she'd just managed to convince herself that she was in some kind of danger. She was creating fictional scenarios and problems for herself, most likely seeing more in the couple's actions than was there. Still, the fear wasn't fully leaving, either. Fear often led to loss of control.

And Kate didn't like losing what little control she had.

She cleared her throat before continuing with a much stronger voice. "I never liked being called Kathryn."

"Okay, *Kate*," he started, brows pulling together. "Who did you see?"

"Never mind," she said. She straightened her back and took a deep breath. There was no way she was going to let the bodyguard's paranoia and her fear make her lose her focus. "Let's head back," she said, no longer wanting to explore.

Kate might be able to write off how the woman in the green coat had seemingly been looking for her as a coincidence, but she wasn't about to take off from the bodyguard's side again.

She was in denial, but not *that* much.

THE WALK BACK to the hotel was quiet. More than anything Jonathan wanted to reprimand his charge for running off, but after seeing her expression in the alley, he'd refrained. Whatever—whoever—she'd seen had spooked her. While seeing Jonathan had done the opposite.

She'd let out a deep sigh that had seemingly passed through her entire body at the sight of him. Seeing such poignant relief because of his proximity had affected him almost as much as the look of fear she'd harbored seconds before. The absurd amount of annoyance he'd felt for Kathryn—*Kate*—had taken a backseat to a resounding protectiveness that went beyond his usual job duties.

He suddenly not only needed to keep her safe, he *wanted* to do it, and to the best of his abilities.

The silence stretched past the sidewalk and up to their rooms, and when it finally broke, it wasn't by much.

"I'm a little tired from traveling," Kate muttered. "I'll let you know if I want to leave." There was an undercurrent to her words, but Jonathan couldn't place the emotion creating it. Was it guilt at ditching him earlier? Or residual fear from whatever had happened when he hadn't been right on her heels?

"Thank you," was all he could say.

She nodded and opened her door. He waited until it was closed and the top latch was thrown in place. It made him wonder if she'd done it by habit, or if Kate was more worried than she was letting on.

Chapter Six

Kate closed the top latch over the door and took a step back to look at it. She heard Jonathan's door close.

You aren't in any danger, she thought. *Don't let his overprotectiveness worry you.*

But even as she gave herself the advice, she couldn't help but feel an influx of nerves tighten her stomach.

"This is why I didn't want a bodyguard," she muttered, rubbing her stomach. "Now I think I have problems I don't really have."

Trying to forget about the man next door wasn't as easy as she'd hoped.

Talking about his past, including Orion's origin, had softened her otherwise harsh opinion of the man. He wasn't some faceless hunk of meat sent to stalk her in hopes of keeping a potentially imaginary predator at bay. He was a man who had persevered through tragedy and had made a life of preventing it from repeating again.

And wasn't that exactly what she was doing, too?

She tried to banish thoughts of the brooding dark-haired man and fell onto the bed. The jaunt right after eating a full meal plus traveling combined to make her eyelids unbelievably heavy as soon as she hit the pillow.

The feeling of exhaustion and the desire to give in to

the comfort of the bed surprised her. Taking naps wasn't something she was used to doing. In the last few years, if there was time to sleep, then that meant there was time to work. She'd rarely picked a nap over lab time. It was a choice that had turned into a habit.

A yawn tore itself from her lips and she knew it wouldn't be long before she was asleep.

This trip was already turning out much differently than she had originally planned.

THE ROOM WAS DARK.

Barely any light filtered in from behind the curtains. It was so dim Kate placed them as streetlights. Which meant her nap had stretched longer than she'd meant it to.

She rolled onto her back and yawned. Even though she'd been sleeping, she felt exhaustion still weighing her down. If she closed her eyes again, she was sure she'd sleep until morning.

So what had woken her up?

She tilted her head, listening.

A car horn blared outside, promptly followed by two more.

Ah, the sweet sounds of New York City, she thought.

She contemplated her next move, listening to a symphony of agitated drivers vent via their respective vehicles when another sound caught her ear.

Confused, she turned her head, peering into the dark for the culprit. It stopped.

Kate's heartbeat began to pick up. She waited. There it was again.

Someone was in the hallway.

But what were they doing?

Curious—always curious—Kate got off the bed and

made her way to the door. She peered through the peep-hole but was met with a cloudy circle with no help identifying who was outside. If there was anyone at all. She dropped back down to flat-footed and bit her bottom lip, waiting.

Seconds turned into minutes. Kate remained perfectly still until she was positive the sound, whatever it had been, had stopped. Slowly she unlatched the top lock and eased the door open a crack.

No one was there.

Cautious, Kate stepped out into the hallway. It was empty. She let out a breath she hadn't realized she was holding.

See? That bodyguard has made you paranoid, she thought. *No one is after you. No one even knows where you—*

Her current thought bubble popped as she turned.

Taped to the door was a piece of paper with a single word written on it: *Stop*.

However, it wasn't the message that made her throat catch.

Soaking the paper, blurring the one bold word, was blood. It ran off the paper and down the chipped paint of the door.

And this time, Kate didn't think it was fake.

Chapter Seven

Jonathan was barely out of the shower when a pounding sounded against his door. Adrenaline spiked at the urgency behind each knock. He dropped the towel to his waist and had the door open within seconds, water dripping off him and on to the carpet.

"I think it's real," Kate greeted. She was still wearing her clothes from earlier but the impression of a pillow lined the right side of her face while her hair was ruffled. Like he'd suspected, she had been sleeping for the last few hours. Her expression, however, was not in the least rested. Her brows were pushed together, a wrinkle between them, and she wore a frown so pronounced it seemed to drag down every line that made up her face.

"What?" Jonathan asked, an umbrella question to everything.

"This time I think it's real," she repeated.

"What's real?" Jonathan moved closer, out of the doorway. He was trying to get an answer that made sense. What he got was Kate's shaky hand pointing to her door.

And then he understood.

"It's real blood," he said, senses going on alert as he took in what was taped to her door. This one undoubtedly looked more menacing than the other letters she'd received.

"Yes. The coloring, the way it drips," she added. "The way it smells."

Jonathan didn't need to sniff the dark crimson to agree with her assessment. When he was a teenager, he'd gotten into a bad fight with a kid in foster care over which bed was his. The kid had been older and bigger and had hit Jonathan so perfectly in the nose that he busted it on impact. For nearly an hour it had bled. The color and consistency matched what was on the door now.

That was real blood, all right.

"Did you see who put it here?" he asked. His head swiveled back and forth down the empty hallway.

"No. I heard something and when I came out here to look I found—" she motioned to the note, eyes wide "—that."

Jonathan spotted the bubble cameras at each end of the hall.

"I bet those did," he muttered. "Have you touched it in any way?"

Kate shook her head.

"I just saw it and then knocked on your door."

"Good, come on."

He motioned for her to go into his room. Her concerned look turned stubborn immediately.

"Shouldn't we call someone?"

"We will, but inside the room," he said, holding back a building tidal wave of frustration only she seemed to be able to produce within him. "If you haven't noticed, the longest trail of blood hasn't even made it to the carpet yet."

Kate whipped her head back to the door and he knew when she saw what he was talking about.

"Which means—" Jonathan started before she cut him off.

"That it hasn't been there long at all."

"A plus for the scientist," he said, waving her through again.

This time she followed instructions without resistance.

"Call the front desk and get the manager up here," he said, following her in and immediately going to his still-packed bag. "Let them know that you're also calling the cops." Kate's mouth opened and closed, like a fish out of water. "Listen, there's no doubt in my mind this letter is connected to the others you've been receiving. Which means his anger is escalating." He held up his fingers to tick off his points as he made them. "One large 'stop' instead of a page filled with the word. Real blood, not fake. On your hotel-room door, states away from home. Even that stubborn brain of yours has to see that whoever is behind these letters is getting angrier."

He watched as the urge to fight back—to be the one making complete sense—flashed across her face. Thankfully, it disappeared quickly. In its place was the face of a woman who finally agreed with him. She nodded.

"Which asks the question…what's next?"

"Let's make sure we never have to find out. Now call the front desk and, if you don't want to see me naked, turn around."

Jonathan saw her cheeks redden, but he didn't have time to dwell on it. Someone had left a letter soaked in blood as a warning to Kate—a violent threat. Jonathan not only wanted to protect her from that person, he wanted to find and stop them, too.

He changed into a white T-shirt and covered it with a gray button-down and a pair of khakis that were a bit tighter than he liked thanks to his recently changed leg workouts. Once he put on his boots, though, he wasn't thinking about how his clothes looked. His mind was already focused outside the hotel room.

"The front-desk guy, Jett, the one who checked you in, said a manager is on the way up," Kate said, eyes still averted. "He sounded more than concerned."

"Good, he should be."

Jonathan grabbed his cell phone and rummaged through his bags until he found something he had hoped he wouldn't even have to think about while on contract.

"Orion prides itself on always trying to use nonlethal means to protect our clients," he said, walking to the other side of the bed where Kate sat with the phone. "But since you refused a second bodyguard and now you're getting bloody letters on your door, I'm going to give you this and warn you to be careful." Jonathan extended the small block of plastic to her. It was black with a strip of school-bus yellow across the grips on either side and about as heavy as it looked. "Do I need to show you how to use it?"

Kate's eyes had widened when she realized what it was, but the surprise didn't last long.

"I'm a woman who lives by herself," she said, taking it carefully and placing it on the nightstand. "I know how to use a Taser, Mr. Bodyguard."

"Good to know, Miss Scientist," he said, resisting the urge to roll his eyes at her. "Now call the police and don't open this door until I come back."

"Where are you going?"

"To find out who left that note," he said, already at the door and opening it. "And to find out how they knew exactly what room you were in."

THE MANAGER WAS a woman named Lola Teague and she was as concerned as she was determined to help. She met Jonathan at the elevator, sporting a dark navy pant-suit, heels and a name tag that caught the fluorescent lights. Jonathan placed Lola in her fifties, with impeccably styled dark hair, matching pristine posture and laugh lines at the corners of her eyes.

When she saw the note on the door, she definitely wasn't laughing.

She let out a low whistle.

"This is a first for us. And that says something, coming from someone who has been with the hotel since day one." She leaned in close but was careful not to touch, a consideration that made Jonathan instantly respect her. "To be perfectly candid, where other managers might want to call the hotel owner before the cops, I don't share the same school of thought." She straightened and gave him a severe look.

"Don't worry, we already called."

Lola gave a quick nod before giving him an appraising look.

"You're the bodyguard, then?" she asked before tacking on, "Jett heard the two of you talking when you checked in earlier."

Jonathan's jaw tightened.

"I hope he wasn't broadcasting our stay here," he said, voice dangerously low. "Because, I'll be candid, too—very few people knew we were staying at this hotel. We haven't been here for more than a few hours and someone knows exactly what room she was in."

Lola didn't miss the implication that Jett might have told someone where they could be found. He saw her tense up. Professional distress.

Welcome to my world, he thought.

Instead of trying to defend her employee, however, her eyes flitted down the hall. He followed her gaze to the security camera.

"I think it's time to see what our cameras picked up."

"I think you're right."

Jonathan paused to take a picture of the note and door before following the manager into the elevator and down to the lobby. Jett sat at the front desk, eyes darting to each new face that entered. Jonathan was doing the same thing, though he hoped a little more slyly than the young black-haired man. His head jerked around like he was on a roller coaster.

"Jett," Lola greeted, voice as even as it had been when she had spoken upstairs. "Did you by chance tell anyone that Miss Spears or Mr. Carmichael were staying here?"

"Or mention which rooms?" Jonathan added.

Jett's eyes widened a fraction but he didn't sag with guilt or pucker up with resentment at the question.

"No way," he exclaimed to them. He turned to Jonathan. "You were the only one who even asked about her. No one else has called or come to me asking about either one of you. Especially not room numbers. I swear!"

Lola gave a curt nod and shared a look with Jonathan. One that asked if he was satisfied with her employee's answer, because she was.

"Okay," Jonathan consented.

"Jett, please come get us when the police arrive," she said. "Also, send Norman up there to make sure no one touches that letter until the cops get here."

"Yes, ma'am."

"Norman?" Jonathan asked.

"The head of our cleaning staff," she answered before addressing Jett again.

"And Jett? If you see *anyone*, and I mean *anyone*, you don't recognize as a guest, come get me immediately."

Jett nodded and went back to hawk-eyeing each guest who walked past.

Lola led them around the front desk to a door in the corner marked Employees Only. It opened up into a small hall that forked right up to another door. It was marked Security. The manager got a key out and unlocked the door.

"I just realized," she said, not at all happy, "whoever put up that note did so during our security guard Bernie's dinner break. What are the odds?"

"Who says it's a coincidence?" Jonathan pointed out. Lola paused a moment, taking in his meaning, before pushing into the small room. Whatever was happening, Jonathan wasn't liking it one bit. Escalating threats, obvious malice and now a coincidence like the one guard supposed to watch the security camera just happened to be on break when the note was delivered?

This contract—protecting Kate Spears—had taken a turn he hadn't anticipated at all.

The security room wasn't much to look at. A desk ran the length of the wall with two flat-screen monitors on top. Eight frames were displayed within each.

"This is your floor," Lola pointed out, sitting down in the desk chair. "What one camera caught, so did the other." Jonathan came closer and looked at the real-time feed. Kate's door was square in the middle of the two, close enough that anyone who went up to it would be seen but far enough away that the note on the door wasn't as noticeable. Even the blood.

Lola clicked around the computer while Jonathan's attention roamed over the rest of the live security feeds. There was not a lot of movement and, even if there had been, it wasn't like he could question each and every guest in hopes he'd get lucky and catch the culprit. He had a feeling it wouldn't be *that* easy.

"How far back should I go?" she asked, both of the hall's feeds the only images on one monitor.

"Try fifteen minutes."

She did as he said and they watched as three different people moved down the hall and into their respective rooms. Not one of them stopped at Kate's door.

"Go back a few more minutes."

Lola started to move the frames back by five minutes when Jonathan held out his hand.

"There," he said. "He's in front of her door."

The two quieted as she hit Play. They watched as a man took out what looked like a large plastic sandwich bag from beneath his jacket.

"That's the paper on her door," Lola said.

Jonathan nodded.

"He had it in a bag so the blood wouldn't get everywhere."

The man carefully took the note out, not at all worried that someone might see him. He pressed the paper against the door. With his free hand he produced a roll of duct tape and yanked off a piece. If Jonathan hadn't been in the shower, he surely would have heard that. Like he was hanging a birthday banner, the man taped the blood-soaked paper to the door. When he was satisfied that it would stay up, he turned and began to walk away.

Lola paused that particular frame.

"I'm going to print this out," she said, already doing just that. Jonathan didn't respond. All of his attention was on the man's face. Anger, hot and fluid, moved over every inch of his skin. "Wait," Lola said, pausing in what she was doing to look back at him. "Do you know this man?"

"No," he admitted. "I saw him earlier today, though. He had a woman with him then."

But, what Jonathan really wanted to know was, where were they now?

Chapter Eight

Kate rubbed her arms as if the motion would scrub away the feeling of unease that had crept in. The two NYPD officers who had shown up had eyed the bloody threat with a good dose of concern, but it hadn't lasted long. They took pictures, removed the letter and bagged it.

"We'll check the blood to see who or what it belongs to," one of them said. "If anything comes up, we'll let you know."

Kate watched as Jonathan's mood darkened. He had expected more.

"And the man?" he asked when the two looked like they were ready to leave.

"We'll run his name and pay him a visit," the most senior of the two said. "What happens during that visit depends on if this is real blood or not."

They didn't stick around past that. Kate watched them walk down the narrow hallway to the elevators with a flush of frustration she'd bet the bodyguard was also harboring.

"I thought they'd be more helpful, somehow," she admitted when the officers were in the elevator. "They didn't really even seem to be too concerned about it. I mean, I know they've probably seen much worse than a blood-soaked letter, but still…"

Jonathan muttered something angrily beneath his breath before motioning to her door.

"Go ahead and get your things together."

Kate's eyebrows flew straight up.

"What? We aren't leaving," she exclaimed. "I don't care if some sadistic person is trying their best to freak me out. I have work to do and I'm not—"

"Kate," Jonathan interrupted. He held his hand up to further emphasize the need for her to stop. "I had a feeling you wouldn't leave, even if I asked. The hotel manager is letting us move to another set of rooms off book."

Kate felt her face heat slightly.

"Oh."

"Yeah, so please go get your things together so we can go to our new rooms."

Kate nodded, but paused before opening her door.

"What do you mean, 'off book'?"

"In the computers we'll still be registered as staying in these rooms. The ones we'll be using are now booked under different names. Hopefully that will keep our letter writer from paying us another visit." He quieted a moment. "I don't think they will rebook this room on the off chance the writer decides to escalate, either. Also, may I point out that you *should* care that some sadistic person is trying their best to freak you out. Caution isn't for stupid people, Kate. It's smart people who've realized that they should be careful."

Kate felt the low thrum of nerves in her stomach get a touch louder. She nodded to Jonathan and his words of wisdom, and again she wondered what that next step might be. Either way, Jonathan wasn't taking any chances. He waited for her to go inside and lock her door before she heard him go to his own room.

Packing quickly made the methodical side of her cringe. What normally would have her taking her time—finding each article of clothing and accessory a specific place—had her cramming her luggage full. The room, she realized, now felt tainted in a way. Whose blood had been on that letter? Was it the man she'd seen earlier on the street? Or had he taken it from someone else?

Kate's eyes traveled to the side pocket of her bag. Within it was a small leather-bound notebook.

What you're doing is important, Kate, she thought. *Don't let them scare you.*

She took a deep breath.

Jonathan was already packed and waiting for her in the hall when she finished. Without a word he took the bag from her and began walking. She gave the door one last look. The hotel manager had said she would be cleaning it off personally. Kate hoped she'd do it soon, or some late nighters would get more of a scare than they'd bargained for.

"We need to talk more about tonight," Jonathan said as soon as the elevator doors closed them in. Kate followed his finger as he hit the third-floor button. She didn't want to look him in the eyes. She didn't want to fight.

"Aren't bodyguards supposed to be quiet observers?" she asked with a small smile. Even though she'd taken a nap earlier, fatigue was pulling her body down. Her adrenaline had spiked when she'd seen the present left on the door. Now it had all but worn off, leaving exhaustion in its wake. She didn't want to talk about any of it right then. Not even with the man who was obviously trying his best to keep her safe without knowing whom he was protecting her from.

"I thought you didn't like men who quietly watched you from a distance." Though the reference was done in a humorous way, Kate detected no lightness to his mood. She cut her eyes toward him.

Looking straight ahead, there was no denying Jonathan Carmichael had an absolutely handsome profile. Hard angles to his jaw, chin and nose gave him a sculpted, tough look, while his eyes...

Jonathan turned and met her stare with his own. Those very eyes she'd just been trying to find descriptors for were now focused squarely on her.

Kate prided herself on being meticulous in work and in life. She labeled things—and people—with no second thoughts. She paid attention to the smaller details while often losing sight of the larger picture, as her father liked to say. To know the name of something—the essence of what made it up—was a natural and necessary ritual for her. A reflex of sorts that had made her work life flourish while, perhaps, stunting her personal one. Her emotions were included in the latter. Kate wouldn't go as far as to say she didn't have feelings—she did— but they were calculated and timed with reason.

Yet, in that moment, Kate found a part of her floundering to make sense of a new warmth that had taken place within her. What's more, in all of her vocabulary and thought, she couldn't seem to find one word to describe the dark blue of her bodyguard's eyes.

And certainly not how they made her feel all of a sudden.

"Are you okay?" he asked, the world beneath their feet stopping. The elevator beeped. The door slid open. "Kate?" His voice dipped low, concern clearly there. She'd known him for less than a day and here he was, showing genuine concern for her well-being. Was that just part of the job?

Kate blinked.

"Sorry. I just—I'm tired. I guess I was more worn out from traveling than I'd thought." To prove her point, she stifled a yawn, stretching her arms out wide. "Don't you want to get some sleep?" Jonathan held her stare a moment longer before she slid into the hallway, trying to escape whatever fog she'd just found herself in. Why would it matter if he cared for her beyond his bodyguard duties? Or if he didn't? Kate didn't detest the idea that Jonathan could genuinely care. Instead it created an anxious feeling inside her. What would she even do if he did?

"I've learned to operate on little sleep," he said matter-of-factly, following her out. "Call it a trick of the trade."

They moved down the hall and to their new rooms, Jonathan unlocking the first before going inside. He did the same sweep he'd done that morning, checking every inch of the space before giving it the okay. When he was finished, however, he went to the door and threw the top latch.

Locking the two of them inside.

The fog from earlier rushed back, but this time lightning jolted through it. Heat rose up her neck and spread to her cheeks. She raised her eyebrow, questioning the man. Was he staying the night with her?

Quickly her eyes flitted to the one king-size bed in the room. Her skin grew hotter.

If Jonathan noticed her burning blush, he didn't say anything.

"I know you're not a fan of adjoining rooms," he said, walking to the one next to her. "But given what's happened, I thought it might be smart to have access to one." He pulled another key card from his pocket and slid it into the lock on the door. It clicked and he opened it wide. Kate peered in to see another duplicate room. One with its own king-size bed.

The heat that should have abated at realizing the bodyguard wasn't trying to stay in her room didn't. Kate turned to her bag on the floor and unzipped it, talking over her shoulder while she hoped her face wasn't too red.

"As long as you don't decide to turn into a creep and come into my room while I sleep, I think I'll survive."

He laughed.

"I won't come stare at you sleeping if you don't do the same to me." She turned as he placed a second key card on the TV stand next to the door. "If you need me, just knock. Good night."

He started to close his door when Kate moved toward him. He stopped as she called his name.

"Jonathan?" He turned and once again she was slammed with the full impact of his eyes. She didn't let it divert her current thought process, though. "I don't know exactly how Orion and its agents work—if you call in and give updates—but I'd really appreciate it if you wouldn't mention to my father what's happened." She gave him a small smile. "I know technically he's the one who hired you, but he worries too much."

The bodyguard looked like he was going to say something but decided against it. He didn't return her smile.

"You know, it's okay to have people worry about you. That's all some people want in this world." The way he said the last part pulled at her heart. It also piqued her curiosity about the life of the man in front of her. Regardless, she pressed on.

"My father has had enough worry to last him a lifetime," she said. "I don't want to add to it until I have to."

She searched his face, looking for the cause of the hardened man.

"When this is over, I'll give a full report to my boss and then she'll debrief the client. But, for now, I think we both need some sleep."

It wasn't a yes to her request, but it wasn't a no, either.

No THREATENING LETTERS covered in blood appeared during the night. The hotel's day manager, a balding man named Ted, kept a vigilant eye out for the man caught on the security footage as well as any other suspicious activity after Lola explained what had happened. Like Jett, his enthusiasm worked to their advantage. It was like he'd been asked to be a spy temporarily. He seemed to enjoy a break from his normal, everyday activities.

When Kate and Jonathan came down to the lobby to introduce themselves, he was more than accommodating.

"If you'd like to have breakfast, it's on the house," he chirped at them. Kate's stomach growled in response. She hadn't eaten since the Chinese restaurant the day before.

"That's nice," she commented. Ted in turn kept smiling even as he leaned in close to ask for any updates from the police.

"I called in before we came down but was told there was no new information," Jonathan answered with a shrug. "I suppose we just have to wait."

Ted nodded to that, and Kate and the bodyguard took

advantage of their free breakfast. It wasn't until they were halfway into their eggs and bacon that the man across from her asked a question she'd been expecting.

"So, what exactly is this convention all about?"

Kate paused her fork in midair.

"What do you know about it already?" she asked, curious.

"Nothing other than you need to be invited and wear something nice."

Kate smirked.

"The convention, typically, isn't a public affair. Depending on your field of study, what you're working on and your connections, you get invited to showcase your research or invention. You basically present to potential sponsors for funding." She felt her smirk transform into a more genuine show of excitement. "I had a breakthrough with the work I've been doing and was invited to present my research." Jonathan nodded, seemingly impressed. If he wanted more details than that, he was going to be disappointed. Only those who needed to know did. "That's actually why we're meeting Greg for coffee. He's more of a mentor and, I'm hoping, has a present for me."

Jonathan raised his eyebrow.

"What kind of present?" he asked.

Her smirk came back in full.

"The game-changing kind."

Chapter Nine

Greg Calhoun was short, round and had little hair. His dark skin was a complete contrast to his chemically treated white smile, and his glasses were as awkwardly shaped as the crumpled handkerchief he always carried in his pocket. He entered the coffee shop with a narrow focus that didn't dissipate until his eyes landed on Kate. He shone his sparkling smile and made a beeline for her.

"Kate," he exclaimed in greeting. "What a sight for sore eyes."

Kate stood and accepted his embrace. She felt the corners of her lips lift. Her social life might have been stunted by her professional one, but she considered the older man a true friend.

"Nice to see you, too, Greg. It's been a long time since we've talked to each other in person," she said, sitting back down. Jonathan sat to her left and extended a hand to Greg as he sat opposite. "Greg, I'd like to introduce you to Jonathan Carmichael." Kate hesitated before explaining their relationship. She hadn't told anyone aside from a friend about her father's need for his daughter to be protected. Was it against the rules to tell him now that Jonathan was her bodyguard? She trusted Greg. Few people in her life had garnered such intense trust and loyalty from her. Shouldn't she pay him the same courtesy?

"I'm her bodyguard." Jonathan spoke up while she was still deciding what to say. Surprised, she tilted her head. "You seemed to be struggling with what to label me," he whispered before turning back to the man.

Greg shook his hand without issue and nodded.

"I'm glad you hired one, to be honest," he said. "Once your father told me about the letters, I was concerned you weren't being cautious enough."

Kate's eyes widened and a slow burn crept to her face.

"My father told you about the letters?" she asked. Greg paid her enough respect to look sheepish.

"He phoned me after he found out. I think he made the call to find out if I sent them or had received any like them. When he was convinced I really hadn't known about their existence, he told me to keep an eye out for you at the convention." He patted his pronounced stomach and then motioned to Jonathan's flat front. "I'm glad you decided to get someone a bit more qualified."

Jonathan let out a small laugh, but Kate wasn't in the mood. Her father had gone behind her back. She could already imagine the unapologetic look on Deacon's face when she eventually confronted him about it.

"Listen, don't be mad at your father," Greg added. "He's worried about you and—" he put the silver case he'd been carrying on the table and gave it a pat "—I don't blame him."

Despite the subtle warning, Kate couldn't help but grin.

"You actually got it," she almost yelled in excitement. Suddenly the anxiety of the last twenty-four hours disappeared. "I was worried it wouldn't be ready in time!"

Greg smiled.

"You may not be able to use it, but I think it will help to have at least one physical example of the work you've been doing. Seeing is believing and all of that." He pulled the case off the table and set it on the ground beside him. Jonathan looked between the two without saying a thing. If it had been Kate, she would have questioned the exchange, but she had a feeling Jonathan was staying professional. He was there to guard her, not nose into her business. Again, something she definitely would have been doing if the shoe had been on the other foot.

"Well, thank you," she said. "Hopefully this will get people's attention."

Greg sobered slightly.

"I hope so." He turned to Jonathan and gave him a sly smile. "Speaking of hope, I hope this one here hasn't made your life too difficult. I know she can be a handful."

Jonathan laughed.

"She's not the most difficult client I've had," he answered. "She's not the easiest, either."

Greg gave a hoot of laughter.

"I'm right here, you know," Kate pointed out. Jonathan cut her a quick smirk. It jump-started parts of her she hadn't realized needed jump-starting. Once again, warmth started to spread up her chest and neck. She hid behind her coffee, taking a big swig. Had he been this attractive when they'd first met? Or had she been too distracted by her disgruntled attitude to really feel it?

"That's a very politically correct way to phrase it," Greg said. His expression softened. "Cassandra was the same way. She liked to say she was just spirited. Kathryn here definitely could fall into the same category." Kate lowered her cup. Her mother's name impacted her in two ways every time she was mentioned. She remembered the woman who had loved her and whom she had loved back. Cassandra's inspiring compassion and untouchable determination had left a lasting mark on her only daughter. Kate felt the same love she'd felt all those years ago every time the woman was brought up. Yet, at the same token, she also felt the emptiness her death had left behind. A blank space that should have been filled with memories of growing up with her. Memories that should have included school dances and birthday parties, teenage love problems that only moms knew how to fix, graduations and celebrations, quiet nights spent watching TV together, oblivious to the pain that would be felt if all of it were to be taken away.

Greg reached forward and patted the top of Kate's hand. He wasn't a stranger to the pain that Cassandra Spears's death had brought. Jonathan once again remained quiet, obviously trying to respect the turn in conversation. He searched her face, though, as if there was something in her eyes that could lead him to the answer. In the moment, she felt an odd sense of obligation to him.

"Greg used to work with my mother when she needed some scientific expertise for her job. He became a family friend," she explained after clearing her throat. "When he found out about my research, he reached out and helped me connect with my current lab and secure start-up funding. He's had an integral part in how I got to where I am now."

"Sounds like a good man to have on your side," Jonathan observed. Kate nodded.

"One of the best!"

Greg put his hands up, smiling.

"And here I thought I was just coming to deliver a package, not have my praises sung among the smell of roasting coffee beans and budding writers working on their screenplays." They glanced over to a younger man with bright blue hair, head bent over his laptop and two empty coffee cups next to him. Kate couldn't help but laugh.

"So, is what you do as secretive as what Kate does?" Jonathan asked. Apparently he could curb his curiosity for only so long.

"Not particularly," Greg said with a grin. "I used to be an adjunct professor at Harvard—science was my game—when I decided I'd like a change of pace. I'm a business consultant now, with an unperturbed affinity for scientific pursuits on the side. That's to say, I dabble in lab work here and there, and am occasionally hired as an adviser on more complicated projects." Greg shrugged. "Mostly boring work, I'm sure, especially compared to the life of a bodyguard."

Jonathan cracked a smile.

"It has its moments. The travel is great and the people I've met have been—" he gave Kate a pointed glance "—interesting."

"I'd imagine so! It sounds like a dream job for some."

Jonathan's smile at talking about his job—one he seemed to hold very dear—lost some of its mirth. The corners dropped slightly.

"It used to be mine," he admitted. "But, actually, this is my last field contract."

That caught Kate off guard.

"You're leaving Orion?"

Jonathan shook his head.

"I'm not leaving Orion unless Nikki Waters tells me to," he said with a laugh. "Until then she's agreed to help find me a job at the office. One where I'm not constantly traveling."

"Roots," was all Greg said, as if all of his wisdom leaked into the one syllable. Jonathan nodded. The two men shared a look of what Kate believed to be understanding. She, however, hadn't yet caught the meaning behind it. If Jonathan loved his job so much, why give it up for a glorified desk job?

"So does that mean you have someone back home you'd like to grow those roots with?" Kate's idea about questioning why a seemingly driven man like Jonathan would give up fieldwork came to a screeching halt. Since she'd met the bodyguard, she hadn't once asked him about or even pondered his relationship status. She hadn't seen a ring on his finger and had assumed he wasn't married, but beyond that she'd not thought about it. Not even when realizing how attracted to him she was.

Jonathan's weakening smile found a dose of strength. It grew alongside a sinking, cold feeling of disappointment in Kate. Why?

Why did it matter if he had someone back home? He was her bodyguard, nothing more.

"Sadly, no. Aside from friends, it's only my roots that will be growing." The cold in Kate's stomach found a spot to settle. Greg's eyes swept her expression and once again she hid behind her coffee cup.

"I'm sure you'll find someone to share your life with," Greg said. Then, with another loud hoot of laughter he added, "And if not, you could always get a dog."

Both men burst into a fit of laughter. One Kate found herself joining in on. She'd been unsure of how this meeting would go. Greg was and always had been a nice man. However, like her, there were moments when he'd become clipped and detached, his thoughts trailing back to whatever project he was currently on. Kate was glad Jonathan was able to meet the carefree and personable Greg Calhoun. For some reason, she found she wanted the bodyguard to like him. And vice versa.

"Well, Kathryn, it's only fair I reiterate the same question to you," Greg said once their laughter had died off. "I know we talk a lot, but it's been a while since the topic centered on anything other than work. Are you still dating that man? What's his name?"

Kate felt her cheeks heat. She cast a quick look at Jonathan, who seemed to be paying rapt attention. His dark blue eyes were honed in on her face. She guessed she wasn't the only one who had been in the dark about the other's romantic attachments.

"If you mean Caleb, and I'm pretty sure you do, then no," she admitted. "We didn't make it past year two of the project." Three years later and she hadn't dated, let alone been interested in, anyone since. Though she thought she had filled Greg in on the matter since then, she wasn't surprised she hadn't. When they spoke on the phone it was all about research and data and theories. Not their love lives. She shrugged before either man could comment. "More time to work, if you ask me."

Greg reached out and patted her hand against the coffee cup again, mouth opening to say something she'd bet would be profound, when Jonathan spoke up instead.

"You know what they say about all work and no play." Kate's breath caught just as Jonathan gave her a wink. For a moment all she could do was stare.

"I like you, Jonathan," Greg said. "Which is another reason I hate to say I need to leave." He started to stand and Kate and Jonathan followed suit. "I'm currently working on a project that requires my close attention."

"Well, thank you for coming to meet me," Kate said,

reaching down for the silver case. "And thank you for working on this."

The three of them walked out to the sidewalk, the morning light making Kate squint as her eyes adjusted. The case was hardly heavy in her hands. Her mind had already begun to form a mental picture of what it looked like. While she'd more or less created it, she'd never seen it take a physical form.

"It was nice to meet you, Jonathan," Greg said, pausing for a handshake. "I wish you luck with growing roots, and also for keeping up with this one."

"She's spirited," Jonathan said.

Greg laughed.

"Bingo." He turned to Kate and enveloped her in a quick hug. "Your mother would be so proud of you," he whispered in her ear. "As am I."

"Thank you," she said, a different kind of warmth spreading through her. "That means a lot."

They parted and he gave her one last pat on the hand.

"Let me know if you need anything, and good luck with the convention." He gave a small nod to Jonathan, who returned it, and then started to cross the wide crosswalk toward a parking garage. Jonathan began to turn in the direction of the hotel when Kate remembered a question she needed to ask.

"Wait, I have to ask him for the code on this thing," she said, motioning to the case. Greg was already halfway across the street, surrounded by pedestrians. The Walk sign was still white.

"Greg," Kate called as she and Jonathan hit the crosswalk. He heard them and turned, pausing his stride.

Even though he didn't know why she'd called him, there was a smile pulling up his lips.

It was bright and happy and genuine.

Then the screaming started.

Chapter Ten

The car lurched forward without any indication that it was going to stop. Not even as the front bumper connected with a man and woman midstep. They didn't have time to scream as they were run over, but the pedestrians around them didn't let that stop them from yelling in terror.

The car, a few feet to their right, was merely slowed by the people it had hit. Jonathan tried to look into the driver's side through the windshield but didn't have time to focus on the face behind the wheel. The sound of a revving engine mixed with the screaming around him.

Like the fight between him and the thug during his last contract protecting Martin, Jonathan would later realize what happened next might have gone a completely different way. If he hadn't moved slightly ahead of Kate, right in between her and Greg, he never would have had enough time to pull her out of the way. As it was, he was lucky. He pivoted and slung his body into hers. His height and muscle—and her sheer surprise—knocked the two of them out of the way just as the car continued through the crosswalk.

Arm over Kate's chest, they hit the asphalt hard. Pain burst in his side and elbow as they took the brunt of his fall, but Kate wasn't as lucky. Amid the cries around them, he was able to hear Kate's own cry of pain as her head whipped back against the road.

"Are you okay?" Jonathan yelled out, already scrambling to stand. Lying in a crosswalk while people were getting run over wasn't something he wanted them to do. Kate shut her eyes tight with another cry of pain. Her hand flew to the back of her head, and when she pulled it away it was bloody. He turned as another wave of screaming intensified. The car's back bumper was only a few inches away. They'd just missed being run over. "Kate?" he asked, turning his attention back to her, wanting to get her away from the carnage.

"My head," she said, reaching out to take his hand. He got her to her feet, barely steadying her before she yelled again.

This time it wasn't in pain.

"Greg!" Kate rocketed around Jonathan, stumbling once before making it to the man. He lay crumpled on the asphalt, unmoving and bloodied. Jonathan hurried over just as Kate dropped to her knees beside the man's head.

The car that had inflicted the damage had finally stopped, ramming into a parked car waiting for the light to change. It was immediately swarmed by angry bystanders while others were seeing to those who had been hit. From a glance around him, Jonathan counted five people lying on the ground.

Kate grabbed Greg's wrist, checking for a pulse. A woman who had missed the car's path through the crosswalk caught Jonathan's attention.

"He didn't go under. He bounced off the side."

Jonathan knew that was good. Better than being run over and crushed. But the way Kate's entire body fell as she fished for the man's pulse made him believe maybe that one saving grace hadn't been enough.

"No, no, no, no, no," she whispered in quick procession. "Please, Greg, please!"

Jonathan was about to kneel to check the man out when a yell grabbed his attention.

"She's running!"

He turned to watch as the driver got out of the car and punched the first person next to her door. She threw another few hits to get the people around her to step back long enough to make a break for the sidewalk. It was then that he got a good look at her.

It was the woman who had been following them the day before, arm bandaged and expression determined.

Jonathan half expected the man who had left the letter to get out of the passenger side to join her, but the door never opened.

"It's her," Jonathan yelled to Kate, rage building in his system. Surely it was no coincidence she of all people had driven a car that nearly killed them.

No, it couldn't be a coincidence.

Kate looked up to see what he meant and realization washed over her face. That was all Jonathan needed to get ready to chase down the woman. She was a deadly threat. One who could answer a lot of their questions.

"Don't leave me!"

Every muscle that had been ready to spring to action hardened. Jonathan turned back to Kate. She held Greg's hand in hers while the other rested under the side of his face against the asphalt. She wasn't crying, but the way her beautiful dark eyes reached out to him let him know that she was close. "Please, stay with me."

It was in that moment that he knew there was no other place he wanted to be.

He pulled out his phone and took a picture of the driver booking it away from the crime scene. A few bystanders were giving chase while he spotted a couple of drivers who had been waiting in line doing the same thing he was doing, taking quick pictures that would hopefully lead to an arrest once she was caught. With this many people eager to find her, Jonathan doubted her escape would be easy.

"It was the woman who followed us yesterday," Kate said as Jonathan crouched next to her. He nodded and watched as anger flashed across her face. When she looked down at Greg, it seemed to dissolve a bit. "He's breathing. I'm afraid to move him, though."

On a reflex he didn't know he had, Jonathan put his hand against her cheek, cradling it softly. Slowly she dragged her dark eyes up to his. The smile that graced her lips for only a second was small.

And then it was gone.

"It'll be okay," he said. "I promise."

Sirens could be heard in the distance. The crying and yelling still sounded around them. The woman and those chasing her were out of sight. Someone had turned off the car, but its exhaust created a nauseating smell in the air. Jonathan kept looking into Kate's eyes as she held a man she cared about deeply, praying he'd be okay.

For the first time since the accident, he realized the silver case hadn't left Kate's side. She'd kept it with her through it all.

What was in it?

And why was it worth killing for?

THE POLICE ARRIVED FIRST, then the ambulances. Jonathan, along with two others who had witnessed the entire thing, gave their statements first while EMTs rounded up those who were badly hurt.

Kate didn't leave Greg's side until the EMTs came for him. She quickly recalled his medical history and her fear that he had internal bleeding as they wheeled him to the vehicle. When they asked if she'd be riding with him, however, she said no.

"I've already called a close friend of his," she said. "He'll make it to the hospital before you will."

Kate clutched the silver case while she watched the ambulance take off. Jonathan was shocked she had declined riding with him, but before he could ask her reasoning, an EMT caught her attention.

"Miss, you're bleeding." The young man motioned to the back of Kate's head. It prompted her to look down at her hand, where the blood from a little while ago had dried.

"It's just a superficial wound from hitting the asphalt," she said, dismissively. The EMT wasn't having any of it.

"Can I have a look?"

"It's fine."

The EMT smirked.

"Then you won't mind me having a quick look if it's no problem."

Jonathan couldn't help but mimic the man's smile. He got her there.

"Fine," she huffed. "Let's get this over with."

They followed the EMT back to an empty ambulance, where Kate perched on the lip of the vehicle. Jonathan was able to get a good look at her as she waited while the man did a quick examination.

The white blouse she wore was covered in dirt and grime, as were her navy dress pants. He even spied a tiny hole in the knee of one leg where she'd been resting on the ground next to Greg. Along with the blood on the back of her head, there was a patch of rubbed-off skin on her elbow where she'd hit the ground trying to get away from the car. Her hair was ruffled while her bangs had a gap in them where she'd rubbed her forehead due to the stress of everything. Her cheeks were tinted and her lips were still red, but her eyes had changed. While they had been playful during their talk with Greg in the coffee shop, now they were sharp. And angry. Not at the EMT poking at her head or Jonathan for hovering, but at the cause of what had happened.

The woman who had driven the car.

The man who left the bloody letter.

The same two he had suspected of following them the day before.

"Ow," Kate exclaimed, turning back at the EMT. "Watch it," she warned. Okay, so maybe she did have some anger for the man.

"Sorry," he muttered. "The cut isn't that bad back here. You don't need stitches, but it will be sore for a while. And, I'll state the obvious, you probably have a concussion and should go to the hospital to get it checked out."

The EMT stood back and swept his hand out to show he meant she should ride with him to the hospital. Kate didn't care. She got down and flashed him an apologetic smile.

"I'll be fine," she insisted. "Thanks for the concern."

The EMT looked to Jonathan.

"Are you sure, Kate?" he asked.

Kate nodded.

"When I was in college, I got into a car accident and had a bad concussion." She pointed to her head. "While

I have a headache, this isn't bad. I just want to go back to the hotel now."

Jonathan wanted to push more, but he couldn't make her go to the ER. He looked back to the EMT.

"Sorry, man, but thanks for checking her out."

The young man shrugged and went back out into the still-lingering crowd. Jonathan and Kate finally made it back to the sidewalk in front of the coffee shop. As they started their trek back, a coroner's van split the crowd in the street.

They paused in a moment of silence.

"This shouldn't have happened," Kate whispered when they started walking again. Jonathan kept his body between hers and the street. She kept the case between the two of them. He wondered if she'd let it go even once since leaving the coffee shop. "I just don't understand," she added. "I mean, if that's the same woman, then surely this all can't be a coincidence. Did you tell the cops about her and the man from the hotel?"

Jonathan nodded.

"He said, as of right then, they believed it to be an accident and the driver fled because she was either under the influence of something illegal or sheer fear and embarrassment of losing control of the car. But he would take down what I had to say and look into it." Jonathan was hiding his frustration. No matter how immense it was. Kate had already been through enough. He didn't need to escalate her nerves by adding his own. Still, she reacted badly to the news.

"An accident?" she squawked, attracting attention from the people walking around them. She didn't lower her voice. "She had an entire intersection to hit the brakes. Heck, after she killed those first two people by *running them over*, she could have put her foot on the brake pedal. No, what she did, she did on purpose. Greg is on his way to the hospital because that woman knew exactly what she was doing." Her free hand had fisted and her breathing had quickened. The passion she had exhibited when talking about the convention that morning was back. With a healthy dose of anger mixed in. She shook the case in her hand. "This is supposed to save people, not hurt them."

They were a block from the hotel. Jonathan looked away from Kate and kept his eyes peeled for any suspicious activity. He didn't comment on what she said until they finally made it to the hotel's elevator. When it closed them in, he turned and asked a question he'd been wanting to ask for a while.

"Normally Orion agents don't have to get too specific on client details," he started. "We give you the privacy you deserve. That is, until whatever information you're withholding puts you in danger. I'm not saying that woman was targeting you, or trying to scare you, or if she was desperate to get her hands on that silver case. However, if any of that is true, then I have to ask you one question." Jonathan grabbed her chin in his hand and tilted her eyes up until they were locked with his. "Kate, what's in the case?"

Chapter Eleven

The elevator beeped at their floor before Kate let out a breath. Jonathan held her face in his hand, but it was his eyes that once again had all of her attention. The fact that she could see every swirl of blue, a dark pond as still and beautiful as a painting, only highlighted the realization that the bodyguard was less than a few inches away from her lips.

Did he feel the urge to kiss her?

Did *she* feel the urge to kiss *him*?

No, Kate, she thought. *He wants to know what's in the case, that's all.*

"You saved my life, Jonathan," she stated, hedging around a response. "Thank you."

The bodyguard didn't want to relent—she could tell by the way he stayed still, not budging physically—but then the elevator doors started to close again. He stuck his hand out to stop them, turning away from her and letting her face go in the process. She felt the warmth of his skin even after the contact was broken.

"Are you sure you're okay?" Jonathan asked as they walked toward their doors. She was thankful he'd dropped his earlier question but knew it was a matter of time before he'd ask again. If she was him, she would have kept nagging. Then again, Jonathan didn't seem like the type of person who nagged. "Yes, just a headache." She got her key card out and paused. "I didn't want to take this into the hospital," she said, motioning to the case in her hand. "But I would like to go there to check on Greg. Even though it's also not on the itinerary."

Jonathan's expression softened.

"That's no problem. I'd like to check on him, too."

Kate smiled a genuine smile at the man tasked with protecting her.

"Let me rinse off and then we can go."

They parted ways. Kate threw the top latch when her door was shut and took a moment to stare at it.

You aren't in any danger, she remembered thinking the day before. Thinking Jonathan's overprotectiveness had led to paranoia that had started to leak into her.

It's just in his head.

But now, could she claim the same?

The sound the car had made as it slammed into the first man and woman replayed in her head. She would have stayed frozen to the spot, terrified and unable to move, and been hit head-on had Jonathan not acted quickly. Sure, she'd hit her head in the process, but he'd saved her life by getting her out of the car's path. In that moment he'd truly done his job as bodyguard.

Greg's motionless body, crumpled against the asphalt, slid into her mind. The terror and anguish she'd first felt at seeing him started to grow within her again.

Had the woman really done that to him—to the rest of those walking over the crosswalk—because of Kate?

Her thoughts turned rapid, firing off in quick succession as she went through her interactions with her mentor in the last two decades. They went back as far as to include her mother in some.

I can't be the reason why he's hurt, she thought, moving back from the door like it had suddenly caught fire. *I just can't be.*

She turned her thoughts to the case in her hand and decided to slide it under the bed. Right then she needed to rinse the dirt and blood off her and head to the hospital. Until that morning she hadn't even known if she would get Greg's gift before the convention. She could wait another few hours before opening it.

A sigh escaped her lips as she stepped into the hot shower a minute later. Its temperature was instantly welcomed as each stream began to unknot the tension in her body. Trying to forget about how five years of her life were now being outshone by the last twenty-four hours in New York City was difficult to comprehend. Able to sidestep the violent, life-threatening parts, her thoughts turned to the man next door.

She ran her hands up and over her face, comparing Jonathan to herself. Before their talk with Greg she'd believed him to be as single-minded as she was about his work. But then he'd admitted he wanted roots.

Roots. Family. Love.

Could she claim the same? For the last five years and, to some extent, before she'd even begun her research, her life had revolved around the pursuit to save others from dealing with the same tragedy she had. She'd kissed, liked, dated and even shared her bed with a few suitors, but none of them had had staying power. They'd mistaken her unyielding determination for obsession instead of passion.

Kate paused to watch some of her blood swirl down the drain.

Had she blurred the line between the two?

Had her dream to prevent the senseless loss of life had the exact opposite effect on hers?

Pain exploded, hot and electric, on the back of her neck. Kate slapped at it, but by the time her hand touched the spot, the pain was gone. Confused, she ran her finger across the skin. The shock of pain didn't come back, but she realized there was a dull soreness radiating downward.

"What the—"

Kneading the skin around the source of the pain, she ran across a patch of skin that was raised. The dull soreness began to burn as it made its way down her body.

"Oh, my God."

Her thoughts began to race, her heart rate accelerating. She knew what this was. What solace or calm she'd tried to get from the hot shower definitely wasn't going to be obtained anymore. Turning off the water on reflex alone, she stumbled out of the shower and tried to take a breath.

It came out easily enough. Perhaps too easily. It turned into an extended yawn. Though the shower had woken her up considerably, Kate found her eyelids were growing heavy.

Too heavy.

Too fast.

Concern and confusion turned to fear as the feeling of wariness intensified.

Kate fumbled for a towel but missed it altogether. Her mind was trying to work overtime to make a plan of action while a haze was growing rapidly around her. She fumbled for her phone next to the sink. One thought was still bright enough to see among the enclosing fog. She quickly cycled through the names in her contacts before landing on one.

Quickly her fingers flew across the tiny keyboard while her vision began to blur. Her fear doubled, but it was just a thought. One her body wasn't responding to anymore. She hit Send, but her vision was spotting. She couldn't see if she'd hit the right button.

That worry alone propelled her out of the bathroom and to the adjoining door between her room and Jonathan's. She hoped the text had gone through. The way she was struggling to keep her eyes open made her doubt she'd have enough time to tell him what he needed to know.

The card to open the door was still on the TV stand. Kate dragged her palm against its top, trying to grab it. She was able to curl her fingers around the plastic, but when she turned back to the door, her legs buckled beneath her. The card fell along with her body until she was on all fours, struggling to manage a last-ditch knock.

However, the weight of unconsciousness was too much. It crushed her before she could even try to think of another plan.

And then Kate was naked, wet and alone.

"WHAT?"

Jonathan looked at his phone with his head cocked to the side and eyebrow raised. He hadn't expected and didn't understand the text on his phone from Kate.

Call jake not 922!!!

Jake? Nine hundred and twenty-two?

"What?" he asked the room again. His eyes traveled to the wall that separated their rooms just as his brain made sense of the random text. *Nine-one-one!*

Jonathan's body went on alert. He went to the adjoining door and knocked.

"Kate?"

He didn't hesitate.

Grabbing the key card, he unlocked the door and pushed it outward, but something kept it from swinging all the way open. He moved around the door and looked down to see what was blocking it. The scene he was met with was just as confusing as the text had been.

"Kate!"

She was lying on her side, slumped over on the ground, the door hitting her right shoulder. Her hand was out but empty, the card for the door discarded next to it. Like she had been trying to get to him but couldn't. Not only was she unconscious, she was also naked.

Jonathan didn't immediately check her. He had his fists up, ready to attack the man or woman who was behind her current state of distress. There was no one in the main room or bathroom. All he found was a bathroom filled with steam and a wet, naked woman against the carpet.

Then what had happened? Had her head injury caused this? But what was this?

"Kate," he said, urgency clear in his voice. Its tone or volume didn't stir the woman. Jonathan dropped to his knee and inspected her closer.

She had a pulse. It beat to a rhythm that wasn't strong but also wasn't weak. It thumped against his fingers on her neck with a steady beat that inspired an outpouring of relief on his end. He moved his attention to her chest, mindful not to focus on the more intimate parts, to find her breath pushing her body up and down with no apparent difficulty. Jonathan's eyes traveled the rest of her body, once again not with a focus that crossed the line between bodyguard and client, and couldn't find any identifying marks that suggested she'd been physically attacked.

"Kate?" he asked again. Moving her hair across her cheek and away from her face, Jonathan saw a woman who looked almost peaceful.

Jonathan started to grab his phone—clearly Kate wasn't waking up—when he remembered the text.

Call jake not 922!!!

He had no doubt in his mind that she'd meant to say, "Nine-one-one," which meant she'd known something was about to happen to her. But why not call the one service you were supposed to call in a situation like this?

He cast a quick glance at the still brunette. He also had no doubt that the woman was smart, brilliant even. So it was no stretch of the imagination that Kathryn Spears knew more than he did about her current condition.

Jonathan just hoped this Jake person did, too.

Kate's phone was on the bathroom sink, still on the screen with the text she'd sent. Under different circumstances, he would have either been annoyed or amused to find his contact listed under the name *Mr. Bodyguard*. Instead he didn't have time to dawdle. He scrolled through her contacts to the one and only Jake. He hit Call without hesitating.

It rang twice.

"Kate?" a man answered, sounding surprised. "Can I call you back in two seconds?" A flurry of voices sounded on his end.

"This isn't Kate, and we need to talk *now*."

Jonathan might not have known anything about the

man, but he could tell what had been surprise at getting
Kate's call had tripled. With added aggression.

"Who is this? Where is Kate?" the man asked, au-
dibly moving away from the voices in the background.

"My name is Jonathan Carmichael, I'm—"

"The bodyguard?"

That gave Jonathan pause.

"Yes," he admitted.

"What's wrong with Kate?" While Jake had been
ready to go on the offensive with Jonathan, his tone
had changed to one of acute concern. A whiplash effect that spoke volumes about him. Whoever the man
was, he cared about Kate.

"Honestly, I don't know," Jonathan answered. "She
sent me a text that said to call you and not nine-one-
one. Less than a minute later I found her passed out on
her hotel room floor." Jonathan didn't know why, but
he left out the part about her being naked. Whether it
was a weird jealousy he felt or a wild notion that he was
somehow protecting her virtue, he had no idea. "She's
breathing fine and has a normal pulse, but she's unresponsive. Less than an hour ago she got a concussion
but said she knew it was fine."

The sound of a beep, maybe an elevator, Jonathan
thought, popped in the background. Wherever Jake was,
he was moving.

"No. If Kate said to call me and not an ambulance,
then I can guarantee you she didn't pass out from a
concussion. Have you called or told anyone about her?"
he asked.

"No," Jonathan admitted, wondering for a second if
he *had* made a mistake by calling Jake. "But since telling me to only call you was probably the last thing she

did before she lost consciousness, I figured that was the best route to take."

"Good, that's good." Another faint beep traveled through the connection. "Has anyone come into contact with her in the last half hour?"

"Like I said, she was in an accident where she hit her head against the road."

"No, I mean, did anyone have physical, skin-to-skin contact with her?" Jake's frustration put Jonathan on edge. Instead of combating the feeling and the man it came from, it made him focus on the question.

"Aside from me and an unconscious work associate of hers, no." Then he remembered something. "Actually, an EMT checked her head in the back of an ambulance. Less than a half hour ago." As he said it, Jonathan knelt back down beside Kate. He put the cell phone between his shoulder and cheek to free up his hands. Gingerly, he ran his hands over the back of her hair, trying to find the wound. He found it and the dried blood over it.

"Check the back of her neck for any raised skin or mark," Jake rushed to say.

"Already ahead of you," Jonathan muttered, running his fingers down from the wound to the skin of her neck. Kate's skin was warm, wet and soft. "Wait." Jonathan paused as his finger ran over a small bump on the back of her neck. He moved her hair out of the way and leaned closer, narrowing his eyes at the raised skin. "There's a bump in the middle of her neck. It isn't red or pink. I would have missed it had I not been feeling for it. There's also a tiny hole in the middle of it." Jonathan looked back into the bathroom. Aside from her clothes, there was nothing out of the ordinary as far as he could tell. "Did she do that to herself?"

"If she did, she's crazier than I thought," Jake said.

"No, I think that EMT wasn't your run-of-the-mill paramedic."

"What?" Jonathan felt his muscles tense again. Getting warm, ready to attack. "Why would he do that?"

He looked down at Kate's relaxed face.

"I can only make a few guesses, and that would take up time we don't have." The warning behind Jake's words amplified the urgency Jonathan had carried moments before. "Text me the hotel address and room number. I need to make some calls on the way over there."

Jonathan's instinct to protect the privacy of his client flared to life.

"What's going on? Is she going to be okay?"

"No. Not if you play hardball with me," he spit out. "If you make me go through the trouble of tracing this call, we're going to lose minutes that could save her."

"Listen, buddy, I don't even know who you are," Jonathan pointed out.

Jake let out an aggravated sigh of frustration, barely dimmed by the sound of a car door shutting.

"You don't know me, but Kate does," he said. "She wanted you to call me and not the authorities because I know why she's in New York. I can't imagine she even told you that last part, did she?"

"The convention—" Jonathan started. The man was quick to interrupt.

"Is only the tip of the iceberg."

Chapter Twelve

Jonathan carefully picked up Kate's naked body and moved her to the bed. In any other situation, that alone would have been exhilarating in its own right. Taking a beautiful woman to bed without a stitch of clothing on her body would be followed by him joining her, also sans clothes.

However, Jonathan wasn't aroused in the least.

Instead, he was close to overwhelmed with concern.

"Don't worry, Kate," Jonathan whispered as he pulled the sheets and blanket up to her shoulders. "I'm going to fix this. Whatever this is."

Kate remained as unresponsive as she had been when he'd first found her. A fleeting thought that he should dress her crossed his mind, but he batted it away, afraid that jostling her too much might worsen her condition.

Not that he knew what her condition was, except that someone had injected her with something that had left her unconscious.

He looked once again at her relaxed face—peaceful—and was bowled over by how beautiful she was. The concern he felt for her future ran deep. How had a woman he'd only known for two days gotten so far beneath his skin? Was that even possible?

He watched as the sheets moved up and down as she breathed softly.

Yes, somehow it was possible.

Jonathan didn't leave her side until a knock sounded on the door to his room. He gave her one more quick look before going through the adjoining room—shutting the door behind him—and heading to answer the knock. His body was tense, like a snake readying to strike at the first sign of a threat. He peered through the peephole to see a man standing by himself.

Jonathan pushed aside the lingering fear that he had made a huge mistake in listening to Kate's text and opened the door.

Jonathan placed Jake around the same age as him. He was shorter, around six feet, but lean just like him. Jonathan bet the black blazer that matched his slacks hid toned muscles that worked in tandem with a trained posture. Beneath the blazer was a white button-up and a black-and-dark-blue-striped tie. The outfit was finished off with dress shoes that almost reflected the hallway lights. His hair was also neat, dark blond and cropped short, while his face was cleanly shaven. Even his eyes, a pale blue, seemed to be proper. Jonathan would bet money this guy was some type of law enforcement. Then again, that didn't mean Jonathan trusted him any more in the moment.

"Where is she?" the man greeted, body already angling like he had been invited inside. Even though he didn't introduce himself, his voice matched the one on the phone. But Jonathan had to be sure he could trust him before allowing him anywhere near Kate.

"How do I even know if you're here to help?" Jonathan asked, voice as cold as steel.

The man didn't hide his frustration. It turned his expression into a scowl.

"You don't," he admitted. "But I swear to you if Kate dies while you're out here trying to be a good bodyguard, then wouldn't that be a kick in the professional ass?"

There was no humor in his words, just sincerity.

It was that sureness that made Jonathan turn around, key card already in hand for the adjoining door.

"If you do *anything* I think is hurting her, I'll kill you," Jonathan growled.

The man followed him into the room.

"I thought bodyguards protected, not killed."

"I'd make the exception for her."

Jake didn't respond as they moved to the other room.

"I moved her off the floor," Jonathan said, pointing out the obvious just in case it affected whatever magic Jake was supposed to generate to fix the situation. "She had just gotten out of the shower."

Jake went over to Kate so fast that Jonathan fisted his hands. He kept the man's pace and watched as he bent over her.

"Careful," Jonathan warned. Jake didn't pause in his actions. He turned her head carefully to the side to look at the mark on her neck himself. It lasted less than a second.

"This paramedic looked her over after the car ran Greg down?" he asked, attention falling away from Kate.

"Yes," Jonathan answered, surprised. "How did you know about the accident?"

Jake pointed his thumb back at Kate.

"She called me after it happened." Jonathan connected the dots. So Jake had been the close friend Kate had called to go to the hospital when she couldn't. That eased some of Jonathan's suspicion of the man. But only some. "I'm working on a project with Greg here in New York," he added, as if that explained anything, but Jonathan was only concerned about one thing.

"So what's wrong with Kate?"

For the first time since the man had walked through the door, he looked Jonathan straight in the eyes.

"How seriously do you take your job as her bodyguard?"

Jonathan squared his shoulders.

"Very."

"Then we need to leave *now*." Jake was already walking away, head lowered in an obvious show of determination. But, once again, nothing was being explained.

"Wait, leave?"

Jake turned quick, angry.

"Listen here—" he started, but Jonathan had had enough. He pushed the man until his back slammed into the wall. He didn't stop there, lifting him slightly by the collar of his shirt.

"No, you listen here," Jonathan fumed. "I don't know you, I don't even know your last name and I don't know where it is you expect me to go. But I'll tell you right now, I'm not one of those people who run on pure faith alone. I need some answers."

Jonathan's adrenaline was pumping through his veins. He could have done some serious damage to the man—shown him exactly how physical suspicion could be—but Jonathan was letting one fact and one fact alone hold his anger back.

Kate had asked him to call the man.

Jake appeared to be wrangling his own knee-jerk

reactions. When he spoke there was a sharp edge to his words.

"My name is Jake Harper and I'm a federal agent. My badge is in my blazer pocket, right side," he explained. Jonathan lowered the man back to the ground and motioned for him to show said badge. He pulled out the black flip wallet and, just as he said, Jake Harper, FBI, was on it. "I've known Kate since she was eight, and I've worked with Greg for the last five years."

"You know what she was injected with," Jonathan stated.

Jake nodded.

"I wouldn't have, had she gone to the hospital, but if she truly asked you to call me instead, then she must know I can help. And there's only one thing I would even guess could make her drop like that." He put his badge back into his pocket. Jonathan caught a glimpse of the holstered gun beneath his jacket. "If I'm right, and there's a good chance I am, then we need to give her another specific injection from Greg's lab."

"And if we don't?" Jonathan was almost afraid to ask.

"Then she dies." Jake didn't pause to let that sink in. "So, bodyguard, you said you were willing to kill for her. Now the question is, are you willing to help steal for her?"

It was raining.

The pitter-patter of drops hitting the tin roof was an ocean of sound around her, filling the tiny bedroom with comforting white noise. The soft glow of her bedside lamp projected hundreds of tiny stars on the ceiling. She looked up at them from where she'd fallen asleep on the rug and drew a line in the air connecting a cluster, creating Orion's belt with ease. She'd never been able to spot the constellation before, but now she was sure of how its placement looked. It made her happy, though she couldn't figure out why.

The rain got harder and tore her attention away. She heard a distant slam followed by voices. Quickly, she jumped up and crawled into bed. She wasn't supposed to be awake.

The rain got even harder and the stars went out, bathing everything in darkness. Something was wrong. Fear twisted around her heart at the sound of footsteps in the hallway. They weren't heavy like a man's, but softer. Excitement banished all fear. The star lights flashed back on and even the rain quieted as the door to the bedroom cracked open. A woman's face appeared in the space, searching for her.

"Kate, aren't you supposed to be asleep?"

Kate giggled.

"Mom, I was waiting for you," she said matter-of-factly. "You were gone for a long time!"

Cassandra opened the door wide, already kicking off her boots and throwing her jacket to the floor. She came up to the bed and said, "Scoot!"

Kate did as she was told and soon they were both squeezed into the twin-size bed. Kate didn't mind one bit.

"I told you not to wait up for me," Cassandra said, putting her arm around Kate and smooshing her into her side. "You have your first day of third grade tomorrow. You're going to be tired." Cassandra tickled her side a few times until Kate laughed.

The sound became so loud it blocked out all other noises. The stars flickered. A wave of cold wrapped around Kate.

"Don't be scared," Cassandra whispered.

And then everything felt right in the room.

"I'm not scared," Kate said, pouting. She didn't want her mother to think she wasn't strong. She slid her hand down to the badge on her belt and ran her finger over the gold. She'd always loved tracing the three letters with her fingertips.

Cassandra kissed the top of Kate's head.

"Just because someone's scared doesn't mean they aren't strong."

Kate felt her cheeks heat, embarrassed that she'd had to be taught a lesson and hadn't learned it on her own.

"Jake says *he's* not afraid of anything, because his dad gave him a badge like his to carry around," Kate said. Cassandra laughed, but the sound was off. Like being underwater. Kate tilted her head up to see what the cause was. Cassandra's eyes were closed, lips turned downward like she was sleeping.

"Mom?" Kate whispered.

Cassandra didn't move.

"Is that what you want? A badge?" she asked, and though her lips still didn't move, Kate knew it was her mother asking. Her voice filled the small room like it was coming through a school intercom. She felt a finger press lightly against her temple. It was cold. "Because I believe *this* is your greatest weapon, and you should, too. You're smart and clever and the world will quake beneath your feet if you ever decide to conquer it."

The frozen Cassandra thawed in a fit of laughter. Kate joined in, liking the way the sounds harmonized.

"If I ruled the world, I'd make everyone have brownies for dinner," Kate said. "And bedtime would be whenever I wanted."

"That's my girl."

She looked up to see if her mother really did approve,

but Cassandra was gone. Kate scrambled out of bed, trying to escape the growing feeling that something terrible had happened. Something was horribly wrong. She ran through the doorway, with her parents' room in mind, when suddenly she was no longer in her house.

Where she was now smelled old and weird. Half of it Kate could process, the other half she didn't understand. It was dark, too.

Someone tugged at her hand.

She turned her head to see them.

"Kate?"

Jonathan was staring back at her, blue eyes nearly lost in the darkness around them.

"Where's Jake?" she asked, unease building into panic. "We rode our bikes here."

Jonathan didn't seem to care. Instead he looked over her head, focusing on something with interest. Kate turned and saw what caught his eye. A figure in the distance, sitting in an open room all alone.

"We shouldn't go in there," Jake's voice whispered now at her side. There was real fear in it. Fear that coursed through their hands held together. "We need to go get help."

"Just because we're scared doesn't mean we aren't strong," Kate chanted. She started forward, slowly moving closer to the person in the chair.

Kate heard Jake follow—heard his footsteps echo in the abandoned building—and felt braver. She could be strong just like her mom. She could find out who the person was. She could help them.

The closer she came, though, the farther away she ended up. The never-ending hallway became darker and darker until the old building, Jake and the person in the chair disappeared altogether.

"Don't worry, Kate," Jonathan's voice said, now the only thing around her. "I'm going to fix this."

One by one the stars on the ceiling turned back on. Kate was back in her bedroom, but this time it was different. Sitting on the rug, tears in her eyes, was a little girl dressed in black. Between her small hands was a shiny gold badge.

Jonathan's words continued to echo around the two of them. They were strong and powerful, but Kate knew they were just words.

"You can't fix this," she whispered. "No one can."

Chapter Thirteen

Jake blew through a red light, swerving around a car driving past the intersection. Jonathan gripped the handle of the passenger door. He wasn't afraid, but he couldn't deny that he was anxious. He'd just met the man ten minutes ago and now they were speeding toward an apparently secret lab for an equally secret antidote.

It was all very James Bond.

"I know you have no good reason to trust me, but I'm afraid you're going to have to," Jake reiterated. "After we get what we need and administer it to Kate, I'll let her explain everything she's willing to—she can do that better than I can, at least—and everything will make more sense."

Jonathan was starting to doubt anyone had all the answers to connect the dots that had sprung up in the last two days, but he was willing to hold out hope.

"Are you at least going to give me more info on this 'secret lab' of yours?" he asked, making finger quotes around the part that undoubtedly made it sound like he was in a spy movie. "Is it a part of the FBI?"

A car horn blared at their side as Jake did some more defensive driving. Instead of hitting the brakes, he smoothly dipped into oncoming traffic before swerv-

ing back to the original lane, passing the taxi that had
thought it a good idea to cut them off.

"Yes and no," Jake answered, unaffected by the high
speeds and subsequently more dangerous obstacles in
their way. It made Jonathan think he'd done it before.
"The lab was created and is currently funded and main-
tained by the FBI, but only a few know about it. The
facility is run by its lead scientist, Greg Calhoun."

"He said he was in business consulting now, only
dabbling in scientific pursuits," Jonathan interrupted,
paraphrasing what the man had said earlier.

Jake snorted.

"He lied," he said. "And before you get your panties
all in a twist about being lied to, you must understand
that even Kate doesn't know about his involvement with
the FBI or, for that matter, that Greg in no form or fashion lives or works in Buffalo. He's never even been to
Buffalo. Hell, she doesn't even know of my involvement with Greg."

"Which is what?"

Jake cast him a look that perfectly exhibited pride
and simultaneous defeat.

"I'm his handler." The defeat—the guilt—now
made sense. "Normally I wouldn't have been assigned
a job like this—it was given to me barely out of the
academy—but Greg said the only way he'd agree to
work with the Bureau was if he could pick who oversaw
his work and the day-to-day operations. He picked me."

"You grew up with Kate," Jonathan added, realizing
the connection. "That means you—"

"Also grew up with Greg around," Jake finished.
"That's why he chose *me*. He trusted me, and now—"
Jake cut himself off by slamming his hands against the
SUV's steering wheel. "He's in the hospital, and now

Kate?" He quieted a moment but didn't give Jonathan enough time to say anything before he spoke again. "The power went off in my building last night and killed my alarm clock. I'm not one of those people who can just wake up to the sound of their phone. I need both. Without the first, I woke up late and missed a call from Greg saying he was going to meet Kate. I was supposed to go with him. I was supposed to be there. I was supposed to protect him." Again, Jake's anger at fate, or himself, boiled over. He punched the steering wheel. Normally Jonathan would have stopped the rant. He didn't know Jake, so how could he relate to him?

But, the thing was, he absolutely could.

In a way Jake was Greg's bodyguard, just with a different title. He was responsible for keeping him safe. For protecting someone he cared about. As soon as that car had floored it through that intersection, he had failed.

Just as Jonathan had with Kate.

Empathy started to create a fondness for Jake, but that didn't mean it would last. There were still too many questions he needed answered first.

"So what does Greg have to do with what happened to Kate? And why are the injections we need in his lab?" he asked, trying to grasp *something*.

While Jake had admitted freely that there was a secret lab and he was Greg's handler, these questions made him hesitate. "Listen, if I'm about to help you *steal* from a lab operated by the *Federal Bureau of Investigation*, then you're going to tell me why."

Jake turned on his blinker seconds before taking a quick turn. Another series of car horns went off. So far the traffic hadn't been too bad, a fact that made Jonathan again realize Jake had done this before. When they were heading straight again, he let out a long breath.

"Kate has been working on the beginnings of a drug that could help law enforcement in a phenomenally big way. One that could help turn the tides on interrogation while remaining one hundred percent humane," he explained. "She brought the idea to Greg, who was an FBI consultant at the time. To his surprise, it actually seemed plausible. He pitched the idea to an FBI task force dealing with scientific pursuits. Instead of simply taking the idea for themselves, Greg convinced them that Kate's singular focus and passion for the project would benefit them more than a bunch of old scientists trying to become famous. I guess they agreed, but only in part. They let Greg find funding and contacts for her to start her research while giving Greg the same tools. He was told to oversee her work while simultaneously trying to work on it alongside her. While some believed in Greg's vote of confidence for Kate, others thought she was too young, too inexperienced, to come up with any usable end goal, especially before they could." The FBI agent cut Jonathan a quick smile. "But she did."

"She doesn't know about Greg working on the same thing then, does she?" Jake shook his head. "So what was supposed to happen when she finished?" He didn't understand how the convention fit into the picture. Jake seemed to pick up on that thread of thought.

"The convention is a somewhat private event where scientific and technological inventions and ideas are presented to potential investors to try to get more funding. It's also a way to monitor possible future security threats—shutting down could-be mad scientists," he added with a tone that said he was joking, though Jonathan was sure he wasn't. "I think the idea was to get her to the convention, have her make her case and then offer her a job. Then let her know what Greg had been up to."

"And if she didn't take the job? What was the plan then?"

"They would have continued her work and made all attempts to keep her from receiving any other funding. Until she'd have to accept." At least Jake didn't sound happy about that plan. "And before you ask, yes, she would have eventually accepted. Kate might not have gone the exact route I did, but she's always wanted to be part of the FBI. It's just in our blood."

Before Jonathan could ask what he meant by that, another flurry of questions came to mind.

"So what the hell was she injected with? The drug she created? And how did she know to call you if she didn't even know about Greg's laboratory here?"

Jake's jaw tightened.

"Kate is a very cautious person. Up until now she hasn't started testing on her finished product—that's what the next step is supposed to be. However, Greg isn't as cautious. He synthesized a version of it off her current notes and gave it to her as a present during a visit, a memento of all the work she'd done so far."

"She took it," Jonathan guessed, already picking up on his hardened body language.

"Yes. Frustration got the better of her. It was too early in the research stages and the effects were dangerous. If Greg hadn't been there to counteract them... Well, let's just say you wouldn't be in New York right now." For the first time since Jonathan had gotten into the SUV, they began to slow. "He said he'd make a few more vials just in case someone ever accidentally did it again. Being his handler, I was also there with them. I suppose that's the only reason Kate wanted you to call me."

"She knew you would put it together."

"She doesn't know that I know the location of Greg's lab, but I'm guessing she assumed, being FBI, I'd have a good chance of figuring it out."

"That would also mean that she knew she was injected with the failed drug," Jonathan said. "A failed version of *her* drug. One that was made in an FBI-sanctioned lab..."

"Which means the couple you told me about when we first got into the car had access to the lab and the failed samples Greg kept for further study."

"Or someone helped them get it."

"Let me worry about that later," Jake seethed, knuckles tightening around the steering wheel until they were white. "What we need to focus on now is stealing from a lab that isn't supposed to exist."

"Don't you have access, though?"

Jake shook his head.

"No one except Greg is allowed to take anything out of the lab. Even if I explained, they still wouldn't let me grab the injections and would most likely lock them down instead."

"So what do you need me to do?"

Jake took one last turn into a two-story parking garage. He flashed his badge at the parking attendant before he even had a chance to stand. The gate began to retract and Jake continued inside. He drove to the back corner and parked in a spot reserved for overnighters. He cut the ignition and turned, a smirk clear as day on his face.

"I need you to be a distraction."

THE RAIN DIDN'T come back.

Kate instead only heard the sound of voices floating

down the hallway to her bedroom. She didn't like the voices. They made her cold.

"Want to see it again?"

She turned to look at the boy next to her. He was playing with something in his hands.

"It's not a real badge, Jake," she answered. "It doesn't even say the right thing."

Jake didn't let her harsh words bother him. He shrugged.

"We need to get closer so I can hear," she declared.

"Kate, that isn't a good idea."

A man appeared in the corner, leaning against her dresser.

"I can't hear them," she insisted.

"You don't have to do this," he responded. He didn't blink as he spoke. The stars from her lamp now attached to his shirt.

"If I don't get closer, I won't know what they're talking about," she reasoned again, already getting up. She took Jake's hand and tugged him along after her into the hall. The voices got louder.

"If he's lying, then what?" her father asked. He sounded scared. It made her pause.

"You can go back to your room," Jonathan offered, now standing next to her. "You don't need to do this again, Kate. You can't change what happens."

Kate shook her head, trying to clear his voice out of her head.

"Deacon, they'll find them," the woman said.

A loud ringing exploded throughout the house. Kate threw her hands over her ears and tried to yell, but nothing came out.

Suddenly she was in the office. Jake had the house phone pressed against his ear, hand over the receiver.

Kate watched as he carefully hung up the phone and began to speak to someone else in the room.

It was a girl.

Both of their mouths moved, but no words came out. Kate could tell the two were excited. Afraid, but excited.

She followed them back to the girl's bedroom and watched as they opened the window.

"Don't go," Kate warned, though she couldn't remember why. Jake and the girl didn't listen and soon they were out of the window and running across the grass to their bikes.

"They're worried about their mom and dad," Jonathan said from his seat on the bed. "They're being brave."

Kate shook her head, the intensifying feeling of wrongness making her start to cry.

"They shouldn't go," she cried. "I shouldn't have gone."

Chapter Fourteen

He didn't like the plan.

Not one bit.

No matter that there was still a good chance that this was all some elaborate setup.

One giant lie that would only spell giant trouble for him.

"You ready?" Jake asked, holding the bag up.

Jonathan looked at it with annoyance.

"From what you've said, I don't think we even have time to go back over this very bad plan of yours."

Jake flipped the bag upside down.

"You're right," he said. Jake didn't hesitate putting the bag over Jonathan's head. The world instantly went dark.

Completely and utterly dark.

"Put your hands behind your back now."

Jonathan did as he was told, still in no form or fashion liking the plan. He felt a zip tie go around his wrists but, thankfully, it wasn't tightened all the way.

"Just in case," Jake said, voice lowered. "Now, let's get to walking. And remember, no talking. If we're going to keep this under wraps, I don't need you to incriminate yourself."

Jonathan snorted.

A very, very bad plan.

Jake grabbed hold of his arm and together they began to walk away from the car.

"You know, I've got to hand it to you," Jake whispered. "To go through this, the risks you're taking, you're either really dedicated to your job or Kate's made quite the impression on you."

Jonathan let those words sink in. On the one hand, he was extremely dedicated to his job. When he succeeded, despite unforeseen obstacles, Orion Security Group succeeded. Which meant Nikki, Mark, Oliver and all of their loved ones succeeded, as well. It was a trickle-down effect that he'd always strived to keep positive.

On the other hand, Kate *had* made quite the impression on him. In less than two days, she had annoyed him, frustrated him, angered him and, yet, she'd also surprised him. Her passion—her drive—was so strong it was nearly tangible. Where others, like the ex she'd mentioned, had seen it as perhaps a flaw—an obstacle to getting to know her—Jonathan saw something else. He saw love and perseverance and patience. Kate was so focused on completing something meant to save lives that she'd practically given up her own to see it get done. She'd sacrificed herself for strangers. Sure, she'd been a pain in the backside to him, but Jonathan was starting to see that a woman like Kathryn Spears was much more than her snark. She had a good heart.

And that heart needed protecting.

So, without answering the man Jonathan believed to be Kate's closest friend, he walked in darkness, ready to accept whatever consequences might come his way.

"We're about to get in an elevator that will take us to the basement," Jake whispered after they'd walked for less than a minute. "This isn't the usual way in, so we'll be seen. Don't talk."

Jonathan nodded and soon the sounds of the outside world became muffled and then disappeared. He heard a series of clicks before the motion of moving downward pulled at his stomach. Jonathan half expected to be in the elevator for much longer than it took to get between one floor and the next, envisioning a secret lab much farther down, maybe even in an abandoned subway tunnel or the sewers, but the movement stopped after one floor.

The door slid open and a wave of cold air met them. Still, the bag blocked him from seeing his surroundings. Jonathan moved his wrist around slightly, making sure he could get out of the tie if need be. It silenced some of his nerves.

They walked straight off the elevator and took a sharp left. From there they continued straight for at least thirty seconds before taking a step down. Jake's grip on his arm tightened for a moment.

Jonathan rolled back his shoulders before pulling away from Jake's grip. The agent responded by tightening his grip again before pulling Jonathan forward with obvious aggression.

"If you don't stop fighting me, I'll break your kneecaps," Jake growled loudly. Jonathan continued to fight against him, but Jake had the upper hand. He shoved him forward until Jonathan finally heard the other man.

"What's this?" the third man asked. He was farther away, and soon after he spoke, the rollers of a chair scraped the ground. He'd been sitting.

"Someone who needs to be taught a lesson in manners," Jake said smartly, still struggling with Jonathan.

"I need to ask him a few questions and this was the safest and closest place to do it."

"But no one is allowed down here since the lockdown," the guy said. "Sorry, but you'll have to take him somewhere else."

"Listen, you heard about what happened to Greg?"

There was a silence in which Jonathan guessed the guard nodded.

"I think this guy can help lead us to the people who were behind it." The man must not have looked convinced. "Listen, until we find out who did this, Greg is still in danger, and I'm not willing to let him die because of a traffic jam between here and the Bureau. Are you?"

For added effect, Jonathan chose that moment to break free of Jake's hold and lurch forward into the unknown. The men behind him reacted fast. Someone's full weight crashed into him and pinned him hard to the tile. The second man came up and together they lifted Jonathan back to his feet.

"Take him into the back room so he doesn't break anything in here," said the guard.

"Thanks, Barry," Jake replied, already moving Jonathan forward.

They walked for what felt like several hundred feet before the sound of a door opening and closing met his ears. Jake pushed Jonathan hard, causing him to stumble into what felt like a table.

"Sit down and don't move," he barked out.

Jonathan did as he was told, finding a chair with rollers. Once he was seated, Jake grabbed the chair's arms and pulled him away from the table to the middle of the room, apparently away from anything. Jonathan heard another chair's rollers scraping against the floor before it seemed to be positioned across from him.

"Barry is a good man, but he's very protective of Greg and the people who work here every day," Jake said. "The way he looked at me when I said you might know who is behind Greg's current condition… He may get physical with you, even though I'll tell him not to." And then he heard Jake stand and walk away. He called out to Barry without waiting for any kind of response from Jonathan. "I need you to watch him for a second. I need to take this call."

Barry didn't question or complain this time around. Jonathan heard his footfalls and then a quick exchange of whispered words between the two men. The sound of Jake talking louder came back. He was pretending to be on a call, getting him into the lab while their only obstacle, Barry, was in the same room with Jonathan.

This time the door wasn't shut.

Jonathan hoped Barry's focus would remain on him and not what Jake was doing in the other room.

KATE COULDN'T SEE ANYTHING, but she knew she was in a box. Just like she *knew* she was naked. Those were two facts that she accepted as absolute truth.

She ran her hands over the wood that enclosed her, trying to feel for a way out while also trying to determine why she was there at all. Then the inside of the box lit up.

She wasn't in just any box.

She was in a coffin.

Pain in the back of her neck moved an already terrified feeling to its limit. Tears sprang to her eyes as she threw her fists against the top. It did nothing to damage the wood.

"Help!" she yelled.

No one responded.

She pounded on the lid and its sides for what felt like an eternity, but nothing changed. The wood didn't splinter or crack, and no called out to her.

She was alone.

Unwilling to give up, she scooted as far to the side as she could to see where the light was coming from. Through eyes blurred by tears, she could just make out the shape of star lights against the wood.

"Kate?"

The sound of someone yelling above her made her focus back on the lid. Instead of relief pouring through her, a deep coldness enveloped her. It started against her back and slowly moved up across her skin. The light from the stars flickered. Kate turned her head to see why.

She screamed.

Water was seeping in through each star and rising at an alarming rate. It was already to her ears.

"Help!" she yelled again, resuming her pounding against the lid.

The water moved higher until she had to prop herself up on her elbows, trying to keep her head above water. However, the attempt seemed to make it rise faster. She turned her head, pressing her cheek to the wood, and took one last long breath seconds before the box was completely filled.

The flickering lights stabilized, continuing their earlier, steady glow. Kate wasn't only going to drown, she was going to be able to watch herself do it.

Pain in the back of her neck shot downward and dispersed.

She was going to die.

THE PUNCH PROBABLY didn't come out of nowhere. Had Jonathan been able to see, he would have picked up on

the physical signs that Barry was about to clock him
one good. He would have seen the tension in his arm, in
his shoulder and in his jaw. All tightening as a result of
acute anger or adrenaline or both. He would have also
seen the expression, or complete lack of one, and realized that the man sitting across from him was indeed
very protective of his colleagues.

The punch landed against the right side of Jonathan's
jaw. It sent his head reeling to the left as pain exploded
along the bone. Jonathan didn't know what Barry looked
like, but from his voice alone he'd bet the man was
similar in size to him. By the power behind his punch,
Jonathan guessed the man had less muscle, though. A
blessing given the current situation.

"Who hit him?" Barry asked, voice low so Jake
couldn't hear. "Who is the woman who hit Mr. Calhoun?"

Jonathan snorted.

That's exactly what I'd like to know, too, Barry.

"Are you laughing? Is this *funny to you*?" Barry
seethed. Jonathan braced for another hit. He turned his
head to the other side, hoping to catch the new hit on a
spot that wasn't already throbbing. But then he heard the
man's chair push back. He was now standing in front of
him. No matter where he decided to hit, Jonathan knew
it was going to hurt.

A sound of glass shattering in the lab put a halt to
Barry's wrath. Jonathan froze. If Barry got at all suspicious of Jake's intention, then Jake would have no
choice but to keep him quiet.

"If there's a chance someone on the inside is involved
with whatever is going on with Greg and Kate, then I
want to find out on my own," Jake had said after they'd
run through their plan in the parking garage. "I'm sure

Kate will tell you later why I have trust issues, but until I figure this out, I'm not going to trust anyone. That's why I couldn't do this by myself. I need to stay in the clear if I want to see this through."

Jonathan saw the same determination in Jake that Kate displayed about her work. The agent suspected someone had betrayed their task force—their team—and was going to do everything in his power to crack the mystery wide open.

But not if he got caught.

"Jake, what are you—" Barry started to ask. He didn't get the chance to finish the question. Jonathan rocked up on his feet and threw his shoulder into the man's chest so quickly that he didn't have time to dodge the attack. The two of them toppled over Barry's chair and once again Jonathan hit the ground hard, but not harder than Barry. He could hear the man's breath wheeze out and decided to use that against him. He slid one hand out of the tie binding his wrists together and struck out, connecting with the man's face. He made a grunt and then went limp.

Jonathan waited a moment.

Barry still didn't move.

Slowly, Jonathan rose to his feet and lifted the bottom of the bag. Barry was most definitely unconscious.

The sound of quick footsteps made him turn around just as Jake slid into the doorway. He looked at Jonathan and then down at Barry.

"It was either that or you would have been caught," Jonathan said, answering the unasked question. "Plus, you were right. He did get physical."

Jake let out a quick breath but nodded. In his hand was a small black bag.

"We need to leave."

Jonathan followed the man into the lab and paused. Workstations covered in machines, vials, papers and things Jonathan didn't recognize littered the room. He pictured Kate among them all, head bent over a microscope before going to one of the walls that was nothing but a whiteboard, concentrated yet just as excited. Imagining her working made him smile, but at the same time soured in his stomach. This was her element. Her life.

One he just didn't understand.

"Fast thinking, taking him down. I accidentally knocked over an empty vial," Jake said, running over to a small office in the corner next to the hall they had originally come down. "I'm going to reboot the security cameras. It should give us enough time to make it back to the car."

"Are there cameras in here?" Jonathan asked, following. Jake still had the bag in his hand.

"No, lab work isn't supposed to be monitored, just the exits."

"What about when Barry wakes up? Won't he realize you helped me?"

Jake's hands flew across the computer's keyboard.

"I wouldn't be leaving here with you if I didn't have a plan," he said when he had finished. "Now, run!"

Jonathan followed as Jake ran into the hallway. Unlike the lab it was narrow and cold, its walls a crumbling white that barely reflected the lights. They ran until they took a sharp right to the elevator. It wasn't as old or as high-tech as Jonathan had envisioned. It looked like a normal elevator with only two floors as options, disappointing his inner James Bond fan.

They didn't speak as Jake punched the two buttons in a quick five-figure sequence and the elevator began to ascend. Seconds later it dinged, opening up to the first floor of the parking garage. In the distance Jonathan could see the SUV.

"Your secret lab is under a parking garage," Jonathan said, sarcasm lacing his voice, as soon as they got into the vehicle. Jake started the engine and handed Jonathan the bag.

"Hey, until just now you didn't know it was here, so mission accomplished."

Jonathan had to agree with that.

"We should have brought Kate with us," Jonathan said. "We could have given this to her now."

Jake shook his head.

"I wasn't sure how this would shake out," he admitted. "Things could have gotten much more intense. I would have hated for Kate to get hurt while we're trying to save her."

Jake was right, but that didn't mean that Jonathan didn't feel the pressure of time against them. Kate had been unconscious for far too long for his liking. He looked down at the bag in his hands. It was small and not at all heavy.

"Are you sure this will save her?" he asked, back to serious.

Jake matched his tone.

"I sure hope so."

Chapter Fifteen

A fist broke through the coffin's lid just as Kate's body floated to the bottom. She focused on it, inches from her face, as cracks from the new hole spiderwebbed through the rest of the lid. Slowly, and then with startling speed, the water began to drain upward and out of the coffin.

Kate kept her focus on the fist, still balled, even as she coughed, gasping for air.

"Who are you?" she asked once she could breathe again.

The fist finally opened into a hand that reached out for her, beckoning her to take it. So she did.

It pulled her from the coffin with ease, shattering the lid and leaving the horrors behind. Its warmth guided her through a moment of darkness before she was standing, naked and wet, in a warehouse.

The warehouse.

Kate wanted to turn to see if her savior was behind her but couldn't move. All of her attention was at the end of a room in the distance. People were standing, backs to her, all looking at the person in the center.

The person hunched over in a chair.

Kate's feet slapped against the cold concrete, but didn't make a sound as she walked toward them. That room. That person. She couldn't remember what they had to do with her. Why she was there.

She needed to finally find out.

She needed to remember.

Kate stopped among the people gathered around the person in the middle. Even though she was so close, she couldn't make out who it was. However, the faces around her she had little trouble recognizing.

Jake, tall and in his FBI uniform, stood closest to her, eyes never leaving the person in the chair. Next to him was Greg, smiling like he always did, a silver case in his hand. Her father was there farther back. He was young and upset. She couldn't remember why.

"Kate, we shouldn't be here."

Able to finally turn around, she saw a little girl holding a little boy's hand. The girl didn't care about his warning. She looked through Kate at the woman in the chair.

The woman.

Terror and anguish collided in her chest as she remembered where she was.

When she was.

And who the woman was.

Kate turned and was suddenly kneeling in front of her.

"Mom?"

The rope around Cassandra was tied so tightly to the chair that at first it appeared as if she was sitting up on her own. Her hair that she'd always worn back in a ponytail for work had fallen out of its holder and covered half of her face. The other half was covered in blood, still dripping. Her eye was swollen shut and there was duct tape across her mouth.

Kate stumbled backward just as the little girl walked

forward. Her eyes were wide, glazed over. With shaking little hands, she reached for the tape and took it off.

"Mom?" she whispered.

The little boy started to put his arms around her when his focus caught on something in the corner.

"Dad?" he yelled, dropping her hand and running out of view.

Kate didn't watch—instead she looked back at the girl.

But she was gone and so was everyone else except for Cassandra.

"I found you," Kate whispered. "Dad thought the call was a fake, but we didn't listen and we found you first." Kate took an uncertain step forward. "You weren't breathing. I heard them tell Dad you'd been gone for hours. I tried to untie you," Kate continued, voice shaking, "but it was too hard. I wasn't strong enough."

She looked down at the ropes again, angry at them like she had been all those years ago. Suddenly, she felt the need to try again. Kate moved to the back of the chair and found the three knots. She tried to undo them, a feeling of defeat already rising, but the first one came undone. She paused, surprised, but then moved to the next one. It too came undone in her hands. She moved to the last one and, with a cry of joy, it unknotted.

Kate squeezed her eyes shut, trying to stop her tears.

"I did it," she said, voice wavering. "I finally untied them."

"Good job."

Her eyes flashed open and she was no longer standing. She was back in the coffin. However, this time, the lid was gone, open to a white ceiling. Panic started to seize her once more when the feeling of running water moved across her bare skin again. She began to flail around.

"Don't worry, I'm here," said a voice next to her. "Kate, I'm here."

It was Jonathan.

He held her against his chest while the water moved higher and higher.

"Don't worry, you're safe now," he said.

And Kate decided that was all she needed to hear.

KATE STOPPED STRUGGLING against him.

"I think she heard you," Jake said from next to the tub. "That means it's working."

Jonathan stroked Kate's hair away from her face as the cold water rained down on them both from the showerhead. He had her body cradled against his chest, trying to keep her as calm as he could.

"Kate, it's Jonathan," he said. "Can you hear me?"

At first he thought he imagined it, but then, slowly, Kate's eyelids rose.

"Kate?" Jake asked, bending slightly to try to level his gaze and grab her attention. It worked.

"I untied her," she whispered. Jonathan's eyebrow rose on reflex. He didn't understand, but apparently Jake did. The agent's entire face fell, but then he gave the smallest of smiles. She tilted her head up to look at Jonathan next.

"I'm glad this isn't a coffin," she said, voice tired.

Jonathan couldn't help but laugh at that.

"Me, too," he said. "How are you feeling?"

Kate quieted a moment, making Jonathan fear that she'd lost consciousness again.

"I feel like I'm the only naked one in here," she finally said, voice notably stronger. Jake laughed this time and retreated into the hotel room. Seconds later he was back with a floor-length robe. Jonathan reached back and turned the water off while the agent held the robe out and closed his eyes.

Kate started to stand, but her legs shook and she couldn't seem to get the hang of it.

"Looks like I need your help still, Mr. Bodyguard," she whispered. Jonathan didn't realize how good it was to hear the sarcastic nickname again. Slowly he stood, bringing Kate with him. Keeping his eyes averted to above her chest so she'd know he wasn't taking advantage of the situation, he helped maneuver her arms into the robe and even tied it once it was closed.

"What time is it?" she asked.

"Almost three," Jonathan answered, still unhappy with how long it had taken to get her the antidote. The two men guided her back to the bed. Jake piled the pillows behind her so she was sitting up straight. He turned to Jonathan after.

"She needs to stay awake for at least a few more hours," he said. "Just in case."

Jonathan nodded.

The agent turned back to his friend.

"How are you feeling, Kate?" he asked, voice kind.

"My body feels tired and my head hurts a little," she admitted. "There's a slight throbbing in my arm, but I suspect that's from the injection."

Jake nodded.

"We were rushed for time. Sorry if I was a little sloppy with it."

Kate shrugged. "I'm not complaining."

She gave the two men a passing smile of gratitude. Jonathan was once again happy to see another sign that Kate was better. The smile didn't last long.

"The EMT," she started, brow creasing. "I think he was the one who injected me."

Jake nodded.

"Jonathan suspected that much. I'm already looking into it."

Kate cast a quick look of surprise at Jonathan before asking the million-dollar question.

"The fact that I'm alive and functioning means that what he pumped into me was my failed drug from years ago, but how did he get it?"

"I'm about to leave to go find that out," Jake said. "But first there are some things I need to tell you that I should have told you sooner."

He turned to Jonathan and he took the hint.

"I'm going to go change while you two talk," he said. "I'll be right next door."

Kate held his gaze with her own dark, mesmerizing eyes before nodding.

Jonathan walked to the adjoining door as Jake began the story about Greg and the FBI's involvement with her research. He wondered how she would take the news.

Jonathan shucked his wet clothes back in his bathroom. He toweled off and took a long, long breath. He'd been a bodyguard for years. He'd taken on clients where nothing out of the ordinary had happened and he'd taken on clients where things had gotten interesting. However, two days with Kathryn Spears and he'd never forget what had happened for the rest of his life. The FBI, secret labs and experimental drugs. He was no longer in his comfort zone as a bodyguard.

But hadn't he already decided that he'd see this contract through? Hadn't he already made a deal with himself that he'd stop at nothing to keep Kate safe?

Jonathan looked at his reflection and nodded to it.

Yes, he had.

He went back to his room and changed into a pair of green khakis and a shirt that was white with a gray trim and went down to his elbows. He ruffled his wet hair and even touched up his goatee with a razor. By the time he stepped into his backup pair of boots, a knock sounded against the adjoining door.

It was Jake. He stepped aside.

"I told her everything," he greeted. "And now that she knows all of the same players as we do, maybe it might help the two of you keep safe. Whoever is behind this, I'm sure they're trying to take what she has before the convention, so I can't stress enough how important it is that that doesn't happen."

"Then why don't we go into some kind of protective custody or, since she's already going to be offered the job, skip the convention altogether?" Jonathan asked.

"Normally that's exactly what I'd do, but we still have no idea who is behind this. Someone had access to the lab and I'm not confident that they wouldn't find out about her protection detail, too. The best I can do is this." Jake went over to the desk and used the complimentary pen and pad to write down an address and number. "On the way over here earlier, after you first called me, I called in a favor to one of the few people I know I can trust. If someone within the Bureau tries to track Kate's or Greg's cell phone, I'll be the first to know. That being said, I can't promise this hotel is safe anymore. I've already told Kate and she turned me down, but this is my apartment. Kate knows where the spare key is." Jonathan took the paper.

"Will she be okay now?"

"I think so." Jake turned for the hotel door, but paused before he opened it. "And Jonathan, what Kate said when she first spoke in the tub…you should ask her what she meant." Jonathan raised his eyebrow at that. "One of the drug's side effects that she experienced when she took it once before was a form of lucid dreaming. I feel like it might do her some good to talk about it." Jake's lips turned up into a small smile. "And you obviously seem to care about her enough to risk some serious jail time. Why else would you, as you said, break into a secret lab for her?"

THE TWO MEN in the other room were undoubtedly smart. Kate knew that much with certainty. However, as she turned her head to try to hear their conversation through the adjoining door, she questioned their intelligence just a bit. Did they really think she couldn't hear them?

"Will she be okay now?" Jonathan asked, sounding as if he was *trying* to be quiet.

Jake responded with an indecisive, "I think so." But Kate knew that if he thought the injection hadn't counteracted the drug, he wouldn't be leaving. Even though he had some quick explaining to do about the man they'd left unconscious in Greg's lab.

Greg's lab.

Kate closed her eyes. Among everything she'd just learned, that was a revelation she hadn't even suspected existed.

"And you obviously seem to care about her enough to risk some serious jail time. Why else would you, as you said, break into a secret lab for her?"

Kate's eyes flashed open. A fluttering actually moved across her stomach at Jake's words. It was such a foreign feeling of excitement that she tilted her chin down to look at her stomach, as if she could spot a physical object that explained the feeling. But even someone as emotionally stunted as Kate had an inkling of the emotion that made her cheeks heat.

She took a deep breath and slowly let it stream out. The door to Jonathan's room opened and shut. She heard the bodyguard throw the top latch and the dead bolt. For one wild moment Kate became self-conscious of how she looked. With hands that still shook slightly, she felt her hair and sighed again. Without looking at her reflection, she knew the frizz was out of control. It was a nice distraction from the fact that Jonathan had seen and had to touch her naked body. Fleetingly she cursed her past self for canceling her gym membership the year before.

"Can I come in?"

Kate tore herself out of her scattering thoughts and nodded at the man in the doorway. He took the desk chair and rolled it to the side of the bed.

"To be honest, I assumed you wouldn't give me the option of being alone," she admitted. "Considering everything that's happened."

"To be honest, I don't think you want to be alone anymore," he responded. The simple statement made the earlier heat in her cheeks reignite. She held his gaze despite the powerful urge to avert her eyes.

"I'm not afraid to be alone. In fact, I enjoy being alone," she said after a moment. The bodyguard sat up straighter, as if he was ready to highlight all the bad that had happened to point out that she *was* in fact in life-threatening danger and his protection was needed. Kate didn't want to argue. That wasn't the point she was trying to make.

She reached out and took the bodyguard's hand in hers. His skin was warm against her. "But I'm finding that being with you is the exception."

Chapter Sixteen

Jonathan's training throughout the years had helped his reaction time considerably when it came to surprises. Case in point, he'd been able to get Kate out of the way when the car had barreled across the intersection. But as he looked into her eyes while she admitted she wanted to be with him instead of alone, he had no idea how to proceed.

Was she just talking about wanting him around because of his duty as her bodyguard, or was there another truth to her words?

Jonathan felt the walls he'd built around himself try to slide up—to cut off any emotional response to her words—but he didn't have time to think on it for too long. She retracted her hand. Jonathan cleared his throat. The moment, whatever it meant, had passed.

"That was smart of you, by the way," she continued. "Jake said it was your idea to put me under the water to help wake me up faster. Putting me in the shower probably saved my life, or at least its quality."

"Once Jake gave you the injection, you wouldn't budge. He said it had been too long and if you didn't wake up ASAP you could have some permanent brain damage." Jonathan shrugged. "If I'd had a bucket of water I would have thrown it on you. The shower seemed like a better option. More polite."

Kate laughed a little. It was a good sound to hear.

"Well, thank you," she said. "As far as I can tell, everything up here is as normal as it ever was." She tapped her temple and winced. Jonathan moved closer.

"Are you sure you're okay?" he asked, concern leaking out into every word. Kate rubbed the side of her head but nodded.

"It's just a headache, one I definitely have had before."

"When you took the drug a few years ago," Jonathan supplied. Kate paused the rubbing motion against her head before dropping her hand to her lap.

"Yes. It's like the beginnings of a migraine mixed with the middle of a hangover."

Jonathan made a face.

"That doesn't sound pleasant."

Kate sighed.

"It isn't."

Jonathan contemplated grabbing Kate's hand to ask the next question. He decided against the action but not the question.

"Kate, I know you probably don't want to but—"

"You want to know about the drug," she interjected. He nodded. "You saved my life at least twice today. I suppose the truth is the least you deserve." Jonathan leaned in a fraction. He had a feeling he was about to learn a lot about Kathryn Spears.

"When I was a little girl, I wanted to be a dancer," she started. "A tap dancer, to be precise. I just couldn't get over my love for how the shoes sounded when they hit the ground—I still can't seem to find anything but joy in the sound now." A smile swam up to her lips for a

moment. Then it dived back under in the next. "Jake will
tell you he always wanted to be in law enforcement—
he used to walk around with a plastic badge and pull it
out on kids in the playground citing offenses he'd seen
them commit—but I think, given time, he would have
pursued something like architecture. He had a fixed
fascination with building." Kate quieted. While she had
offered to finally tell him the truth, she seemed to need
some help moving along.

"What changed?" he asked.

"The reason I grew up around Jake was because his
father was my mother's partner."

"FBI?" Jonathan guessed. Kate nodded.

"Our parents became good friends and so did we.
There were some rough patches at first between my
mother and Bill, Jake's father, but they worked it out
and had several years of friendship and success. That
is, until one night when neither came home." She took
a deep breath to seemingly give her strength, but then
it seeped out slowly. Jonathan felt a pull in his chest,
knowing she was opening a deep wound. "One night
turned into two. My mother's car was found abandoned with signs of a struggle and Bill's office had
been trashed. I didn't know this at the time. What I
also wouldn't learn until later was, while searching my
mother's car, they found evidence that she and Bill had
been investigating something on the sly. Something
that hadn't been reported or sanctioned." She paused
and gave a quick smile. "You think I'm stubborn when
I'm focused—you should have met my mother." Jonathan couldn't help but return the show of affection.
"For the last two years, a lot of their cases fell through
last minute. Evidence disappeared. Witnesses suddenly
didn't know anything. You name it and it started to

happen. Bill and my mother had a theory that some-one within their team was behind the scenes, working against them."

"A traitor," Jonathan said.

"Yes. Their boss found their notes and was able to guess the identity of the man. They picked him up and immediately started interrogating him. From what I've been told by my father and Greg, the man let it slip that Mom and Bill were running out of time. They leaned on him until they got an address just outside town. My father had made friends with Mom's boss and was kept in the loop. I remember he called Jake and his mother over to wait. She didn't trust the information, said it was too easy to get." Kate's frown deepened. "She was right. He'd lied, and it wasn't until hours later that he came clean about the real location. My mother's boss called the house to tell them they had a lead. Jake and I overheard the address. It wasn't too far from the house and we knew a shortcut, so we snuck out and rode our bikes there in hopes of saving our parents."

Kate's eyes began to gloss over. She paused to swallow, trying not to cry. Jonathan didn't say a word. He waited as she composed herself.

"To this day, I've never felt the amount of unease I did walking into that warehouse. That feeling where you know something is terribly wrong but can't place it. Jake wanted to leave—he felt it, too—but I was too stubborn. My mother had a saying that just because you were scared didn't mean you weren't strong. And all I was trying to do was be strong." One lone tear slipped out and trailed down her cheek. Before it could keep going, Kate caught it with the back of her other hand. "We found them in the back room. Mom was tied to a chair, beaten badly. Bill was there, too, but in the corner. He wasn't tied up but had been shot—we were told later he'd most likely been trying to save his partner." It was Kate's turn to clear her throat. "We knew the moment we saw them that they were gone, but the kids in us didn't want to believe it. Jake tried to wake up his dad and I tried to untie Mom, as if that would somehow help, but the knots were too tight. I wasn't strong enough."

"'I untied her,'" Jonathan said, quoting her. "That's the first thing you said when you woke up."

Kate nodded.

"I dreamed that I finally freed her. I guess it's been bothering me for a long time." She shrugged. "In the moment I thought if I could untie her, I could have saved her. There was no time, though. Probably less than a minute after we found them, the cavalry showed up. They had enough evidence to send that horrible man away for both of our lives combined, ending his years of betrayal. After all of that, our families stayed together. Jake and I eventually stopped having nightmares, but we knew we had been changed. Jake decided his only goal in life was to become an FBI agent like his father, trading in a plastic badge for the real thing, while I became obsessed with one notion."

Jonathan raised his eyebrow.

"If that man had told the truth the first time he was questioned, Mom and Bill would still be alive."

"That's why you started working on the drug," Jonathan said as he realized.

"I just couldn't get over the fact that one lie destroyed two lives—two families. However, I wasn't so blind with despair to realize that no matter who you are interrogating, there should be an ethical and moral line you don't cross. I know that some would disagree, but, for me, it was important to come up with a nonharmful solution." For the first time Kate gave him a smile that convinced him she was now out of the past. At least the bad parts. "I had a series of lucid dreams in college one month. Ones in which I was a child again and talking to my mother. I told her everything, all of my secrets, without a second thought. I suppose that was because I knew I was dreaming. But that gave me an idea, one that I presented to Greg, who I now realize took it to the FBI. If I could create a drug that replicated the feeling of lucid dreaming, then any question you asked the subject while under its effect would be answered without hesitation."

"Because you trust you're only dreaming," Jonathan guessed.

"Yes. A temporary window in which the person being questioned isn't harmed physically in any way, yet has no imaginable reason why they wouldn't answer the questions asked of them."

"A humane way to interrogate."

Kate nodded. Despite the pride she seemed to take in the idea, her brows drew in together and her lips pursed. Before he could stop the thought, Jonathan imagined the feel of them against his own lips. He shook his head slightly and played it off by cracking his neck.

"The day Greg gave me a physical serum to help remind me of all I'd done was already a bad day. It was the anniversary of Mom and Bill's deaths and frustration took over. As you might have been able to tell, I tend to like my control. Taking the drug, even though I knew it wasn't ready, was my way of trying to get control. Instead, it nearly put me in a coma. It put me in a constant state of lucid dreaming with little hope of ever waking up. Reliving my mother's death over and over again until I died. Not something I want to subject anyone else to. The drug has many years of testing to go before it's ever ready to be used. What Greg gave me in the coffee shop, in the silver case, is another physical copy of the up-to-date drug. A physical representation of everything I've been working toward."

Jonathan sat back in his chair and let out a breath. His last case was sure turning out to be a doozy.

"Sounds like a drug worth trying to steal," he said. From threatening notes before she'd ever left home to nearly being killed by the very drug she'd created, someone wanted what Kate had spent the last five years researching. The couple in the jackets were directly intertwined with that attempt, but Jonathan had a hard time thinking they were doing it alone. When Jonathan and Jake had first gotten into his SUV on the way to the lab, Jonathan had forwarded the picture of the man who had left a note on Kate's door to his phone. Maybe Jake would get lucky and find out his identity. Because the cops still hadn't called him back with any new information.

Just more questions than answers.

KATE'S HEADACHE EXPANDED and consumed. Jonathan's concern seemed to double. It took her several attempts to convince him that the headache was a side effect of both the drug and the fall against the asphalt on the crosswalk. What she needed was some caffeine to help make her feel more alert and normal, something neither of them had.

"I'm not leaving this room," Jonathan said, stern.

"And neither am I," she said, motioning to her robe. "But I'm also hungry."

Kate's stomach growled loudly, egging his decision on. Finally, the bodyguard sighed.

"How about I do this instead?"

He disappeared into his room for a moment. Then she heard him on the phone. She nuzzled back into her pillow, trying to ignore the dull throb that only seemed to be getting worse. She might be able to lose it if she gave in to the urge to sleep, but she'd had enough of that in the last few hours. She loved her mother, but she didn't want to chance reliving her death again any time soon.

Even if Jonathan had been in her dream.

Kate couldn't deny she was more than surprised the bodyguard had made not just one appearance but many within her sleeping mind. From the star lights she'd never owned to the man holding her child form's hand, warning her against all of the badness, saving her from drowning in a self-made coffin, her bodyguard had done his job in both the real world and the one within her mind. She smiled to herself, wondering how she would phrase that in a job performance review.

"Okay, Jett is back on front-desk duty and is personally bringing up the pizza as soon as it gets here. And some coffee for us," Jonathan said. "I'm pretty much not leaving your side until we're on a plane back home. Which should be tomorrow, if you ask me."

Kate put her finger up and placed it against his mouth. It was an impulsive, harmless move on her part, but the feel of his lips against her skin sent a shock through her. One that wasn't unpleasant in the least. Jonathan's body tensed. Had he felt it, too?

"Jonathan," she started, voice much softer than she'd meant it to be. "Let's not talk about this until we've at least eaten. Please."

Jonathan's eyes searched her face. The self-consciousness she'd felt earlier wasn't there anymore. The way he was looking at her somehow made her feel oddly beautiful. She lowered her finger, dropping her hand back to her lap. The corner of his lips pulled up.

"Okay, Miss Scientist," he said. "Now, I'm going to go check in with the boss to let her know we're okay. While we were at the lab, she sent quite a few texts. And, before you ask, no, I'm not going to tell her everything that's going on. Not until we figure out who's behind this. I don't want to put her or Orion in any unnecessary danger."

Kate watched him go back into his room. The adjoining door she'd loathed the day before had become an unforeseen perk.

Giving him privacy, as much as she could while being so close, Kate tried to clear her mind and relax. Or something similar given that relaxing wasn't possible under the circumstances. She focused on her breathing and it seemed to work. She didn't even realize when Jonathan started talking or when the knock sounded against his door.

However, she didn't miss the sound of someone's body slamming into the wall.

Kate moved out of bed as quickly as she could. The sound of another body hitting the wall made her pause, frozen in the middle of the room.

"Jonathan?" she asked into the quiet that followed. There was a shuffling noise and the bodyguard appeared in the doorway.

"You're bleeding," Kate said, looking to the blood on his lip. He shook off the concern.

"Get into the bathroom and lock the door. He's here."

Chapter Seventeen

Kate wanted to complain—wanted to help—but she realized her running into whatever fray there was in the next room wouldn't help anything. She did as she was told and retreated to the bathroom, locking the door behind her. The floor was still wet and cold against her bare feet, but her attention was outside the room. *He* as in the man who had left the note?

What was he doing here now?

No sooner had she questioned it than her stomach dropped. The woman who had driven the car over Greg had been aiming at her. If she showed up with the man again, then it was safe to assume he wasn't there to sit down and chat.

Kate strained as she tried to listen to what was happening in the next hotel room. No sound was getting through. Worry about Jonathan crept into her mind and exploded. Which only intensified when a door in the next room slammed shut.

Kate held her breath and waited.

A pounding sound began on the other side, but not against the bathroom door. Whoever had slammed the adjoining door between rooms must have been in her room now. Which meant whoever was still in Jonathan's room must have been trying to get in hers.

The question now was, who was in there with her?

Before she could weigh the pros and cons of flinging open the door and checking on Jonathan, hoping it was him on the other side, someone tried the door handle.

Kate nearly screamed. The lock wasn't sticking. The handle began to move and slowly the door began to open. Whoever was behind it wasn't Jonathan. He would have called out to her, that much Kate was certain. So, with mounting terror, she turned and threw her back against the door, shutting it the small distance it had opened.

A man cursed loudly on the other side.

Definitely not Jonathan.

Kate braced her feet against the slick tile and waited for the man to try again. But how long could she really keep the door closed?

Looking around the room, she tried to spot something that could be used as a weapon. The only thing that looked remotely dangerous was the towel rack. It was too far away and she doubted she'd be able to pull it free from the wall. Feeling increasingly defeated, Kate's eyes traveled across the counter next to her.

And stopped.

Reaching out, she grabbed her travel-size hair spray. Quickly she tossed off the cap. The man slammed into the door hard. Kate tried to push against it, using her legs to apply pressure backward, but he was stronger. In a last-ditch effort at self-defense, Kate put her finger on the nozzle and jumped away from the door, flattening herself against the wall.

The bathroom door flung open. If the rubber doorstop hadn't been attached to the wall, the handle would have made one big hole. The man stopped just inside the room. For one moment they looked at each other.

It was the man who had followed them and who was on the hotel security footage. Without his coat he stood tall and well-built and looked quite a deal younger than she had originally suspected—perhaps early thirties. Like her, he had dark eyes and hair. Unlike her, he was smiling. Kate didn't wait to find out what his plans were.

Wielding the only weapon she had, Kate sprang forward and sprayed the hair spray at the man's face. It was a move he hadn't expected, and even though he grabbed the front of her robe and slung her into the hallway, she'd hit her target. It was a delayed reaction but one that wasn't lacking. The man let out a yell and let her go, fisting at his eyes. Kate used his pain to her advantage. She moved her foot up and connected hard with his groin.

He doubled over, a stream of expletives bursting from his lips. Kate backed up to the wall and moved along it until she was at the door to the hallway. The pounding she'd heard earlier became louder, terrifying her even more and scattering her thoughts, seconds before a loud crack. Kate already had the door open, one foot in the hallway, when another crack followed. She started to turn to place the sound when a ding from the elevators floated down the hallway. If she could get someone to call security, that would strengthen their chances against the unnamed assailant.

However, they weren't so lucky.

The woman, counterpart to the man bellyaching in the room behind her and driver of the car that had put Greg in the hospital, walked off the elevator and fixed Kate with a stare that made her blood run cold. For a moment all Kate could hear was the soft hum of the hallway lights.

She too appeared to be younger than Kate had once thought. Her hair was dark blond and even from the distance between them she saw dark eyes that narrowed at her. In her right hand was a gun.

"Well, hello, Miss Spears."

And then she lifted the gun and shot.

THE DOOR DIDN'T fly off its hinges or break clean in half, but as Jonathan kicked out with all the force he could summon after being temporarily knocked off his feet, the door between his room and Kate's gave way. It splintered unevenly, making him work more to clear the debris until he was standing in his room, fuming.

When he'd gone to answer the door, he'd looked through the peephole to see someone he thought was Jett. The glass was more foggy than clear and Jonathan's mind was still on his call with Nikki. He'd been distracted and it had cost him. Less than a second after he'd opened the door, the man who had delivered the bloody letter had pushed inside. They'd fought in the small hallway and Jonathan had been lucky to land a good hit that dazed the man, giving him enough time to warn Kate. When he'd returned, the man was ready. His fists dealt out blows that Jonathan hadn't been prepared to receive. Especially the right hook that had knocked him dizzy.

By the time Jonathan had regained his footing, the man had slammed the adjoining door shut. The key cards able to open the door were both on Kate's dresser.

Now Jonathan stood in the hotel room with a heaving chest, looking at a scene he didn't quite understand. The man was outside the bathroom, hunched over and cursing. His eyes moved up to Jonathan but they were angry red slits. The bathroom door behind him was open and Kate was nowhere to be seen.

Jonathan wanted to smile, realizing that the scientist had fought back and disabled her attacker, at least temporarily. But what happened next pushed any victorious thoughts clear from his mind.

A gun went off in the hallway.

Kate!

The man, despite struggling with the pain inflicted on him by Kate, whipped his head around to the door so fast that Jonathan thought he heard it snap. Apparently he wasn't the only one caught off guard by the discharge. Jonathan rushed the man.

He might have been hurt, his eyes might have been watering, but the dark-haired man wasn't down for the count. He turned and ducked out of the way at the last second. The hit he couldn't land left Jonathan exposed in front of him, giving the man an easy target. Much like Jonathan did to the door, the intruder hiked his leg up and pushed his foot against Jonathan's stomach. The force sent him back into the wall. A cracking sound split the air as a part of the wall gave out under his weight.

Jonathan let out a groan that hitched a ride on the pain pulsing through his body. But that didn't mean he was down for the count, either. He pushed off the wall with his elbows and threw a punch. The man brought up his arms in time for the hit to be absorbed by his forearms. Still, it did enough to push him back, stepping into the bathroom.

Jonathan came at him again, not wanting to lose the small momentum he had gained. He torqued his left arm back before moving it around to make a solid arc. Imagining, as he always did, going *through* the target and not simply *to* it, he pictured his fist going clean through the man's jaw. It worked. The skin of his knuckles kissed the man's jaw with hot anger, a hit he couldn't dodge. As though the sound of the impact alone was powerful enough, he staggered backward. Jonathan moved closer, ready to keep going, when the man's struggle to remain standing failed. His shoes slipped on the water pooled on the floor, sending his feet flying out from beneath him. He hit the tile hard and his head hit the lip of the tub with a smack. The man's head lolled to the side and the rest of him went limp. Whether the man was dead or simply unconscious, Jonathan didn't have time to find out. He ran out of the hotel room and into the empty hallway. Relief that Kate wasn't lying on the ground anywhere in sight made him exhale. But where was she now?

Their new hotel rooms were between the elevators and the stairs. He took off to the left, hoping she'd gone that direction instead of toward the other stairs.

He needed to find her.

He needed to protect her.

He needed her to be safe.

The doors to the elevator slid open as he neared the end of the hall. An older man with a straw fedora and a smart blue suit looked wide-eyed at him as he flew past. Before Jonathan could warn him that it wasn't safe, another gunshot sounded. The man shrank back into the elevator and pressed the Close Door button while Jonathan tore open the door to the stairs.

"Kate?" he yelled. His voice echoed off the concrete. The stairwell was too small for him to see to the floors below or the one above. No one replied. He started to run down the steps, but then stopped and reversed his path, going to the fourth floor, convinced that that was where the shot had come from. Why had Kate gone up instead of down?

Jonathan pushed open the door just as someone else was trying to open it.

"Kate," he exclaimed, more relief than he thought possible exploding within him at the sight of her. She rocked back on her heels, surprised, and clambered for his hands. He gave them, helping to steady her.

"Run," she said, breathless.

Another gunshot—louder, too close for comfort— added emphasis to the command. Jonathan pulled Kate into the stairwell and guided her along with him back down the steps to the third-floor landing. He pushed them through the door while Kate sucked in a breath. Jonathan glanced back at her and barely caught her as she stumbled forward.

"Dizzy," she wheezed out.

He looped his arm around her middle and pulled up to support some of her weight as they continued to move toward their rooms. Jonathan knew there was a chance that the man was still alive and kicking, but he also knew that man hadn't had a gun. Or at least wasn't willing to use it like his partner. Plus, running down narrow hallways wasn't going to do them any good. Not with Kate unable to run on her own.

Jonathan reached for his key card in his back pocket when another kink in his ever-evolving plan popped up. The door to Kate's room began to open. He let out a long stream of expletives as he used all his power to hoist Kate's body up and keep running down the hall. The fast escape he wanted to make turned into less of a run and more of a pained jog.

"Don't shoot, you idiot," the man behind them yelled seconds after the stairwell door banged open. Jonathan didn't dare look back. Not even when he swung Kate around, using his body as a shield, and hit the elevator Down button. Their one dose of good luck came at the sound of a beep as the doors slid open seconds later.

"Get them," a woman yelled from farther away. It was the confirmation Jonathan needed that the woman who had run over Greg was also after Kate.

Jonathan punched the Lobby button and the Close Door button while flattening Kate against the wall with his body. The doors slowly began to close. He felt Kate exhale, her entire body relaxing against him. Once they got to the lobby he'd be able to hide her until the cops came. He'd be able to keep her safe.

When there was less than a sliver left of open space between the closing doors, a hand snaked through. Jonathan jumped forward, trying to push the man out, but the doors opened enough for him to push inside. Jonathan fully expected him to keep the doors open for his gun-wielding friend, but he surprised him.

The dark-haired man hit the Close Door button. His partner yelled angrily as they slid shut. Jonathan reached out and pulled Kate over to him, moving her once again behind his back. The man across from them let out a devilish smile.

"My friend doesn't like sticking to the plan," he said. "But don't worry, I do."

Chapter Eighteen

Kate screamed.

The man's fist connected with Jonathan's cheek while his other hand reached for Kate. He managed to grab a fistful of her hair, but before he could pull, Jonathan hit above his elbow in an impressive rendition of a karate chop. It generated enough pain that the man let go of her hair, but not before yanking down. She barely had time to yell before Jonathan threw his forearm out to keep her pinned to the wall. He didn't want her anywhere near their attacker.

And she didn't, either.

The man recovered quickly and sent a volley of attacks at the bodyguard. Instead of dodging them, though, Jonathan used the hand not grabbing Kate to cover his face. The man had them in the corner, and if Jonathan so much as moved an inch to either side, he'd hit Kate square on.

Jonathan was protecting her and getting hurt in the process.

She didn't like that.

Not one bit.

The elevator dinged as they slowed to the lobby. The man, in one last desperate attempt, hit Jonathan so hard in the ribs that he doubled over. It left Kate open to him once again. He lunged forward and grabbed her hair. She fumbled in the pocket of her robe for her travel-size hair spray. If she could get his eyes again, then Jonathan could take him out.

"Not again," the man growled when she held the bottle up. He yanked her hair hard toward him, walking backward out of the now-open elevator doors. The pain from her headache intertwined with the burn from her hair being pulled created a wave of nausea. She lost her focus and the hair spray hit the ground.

"Help," she yelled. Murmurs from the lobby turned into shouts. The man moved quickly, dragging her along by her hair. She couldn't see the people around her and she couldn't see the anger on her bodyguard's face.

But she could hear it.

Large footfalls moved around her before the sound of someone being used as a punching bag met her ears. Soon after, her attacker released his hold. Kate fell on her backside, whipping her head up, ready for the next attack. What she saw instead was Jonathan pulling the man's dark hair, both of their faces bloodied.

"Doesn't feel good, does it?" Jonathan bit out. He punched, but was knocked to the side by another well-aimed kick from the man. Kate looked around the lobby to the handful of bystanders. An elderly couple sat on the couch closest to the windows facing the street, two teens stood with a man who had his hands full of luggage and a young mother guarding her toddler at the front desk began moving away. Kate expected someone to step forward but no one did. Until a man yelled from the front door.

"The cops are on their way," Jett warned. Just on the tail of his announcement was the sweet, sweet chorus of sirens in the distance. The man grappling with

Jonathan didn't miss the new information. His attacks became faster, trying to break Jonathan down in the limited amount of time he had left.

Thankfully, Jett wasn't done helping yet. He ran up to the fray and tried to pull the man off the bodyguard. His fearless act inspired a chain reaction. The father of the teens dropped his bags and jumped in, too. They disengaged the unknown man from Jonathan just as the elderly man from the window stood up.

"I can see them comin'," he called.

The realization that the cops were nearly there and it was now three against one seemed to finally push a flight instead of fight response in the attacker. Jett tried to grab for him again but he moved quickly, and he moved around the father as he tried, too. Apparently the man was strong *and* fast.

Kate could see Jonathan getting ready to run after the man who was heading toward the front door. His body had already tilted forward a fraction, more than ready to do whatever he could to stop their attacker.

But Kate couldn't claim the same thing.

She didn't want her bodyguard to get hurt anymore. Not because of her.

"Jonathan," she called out. He turned and she nearly stopped breathing. His eyes were filled with an anger so intense some of the feeling transferred to her. She took in his injuries—his busted bottom lip, bruised jaw, split eyebrow—and felt a fury she didn't think could ever be extinguished. Whoever was behind all of this, whoever the couple was, they would get their due. That train of thought was nearly doused by the cold that crept in. "Jonathan, what about the woman?"

Jonathan's eyes widened. Kate knew he wouldn't leave her now, not even to chase down the man. He quickly yelled to Jett about the woman with the gun. Then Jett ushered the people in the lobby behind the front desk and into the part of the building only accessible to employees. Jonathan picked Kate up off the floor and helped her along with them.

"Are you okay?" Jonathan asked as soon as they stopped moving. He held her chin up so her gaze had no other place to go. And maybe she didn't want to look anywhere else, either.

"I am now," she said honestly. It created a reaction in his face she couldn't quite place. She felt her brows pull together in question. "What about you?" She started to reach out—to hold *his* face and make sure *he* was okay—when Jett hurried over to them.

"We called the cops when we heard the first shot," he said. "We also can't find Arthur."

"Arthur?" Kate and Jonathan asked in unison.

"The security guard on shift. He wasn't back here, so—"

A door down the hallway opened with such force the sound echoed throughout the lobby. On what had to be reflex Jonathan moved Kate around him again. The teens' father did the same with his kids and the elderly couple, putting them behind him. Jett even stepped back to put himself in front of the young mother and her toddler. Everyone seemed to be holding his or her breath until a woman walked around the corner.

It was the hotel manager, Lola Teague, and she was clearly fired up.

"I just watched that woman on the security camera go out the fire exit in the kitchen," she said. Her hair, which had been impeccable the night before, was now visibly ruffled. The laugh lines at the edge of each eye definitely were not being exercised. "I'd ask for everyone's calm and patience as we deal with this matter quickly." The sound of the sirens could be heard clearly from where they stood. Soon the cops would be in the lobby. Lola hurried to the door, pausing just long enough to whisper to them. "Whoever that couple is, they sure are determined."

Lola had no idea.

THE COPS WHO had come the day before for the letter were much more interested in what Jonathan and Kate had to say this time around. While they decided not to reveal that Kate had been drugged earlier in the day, they didn't stop from pointing out what had also happened at the crosswalk. Even a rookie cop could see there was a connection there.

"We ran the picture of that man through our criminal database but didn't get anything," one of them admitted. "The blood was real, but we got no match. But now that we have his accomplice on camera, we should be able to get a name."

Should and *would* were two very different things, but Kate kept her mouth shut. The officers didn't know the entire story, so how did she expect them to do their jobs?

Frustrated, Kate cracked the seal of the bottle of water she'd been handed. Her decision to pursue a drug that could potentially save lives in situations where time was the enemy was one she'd never regretted. Even now she couldn't come to second-guess it. When something consumes your life that much, for so long, the mind begins to treat it like a piece of the foundation that makes you who you are. Part of who Kate was, intrinsically tied to her life, was a drug that turned life into a dream.

"Oh, my God," Kate breathed out, nearly choking on her water. Jonathan stood a foot or so away, still in the lobby, talking with Lola. When he heard her, he did a U-turn so fast it almost made her dizzy again.

"What's wrong?"

She stood, stronger than before, but nowhere near as agile as she wanted.

"The case," was all she said.

It was enough.

Jonathan took her by her elbow and maneuvered her into the elevator. The one they hadn't fought in. She replayed what had happened in the other before recalling all other attacks that had taken place that day.

"I don't understand," Kate started. Jonathan didn't turn his gaze to her. He was more than focused on the elevator doors. Or, more aptly, what might jump out at them when they opened. "The woman would have killed me with her car had you not pushed me out of the way. She'd also have shot me had I not been able to stumble to the stairs. The man, though, seemed to want to take me with him." The elevator reached the third floor. Jonathan angled his body in front of her again. He stepped out, a man born of cautiousness, and nodded when it was clear. He resumed his position at her elbow. "So they don't seem to be on the same page. Plus, killing me wouldn't benefit anyone. I'm no longer, and really never was, the sole researcher of the drug. However…"

They stopped outside her hotel room. Jonathan pulled out the key card.

"I might be the only one with the prototype."

Jonathan did his due diligence again, heading in first and clearing the room before Kate stepped inside. She took in the details of a few holes in the wall where the men must have struggled and the water pooled on the bathroom tile.

"I thought he was dead," Jonathan reiterated, pointing to the tub. "I thought he broke his neck, but I was wrong."

Kate patted the bodyguard on the shoulder and went straight for the bed. She started to bend down but became dizzy. Jonathan was at her side in a flash.

"I'm okay," she said, shooing away his hands. "Is the case there?"

Before he bent down to look, she already knew it wasn't. Why go through all of that trouble without a parting gift?

Jonathan shook his head.

"What could they do with it, really?" he asked.

Kate shrugged. "Destroying it would be useless, since it can be replicated with the research. Using it, or selling it, would be a one-shot deal, and honestly, we don't even know if it works. There's a high chance that it'll have the same effect that the earlier stage of the drug had. My guess would be whoever they are, they're trying to reverse engineer it. Break it down to figure out what's inside so they can make more. Then again, if they have access to the labs, they wouldn't need to go through all that trouble."

"Well, what if we are wrong about that?" Kate raised her eyebrow. "What if they don't have access to the lab? What if it isn't an inside job? What if we know too much and it's skewing our perception of everything that's happened?"

Kate's mouth dangled open a fraction, making her guess she looked like a cartoon character. She could tell her surprise confused him. He tilted his head, giving her a questioning look.

"What?" he asked.

"That was just really attractive," she admitted before

she could censor herself. Jonathan broke into a grin that only made him more mouthwatering.

"What? Objective thinking or problem solving?"

Kate felt her cheeks burn, but she laughed.

"Both."

Jonathan joined in. When the laughter died a moment later, he took a step toward her. Something in the chemistry of the moment changed. The heat from her cheeks burned hotter. She hadn't been with a man in so long and not just in an intimate way. Jonathan Carmichael was looking at her like she'd seen other men look at other women, seeing not just a physical body but also a potential future. What could he see when looking at her?

Kate averted her gaze. This wasn't the time to find out.

"We need to call Jake and tell him what happened," she said. "If you're right and these people didn't have access to the lab, then finding out how they got the failed drug may be the key to figuring out what's going on. Plus, now that we have the woman's picture, maybe he can use the FBI database to find out who she is."

Kate didn't look up to see if Jonathan agreed. Instead she turned to the dresser. Opening the top drawer, she moved past her intimate apparel and pulled out a screwdriver.

"Should I be worried about why you had that in there?" Jonathan asked. Kate turned with a half smile. Whatever their moment had been, it had reverted back to normal. She moved over to the air-conditioning unit and got on her knees. She began to unscrew its cover.

"My mother taught me many things at a young age. Like how it's important to protect the things you care about. And how, sometimes, that means we must hide those very things." She removed the last screw and gently took off the cover. Taped to the inside was a small Moleskine notebook. Gingerly she removed it. Jonathan came to stand beside her, looking down at the book. "While I had digital files on what I was working on, I didn't put them all in the computer. I was always afraid that somehow the information might be leaked." She shook the notebook. "So I kept a secret hard copy that detailed everything. If our mystery crew has no access to the lab and its notes, then *this* is what they should have taken."

"And if they find out you have that, they might pay us another visit," Jonathan breathed out. He sounded split between anger and exhaustion.

Kate flipped open the notebook and let her eyes trace her handwritten scrawls. Notes, figures and calculations she'd devoted the past five years to—but really, her whole life.

A part of her.

A part of her mother.

And now a part of Jonathan.

Chapter Nineteen

Jake didn't answer his phone when Kate called and they decided against leaving any specific information on his voice mail. A vague "Call as soon as you get this—we need to talk," was all the scientist said. Still, Jonathan parked his rental outside an apartment complex on the Upper East Side of Manhattan with every intention of making it their permanent residence until they left New York.

"His apartment is on the third floor," Kate said, pulling her luggage over the sidewalk and up to the front door. No longer in her robe, she'd changed into a long-sleeved blue blouse, a pair of jeans and comfortable-looking flats. She twisted her hair up into a bun and had taken pains to spray down her thick bangs. She hadn't fooled with applying makeup. It was nearing night and they'd be staying put.

"You've been here before, right?" Jonathan asked as he helped her inside. Immediately they were met with stairs to their right. Kate exhaled.

"Yes, once, which means I sadly know there's no elevator. Because I haven't already had my fill of stairs for today," she mumbled. "At least now I won't be getting shot at."

Jonathan smiled, thinking her frustration was perhaps a great deal cuter than it should have been, and started the trek upward, all the while fussing over the woman like she was a child. She'd already been the target of attempted murder three times in two days. Jonathan reasoned his worry was more than warranted.

There were four apartments on the third floor and Kate directed them to one facing the street they'd parked on. A brown and black doormat with the word *Welcome* greeted them.

"Surely an FBI agent doesn't just keep his spare key beneath the mat?" he asked, worrying that maybe Jake wasn't as careful as he'd thought.

Kate chuckled. She lowered her bags to the ground. Putting her foot on the black rubber part of the mat, she bent and burrowed her fingers beneath the raised brown plastic on top. She pulled up and the sound of Velcro coming apart followed.

"It's not Fort Knox, but I don't think many would look here," she said, spying the key tucked in the open space. She pushed the middle back down and turned to Jonathan. Her eyebrow arched.

"Are you jealous of Jake's doormat?"

Jonathan rolled his eyes.

"Just unlock the door."

The apartment opened on a small L-shaped white kitchen that attached directly to the living area with an exposed brick accent wall at the back. Between the two was a small square dining set, a dark green patterned couch, a barrel that had been converted into an accent table and a large flat screen atop shelving bolted into the brick. On the rest of the walls making up the living and dining space were various framed pictures ranging from posters of cop movies to random road signs to pictures of family and friends. Kate watched as Jonathan took in these details and elaborated on a few.

"The only rebellious phase Jake ever went through when we were younger was stealing street signs. He's quite proud of them still." Her attention moved to the converted table. "That was a gag gift my father got Bill a year before he died. I don't think Jake's ever been without it." She pointed to the door across from the table. It was small, as he guessed the room behind it also would be. "Guest bedroom," she said, then pointed to the door next to it. "Very tiny, badly tiled bathroom. Leaving the last door as his room. Also not the most attractive room."

Jonathan laughed and parked his bags next to the couch. He headed back to the kitchen. Their pizza had never shown up at the hotel and he hoped Jake had something that could pass as a meal.

Kate dropped her things off in the guest bedroom and disappeared into Jake's room soon after. To do what, he didn't know. The agent didn't have anything to make a three-course meal, but he had enough to make turkey sandwiches with a side of chips. Jonathan didn't know much about Kate's eating habits aside from her love of the Chinese restaurant, but he was almost positive she was as hungry as he was and would take the food without complaint.

"Food's ready," he called, plating each sandwich.

Kate appeared as he put the plates on the dining table. Her cheeks were rosy and she didn't meet his eyes right away.

"You look suspicious," he commented. Kate tried to play coy and waved a hand at him as if to bat away his concern. "What did you do?"

"Nothing," she said, as if pretending she hadn't gone

into the agent's room in the first place. She took her seat across from him. He was happy to see the flash of pleasure that crossed her face as she spied the food. She didn't hesitate in beginning to eat.

"You know, I don't think I've snooped through Mark's or Oliver's places before, which is what I'm assuming you just did, and definitely not Nikki's," he pointed out with a smile. "I think you're nosy."

"From the little I know of Nikki Waters, it's probably a good thing you don't," she replied, not denying the accusation. "I would think the founder of a security agency appreciates her privacy." He gave her a thumbs-up to show she was right on the money. "I only snoop when I think there might be something worthy of the effort." She cut her eyes back to Jake's room. "Something that might help us make sense of everything."

"And did you find anything useful?"

"No, but I didn't really have enough time, now did I?" She threw him a wink that induced a different kind of pleasure within him than when Kate had eyed her food. It caught him off guard. So much so that he tried to cover for whatever his expression might have given away. He turned to the pictures on the wall beside them.

"Is that Bill?" he asked, honing in on one of a dark blond-haired man smiling wide. The ocean was behind him and he squinted a bit from the glare of the sun. The picture was aged.

"Yes, that was a few years before—" Kate stopped that thought and continued with a new one. "I think my father was the one who took that picture, actually." She put her half-eaten sandwich down and stood. She went along the wall, nose close, investigating each picture until she found the one she was looking for. "Our parents decided to do a joint family vacation one year.

It had been a long time since Jake's mom had been to the beach, so we packed up for a few days and went."

Jonathan joined her in front of the picture. Bill was sitting in the sand behind Jake as a little boy, while a smiling fair-haired woman was farther back in a striped beach chair. Jake wasn't looking at the camera, his concentration on a half-constructed sand castle in front of him. Jonathan recognized Deacon from Kate's Orion file—the younger version was seated in his own striped chair next to Jake's mother, caught in midlaugh. A woman in a black one-piece stood near him, but her eyes were on the little girl with her hands in the sand castle, a small smile on her face. That little girl, undoubtedly Kate, was the only person in the picture looking directly at the camera. They all looked so happy. So content. "You look just like your mother," Jonathan said, looking back at the woman. When the picture was taken she'd been older than Kate was now, but the resemblance was unbelievable.

Kate smiled.

"Thank you. This was actually the first attempt at a nice, smiling picture another tourist was kind enough to offer to take, but then something made my father break out into laughter." The smile from receiving Jonathan's compliment extended. It seemed to strengthen with the power of what must have been a good memory. "After that no one could get their acts together. I don't even know that we have a normal one. A few years back Jake's mother found this and made copies for us and my dad. It's one of my favorite pictures." Kate turned and Jonathan felt the bright light of the love she felt for her family, including Jake and his parents, move to him. Inadvertently he took a step away. He wished he could share the same type of memories—childhood ones of family—with her, be able to share stories of growing up, even the bumps along the way. But he had none.

He moved back to the table and picked up his food again. He was aware that Kate watched him, but she didn't comment on the change in his mood. Instead she, too, went back to eating, and in silence they each finished their food. Still without talking, Kate collected their empty plates and cleaned up. Jonathan tried to shake the mood he'd fallen into but was coming up short. The walls—the emotional barriers—around him built up once again. So high, in fact, that he didn't notice when Kate took her seat opposite him again until she spoke.

"Foster care?" Jonathan felt his eyes widen, finding hers with a questioning look. She gave him an apologetic smile and explained, "Yesterday you mentioned you moved around a lot as a child, something that you seemed angry about but not annoyed with. You also have an intense desire to plant roots and a fierce loyalty and, I bet, protectiveness of your friends and Orion. You talk about them as if they are your family. Plus—" she motioned to the back of her upper arm "—your tattoo. It's of a house."

"That's a big assumption you're making," he said. His even tone didn't faze her. Her dark eyes were kind, searching his face for what, he didn't know. She remained quiet until finally he decided to tell her a story he'd never told anyone before. "My mom died right after I was born and my dad had no business being a parent. So he decided not to be." The anger that he had once felt—the resentment—toward his father all of his childhood wasn't there anymore. He was just stating facts now.

"Like thousands of other children in the country,

I was never adopted and constantly moved around through foster families. For one reason or another, I couldn't make a meaningful connection with the adults. I couldn't seem to make friends with any of the kids, either. Not that it would matter if I had. There were some kids who had siblings in the system they hadn't seen or talked to in years." He exhaled. He might no longer feel the ill feelings he once had about his father's abandonment, but he didn't think he'd ever forget the overwhelming weight of loneliness.

"In high school I was sent to live with a woman who was rumored to only get kids with no hope of being adopted," he continued. "I'll never forget her, if only for her tattoos. She had these large, intricate works of art covering almost every inch of skin. One day I asked how she picked them. She said it had started with one. She'd sat down and thought about what she loved or wanted most in life and got a tattoo that represented it. Every one after was something else she loved or wanted until she was running out of room. So, one day I sat down, too, and while I was trying to think of what I loved more than anything, I drew this." He turned a bit so she could see the tattoo better. He didn't have to look down to recall the little box outline with its triangle on top, squares for windows and a small rectangle for the front door. It was an exact replica of the one he'd doodled on the corner of his notebook. "I guess I'm a cliché. The only thing I'd ever loved was the idea of a home."

Kate stood up so quickly that her chair scraped against the hardwood. Jonathan tensed, ready to put out whatever fire she'd just remembered, but the brunette came around the table and threw her arms around him. She put her chin against his shoulder and buried her face against his neck.

"You're not a cliché," she said, slightly muffled.

Jonathan felt the walls around him shake. Not on reflex—because he didn't have one for this kind of situation—he returned the embrace with a smile. Kate's body was warm against him. The perfume she'd put on before they'd left the hotel was flowery and perfect.

"Thank you," he said, voice soft, almost afraid to spook her. Kate stepped back and what Jonathan saw alarmed him. "Are you crying?"

Kate brought the back of her hands up and wiped away the few stray tears that had found their way to her reddened cheeks.

"Well, excuse me," she exclaimed. "My heartstrings were just violently strummed." She started to move away from him, backing up like she'd been burned. He'd embarrassed her.

"No," he said, capturing her hands so she couldn't escape. "I just don't want to see you cry. Not because of me." Kate stopped moving. Another tear leaked out and all Jonathan could think about was stopping it. He dropped her hand and lifted it to her cheek, running his fingers across and wiping the tear free. "I'll admit that my childhood wasn't ideal, and there are times when I still wish it had been different, but then I remember if it had, I never would have met Nikki. She never would have referred me for a job at Redstone and I'd never have met Oliver and Mark. I'd never leave and join Orion and meet some of the best people I've ever known."

He heard his voice go low on the last part, saw Kate's expression soften and felt the urge to tell her she was now included in that list of people all at the same time. "Don't worry about me, Kate. Let me worry about you."

Chapter Twenty

Every part of Kate was telling—no, screaming at—her to kiss the man in front of her. To create a different kind of embrace than the one they'd shared moments before. To open up and lose herself in something other than her work.

But Kate's body drew away from him before her mind could reason out why. She gave him a quick smile she hoped said everything she couldn't and moved out of his reach.

"The convention is tomorrow afternoon, and no matter what happens, I feel like I should get some sleep," she said.

It was like a fog lifted from Jonathan's face. He straightened his back, cleared his throat and nodded. Guilt, though she didn't quite understand its place, slowly turned within her. Like she'd deflated him somehow.

"Yeah, I don't blame you for being tired," he said. "I'm going to stay out here and wait for Jake to get in."

"Could you wake me up when he does?" Kate was already moving away, as if she could physically separate herself from the foreign feeling of desire she realized had started to grow.

"Sure thing," he said, "Good night, Miss Scientist."

Despite her unease, when she got to the guest bedroom door she turned with a quick response.

"You, too, Mr. Bodyguard."

She shut the door behind her like she was running from a nightmare. But hadn't Jonathan been the one good thing in her dreams? Kate put her back to the door and tried to compose her skittering thoughts.

The man had opened up to her—had been undeniably vulnerable—and what had she done with the moment? Run. The way he'd looked at her, the way he'd wiped her tears away yet left his hand caressing her face had given her the perfect moment to grab hold of something.

But she couldn't do it.

Jonathan wanted roots. He wanted friends, a family, a home. Aside from her father visiting and the occasional email or phone call from Greg and Jake, Kate's life revolved around her work. Her one goal in life. She didn't know how to cope or deal with anything else. Like her father said, she was narrow-minded. Seeing the big picture wasn't just hard for her, it was sometimes downright impossible.

One thing she was sure of in the midst of all of the new uncertainty that had surfaced in her life was that the man in the next room deserved more than an emotionally stunted woman stumbling through what others did with ease.

He deserved a life without her as a complication.

KATE ROLLED OVER, getting wrapped up in the mismatched blanket and sheets, and looked up into the darkness. She'd been in bed for at least two hours and hadn't gotten a lick of sleep, but not for lack of trying.

The first hour she wondered if it was her fear of slipping back into her dream world from earlier that day. Reliving the discovery of her mother and Bill's bodies was frightening enough to make her mind try its best to stay awake. It was a niggling thought that finally got her to call her father. She'd ignored his few calls over the last two days, responding with a quick text that she was fine, just busy. She didn't want to worry him more than he already was. Despite the late hour, which she let him assume was because she'd been working and lost track of time, he'd been happy to finally hear her voice. She promised to call him after the convention the next day. She made sure to tell him she loved him. The rest of that hour had then crawled by. Yet, as she rolled into the next hour, she started to realize what she was really afraid of.

The dark.

The world when she was awake.

The couple that had made very public and violent attempts on her life.

Thoughts of the man and his dark, narrow eyes made her hand flit to her hair. She massaged her scalp, remembering the pain of having her hair pulled without an ounce of remorse.

It was that man and his partner that kept her tossing and turning. The tiny window that faced the side of the building next door didn't help with its lack of light that filtered into the small room.

After more time had passed, Kate finally gave up. As quietly as if it was Christmas and she was trying to get a glimpse of Santa, she tiptoed to the door and slowly opened it. She winced as it creaked something awful. The lights from the kitchen and living area were off, save for a floor lamp next to the TV. It was enough light for her to see Jonathan quickly turn at the noise.

She held her hands up in defense.

"Sorry," she whispered. "I meant to be a bit sneakier than that."

Jonathan visibly relaxed and put down what looked like a sports magazine he'd been reading.

"Is everything okay?"

Kate nodded.

"You having trouble sleeping?"

Jonathan grinned.

"I'm not trying to."

"You have to sleep sometime," she pointed out.

"Sometimes that's not in the job description."

Kate was going to argue, but who was she to tell anyone what to do within the bounds of their job. She certainly didn't listen to others. Still, she bounced from foot to foot, trying carefully to say the right thing.

"So," she started, cheeks already blazing hot. "You're not going to try to sleep any time soon?"

Jonathan raised his eyebrow but nodded.

"I've worked on a lot less sleep," he explained. "Why?"

Kate's blush was an all-out inferno. She could feel its heat even moving to her ears.

"Well, I was wondering, if it's okay with you, if maybe you could come stay in here with me?" Jonathan's eyebrow rose so high that it almost seemed to get lost in his hairline. "It's just, well, I can't fall asleep," she added quickly, rubbing the side of her arm, self-conscious. "I think I'd feel safer if you were closer."

"Oh," Jonathan said, two beats too late. Kate started to back into the bedroom again, waving her hands to dismiss her request.

"Never mind, it's okay, really," she said. "I can—"

Jonathan stood and started laughing. It stopped her words before they tripped off her tongue.

"Kate, it's okay," he said. "I don't mind in the least. Plus, this couch is really uncomfortable."

Kate felt her lips pull up at the corners. She'd bet that last part was for her benefit. The bodyguard moved toward her and she flipped the light back on so he could see the room. It was small and only housed a queen-size bed, a nightstand, a closet and a strip of carpet for limited foot traffic. Kate turned to see him sizing up the space and realized he might not have known what he was agreeing to do.

"There's nothing in here but the bed," she said, blunt. Jonathan let out another howl of laughter. Instead of backing out or teasing her, he kicked off his shoes and sat down on the side closest to the door. It sagged a bit beneath his weight as he lay down, so long his feet nearly went off the foot, and put his hands behind his head.

"If I turn the light off, won't it make you sleepy?" Kate asked, moving her hand over the switch. Jonathan shook his head. So she clicked it off and moved to the other side of the bed. If she hadn't been in her long T-shirt and pajama shorts, she wouldn't have suggested his supervision in the room. But, truth be told, she *did* need to get some sleep.

The bed dipped considerably less as she quickly shimmied under the displaced sheets and blanket. The bed might have been queen-size, but as she found the warm spot that her body had created before, she realized just how close the man next to her was. Although he was wearing the same shirt and pants from earlier that day and there was a swath of fabric between them, she could feel warmth from him seeping into her. It was more than just comforting.

Kate waited for her eyes to adjust to the darkness and the smallest ounce of light from the window while she rolled on her side and finally looked up at the man. Able to make out a wisp of his profile, she found her earlier thoughts on whatever moment they could have shared weighing on her just as heavily as her desire to save him the trouble of having her in his life. She pulled her hand out of the covers with the intention of taking his while the internal struggle between her happiness and his waged within her. Her hand paused in midair.

Do it, Kate.

But she couldn't. Her hand slid beneath her pillow.

"I'm sorry," she whispered into the dark. The sound of him moving his head toward her made the heat in her cheeks flare back to life.

"What for?"

Kate was sorry she'd been mean to him, callous and tactless about his profession when they'd met. She was sorry she'd been difficult and her singular focus had put him in danger. She was sorry that, despite the fact that he'd saved her at least three times, she didn't know how to really say thank-you. She was sorry for a lot of things, but couldn't find the words to connect that feeling to one thought.

"I'm not good with people," was all she said. In her mind it encompassed everything she felt guilty for right down to the moment she'd let slip away.

Jonathan moved some more, but in the darkness she couldn't pinpoint how.

"You're just fine for me."

Despite the lack of light, Jonathan's lips found hers with undeniable precision. Like his body, their warmth coaxed out a desire in Kate that she'd been trying to keep at bay. One that she felt growing stronger and stronger.

Jonathan broke the kiss and moved back.

"Sorry," he started, voice suddenly very low. "I—"

Kate pushed her body forward, hand out, taking his face and bringing his lips back to hers. She'd interrupted him, but manners be damned. Jonathan's apology evaporated like the space between their two bodies. His lips were as hungry as hers, and soon their tongues joined each other in a tangled fray.

Kate moaned against him, against his taste. The sound seemed to charge the bodyguard even more. He rolled on top of her, elbows out to prop himself up, all without breaking their bond. Kate more than approved of the new position, putting her hands around his neck and pulling him down to her. For years, and maybe her entire life up until this point, she hadn't craved anyone as badly as she now craved this man. Kate moved her hands down to the bottom of his shirt and tugged upward with enthusiasm. Instead of it peeling off easily like she'd seen in countless movies, it stuck. Frustrated, she accidentally made a huff sound against his lips. She felt the same lips curve up into a smile. Jonathan broke their kiss, much to her dismay.

Without a word he sat up, now fully straddling her. Kate's chest heaved up and down, her face hot, but not as much as the rest of her when the bodyguard did something that really raised her temperature. With her eyes fully adjusted and able to make out what he was doing, Kate watched wide-eyed as the bodyguard pulled off his shirt and threw it on the floor. He lowered his lips back down to her, and instead of the hard crush of the last one, this kiss was a soft brush that left her wanting more. He moved his lips to her ear and whispered something that let Kate know exactly where she wanted this to go.

"Your turn."

LIKE LIGHTNING HAD struck her, Kate's eyelids flashed open. Something that had been hanging in the back of her mind was about to fall free. An idea, a theory on the tip of her tongue that bothered her on an almost emotional level. Something her mind was grasping for with such enthusiasm she'd woken up to help solve whatever problem it was attached to.

She started to get out of bed when an odd heaviness brought her attention to the man beside her, derailing her train of thought. Jonathan was on his side, fast asleep, his arm thrown over her—protective still. Kate smiled. She'd had a feeling the man had been just as tired as her.

Kate took a moment to watch the bodyguard sleep. In the soft light of early morning, she had an unobstructed view of his well-muscled chest with its light brushing of dark hair that slid down his stomach and disappeared beneath the sheets. She felt her cheeks heat with the knowledge of exactly what was beneath them. Despite her need to get some sleep, they'd spent quite a big portion of the rest of the night doing anything but.

She used all of her grace to move the man's arm off her and slip out of the bed without jostling him too much. He stirred but didn't wake up. Kate once again tiptoed across the room. Her body, she realized, was sore, but in a pleasant way. It reminded her of the way the bodyguard had felt with her. In every way. She smiled, still able to feel the impression of his lips against her skin.

Kate, as naked as the day she was born, collected her toiletries and clothes. She went into the badly tiled bathroom and showered quickly. Her mind had finally detached itself from the naked man in the room next door and focused on the feeling that was sticking out like a sore thumb in her mind. It felt like a hunch, but she didn't yet know what it was and why it was suddenly bothering her so much. Since she was positive she wasn't going to be able to fall back to sleep any time soon, she dressed in the clothes she'd packed for the convention without a second thought—a slightly sheer quarter-length sleeved burgundy blouse with a black camisole beneath that tucked right into wrinkle-free black slacks. Mind elsewhere still, she went through the motions of applying eyeliner, blush and dark red lipstick. She started to towel dry her hair when she remembered everything that had happened. Slowly she lowered the towel. Chances were attending the convention wouldn't be easy. It didn't seem like the couple was done yet, especially if they were working for anyone with half a brain. It wouldn't matter if they somehow were able to reverse engineer the drug. There wasn't enough time to do it before Kate presented her research.

She watched in the mirror as her expression hardened. She threw the towel over the shower rod and furiously brushed out her hair. When done, she gave herself one curt nod.

It was time to try to put an end to this.

Slipping into the flats she'd taken off in the living room, Kate padded to Jake's bedroom. To her surprise he still wasn't in the apartment, but then again, she knew that cases could often keep an agent away from home for days at a time. The larger room had a bed, desk and three waist-high filing cabinets. All with locks. Kate went to the one she'd jimmied open the night before—right before Jonathan had called her to dinner, noting she looked suspicious—and pulled it open. Jake had an office at the Bureau as well as one within Greg's lab. In both he had files and places to keep them safe. However, just as Jake had learned to become neat, he'd learned the importance of hard copies and backups. The filing cabinet she'd opened had information on dates and events that seemed to be tied to his job as Greg's handler. Most seemed to be written with code names, and as far as she could tell, there was no mention of the drug.

However, she had seen something the night before that was bothering her now. She shuffled through the files, trying to spark whatever trail she'd dismissed already. Minutes rolled by as she thumbed through and pulled out several different files.

What had she seen?

Frustrated, she turned and perched against the cabinet, trying to remember. Her eyes roamed the room around her as her mind went blank. She took in Jake's sparse bedroom decor—some knickknacks he'd saved through the years, pictures of trips he'd taken and memorabilia he'd collected and been given—when suddenly she knew exactly what it was she was looking for.

The theory that she had unconsciously formed even before waking became less of a *what if* and more of a terrifying possibility. With her stomach having dropped somewhere past her feet, she walked to one picture sitting on Jake's desk. Her hands trembled as she picked it up.

There it was.

It all made sense now.

Her phone buzzed in her pocket. She had been so

focused on the picture that the motion startled her. She dropped the frame and winced as the glass cracked on impact.

Then she realized that was the least of her worries.

She fumbled for her phone and read Jake's ID flashing across the screen. Her stomach twisted.

"Jake," she started. But the man who responded definitely wasn't the boy she'd grown up with.

"No, but you can save him."

Chapter Twenty-One

Jonathan rolled onto his side, throwing his arm out so he wouldn't hit Kate. With his eyes still closed, he lowered it to the bed, careful he didn't hurt her.

But there was no Kate beneath it.

Jonathan opened one eye, took in the light from the window and looked at the empty spot next to him with a split feeling of warmth and coldness. Seeing where the scientist had been reminded him of what they had done, bringing a sense of unfamiliar happiness over him. At the same time, the empty spot highlighted the one fact that bodyguards needed to know at all times about their clients.

Where they were.

He swam his way out of the sheets and stopped when something fell to the floor. Confused, he bent over and picked up the book.

"Kate?" he called out into the apartment, pulling on his pants as he realized what he was holding. He opened the bedroom door and saw an empty kitchen and living space. Turning, he scanned the bathroom and found it, too, was empty. Cursing beneath his breath, he went for Jake's room.

Empty.

"Kate?" he called again, even though it was obvi-

ous she wasn't in the apartment. He ran to the front
door, expecting there to be signs of a break-in. But there
wasn't. Everything looked like it had after he'd locked
them in the night before. The door's dead bolt was still
thrown. Jonathan checked the windows next, but they,
too, were locked.

"What's going on?" he asked the empty apartment.

Jonathan retrieved his phone and found no new calls
or messages. He dialed Kate's number. It went straight
to voice mail. The lack of ringing created an instant
feeling of fear laced with panic. He looked down at
the black book in his hand. Kate had left her notebook
for him, he was sure, but why? And where was Jake?
Had they gone somewhere together or had the agent not
come home at all? He opened the notebook to the first
page, hoping she'd left him some kind of clue.

He was disappointed. Kate's past five years of work
were between his hands. Entrusted to him, but why?

Jonathan quickly dressed and decided to search the
apartment for clues once more. All of Kate's things were
still in the bedroom, but he noticed her toiletries had
made it to the bathroom. There was also a wet towel.
She'd showered. He moved on to the kitchen and living area, but nothing seemed to have changed from the
night before. Lastly, he hit Jake's room, the least likely
to hold any clue as to where the woman had gone, seemingly of her own accord.

Or was it?

One of the three filing cabinets beneath the window
had a drawer pulled out. Even from the doorway he
could see the lock had been broken. Jonathan walked
over to inspect it when he noticed most of the papers
were disheveled, like they'd been taken out one by one

before being crammed back inside. *This* was what Kate had been up to before dinner.

Jonathan began to go through a few of the papers, trying to discern what Kate had been after, but without knowing Jake or Greg—whom the files mostly seemed to be about—he couldn't glean whatever Kate had. He slammed the drawer shut and was turning to leave when he spotted a picture lying upside down on the floor near the desk. Without much thought other than to put it back, he picked it up. Broken pieces of glass remained on the carpet. Curiosity piqued, he looked at the picture inside.

It wasn't a picture at all.

It was a letter.

A different kind of coldness came back.

Jonathan reached for his phone and scrolled through his pictures, stopping on the bloody letter left on Kate's hotel door. By the time he'd taken the picture, the words had been smeared by the blood. He opened his email and found Kate's Orion file. He pulled up the photocopies of every letter she'd received before she'd left Florida and scrolled through each. Halfway through he stopped. He didn't need to look any further to know the handwriting was a perfect match with the framed note in his hand.

"How could we have missed this?"

Anger seared through him as he quickly recalled the last three days with his new revelation. The one, he had no doubt, Kate had come to when she'd seen the note. How she must have felt, how she must have reacted, tore at a part of him he didn't even realize had been reserved just for thoughts of her. He put the frame down and was about to dial his boss's number. It was past time to loop her in. He needed help. However, his phone came to life instead. The number was unknown but he answered, cautious.

"Yes?"

"Mr. Carmichael?" Even though the man's voice was lowered, Jonathan was able to pick out who it belonged to easily enough.

"Jett?"

"Yeah, it's me. I thought you should know that man is back."

"Back? In the hotel?"

"I may have kept your and Miss Spears's reservations open in the computers," Jett quickly said. "I thought that it might help to keep you two hidden if they thought you were still here."

Jonathan could have kicked himself for not thinking of that before, just as he could have given the front desk attendant a huge bear hug right about then. This was exactly the break he needed.

"Jett, I need you to do me a huge favor," Jonathan said, already running into the living area to grab his keys. "Kate's gone and right now that man is the only lead I have to finding her. I need you to follow him, but don't say anything to him, and tell me where he's going. Can you do that?"

Jonathan shut the door behind him, not caring that he no longer had a way to get back inside. Kate had a key, and when he had Kate back it would all be okay.

"Jett?" he prodded after hesitation on the other end of the line continued.

"Yes, I can. I'll call you from the car."

KATE LOOKED OUT the window and down into the construction. The building next door was a few stories shorter and currently being built to match the one she was standing in. Though at a much slower pace.

"Progress isn't always as fast as we'd like it to be."

Kate turned in her leather chair and eyed the man who had been pulling the strings all along. A part of Kate withered at the sight of him. The other part flourished in anger.

"It all makes sense now," she said. "I guess the analytical part of me should be happy about that, at least." Kate laughed, a dry, quick sound. "From knowing what hotel I was staying at to knowing my plans while in New York." She laughed again, still as bitter as dark chocolate. "You knew everything, because we disclosed the information to you willingly."

Greg stood at the head of the table but didn't sit down. He wore a dark brown suit with a spotted blue tie she'd actually bought him for his birthday a few years back. A bandage covered his right brow while cuts and swelling could be seen across the same side. He placed his hands on the top of the chair and squeezed the leather. He wasn't smiling, but he sure wasn't frowning, either. Either expression would have incited more anger on her part, but the blank look he was giving her was almost too much to bear. She fought the urge to look down at her hands.

"But how far down does the rabbit hole go, Greg? When did you become *this*? I don't even know how to describe you." Kate felt her eyes begin to water. She hoped she could keep it together long enough to at least understand *something*. "Why have you been terrorizing me—trying to kill me?" Her voice broke on the question and then nearly shattered on the next. "And where is Jake?"

Greg flexed his grip on the chair as if the motions

helped him sort his thoughts. But Kate knew the man well enough—or at least she thought she had—to know it was a show. If Greg really had planned everything that happened so far, then he knew every reason why he'd done it without pausing.

"Do you remember when we first met, Kate? I believe you were eight. I asked you what you wanted to be when you were all grown up. Do you remember what you told me?"

Despite her desire to not play his game—whatever it was—Kate nodded.

"A dancer," she said.

Greg snapped his fingers.

"A dancer," he repeated. "Now, I have nothing against the performing arts or those who seek careers in its purview, but when I looked at you, saw how your mind worked, saw you talk and react to the world around you, I saw exactly what your mother did. I saw untapped potential coupled with an unquenchable curiosity. You didn't just question how the world worked, you tried to understand it. Seeing that raw innocence created within me a feeling of hope for the future so profound that I told you something I'd never told any other soul. Do you remember what that was?"

This time Kate didn't nod. She didn't have to sit there and tell him she remembered anything. They both knew she had never forgotten the words of a man her mother had once proclaimed was the smartest man she knew. Still, Greg waited a moment before continuing. He smiled as the words left his mouth.

"I told you that you were going to change the world." He let go of the chair top and clapped. "And by God, when you told me you'd had a breakthrough in your research, you proved that I was absolutely right!" His excitement began to ebb away, his smile falling slowly. He put his hands on the top of the chair again. Suddenly he looked tired. "I was so proud of you that, at first, I didn't realize what it meant. You, not even thirty, had found answers I hadn't yet been able to obtain despite my vast resources. In fact, your surprising achievements began to highlight my lack of them, showing my superiors that while I had the full force of the FBI behind me, all you had were two part-time lab techs who did menial work on something they had no idea was so important." One of his hands fisted. There was no trace of emotion besides a deep weariness that projected through the slight sagging of his face.

"Talk began to circulate about your achievement, about your work ethic, about your *potential*. For a while they praised me for finding you—for believing in you enough to challenge the Bureau to wait you out, to let you try to work out the solutions and not simply take them from you. That is, until their praise turned to anything but. Maybe I'd convinced them to wait for you because I didn't know how to do it myself. Maybe I had worked *so hard* to keep you associated with the project, without your knowledge, because I knew you wouldn't ask me to leave when *you* finally came on and took over. Maybe I was getting too old and a newer, brighter, younger face was needed." Kate watched as his expression burned white-hot with a flash of anger. It went out as fast as it had ignited. The extreme change in emotion seemed to leave him speechless for a moment. Kate capitalized on it.

"If I was out of the way, then you'd be able to keep your position, your lab and your reputation," she guessed. Even as he nodded, the child that had grown up looking to Greg as her role model tried to reason the admission away. He hadn't done anything. He couldn't have done anything. He was Greg.

But as his chin dipped down and then back up, the grown-up within Kate felt sick.

"I tried to warn you at first," he said. "And then scare you away."

"The notes," she said. It was the connection she'd made in Jake's room once she saw the handwritten letter Jake had received and framed when he graduated from the academy. It was handwriting she'd seen all her life and yet never thought about when staring at the same writing on the letters she'd received.

"I wanted to scare you away, make you realize that the spotlight should be put on someone more experienced."

"Like you."

"Yes, like me."

"But I didn't scare, did I?" she asked.

Greg's expression cracked again, showing another glimpse of anger she'd never seen from the man before.

"No, you didn't. Not even when a note found its way to your hotel-room door with real blood. You didn't even mention it to me the next day. So I had to escalate."

Kate didn't know what to do or say. The world she was currently sitting in didn't make sense. It was like she was back in her dream world. But this time Jonathan wasn't there to save her.

"You got that woman to try to run me over on the street," she breathed. "To just mow me down right in front of you. It was never about getting the case. It was about killing me."

"They don't call it an escalation for nothing," he said, almost teasing.

"But you were almost killed, too."

"That was truly an accident. One variable I didn't count on when we planned it was that Candice was harboring some fierce anger due to Donnie's impromptu knife show when he cut her arm to supply the blood found on the letter on your door." He dragged his finger up the inside of one of his arms. Finally she made the connection with the woman and the bandage. "I guess good help is hard to find sometimes, even from professionals. Her stress caused sloppiness that ended up working well for me in the end. Who would suspect me when I was so clearly a victim? Thankfully, I look much worse than I feel, and, luckily, not only did I have a backup plan, but Donnie was quick to employ it using a contact of his." The paramedic. He had been the backup plan. "But it still didn't work. No, there was another variable I hadn't accounted for."

"Jonathan." Just saying his name made a darkening world momentarily seem to lighten.

"I never thought you'd accept the help of a bodyguard, to be honest. Especially not one who would go above and beyond the scope of his job." He shook his head as if he was scolding her. "Breaking into the lab with Jake to save you was a big risk for him to take for someone he barely knew. Who really could have foreseen that happening?" He shook his head. "And just think, if Jonathan hadn't listened to you and saved you then, none of us would be in this situation we are in now."

Kate twisted her hands together in her lap.

"What have you done with Jake?" she whispered. Her trust in Greg was nothing compared to Jake's. While he'd become a mentor to her, Greg had become a father figure to her friend.

"Getting rid of Jake wouldn't benefit me or my plan.

Being responsible for the death of an FBI agent—more specifically, my handler—would bring me unwanted attention. Not to mention, his affection for me keeps him from seeing exactly what I've done."

"He doesn't know you're behind all of this?" she asked, surprised.

Greg shook his head.

"His passion to avenge my pain and to keep you safe was getting him too close," he explained. "I sent Donnie to retrieve him yesterday. Once this is all over, Jake will be let go. No harm, no foul."

Kate was once again split between two emotions. Relief that Jake was okay and would be okay. Anger that Jake might never know the truth because of his love for the man standing near her.

"You betrayed us," Kate said. Adrenaline and tears made her voice tremble.

Greg nodded solemnly.

"I know your family has already felt this particular sting before, but just know it wasn't always part of the plan." He shrugged. "You simply forced my hand."

Chapter Twenty-Two

Kate's hands fisted. Was this what her mother had felt when she'd realized her team—the people she thought she knew better than anyone—had turned their backs on her?

"What now?" she asked instead. "If you wanted to simply kill me, why bring me here?"

Up until this point, Kate had almost been certain that Greg had needed to share his narrative with her. To explain why he was doing what he was doing. Whether it was cathartic or just a way for him to brag to someone, Kate didn't know. Either way, he answered her.

"I remembered your notebook. That intrepid little thing where you kept all of your notes written down, afraid that the world might take the ideas if they left the paper and ink of its pages. Knowing you, there's something in it that you've left out of the research you shared with me. Something I need to continue. And before you say you don't have it in New York, remember that I know you, Kate. I know you hid it in the hotel room just like I knew you would come here willingly to save Jake." Greg stepped up to the table. He lowered himself until he was pressing down on the glass top, a stance that showed he wanted her absolute full attention now. Not that he didn't already have it. "And once Donnie brings it to me, then I'll say goodbye."

Kate's mouth went dry.

"When they say never meet your idols, they weren't kidding," she whispered. Greg's lips pulled up at the corners.

"And when they said children were our future, how true that was, as well."

Kate watched as the man she had once loved like family turned his back on her. He walked to the door and knocked once before it opened, giving her a glimpse of the woman named Candice.

"No one comes in or out," he ordered. "And if she starts making too much noise, silence her."

Candice cast Kate a quick smirk.

"My pleasure."

Kate held her gaze, not wanting to back down until the door shut, leaving her alone inside. What had started out as a theory was now a full-blown walking nightmare. Not bringing the notebook had saved her life, at least temporarily, but now what if leaving it with Jonathan had endangered his?

Just because you're scared doesn't mean you're not strong.

Kate recalled her mother's words but, for once, found no comfort in them.

In that moment she felt nothing but weakness.

JONATHAN WAS STANDING across from yet another hotel, still in Manhattan but worlds different from where Jett worked.

"He went in there," Jett said, jogging up to Jonathan. He was still dressed in uniform but had taken his blazer off, draping it over his arm to look more casual.

However, Jonathan looked up at the fifteen-story hotel and its glass-walled front and felt that maybe he was the one that looked too casual.

"Of course it is," he said. "This is where the convention is taking place in a few hours."

Jett joined his gaze and whistled.

"I applied for a job here once. It's a pretty fancy place. They have a glass atrium that makes you feel like you're not in a hotel at all."

"So, you've been in there before."

Jett nodded.

"Apparently I didn't have the right look, something about being too shaggy." He shrugged. "I've only seen the lobby, though, and not even for that long. They're pretty diligent about keeping nonguests out."

As soon as he'd been given the address of where Donnie had exited the cab, Jonathan had guessed simply walking in and asking if they'd seen Greg would have been frowned upon.

"So what's the plan?" Jett asked, gaze still turned to the hotel.

"You want to help us?" Jonathan asked, surprised. "Even though you have no idea what's going on?"

Jett shrugged again.

"If I did know, would that make Miss Spears in any less danger?"

Jonathan couldn't help but snort.

"No."

"Then, what's the plan?"

Jett followed along as Jonathan started for the nearest crosswalk and crossed the street. When they were near the double front doors, Jonathan spoke.

"Put this number in your cell phone." He recited the number when Jett's phone was out and made sure the man saved it. "I want you to call that number and tell the woman who answers that I told you to tell her something. Okay?" Jett nodded. "Tell her everything that has happened so far is because of Greg Calhoun. That he's trying to kill Kate and has been since we arrived. He's the one who sent her the letters, too." Jett's eyes widened, but he nodded again. "Tell her where we are and tell her I'm sorry I didn't tell her everything beforehand. Got that?"

"Yeah, when do you want me to do that?"

"Wait out here and give me five minutes and then call. I don't want to tip them off that I'm coming yet."

"And what are you going to do?"

Jonathan pulled out his wallet and counted out two hundred dollars in fifties and twenties.

"I'm going to go lie."

Like the outside, the inside was the complete opposite of the hotels Jonathan was used to. Not only was it as modern as they came—modular sofas and ottomans, white and gray everything with a smidgen of bright orange or blue and smooth, rounded front desks pushed to the side under the low part of the atrium—but as Jonathan walked across the gray tile, he was trying not to marvel at the giant art installations that could be seen from every floor, all the way up to the glass ceiling. It wasn't just a hotel. It was a destination.

He'd barely made it to one of the three front desks when a woman with the nameplate Julie chirped out a scripted welcome. It was all he could do to keep what he hoped was a pleasant and very innocent smile on his face.

"Actually, you can help me and a guest," he said, holding the money up. "I was getting into a taxi right outside when I noticed this lying in the backseat. The driver said it must have fallen out of one of your guests' pockets." Jonathan described the dark-haired man as if he'd heard a secondhand account from his made-up taxi driver. Even as he finished his description, her eyes widened in recognition.

"That sounds like Mr. Smith," she exclaimed. Jonathan wanted to roll his eyes at the name.

"Good! So you'll be able to return it to him," Jonathan said, mimicking her excitement. Julie nodded profusely, picking up the phone next to her. He fully intended to stall as long as he could, pretending to look at the art installations until he could see where Mr. Smith was going, when Julie decided to change the plan without even knowing it. She slid the money he'd put on the table back to him.

"I think Mr. Smith will want to thank you personally," she said after stepping aside to make the call. "It's not every day you find a less-than-greedy man. Most would have kept the money."

Jonathan shrugged.

"That just isn't my style."

Julie pointed out which elevator the man would most likely exit. Instead of skulking in the shadows trying to stalk him, Jonathan figured this bold approach worked just as well. Sooner or later he had bet he would come up against the man again.

Less than two minutes later, Jonathan watched as the elevator doors opened and none other than Mr. Smith was standing in front of him. His look of surprise was hidden quickly as Julie caught his eye and waved.

"I just wanted to return what you left behind," Jonathan said, voice dripping with fake cheer. He smiled for the benefit of Julie just as he suspected the man in front of him was doing.

"How thoughtful," he said, mouth stretched wide. He extended his hand and took the money before motioning for Jonathan to step inside. "To repay your kindness, how about we grab a drink upstairs?"

Jonathan kept smiling and got onto the elevator, now fully facing Julie's approving nod.

"Don't you think it's a little too early to drink?" Jonathan asked.

"Not when I'm celebrating."

The doors began to slide closed.

"And what's the occasion?" Jonathan asked. His entire body tensed as the man pressed the button for the second floor from the top.

"I was about to leave to finish a job," the man said, moving back to his spot against the elevator wall. The elevator doors shut as soon as he finished his next thought. "But it appears that now I don't have to leave at all."

The man reached in his blazer and pulled out a knife just as Jonathan turned and hiked his foot up. He pushed the man away from him just as Mr. Smith swiped at his shin. The knife sliced his pants but didn't cut deeper. Had he not reacted as fast as he did, Jonathan knew that wouldn't have been the case.

Mr. Smith turned the hilt of his knife so he was holding the blade down, arcing it through the air in between them with force. Jonathan lunged forward, grabbing for the man's wrist. He caught it as the man pulled it up, ready for another swipe. Jonathan used his free hand to send a punch against the man's face, but he moved out of range too quickly. The jolt loosened Jonathan's hold on his wrist and he had to jump back, hitting the elevator wall so hard that it shook, to avoid the knife's curved, sharp blade.

Jonathan pushed off the wall, knowing the man wouldn't stop until he had gutted him in the elevator, and grabbed for his arm again. This time, though, he wasn't lucky. The tip of the knife came down before he could push Mr. Smith's arm out of the way. The blade moved across Jonathan's forearm, cutting through his long-sleeve button-up as well as his skin. He made a grunt as the pain registered, but knew the cut hadn't been a direct hit. He pivoted back, moving his left side away from another attack and used the momentum to bring up his right elbow. It connected with the side of the man's nose in a sickening crack and then a spray of blood.

The man let out a howl and swung around in an angry spiral. Once again the knife connected with Jonathan's skin—this time his shoulder.

Jonathan felt the warm liquid before he saw the blood seeping through his shirt. The elevator began to slow and Jonathan just hoped the doors would open soon.

"Fighting an unarmed man seems cowardly." He grabbed his shoulder and moved to the corner. Mr. Smith was also in pain. All humor he'd once had seemed to have broken along with his nose. He held the knife out and wiped the blood from his nose with the back of his other hand. It did nothing but smear the red around.

"Where's the notebook?" he bit out.

"Where's Kate?" Jonathan bit right back.

It angered the man more than the nose break seemed to and he lashed out in another burst of fury just as the elevator doors opened. Without time to glance back to see where he was running out into, Jonathan backed out of the small space and into a much more expansive one. From his periphery he saw more modular couches and closed doors on either side of him. He didn't have time to investigate further.

Mr. Smith wasn't done with him yet.

KATE HADN'T BEEN blindfolded when she was brought into the hotel or the small yet lavish boardroom she was currently being held in. She had given Jonathan her notebook, called a taxi, walked into the lobby and told the front desk attendant she was expected. Then Kate had taken the elevator to the fourteenth floor and walked right into the same boardroom, all without hesitation, to wait for Greg to show up and tell her of her and Jake's fates.

It had been easy to get there.

But she now expected it would be exponentially harder to leave.

She rapped her knuckles against the door and stepped all the way back to the table, trying to show that she in no way meant trouble.

The door opened slowly until the woman's annoyance was seen clearly on her expression. She sized Kate up.

"I just want to talk," Kate pleaded.

Candice snorted, not interested.

"Then talk," she said. Kate took a tentative step forward.

"Do you know who Greg Calhoun really is?" she asked. Candice, an exceptionally pretty woman when she wasn't trying to murder people, paused but didn't release the door handle. "Do you know who he works for?"

"If the money's good, I don't need to know," Candice said.

"He works for the FBI," Kate added quickly. Candice didn't move from her spot, but she did roll her eyes.

"So?"

"So, did he even tell you his plan? His endgame? Or does enough money mean you don't care about going to prison?"

Candice's eye actually spasmed, a quick pulse of hidden emotion breaking through. Once again she didn't move.

"Greg is a scientist. He wants me out of the way so he can take over my work—my research—and continue to work with the FBI after I'm dead. Did you know that?" Kate knew the woman didn't. Her lips had pursed. "My mother was FBI, my friend that Donnie took is FBI and for the last five years I've been under FBI monitoring. Don't you think if I show up dead, not to mention my friend being kidnapped, that an investigation is going to be opened? And if Greg plans to keep his job, then surely he's going to need one strong alibi or one heck of a fall guy…or woman. That case you two stole was given to me by Greg—why do you think he had you steal it back if not to help frame you?" Kate paused for dramatic effect. She noticed Candice's hand had curled into a small fist.

"Listen," Kate began again. "I've known Greg almost all of my life. He's been my role model since I was a little girl. Now he's trying to destroy what I hoped would be my life's work and, well, me. If he's willing to kill someone he once claimed to love like a daughter, do you think for one second he'd hesitate to throw you and your partner under the bus?"

Candice put her back against the door, holding it open still, and crossed her arms over her chest.

"So, what? I should go ahead and kill all of you?" she asked, sarcasm rampant. Kate didn't back down.

"You'd be hunted hard and you know that."

The woman narrowed her eyes.

"If you want my opinion, and I should point out that the FBI wants me for my intelligence, if I was you I would run now. Before all of this gets resolved, you could be out of the state," Kate said. "I'll make sure it's known that you let me go, so if you ever get caught, then you'll look a lot better than if you shot a defenseless woman point-blank. What do you say?"

Chapter Twenty-Three

Jonathan ducked Mr. Smith's next swing. This time he was able to use his right arm to hook the crazed man's arm in a viselike grip. Jonathan squeezed. The hold intensified until the man yelled. The sweet sound of the knife falling to the ground met Jonathan's ears. Mr. Smith wasn't as much of a fan. He used his other hand, fisting it, and delivered a blow to Jonathan's temple that utterly dazed him. He released the man and staggered to the side.

But not before kicking the fallen knife backward as hard as he could.

"You are a pain he didn't warn us about," the man said, half bent, hand to his nose. Jonathan's vision started to fringe black as he went to the closest wall and put his hand against it to try to steady not only his balance but everything else. Jonathan blinked several times, trying to keep from passing out, until the feeling subsided. He pushed off the wall and started to run for the man again. He knew he needed to level the playing field before another player was added to the game. This man might have a knife, but he knew for a fact that his female partner had a gun.

Mr. Smith had no choice but to take Jonathan's shoulder in the chest. He staggered backward but grabbed hold of Jonathan's sleeve to keep from falling. It tugged the man down enough that he got an uninhibited view of something that made his blood run cold despite the exertion they were putting out.

The man used Jonathan's momentary distraction to his advantage. He brought his hand up and pressed hard into the gash in Jonathan's shoulder. Unlike the one in his forearm, this wound was deeper and much more painful. Jonathan once again found himself backing away, fighting a new wave of pain.

"I see you got a good look at my collection," Mr. Smith said, nearly out of breath. He motioned to the inside of his blazer before opening both sides. Jonathan eyed them with an expanding feeling of unease. Attached inside were at least ten knives, ranging in size. "They're beautiful, aren't they?" The man leaned on the wall behind him. He was stalling. "Most people like guns, but me? Well, these are just so much more poetic, don't you think?"

Jonathan didn't pay attention to what the two knives the man pulled out looked like. He knew they would hurt no matter their decoration or size. Instead he ran back toward the elevator, then cut into the small lounge area set up in the corner. While he wished he knew exactly where the Taser was that he'd given to Kate, he spotted the only thing that might give him a small chance to defend himself. Jonathan hoisted the closed umbrella out of the concrete cylinder and brandished it like a sword, wishing again that he'd brought a gun with him to the city. Or at least had had the sense to calm down enough to grab the Taser from his bag before coming to the hotel.

Mr. Smith was nearly on him, like a bull drawn to a matador. In one hand he had a new knife turned downward, reminiscent of a bad guy in a slasher movie, while the other was held up and out, easier for quick jabs. Jonathan quickly judged the surroundings of the small lounge, the elevators to the left and the hall leading to what must have been a corporate meeting floor, and realized he was in the worst possible corner. There was no way to move around the raging, bloodied man.

So Jonathan decided to go through him.

He opened the umbrella wide and rammed it into the man's chest. Using his momentum, he carried the man backward to the far wall before he was able to slice through the material. Jonathan tried to pull the umbrella back so he could use it as a bat, but Mr. Smith's knives got too close again. One went through the fabric and moved through Jonathan's shirt and skin with ease. The umbrella fell between them. Jonathan tried to back away again, but Mr. Smith was quick. He stretched out his leg and tripped Jonathan, sending the man to fall hard without any time to catch himself.

"Like I said," Mr. Smith said, a wild smile pulling up his bloodstained lips, "a pain in my si—"

A gunshot exploded in the hallway.

Jonathan cringed, waiting for the pain. However, it didn't come. It was Mr. Smith who seemed to have taken the bullet. He tipped over and hit the floor in a spray of blood. He'd been shot in the head.

Jonathan turned, confused, to see the dark blond-haired woman lowering her gun in the middle of the hallway.

"Jonathan!"

Farther back, turning the corner, was Kate. She was the most beautiful woman he'd ever seen. The woman between them, however, pulled his attention back. She met his gaze with a smirk and put the gun in the back of her pants.

Jonathan stood as she walked closer and bent over the man.

"That's for slicing me open," she growled. Some other not-so-nice words were said before Kate was at Jonathan's side.

"You're hurt," she exclaimed, already touching his newest cut on his upper arm.

"You should see the other guy."

The woman straightened and snorted at that. Jonathan was ready to fight her for her gun when she turned to Kate.

"Donnie has a suite on the next floor," she said. "That's where your friend is. Use this in the elevator to get there." The woman pulled a gold key card from her back pocket. Kate took it with a nod and looked down at the dead man on the ground. It definitely wasn't a good scene. "If it makes you feel better, even by my standards he was a very, very bad man." As if to emphasize her dislike for him, Candice gave him one swift kick to the ribs.

Kate didn't comment. Jonathan took her hand and pulled her a few feet to the elevator.

"Don't worry," Kate whispered as the doors shut. "She can run, but she can't hide forever."

"I guess telling you we should go get help first wouldn't work," Jonathan said. Kate was already holding the key card up to where she needed to swipe it through.

"Greg doesn't want Jake to know he's involved. I'm assuming Greg will use everything in his power to pin it all on Candice and her partner. Since Jake trusts Greg as much as I once did, that might be easier than it would have been otherwise. I doubt Greg is anywhere near Jake right now," she reasoned. "Plus..." She swiped the card and slowly they began to ascend to the next floor. "I'm not leaving him behind."

"I wouldn't ask you to," Jonathan replied, taking her hand. As far as he could tell, she seemed okay physically. Mentally—emotionally—he'd bet Greg's betrayal would leave a wound that might never heal. But Kate was strong. She would survive this like she'd survived everything else.

THE ELEVATOR DOORS slid open to show an entryway that was the very definition of opulent. Shiny surfaces, detailed decor and modern everything else set the tone for an obviously expensive stay. Kate wondered how a man like Donnie afforded such a place, but then stopped that thought. If Greg had offered them enough money so they didn't ask any questions—and didn't *want* to— she'd bet the man had done similar jobs beforehand, making a penthouse a much more affordable option.

Jonathan, bleeding but standing tall, kept hold of her hand. He didn't ask her why she hadn't woken him before leaving for the hotel, and, in a way, she'd bet he already knew it was to keep him safe. He moved out of the elevator and angled himself so if anyone were to jump out at them, he'd take the brunt of it. She squeezed his hand, hoping he knew how much she appreciated it.

They stepped out of the entryway and right up to a city view that probably made the penthouse as expensive as she imagined it was. Windows that were used as walls stretched to the left, running along a living space, dining and bar area, before dipping out of view into what must have been the kitchen. Off the living area was a hallway that led to the bedrooms. They looked in each massive and lavishly decorated room one by one until they had only the biggest bedroom and its bathroom left.

Kate's palms began to sweat. What if Candice had lied? What if Greg had? What if they'd killed Jake the day before and she'd come voluntarily to exchange her life for his for no reason at all?

"I can't," Kate said, pulling back when they neared the bathroom door. There was nowhere else he could be. Jonathan caught her off guard by turning her so quickly she nearly stumbled and kissing her full on the lips. It was hard and powerful.

"You can," he said after they broke apart. "I'm right here with you."

And that was all she needed to hear.

Stepping forward, she opened the door and didn't hesitate walking inside. The bathroom, like its connected bedroom, was massive and beautiful. A marbled vanity, a walk-in shower that looked like it could fit at a least ten people and a Jacuzzi tub with an FBI agent inside.

"Jake!"

Kate and Jonathan rushed over to the man, whose arms, legs, hands and feet were bound by rope and his mouth covered with tape. For one wild moment Kate felt like she was back in that warehouse all those years ago. Instead of her mother, it was her best friend.

"He's breathing," Jonathan said, cutting through the bad memory. She shook her head. She needed to focus on the here and now.

"Jake? Can you hear me?" Kate asked. She put her fingers against his pulse and sighed in relief. It wasn't strong, but it didn't seem to be too weak, either.

"I think he was knocked unconscious at some point."

Jonathan pointed to the agent's forehead. Dried blood plastered some of his fair hair against his scalp.

Kate bent over and ripped the tape off his mouth. Jonathan undid his hands and started on the arms when a voice paused both of their hands.

"Step away from him."

Kate turned to find Greg standing in the doorway, a gun angled at the space between them.

"Greg," Jonathan started, moving slowly out of the tub and in front of Kate, "let's talk about this."

Greg, who had been the picture of calculated calm earlier, had noticeably changed. His demeanor was slightly rumpled, carrying through his clothes and right down to the crease between his brows. He pushed his glasses up the bridge of his nose, hindered a bit by the bandage, but didn't drop the aim of his gun, instead moving it to Kate herself.

"Let's go have a talk," he said, voice nearly a whisper. "Now, or I'll shoot all three of you."

Jonathan gave Kate a look that quite clearly seemed to say he would take out the man if he could, but she had already judged the distance between Greg's gun and them. He'd be able to get at least one shot off before Jonathan could make a move.

"Okay, we'll come," Kate said, for everyone's benefit.

Greg nodded and began to back out into the bedroom. As if he was pulling on an invisible thread, Jonathan walked with matching speed. Kate followed, but before she cleared the bathroom door, she paused and looked back at her best friend. When he woke up the world would be much different. She only hoped he'd figure out what happened.

As if her intense worry could be heard, Jake's eyes

flashed open. It took everything she had not to give away her relief. The other two men were out of his sight line. Kate hoped he wouldn't call out to her, to let Greg know he was conscious, so then Greg would be forced to silence him, too. However, he kept quiet and even lifted one finger to his lips to silence her.

Kate gave a quick nod and turned back to Greg. She stuck her hand in Jonathan's and they were led back to the living area.

"Backs to the window," Greg ordered, rotating around them so Jonathan was never in range to do anything about the gun pointed at them. Kate squeezed his hand, hoping he'd somehow understand that Jake wasn't down and out for the count. "I *knew* you wouldn't be easy," Greg said when they were in position. While Jonathan had once again positioned himself as a human shield, Kate moved so their shoulders were touching. She was going to face the man. "Within the span of, what, less than an hour, you two have managed to turn everything on its head."

"Or maybe it was just a bad plan," Jonathan said, anger clear. His shoulders were as straight as an arrow, his body tense.

"You have to know the authorities are on their way," Kate pointed out. "Someone must have heard the shot downstairs."

Greg snorted.

"I know they are," he said, an easy smile lifting the corner of his lips. "You two may have been a pain, but you've actually helped me more than you know." Kate raised her eyebrow, questioning. "My two scapegoats look even more guilty than they did before. One obviously used force against you," he said, motioning to Jonathan's cuts, "and the other fled, further proving that's she's just as guilty." Jonathan squeezed her hand several times. Kate's confusion at the pressure diminished when she saw Jake walking along the hallway behind Greg. He was limping, but not enough that it made noise. Still, Kate wanted to keep talking just in case.

"So you're going to just kill us and then what?" Kate asked, anger mounting. "Call the cops and pretend you found us and Jake? Do you think they're really going to believe it all? And, while we're at it, do you think the FBI will really let you take over my work? Surely you've thought about this objectively and seen that if I could figure out it was you behind this based on a hand-written letter, the Bureau could also piece it together."

Kate was trying to keep her eyes off Jake as he got closer, but she had a feeling Jonathan knew exactly what was going on. He applied pressure to her hand again before letting go completely. Whatever was going to happen was about to take place.

"You may be one smart cookie, Kate," Greg said, "but that doesn't mean I'm not, also." He raised the gun and then the world went chaotic.

Jake tackled Greg to the side just as the gun discharged. Kate braced for the hit but was instead thrown to the side, as well. Jonathan's weight sandwiched her to the ground and covered her as the window behind them shattered. Kate closed her eyes tight and waited for the world to quiet.

"Are you okay?"

Kate looked up at the bodyguard and blinked several times.

"Kate?" he prodded, his hand cupping her cheek. They were still on the ground, the sound of the wind roaring past the newly opened window almost carrying his words away.

"Yeah, I think so," she said, quickly cataloging any new pain. Aside from the fall, there wasn't any. "What about you?"

Jonathan got up and nodded as an answer, but moved away quickly, running over to Jake and Greg. Kate scrambled to her feet and followed.

"Oh, my God," Kate breathed.

Jake had managed to push the man to the ground and take possession of his gun, but it was how he'd disabled him that floored her. Greg was sitting up, back leaning against the couch, grabbing his neck. In Jake's other hand was an automated injector.

Empty.

"You injected him with the prototype," she said, not a question.

Jonathan helped the agent to his feet. He nodded.

"I found it in the bedroom. Had to improvise."

Greg looked between them with wide eyes behind his glasses. He looked so helpless without a weapon, without his banter, that a younger Kate would have felt sorry for him. However, now all she felt was a sense of loss.

Kneeling down, she looked him square in the eye.

"Congratulations, Greg," she said. "You just became the first human trial."

Chapter Twenty-Four

"How did you figure it out?" Kate asked. She and Jake sat at what was no doubt a very expensive table in the penthouse as cops swarmed the space. Soon they'd be called off. Jake's boss was on the way.

"I didn't," he answered honestly. "At least not until I came to in the bathroom."

"But he told me you were getting too close," Kate said, confused. "That's why he got Donnie to grab you."

Jake's jaw tensed.

"He was wrong. I was still looking into Donnie's identity as well as that Candice woman's when he jumped me near my apartment." Jake fisted his hand on top of the table. When he met Kate's eyes, there was an immense weight there. One she knew all too well. "The thing is, I never suspected him, Kate. I never once thought Greg could be behind it all. And you and Jonathan were almost killed because of it."

Kate put her hand on his. It was the same show of affection she'd given to the bodyguard, but it was completely different at the same time. Her feelings for Jake had, and would always be, that of an almost sibling type of love. Jonathan, on the other hand…

"Being blinded by love isn't something to apologize for," she said. "Greg knows us as well as our parents. He knew how to work us, how to move the pieces around so we wouldn't suspect him. He used our love for him to his cruel advantage, and that wasn't something either one of us saw coming." She patted his hand and Jake gave a little nod. Although he knew the truth in her words, she knew it would be a long time before he forgave himself.

"I guess your dad really saved the day," he said after a moment. He motioned to Jonathan off to the side, talking to Jett, which had been a surprise in itself, and the paramedic who was bandaging his cuts. Luckily, none were serious. The bodyguard looked over to Kate and she gave him a quick smile. "If Jonathan hadn't been around…"

He didn't need to finish the thought. Kate didn't, either. She knew she owed the dark-haired man her life, many times over.

Jake's boss, a woman named Melanie who looked as if she'd just stepped out of a catalog titled something like Those Who Don't Put Up With Any Nonsense, showed up a few minutes later. She was happy that Jake and Kate were all right, but the anger that she too had been hoodwinked by Greg covered her relief quickly. Jonathan joined Kate as they recounted everything that had happened while Jake was sent to the hospital to get his head wound checked out.

"What will happen to Greg?" Kate asked when they were done. He'd been conscious but unresponsive by the time the cops had come and taken him out of the penthouse, despite Kate's protests. When the FBI had come in, they had collected him and taken him to the hospital. "That stage of the drug hasn't been tested. If its results are like the earlier one, then there's only a limited amount of time in which we can help him. Though, to be honest, unless he has an antidote already created, I probably won't have the time."

Melanie uncrossed her legs. She looked to Jonathan and asked if he'd excuse the two of them. He nodded and returned to Jett, who'd been sidelined by another agent. His involvement had touched Kate, being a stranger but still willing to help. Despite everything that had happened, his hotel would be getting a perfect review from her.

"Kathryn, I understand if you're not that happy with us and the decisions we've made in the past few years in regards to your work," Melanie said, voice all business. "But the goal of this convention was always to offer you a position. One that would consist of your own lab, a team of bright minds to help you and close to unlimited funding and resources. I know getting to this spot took a very different route than either of us anticipated, but this offer is now officially on the table." She pressed her fingertip to the table between them, physically underlining her point. Kate watched the show with little conflict. While she hadn't liked the way they'd gone about it, in the end she trusted Jake's love of where he worked. Just as her mother had.

Betrayal, danger and loss couldn't always be accounted for, but Kate knew that in her line of work the chances of falling into any of them were great. That wouldn't stop her, though.

Instead of giving the answer she knew she always would have given—yes—Kate looked over at Jonathan. What she believed would have been an easy answer suddenly didn't feel that way.

"Looks like you got me to the convention after all, Mr. Bodyguard," Kate said, finally able to have a moment alone with him. They'd been asked to leave the penthouse and were now in the corner of the lobby while all sorts of uniforms bustled about. "One heck of a last field assignment, too."

Jonathan smiled.

"What can I say?" he teased. "I'm just that good."

Kate's smile lit up her entire body, highlighting a nothing short of amazing woman. When that smile began to fade, Jonathan already knew what would happen next.

"They offered you the job," he said, making sure to keep a smile on his face and in his voice.

Kate nodded.

"Apparently Greg is sitting in the hospital right now answering every question he's asked," she said. "I don't know how anyone else will react to the untested drug, but for now we know it works in part."

"That's great," he said honestly.

"They want to go ahead and fly me home to collect my research and come straight back to sift through Greg's." A small blush reddened her cheeks. "It's all happening so fast."

Jonathan didn't have to fake the smile anymore. He was truly happy for her.

"So what happens now?" she asked after a moment of silence passed between them. Her dark eyes searched his face, looking for something he wasn't sure he had. Kate's potential—her dream—was finally being fully realized. Her life was about to change in the best way possible. Even though he wanted more than anything to see that happen, Jonathan knew he wouldn't be a part of it. She was way above his level, and he realized with a drop of his stomach that he'd known that since the moment he'd met her.

"Well, the contract is fulfilled," he said. "I'll return to Dallas and finally get the desk job I always wanted, and you—" He paused, a swell of longing almost making him reach forward and pull her into an embrace she wouldn't forget. "And you, Miss Scientist, will continue trying to save the world."

"I'M GLAD YOU didn't get sick."

Jonathan turned and smiled up at his boss. Nikki was dressed in a long gown, a deep gray a shade darker than the maid of honor's dress. The soft thumping of an '80s throwback had guests and the man and woman of the hour dancing a few feet from his table.

"To be honest, there was a moment I was worried I would," he said. "But then I thought about all of the flack I'd catch from Mark, Oliver and you and knew I needed to keep it together." Nikki laughed and leaned against the empty chair next to him.

"Well, I'll tell you, it was a hilarious, heartfelt best man speech," she said. "I think you almost made Mark cry."

Jonathan couldn't help but laugh at that thought.

It had been two months since he'd returned from New York. Two months since he'd seen or heard from Kate. Since then, Nikki had stayed true to her word and offered him a job that kept him in one place—though, instead of sitting at a desk, he was now the new trainer and recruiter for Orion. Interacting with and vetting current and potential agents was a job he was starting to find he really enjoyed—even though he was surprised Nikki hadn't fired him on the spot when she learned the extent of the events that had happened in New York, and that he'd kept them a secret from her until they'd been resolved.

Then again, he wasn't really that surprised, either.

At the end of the day, Nikki was one of his best friends.

"Well, look at what we have here." Jonathan turned this time to see Oliver Quinn and his wife, Darling, walk up. Oliver was wearing a copy of the tuxes Mark and Jonathan had on while his wife wore a slightly different version of Nikki's dress—one that had had to be modified for her large pregnant belly. "Jonathan and Nikki, the only people *not* dancing." Oliver turned to his wife and smirked. "Why don't we show them how it's done?"

Darling laughed as Oliver held out his hand to Nikki. Jonathan, already knowing his fate, jumped up and extended his hand to Darling, smiling.

"Don't worry," she said as they shuffled onto the dance floor. "All I can really do is sway back and forth."

Jonathan laughed and together they began to move to the beat. He enjoyed the dance and their talk about a case she had just finished working, names redacted, of course, but something inside still didn't feel quite right. Sure, he was surrounded by his closest friends—his family, really—and all of their loved ones and the happiness that seemed to be contagious, but there was something missing. Well, someone.

"Excuse me," a voice said from behind him, "but can I have this dance?"

Darling looked at the woman who cut into their swaying with an all-knowing smile. She gave Jonathan, who had frozen altogether, a wink.

"I'd love that," she said, before backing up to where her husband and Nikki looked on with smiles.

Jonathan turned to the woman and couldn't believe his eyes.

"Kate?"

Kate Spears was wearing a long light blue dress, had her hair curled to her shoulders and had a small, shy smile across her perfect lips. She took one of his hands and placed the other on her hip.

"I'm also a fan of just swaying, if that's okay with you," she said.

Jonathan felt himself nod, absolutely confused. He cast another quick look at his friends to see Mark and his new bride, Kelli, giving him the thumbs-up.

"How are you here?"

Kate gave a tiny laugh that made Jonathan smile instantly. They began to sway to the beat as she answered.

"Well, a man named Mark tracked me down and said this wedding was the place to be. That *everyone* who was anyone would be here." She shrugged. "I decided my handler and I needed a break after all the work we've done the last two months." She glanced off to the side and Jonathan caught sight of Jake, also dressed up, talking to one of the guests, an attractive young woman from Mark's family.

"That makes sense," he said, attention falling back squarely on her. The music could have stopped right then and he wouldn't have noticed. "How is all that going?"

"Interestingly. I consolidated my old lab as well as Greg's and was even able to pick my colleagues. They don't seem to be against my age, which is nice. Did you hear about Candice?"

Jonathan nodded.

"Nikki told me she was caught trying to flee to Mexico."

"Accurate. Now, like Greg, she's answering for her crimes."

Jonathan didn't pry beyond what he was given when it came to Greg. Even now when she mentioned him he could tell it hurt. He let them sway a moment longer before pressing on.

"So, you're living in New York now?"

Kate's cheeks reddened slightly.

"Actually, that's one thing I wanted to talk to you about," she said. "I was hoping you could help us find some good apartments. We're currently staying at a hotel not too far from here, but I don't need to tell you how much I've come to dislike hotels."

Jonathan was afraid he'd heard incorrectly. He almost didn't want to ask and be corrected, but his curiosity got the better of him.

"Wait, you want to get an apartment here in Dallas?"

Kate's cheeks turned a darker shade, but she kept smiling all the same.

"Considering I got my lab moved here, I thought that might be a good idea."

Jonathan felt that missing piece finally fall into place. A smile as true as they came graced his lips. He pulled Kate closer.

"I think I could help with that," he said. He twirled her around before bringing her back into his embrace. She let out a stream of laughter.

"Who knew you could dance, Mr. Bodyguard," she said.

"I just needed the right partner, Miss Scientist."

Together they continued to dance, even as the slow song ended. With a quick look around the dance floor, Jonathan realized he was surrounded by his friends, their families and a woman who made the smile on his face reach all the way down to his heart.

With one thought, he felt a contentment he'd always wanted but never thought possible.

Roots.

* * * * *

MILLS & BOON®

INTRIGUE
Romantic Suspense

A SEDUCTIVE COMBINATION OF DANGER AND DESIRE

A sneak peek at next month's titles...

In stores from 11th August 2016:

- **Laying Down the Law** – Delores Fossen *and*
  Dark Whispers – Debra Webb
- **Delivering Justice** – Barb Han *and*
  Sudden Second Chance – Carol Ericson
- **Hostage Negotiation** – Lena Diaz *and*
  Suspicious Activities – Tyler Anne Snell

Romantic Suspense

- **Conard County Marine** – Rachel Lee
- **High-Stakes Colton** – Karen Anders

MILLS & BOON®

The Regency Collection – Part 1

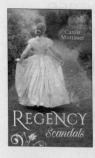

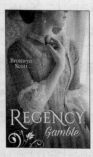

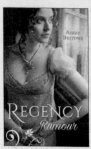

Let these roguish rakes sweep you off to the Regency period in part 1 of our collection!

Order yours at **www.millsandboon.co.uk/regency1**

MILLS & BOON®

The Regency Collection – Part 2

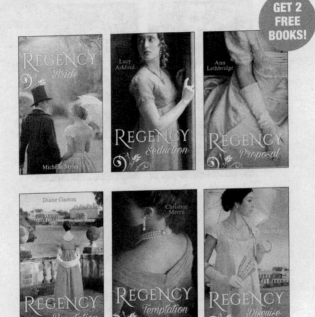

Join the London ton for a Regency
season in part 2 of our collection!

Order yours at **www.millsandboon.co.uk/regency2**

MILLS & BOON®

The Sara Craven Collection!

MILLS & BOON®

The Gold Collection!

You'll love these bestselling stories
from some of our most popular authors!

Order yours at **www.millsandboon.co.uk/gold**

d to look any further to know